MW00916070

Startup

JUL - - 2014

START UP

GLENN OGURA

iUniverse, Inc.
Bloomington

START UP

Copyright © 2013 Glenn Ogura.

All rights reserved. No part of this book may be used or reproduced by any means, graphic, electronic, or mechanical, including photocopying, recording, taping or by any information storage retrieval system without the written permission of the publisher except in the case of brief quotations embodied in critical articles and reviews.

This is a work of fiction. All of the characters, names, incidents, organizations, and dialogue in this novel are either the products of the author's imagination or are used fictitiously.

iUniverse books may be ordered through booksellers or by contacting:

iUniverse
1663 Liberty Drive
Bloomington, IN 47403
www.iuniverse.com
1-800-Authors (1-800-288-4677)

Because of the dynamic nature of the Internet, any web addresses or links contained in this book may have changed since publication and may no longer be valid. The views expressed in this work are solely those of the author and do not necessarily reflect the views of the publisher, and the publisher hereby disclaims any responsibility for them.

Any people depicted in stock imagery provided by Thinkstock are models, and such images are being used for illustrative purposes only.

Certain stock imagery © Thinkstock.

ISBN: 978-1-4759-8855-0 (sc)
ISBN: 978-1-4759-8856-7 (hc)
ISBN: 978-1-4759-8854-3 (e)

Printed in the United States of America

iUniverse rev. date: 5/17/2013

To my best friend and beautiful wife Sheila
and my parents Tad and Eileen

PROLOGUE

When Mary Anne turned the knob, Zack's home-office door swung open without a sound and was immediately swallowed up by the darkness inside. Standing in the dim hallway, she had to clench her hands to stop their trembling.

This was so stupid, she told herself. Despite her father's claims, despite what he had shown her, she didn't believe that Zack could be a traitor to DisplayTechnik. Ever the master manipulator, Allen Henley, CEO and founder of the family corporation, had backed her into a corner, and now she was on the verge of betraying her boyfriend to prove his innocence.

Although her father had soft-pedaled it as "counterintelligence," breaking and entering while her lover slept in a nearby room seemed much less dignified than that—and far more shameful. And she wasn't sure what she'd do if she found something incriminating: hand it over to Allen, or confront Zack with it?

If she turned back now, Zack would never know; and when Allen asked her what she'd discovered, she could tell him to go screw himself—though in words more carefully chosen. For once, she could end one of their arguments having taken the high ground.

But she knew in her heart it was too late to retreat. She had already crossed a line.

She closed the door behind her, exhaling at the soft click of the handle. She'd been holding her breath since she'd slid the key filched from Zack's pants pocket into the lock. Oh, God, there'd be hell to pay if he walked in now, she thought. But maybe that would be better; maybe then it could all be out in the open.

A few weeks prior, Allen had brought up his suspicions in one of their father-daughter "debates." He'd managed to get under her skin as always, and as always, she'd taken the bait. Before she knew what was happening, she'd agreed to search her boyfriend's home office, determined to show Allen that he was wrong about Zack.

Earlier in the evening, she'd tried one last time to elicit the truth from Zack, but he kept dodging her questions about his future plans. Why couldn't he just trust her?

She inched forward in the dark until her shin bumped the side of the desk. Afraid she'd knock something over, she carefully reached out, feeling for the lamp. Her fingers touched papers, a pen, and then bumped the lampshade—hard. For an instant, she imagined the lamp teetering over and shattering on the floor, but that didn't happen.

She found the toggle switch and clicked it. The burst of bright light hurt her eyes. She leaned over the desk, cluttered with heaps of file folders and documents.

God, she thought, how do professional thieves *do* this?

———————————————

Fifteen minutes later, she closed and locked the door behind her, a single piece of paper folded in her hand. She quietly retraced her steps down the hall. She'd left the bedroom door partially open. She slipped through it and tiptoed across the darkened room. Zack was barely visible on the bed, a long lump under the covers. After returning the key to his pants pockets, she picked up her purse and took it into the bathroom, closing the door after her. In the glow of the nightlight, she put the slip of paper in her purse. Then she flushed the toilet and turned on the water in the sink for a moment.

She shuffled back across the room and then got back into the warm bed. A carefully placed poke with her elbow made Zack roll over, and he wrapped a protective arm around her, giving her a gentle, half-awake squeeze before he sighed and slipped back to sleep.

Mary Anne lay beside her boyfriend, muscles clenched, heart pounding. Maybe there was some other explanation for what she'd found, but she couldn't think of it. The last thing she wanted was to be touched by this man, this sudden stranger, but if she got up and left, Zack would know something had happened. He'd want answers. Her father had convinced her that it was in their interest and the interest of DisplayTechnik to keep whatever she discovered a secret from Zack until the proper moment. And her father was always right.

CHAPTER ONE

Upon entering the mirrored-glass and stainless-steel lobby of DisplayTechnik, most people's eyes were immediately drawn to the immense mobile hanging thirty feet overhead. It revolved ever so lazily, its burnished metal dazzling in the California sun. Ultrathin suspension cables concealed by the mosaic pattern on the wall behind the display created the illusion that the massive structure was simply hovering, perhaps by some trick of magnetism.

The mobile reminded Zack of scimitars and guillotine blades. As far as he was concerned, the truly magnificent work of art in the entranceway was the vast floor of highly polished black marble. Walking across it was like stepping into space: looking down at the pinpoints and streaks of glittering white, one strolled through the stars of the heavens, passing by galaxies, and the streamers of some gaseous nebula. Beneath the steel and glass homage to Allen Henley's vanity was the constancy of the universe—immoveable, immutable, and terrible in its beauty. A plush burgundy carpet surrounded the receptionist's area, which stood like an island in the sea of black.

Engineers like Zack weren't supposed to use the main lobby entrance, and he didn't most days, but it was only six thirty and any of the flock of senior vice presidents who might care if he were violating company protocol were probably still in bed. He usually got to work early, though not merely to avoid the crawl over

Highway 680. He liked to take in the surroundings, soak them up, and breathe in the crisp, mechanically filtered air, knowing that one day his own company would never, ever look like this.

But he did hope to have someone as cheerful as Jan as his receptionist. She flashed him her beaming smile and waved him over to her island.

"Yes, okay. Hold, please—" she said, and put the caller on hold before he or she could object. "Hiya, Zack, how was your weekend? You look tired—didn't you get in any sleep?"

"Of course," Zack said. "Whenever I wasn't working or awake."

"You know, weekends mean taking time off, not just not going to the office."

"I know, but the work doesn't get done if someone doesn't do it. I am planning on going skiing next weekend ..." His voice trailed off when Jan disappeared behind the desk, and he leaned forward to see if she'd fallen through some sort of trapdoor.

She popped up with a rectangular block of aluminum foil in her hand. "This is for you," she said. "It's a loaf of banana nut bread I made. It was supposed to be for Jimmy, but you're looking thinner and thinner lately. Haven't you been eating?"

Zack knew better than to argue or refuse the gift. He was about to defend his appetite when Jan turned back to the flashing lights on her board. "DisplayTechnik, how may I direct your call? Oh! Have you been holding all this time?"

Zack mouthed a thank-you as he picked up the package. It was heavier than it looked. Jan gave him a wink and wave as he turned for the bank of glass elevators. He walked past them and swiped his access card to the door to the stairs. Walking up to the third floor, he sampled Jan's bread. He hadn't had breakfast, unless two cups of coffee with cream and sugar counted. The bread was worlds above the preservative-loaded cinnamon roll from the vending machine that he usually had around nine.

At the third-floor landing, he swiped his card again and walked down the hallway to his office. He fumbled in his pocket for the key, and when he couldn't extract it while juggling everything else, he set down his briefcase. The heavy case leaned against the door, and it swung slowly open. He was *positive* he'd locked it. He always locked it before leaving on Fridays.

Zack nudged it wide-open with his knee, reached in, and slid his fingers up the wall until he found the light switch. The overhead fluorescent light flickered and then came to life.

Everything on his desk looked just the way he'd left it, but he immediately noticed that the pine bookcase stood at a slight angle away from the wall. The filing cabinet's key lock appeared untouched. He'd been concerned that someone had been going through his things lately and it bothered him, even if he knew they wouldn't find anything here.

Well, maybe it was the damn careless cleaning staff again, he told himself. It would have been the second time in three weeks that they'd failed to lock his door. The company had, after all, just hired some new staff. And it wouldn't be the first time that they'd gone nuts with their massive industrial vacuums.

He tossed his keys onto the desk and then set his briefcase on the chair. As he opened it, he took another look around. Everything seemed secure. *Wait a minute!* Panic fluttered in his stomach like he'd reached the crest of a roller coaster's first climb and was about to go over the summit. Had he left the drawing here that Dimitre had scratched out at lunch on Friday, the one with the latest specs for the polymer formulation?

Jesus, if someone found that and realized what it meant, he was screwed. They were all screwed.

Then he remembered sticking it in his briefcase before he left. He was going to work on it over the weekend but never got to it with everything else he'd had to do.

As Zack turned to place the briefcase on his desk, his hand slipped, and the contents spilled onto the floor.

Damn it!

He got down on his hands and knees and started piling it all back in the case, checking each scrap of paper and CD as he went—overdue laundry second notice, trade magazines, candy bar wrappers, the latest bulletin from marketing about how they desperately needed specs and colors. He scooped together the half-dozen file folders containing reports he was supposed to have finished up on Saturday and flipped through them, thinking Dimitre's napkin might have gotten mixed up with them. *Boy, wouldn't that have been sweet.*

Zack sat in the middle of the floor, reconstructing events. Okay, the last place he remembered seeing it for sure was here when he put it in his briefcase. So, obviously, it still had to be here, right? No, wait a second. Mary Anne had shown up early on Friday night, and he'd slipped it into his desk drawer at home, along with some other papers he'd been working on that he didn't want her to see. He remembered now seeing the edge of it poking out of the stack. He'd wanted to put it all in the safe later that night but didn't get a chance to because she'd distracted him with that new nightie. He smiled, thinking what they'd—

"Hey, stranger."

Zack jumped at the voice behind him. It was Phyllis, the administrative assistant for the engineering staff.

"So is that what you call filing?"

Zack stood up. "Did you come into my office over the weekend?"

"You kidding me?" Phyllis wrinkled her nose. "Come in here on the weekend? That's not my idea of a fun time. I'm not as crazy as you boys from engineering."

"How about this morning?"

"I don't have a key, remember? Why?"

"The door was unlocked."

"Maybe you didn't lock it."

"I *always* lock the office."

"Uh-huh." Phyllis waved at his cluttered desk. "And you always keep your office tidy as well."

Zack bent down and started to clear the desk.

"Too little, too late," Phyllis chided him. "Anyhow, you don't have time for that. Julie told me to keep an eye open for you. Said to tell you Mr. Henley wants to see you as soon as you came in, but you were to swing into her office first. Think she has the hots for you?"

Phyllis winked at him. There were a lot of rumors about Julie Reynolds's hots. She was a key member of the inner Gestapo of DisplayTechnik, *exactly* the type of person who would invade his office.

Zack ran a hand through his straight brown hair. It was usually a little ruffled and just long enough to make it difficult to manage. This morning he'd seen a unicorn staring back at him in the mirror, and even after a shower, it had still been sticking up a bit.

He hurriedly ushered Phyllis out into the hall, and he made a show of locking the door after him. Arms folded across her chest, she rolled her eyes as he turned for Julie's office.

Why would the Human Resources manager want to see him? She only called in people when she was firing them, or fishing for reasons to fire someone else, or giving them a lower-than-deserved rating for their latest evaluation. In the latter case, she claimed she wanted to head off any problems with poor performance, but the twinkle in her eye hinted at sadistic pleasure.

And what the hell did their esteemed founder and CEO want? He wasn't exactly the type to have personal chats with his engineering team, even though Zack was the head of the department. Maybe this was about the new line of monitors due out next month? They were still having problems with a residual flicker and didn't seem to be any closer to isolating the problem.

Bill Bennet, the general counsel, came out of nowhere and nearly collided with him. Bill clutched a pile of papers to his chest and held out his coffee mug as it slopped over onto the rug.

"Jesus! Watch where you're—oh, hi, Zack." He clutched the papers a little tighter and then turned them upside down onto a nearby desk, shaking the coffee from his hand. "Where are you off to in such a hurry?"

"I could ask the same thing. So, how are the plans coming along to get traffic lights installed on these dangerous intersections?"

"Seen Julie yet?" Bill said.

Zack frowned. "What, are they broadcasting my morning's meetings on the Bay Area Early News?"

"Pardon?"

"You're the second person who's told me that Julie wants to see me."

"Oh, well, you know. We're all supposed to be communicating better."

Sure, Zack thought. DisplayTechnik was such a warm, wonderful place, and management only wanted the best for employees.

"Actually, I was off to see, uh, Mr. Henley first," Zack said. "You know, start at the top. Apparently he wants to meet with me too, in case that didn't make the broadcast this morning."

Bill stared at him blankly and then said, "I just came from the tower, and he's going to be busy for a while. An interview with *Silicon Valley Business*, I believe. Why don't you go see Julie first?"

Zack nodded.

"Hey, catch that Giants game?" Bill said as he started in the opposite direction.

Attempts at small talk by Bennet always seemed forced. The man was more comfortable talking about patent law than even the simplest of human connections. His eyes were cold and judgmental, constantly weighing just how valuable talking to you really was. And if at some point in the conversation you'd somehow confirmed that you were worth more than the carpet he was standing on, he always tried to end with something that would make him appear a real person, a regular guy. He was a perfect fit for DisplayTechnik.

"Yeah, I did," Zack said, "the last four innings anyway ..." He was instantly sorry he'd opened his mouth. Bill turned the corner and walked out of sight without a word.

Asshole. *Asshole.*

Zack took the stairs up one floor to the Human Resources department. He knew that a media interview with the CEO could easily take an hour or more, and it might even stretch on to lunch.

Typical that Allen had made his stopping by a top priority and then failed to leave the time open for their meeting.

Julie was on the phone when he stepped into her office, which had all the pizzazz of a funeral home. The only bright spot was a calendar of Caribbean beaches. She waved him to a seat at the conference table.

The Human Resources manager could have easily modeled for a calendar herself—the kind usually found in a men's locker room. As Zack sat down, Julie leaned back in her chair, arching her back, which made her ample chest look like it was erupting from her business jacket. He grabbed a nearby magazine. It was ironic that someone who inspired such anxiety in her fellow employees should be so irresistible to look at. She had the most wonderful skin, like Bernadette Peters, which made her blue-green eyes look like jewels in a milk bath. Her long dark hair, pulled back from her face by a clever assortment of clips, cascaded around her shoulders.

Julie shifted in her chair. Zack peered over the top of the magazine and watched her cross and uncross her legs, which were regrettably mostly hidden by the desk. He couldn't help but smile remembering a recent, late-night, development-group engineering session at his apartment. Jimmy had recounted his latest Julie fantasy. He had it bad for her. "So, Mr. Morgan, now that you're no longer an employee," he'd said, imitating her voice in breathless fashion, "why don't we get down to business?" With that, she'd cleared her desk for them in a single swipe. The room had erupted into a mix of laughter and catcalls. Someone threw a half a piece of pizza and hit Jimmy smack in the middle of the forehead, and it had stuck there for a good three seconds—

"Mr. Zack Penny. How are you?"

Zack flinched.

"Hi, Julie." He cleared his throat. "So, what's up?"

She joined him at the conference table. "You know Brett Davis, don't you?"

Brett was the Southwest sales rep. "Of course. What's going on?"

"Is he a friend of yours?"

His eyes narrowed. "Yeah. Why?"

"You stoutly defended him in your report after the HP deal collapsed last year."

"I didn't defend him because he was my friend; I defended him because we weren't treating a valued employee right. Okay?"

"Sure, Zack," she said quickly. "But we lost the account to a competitor with an inferior product, and Brett's coming up for another performance evaluation."

Ah, so this was a fishing expedition. Zack studied those blue-green eyes. "And your point is?"

Julie leaned forward, pressing her left hand against her jacket to keep the top from opening. "Are you familiar with our company's employee handbook? It is, after all, considered an addendum to your contract, just as it is with everyone else's."

The contract he'd signed five years ago? Yeah, sure. Like he'd remember everything in a document the size of the New Testament. The first time he'd even glanced at the handbook was three years ago to look up rules for personal days when he'd managed to get tickets to a Monday night game between the Niners and Cowboys. Since then, he'd only ever taken one other personal day, and that had been just a month ago.

"As I'm sure you'll recall," Julie said, "the handbook clearly details that employees are to conduct themselves in a professional manner at all times and also to report any behavior that might be detrimental to the company. Our competitors come up with all sorts of ingenious methods of winning."

"Are you accusing Brett of something?"

"Why? What do you know?"

"I don't have the faintest idea what you're talking about."

She blinked slowly at him. She had very long lashes. "You should take this seriously."

Zack could feel his cheeks heating up.

"I repeat," she said, "what do you know?"

"You're accusing Brett of what, conspiring with the competition to lose the account on purpose? Do you know how insane that sounds? Sales reps earn big bonuses by bringing in accounts."

"It wouldn't be the first time a competitor has paid someone to *not* make a sale, especially if they have a directly competing product that they might be trying to rush to market or to gain a foothold with. It's an insane world out there. Our competitors are stealing our employees, and worse, stealing our ideas. My job is to ensure loyalty, to find out where our own employees stand. And if you can be honest and simply tell me what you know about the competition out there, then it would do a lot to reassure DisplayTechnik of your loyalty and commitment."

The lilt in her voice made him decidedly uncomfortable. "My loyalty is to people," he said. "I'm not going to backstab Brett because of some far-fetched suspicion of yours. And that's all it seems you have—suspicion. As for my commitment, I easily work sixty hours in a slow week, so why don't you just back off?"

The faint smile on her face was frozen in place. After a few moments of silence, she arched her eyebrows slightly, looking past him, as if she'd come to some sort of determination.

There was a tiny knock on the door, followed by Julie's administrative assistant popping her head in.

"Sorry to bother you, but—"

"Yes, Tiffany?" Julie said.

"You told me to interrupt the meeting when Mr. Henley was free. Well, he's free. The camera crew is just packing up their gear, and Louise said that—"

"Fine, fine. Thank you."

Tiffany retreated, and Julie stood up abruptly. "So I take it that you won't help us?" she said.

"If you mean, will I rat-fink on Brett to promote your excess paranoia, the answer is no."

"Then I will see you later."

Not if he could help it. Zack got up and walked past her, out the door, heading for management's elaborate corporate offices.

God, he hated what this company had turned into. It was

infected with warrior politics and the credo of questioning everyone if their motives weren't completely aligned with General Allen's objectives.

Zack took a shortcut through a cluster of gray cubicles. They were arranged so workers couldn't see each other or the hallway traffic. He made his way through the beehive maze to the hallway that led to the Ivory Tower. He had no idea what this meeting was about, and that was unnerving. Despite the fact that he'd been in countless social settings with the man over the years, despite the fact that Allen made a point of telling others Zack might one day succeed him as CEO, Zack was still never completely comfortable in his presence.

He was dating the man's daughter, and so it was only natural to feel scrutinized by him. He knew he'd be analyzing anyone his own daughter was seeing too, but it seemed Allen noted his every comment and action, evaluated and stored it away for future use. It had been more than a year since he and Mary Anne had started going out, and he'd hoped at some point the man would let up, but if anything, of late he had become even more intense. Perhaps word that he and Mary Anne had probed each other's thoughts about marriage had reached him.

God, there was so much going on, he really didn't have time for this. He looked at his watch. Good Lord. Eight fifteen, and he hadn't even checked his e-mails yet.

He thought very briefly about swinging down to Mary Anne's office to see if she could give him a heads-up on whatever it was her father wanted, but he knew that was out of the question. Fraternizing during office hours was strictly forbidden at DisplayTechnik and both of them were aware of the many eyes on them, so they limited their contact to only the most pressing of business issues.

Zack pushed down on the brass lever and pushed the solid walnut door open with his shoulder. The thick burgundy carpet flattened as the door swung inward, revealing a softer cast of light and a quieter mood. The grand-entrance foyer connected the rest of DisplayTechnik to the Ivory Tower, where long-range, strategic business plans incubated. Standing at the base of the stairs, he looked up eight stories to the domed top of the tower. Wind chimes played softly from somewhere; they had to be electronic–there was no breeze.

The gleaming, sculpted wood paneling, textured wallpaper, and avant-garde murals of historical battles, all floodlit from above and below, restated the obvious: there was money here—*big money*. It was the same feeling he'd had when he and his partner in the secret start-up, Paul Ryerson, had visited New York and California investment banks and venture capital firms last year on his vacation days—or when Mary Anne was out of town on her scuba diving trips to the Caribbean and Mexico.

Unlike most of their competitors, DisplayTechnik's upper managers did not share office space with lower-level employees. Instead, the high-ranking employees were closeted here, like drones surrounding the queen bee, in cavernous offices appointed with deep, L-shaped mahogany desks and matching bookcases. Each spacious room had been meticulously arranged using the best feng shui consultants in the Bay Area. Water was featured prominently, but so too were the large potted plants cared for by invisible minions who only crept into the offices long after they'd been deserted for the night.

The Ivory Tower was only four stories, but each level was double the normal height. Tall, narrow, cathedral windows allowed solid angles of light to penetrate the reception area. The foyer, where Zack now stood, was the site for lavish corporate receptions and entertaining important guests, not for morale-boosting Christmas parties.

The system Allen Henley had created was downright feudal, and he ruled over it by what he considered his divine right. According to Mary Anne, her father had told the architect he wanted the top stories to dazzle prospective clients, creating an instant home court advantage, much like the White House. For his part, Zack found the ostentatious display of corporate wealth and autocratic power sickening.

He started the ascent up the stairway to where the executive management team resided. At the landing at the top was a nearly bare desk, behind which was the first gatekeeper, a woman who hardly glanced up at Zack's approach. After all, he was expected.

Zack turned left and took the next set of stairs; these were much narrower and followed the circular line of the inner wall and mirrored an identical set of stairs opposite. The two staircases converged at the top, spilling out into an open area. A short walk along the balcony took him to another pair of staircases, which led to the highest level.

Allen's executive secretary, Louise, gave him what appeared to be a genuine smile as he approached. "Go right in," she said.

When Zack entered the palatial office, he was struck by the strong scent of tropical vegetation, coupled with the soft, white noise of the two waterfalls on either side of the door. This was indeed the holy of holies.

"Good morning," he said.

"Please, have a seat." Allen Henley motioned him to a deep blue, leather chair next to a large rubber tree plant. His head was closely shaven, a relatively new development intended to disguise the spreading bald spot at the back of his head. Abandoning his massive desk, which was off to Zack's right in a recessed alcove, Henley sat next to a small pond filled with koi, the wide stone edge of which served as a side table to his chair.

The CEO and president of DisplayTechnik was one of the most recognizable businessmen in America, though not quite as successful as Bill Gates of Microsoft, Andy Grove of Intel, or Lee Iacocca of past Chrysler fame. He was a distinguished icon of corporate America because he actively sought the publicity. Some first-year MBA student could write a paper and argue that he hungered for media attention because he wanted to put the spotlight on DisplayTechnik, but in reality, the flat-panel display market was a relatively small field. Everybody knew everybody. Unlike the hamburger industry, where plastic toys and party packs—not the actual taste or quality of the product—defined the market strategy, a mega advertising blitz wasn't necessary to convince people to choose a particular product.

Zack sat down and was immediately swallowed by the chair. "So, I heard that the local news boys from *Silicon Valley Business* were here," he said to try to head off the nervousness he was feeling.

"Yes. I believe that *SVB* might even do a follow-up piece on us," Allen said. "They can't believe we're actually going toe-to-toe with the Japanese on the FPD market and gaining ground on Toshiba and the lot. The reporter said it was like the USA kicking butt again after we got reamed by the Asians in the DRAM memory market."

Zack expected Allen to smile at the remembered compliment, but he didn't.

"So what if Japan or Southeast Asia tries to ream us with their technology?" Allen said. "After all, we live in a competitive society. Sun Tzu, had he been alive today, would have said that the art of business is war. Yes, most definitely."

Zack had heard this monologue before and knew once Henley got started, he could go on for a long time. He really should have been a televangelist, except that he had no beliefs in a higher power—other than himself. "Is there something in particular you wanted to talk to me about?"

A slight smile played at the corners of Allen's lips. "Yes, Zack, I did have something particular in mind." He gripped the arms of his chair and pulled himself out. He turned his back to Zack as he walked slowly toward the expansive window.

"When you fight a war against an enemy, generally he's in front of you," Allen said. "But then again, all warfare is based on deception."

Zack had a hard time believing he was here for a lecture on Sun Tzu. He didn't like the references to "an enemy." What was Allen getting at?

"When able to attack, we must seem unable," Allen went on, hands clasped behind his back as he paced the floor. "When we are near, we must make the enemy believe we are far away. When far away, make him believe we are near. Hold out baits to entice the enemy. Feign disorder—then crush him."

Allen turned abruptly to face Zack. "Do you understand what I'm saying?"

Zack didn't, but he nodded in the affirmative anyway. It seemed to satisfy the CEO, at least momentarily. Wasn't there *anything* in Sun Tzu that addressed taking care of your troops in order to assure victory? This was a man who thought nothing of his own employees; they were mere commodities to him, expendable and replaceable. And yet, Zack thought, how could he have raised a daughter as wonderful as Mary Anne and be all bad? If there was a small seed of good in Allen Henley, he hadn't seen it yet.

"The military devices that lead to victory must not be divulged beforehand," Allen said. "Are we clear?"

"Not really," Zack said, standing up. "To be honest, I really don't put much stock in Sun Tzu. I just don't think that's the way things need to operate anymore."

"You don't?" Allen chuckled. "Well, you should. You *should*."

The scalp on the back of Zack's head started to tingle.

"Sun Tzu *is* business, young man. You'd best learn that, and soon. Anyone who wants to start a business had best learn that."

Start a business?

Allen laughed at the stunned reaction he could not hide. "You see? Sun Tzu is working. Appear when you are not expected; attack the enemy when he is unprepared."

Had Allen Henley somehow found out about his plans to leave DisplayTechnik and start his own company, Imagination? But who would have told him? Zack's partner, Paul Ryerson, had been careful to get nondisclosure agreements from the potential investors he'd lined up, but he knew they weren't truly binding. Paul had also picked venture capitalists who had no ties to Allen. Could it have been someone on their design team? Zack doubted that. Every one of them had a serious grudge against Henley and DisplayTechnik. They wouldn't have revealed anything, at least not intentionally.

Had he somehow slipped and said something to Mary Anne? No. He was positive he'd never even hinted at it.

Allen was watching him, clearly enjoying his consternation.

"I called you in here to verify if what I thought was true," Allen said. "And I can see by your face I'm right, you ungrateful bastard. I made you who you are, and you repay me by stabbing me in the back! You were nothing. Right out of college, and yet I brought you here and put the world at your feet, eventually promoting you to director of new technology. For Christ's sake, I even gave you my daughter, my own flesh and blood, and look how you treat my gifts."

Say something, Zack told himself. But his mouth was so dry it was hard to swallow. He dropped back into the chair. There was no doubt about it: someone had turned them in.

As though reading his thoughts, Allen said, "Just as you can be surprised by your enemies, you can also be surprised by your allies. Sun Tzu said that the best way to defeat your enemy in a battle is to never fight the battle at all. Break your enemy before he can mount an attack. Try to find alliances with parties or people or even a single person that your enemy trusts the most. If his forces are united, separate them. Try to create confusion in your enemy's ranks to drain the will of your enemy to fight. Do everything you can to destroy your enemy before you must resort to taking to the battlefield and risking harm to yourself or your friends."

"Where are you going with this?"

"I am giving you a last chance," Allen said. "So we can stop this battle before it starts. Renounce it. Renounce your plans, and I'll let it go. I will, I really will. I just need your word that you're with us. That you're with me."

Screw the pompous ass. The whole point was to get away from him.

"I quit," Zack said and walked out of his mentor's office.

"Come back here! Come back here this instant!" Allen shouted at his back. "If he is taking his ease, give him no rest. Do you hear me, Zack? No rest!"

Zack ignored a wide-eyed Louise, making for the staircase.

"You're history!" Allen bellowed down at him as he took the steps two at a time. "I'll destroy that silly little dream of yours, and you'll never work in the Valley again. Never! I'll bury you, you son of a bitch!"

Zack sidestepped the foyer's gatekeeper, who had risen from her desk. As he reached the walnut doors, they burst open in front of him. In stormed Julie, flanked by Frank, a security guard who ran a football pool that Zack participated in, and another, beefier security guard that he didn't recognize.

"Mr. Zack Penny ..." Julie began, a smile playing at the corners of her lips.

"Shut the hell up!" he said. "I don't want to hear it." He tossed his employee access card at her feet. That wiped the smug grin off her face. "You can't fire me; I already quit."

"So I've been notified. I'm here to escort you from the building. Follow me, please." She turned on her heel.

Zack hustled to keep up with her while the security men brought up the rear. The little convoy plowed down the hall. Astonished employees ducked into side corridors or tightly hugged the wall when there was no escape.

When they reached the engineering section, Phyllis sat behind her desk, a sad, worried look on her face. She didn't say a word. Someone must have tipped off the engineers because their doors were all closed. All except Zack's.

Inside, Bill Bennet was sitting in his chair, scrolling through the files on his computer. There was an empty cardboard box on the floor at Bill's feet.

Julie pointed at the box. "Put your personal things in there."

"If you don't mind," Bill said, "while you go through your desk, I need to take a look in your briefcase to verify, of course, that no company property leaves the premises."

"Knock yourself out," Zack said.

He started piling things in the box: Jan's loaf of bread, pictures, paperweights, books, and a matched set of bookends. From the shelf by the window, he retrieved a small sculpture of a mermaid arching her back, arms gracefully extended as she rose to the surface. Mary Anne had given it to him ten days ago as a one-year anniversary present. It was a beautiful piece that captured a moment of motion. He'd smiled at the time, thinking it a bit ironic that it was titled "Imagination," and had looked forward to being able to share the private joke with her when it was all out in the open. Now the mermaid went ingloriously into the box with the other remnants of his DisplayTechnik career.

He opened the middle drawer and grabbed a fistful of pens, including a fountain pen from his father.

"Wait a minute," Julie said. "You can't take those."

"What do you mean? These are my pens."

"Bill?"

"According to your contract," Bill said without looking up from his task, "unless items deemed personal can actually be verified at the time of dismissal, all such items shall be assumed to be the property of DisplayTechnik. Do you have a receipt?"

"What? Who the hell keeps receipts for their pens at their desks? And you're telling me the company hands out fountain pens now?"

"I can't say we don't. Tell you what. We'll hang on to these for now, but if you can show us a receipt for it, we'll happily return them."

Bill held up a stack of rewritable CDs from the briefcase. "And these are …?"

"Those are all company files except for the one that doesn't have a label. It's music."

"Is it now?" Bill suspiciously eyed the blank silver side.

"Yes. Now if you don't mind—"

"According to your contract," Julie said, "DisplayTechnik retains the rights to search your personal property before you leave the building."

"How about we just take a little look at it?" Bill said. "If it's yours, we'll know soon enough."

When Zack made a step toward him, Frank clamped a hand on his shoulder. He shook his head, his lips tight.

Bill put the CD in the drive. The autoplay engaged, and a Santana tune started to play. Bill frowned. "You realize," he said, staring straight ahead at the screen, "that music piracy is an extremely important issue. Companies lose millions over it." He slowly turned his head and looked at Zack. "I could report this, you know."

"Be my guest," Zack said. "I own the CD. I'm allowed to make copies for my own use, thank you, and I always keep the originals at home."

Bill closed the window and ejected the CD. He placed it in the box with the other items for DisplayTechnik.

"You put it in the wrong box," Zack said.

"No, I think we'll keep it too. It looks a great deal like the other CDs that are DisplayTechnik's, so I imagine it came out of the company storeroom."

"This is ridiculous. I'm sure that's my disk; I have stacks of them at home. Hell, probably all those disks with DisplayTechnik files are actually mine."

"Show me a receipt, and I'm sure we'll reimburse you," Bill said, staring at the screen as he searched through Zack's files on the computer. "Besides, you shouldn't use personal property for company business. Bad for tax purposes."

"Jesus! You people really have gone nuts. What's come over this place? I'm not talking about a fifty-cent CD; I'm talking about the principle of all this."

"Yes," Bill said, appraising him through narrowed eyes. He snorted derisively. "We all know about your high principles." He turned back to the computer. "Well, fifty cents times a thousand employees every week can add up rather quickly. Show me a receipt, and you can have it back."

"Are we done here, or are you going to want to do a cavity search?"

Bill visibly stiffened. "Julie, see him out of the building."

Zack snatched up his briefcase and the box. Julie led the way while Frank and the other guard bracketed him. He was surprised when they didn't take the stairs but instead headed for the lobby elevators. It occurred to him that the idea was to make an example of him, parading him past as many employees as possible.

Fortunately, the lobby was mostly deserted. Jan met his eyes as they crossed the floor, tears brimming. The few other employees who were there looked away. The only person who stared was a visitor just leaving the receptionist's desk. He stopped in his tracks. The beefy guard sidestepped the man and in the process bumped Zack's arm carrying the box. It tilted, the contents slid awkwardly to one side, and as Zack made a grab for it, his foot caught on the corner of the rug.

The box slipped from his hands as he stumbled and fell. He landed heavily on the marble floor, and the box's contents scattered. He remained there, motionless for a few seconds, his face inches from its glossy surface. His elbow screamed in protest as he pushed up.

"This is far enough," Julie announced. With that, she turned and left with the guards in tow.

Zack knelt on the floor, sweeping up his spilled property. The mermaid's decapitated head was halfway to the front doors, still slowly spinning.

CHAPTER TWO

Zack jumped into his car, slamming the box and briefcase onto the passenger seat. He resisted giving vent to his anger until he was out of the reach of Allen's security cameras. Once clear of the parking lot, he pulled over and pounded on the steering wheel.

How in the world had Allen found out about the start-up? Schooled by their CEO's paranoia, they'd taken every possible precaution. No one kept files at DisplayTechnik, and other than that single, stupid, cryptic e-mail from Dimitre that one time, no one—*no one*—ever mentioned Imagination at work. Had someone slipped up? And just how much did Allen know?

He took a deep breath to clear his head and rolled down the window, sticking his elbow into the warm air, and pulled away from the curb to start the drive home. The one good thing about being fired before midday was that the commute up Highway 680 on the east side of the San Francisco Bay would be a breeze.

Against the blue, cloudless sky, a haze hung over the valley. It had its own charm, but it wasn't exactly beautiful. Back in New Hampshire, he'd pictured the Bay Area surrounded by green hills, perhaps because all he knew about San Francisco was that it was near the wine country. What he found instead was a surprising lack of rain, which had the same effect on the hills as wind on chapped skin, leaving them looking scoured and raw and more beige than green. Today as he drove over the Sunol grade, the vacant starkness of those hills against the equally featureless sky made him feel like he was reaching the edge of the world.

In half an hour, he'd arrived at the Pleasanton exit but decided to keep driving, in no hurry to arrive at an empty apartment and needing more time to think.

Perhaps this wasn't so bad, maybe it was even fate. The Imagination team had been in secret product development for six months, and the plan had been to finalize everything over the next three months and then decide once and for all whether to make the break. It was a scary thought to be suddenly out there on their own. For a while Jimmy had advocated that rather than make a clean start with their own company, it might be better to convince Allen to set them up in a spin-off that would still be connected to DisplayTechnik, to make use of its marketing and managerial staff and, more importantly, its financial resources. What had finally convinced Jimmy otherwise was Dimitre asking him if he wanted to do all the work of a start-up while Allen held the plug to their money.

It wasn't as though their plans for the company were now in disarray. Their financing was basically lined up, they already had a building in mind for their plant—another victim of the ups and downs of the tech sector—and Dimitre had finally settled on his latest formulations. The question was, were they ready to take the plunge?

When he reached the bridge at Petaluma, he turned around and headed back to Pleasanton, reaching his apartment complex nearly two hours after he'd left DisplayTechnik. He might have reached the end of one world, but he was confident he'd fallen into a better one.

When he dialed his voice mail, the familiar benign voice of AT&T said, "You have thirty-seven new messages. To hear new messages—"

Zack zipped through them. The first six weren't messages at all. Someone's fax machine had mistakenly dialed his number, and it had repeated its mating call every five minutes. The seventh was from Jan.

"Zack, hi. Listen, I—I'm calling from the pay phone right now, but I … I just wanted to say how sorry I am for everything that happened." There was a muffled sniff. "Call me at home tonight, okay? Promise? I'll send over some baked goods tomorrow with one of your engineers. Bye." The last word was high-pitched, like she was fighting back tears.

The next three messages were all from various colleagues at DisplayTechnik who'd heard the news and offered support of one kind or another. Then the rest of the Imagination team started calling.

"Zack. Is Dimitre. This is being no good. The Metal Queen axed me as well. I smell bad fish here, something stinking to high heaven. My Anna is not going to like this; will call you after she has killed me."

"Hey, Zack … What's up? It's Brett. Give me a call when you can, okay?"

He couldn't tell if Brett had been fired or not. Probably.

"Ditto," followed by the heavy sound of an awkward hang-up. That was Jimmy Morgan.

"Heya, Zack, it's Jerry. Julie and her death squad popped in, and I was popped out. They saved me for last for some reason; I got front-row seats to watch everyone else get kicked out. Like dominos. So, you ready to kick some ass? I sure as hell am! How about a pizza party at your place tonight? Your treat. I'll give everyone else a buzz, and we'll show sixish. Later."

"Zack—is Dimitre again. Is good news. My Anna did not kill me. She said to come home so she could make love to new head engineer for Imagination. Oh. Also, Jerry called me and said pizza tonight at your house. For God's sake, do not get Jimmy's strange pizza. Smell is bad enough, let alone watch him to eat it. Okay, am going home now to my Anna. Will see you tonight if I survive." Dimitre hung up in the middle of his laugh.

"Zack. Paul here. I just spoke with Jimmy Morgan, and he told me what happened. This really complicates things, but I think we can pull a rabbit out of Allen's ass for you, old buddy. It just means we accelerate our plans somewhat. I'm going to go ahead and put that deposit on our building today before someone else grabs it. Looks like we'll need it after all, eh? Lots to talk about, but don't know how much more time this thing has so I'll catch up with you later. Give me a call if I don't catch you first."

There were about a dozen other calls from many different departments other than engineering, most of them calling on their lunch break, probably sneaking out of the office. Many of them offered their help or services if he needed them. One had already heard of a position that might fit him. He wasn't surprised by the number of calls—only by who didn't call.

Not a single message from Mary Anne.

That evening, seven people squeezed into his two-bedroom apartment. In addition to the engineering team of Dimitre Koslov, Jimmy Morgan, and Jerry Steiner, Paul Ryerson, Brett Davis, and John and Molly Baker, branch managers of the Pleasanton Bank of America, were also there. Half of the group sat on the floor, while the others were piled into three pieces of furniture in the living room: a sofa, love seat, and a La-Z-Boy chair.

Jimmy raised his can of beer. He was nearly a head shorter than Dimitre on the opposite end of the love seat. "To Imagination!" he cried.

"No more assholes like Henley!" Jerry said.

Which brought a round of cheers and catcalls.

"To our dream!" Dimitre clinked his mug of champagne against Jerry's tumbler of port.

"To finding Zack a decent lamp!" Molly said.

He joined in on the laughter. The only lamp in the living room cast just enough light to discern the shiny faces of the love-seat occupants. The apartment was warm, despite the air conditioner going full blast. The muted television's screen threw a bit more light on the proceedings.

Zack lay on his side on the floor, propped up by a wiry arm. He didn't have much furniture because he liked to sprawl on the beige carpet—spotted with unidentified stains that he vowed to clean up one of these days. His friends were all looking at him, waiting for his toast.

Zack raised his glass. "To the end of corporate politics and the return of some decency and ethics to the Valley," he said.

There was a moment of silence like someone had just said grace in a beer hall. Allen's lack of morals had pushed them all away; his actions today had strengthened their resolve. Dimitre nodded, and one by one, they all raised their glasses with a quiet, "Here, here."

In the dim glow of the lamp, Brett Davis looked like he had tears in his eyes. He'd flown in from Dallas when he heard the news about the firings, and by the time he'd landed, there was a message on his cell phone that he'd been released and that his personal items would be mailed to him. There was no mention of his final commission paycheck. He was the one person standing, leaning on a doorframe.

John and Molly Baker sat on the floor. The couple had been instrumental in helping introduce Zack to moneymen. They had agreed to take care of the books for the start-up until they were needed full-time.

Paul Ryerson sat beside them, fidgeting, combing his hand through his thick, wavy blond hair. He seemed to be worrying over something. Zack knew it would come out before the night was over. It wasn't like Paul to hold things in.

As the group chatted and chomped their way through the third Round Table pizza, Zack wondered if they were as conscious of the fact that Mary Anne was missing as he was. Even though she hadn't been a part of the planning activities, both he and the others figured after the cat was out of the bag, she would leap into his arms—both figuratively and literally.

"We've already heard Brett's story, so how'd they ax the rest of you guys?" Jimmy asked. "I came back from an early tech meeting, and there was Julie rousting Zack. Her crony, Tiffany, tells me to go wait in my office and then locks the door. Locks the damn door on me! Sheesh, they ought to know I'm claustrophobic. So I've got the window open, considering jumping the ten feet to the ground, when Julie comes in, and she starts in, accusing me of fleeing the scene! Needless to say, I didn't get my final fantasy fulfilled."

Jerry snorted beer out his nose, and the rest joined in the laughter.

"Da. They do much the same to me, except they lock me in my office right from start. Was like KGB raid. I have nothing for them to find, everything at home, so I play solitaire for two hours. They must do everyone else first, save best for last. When Julie and Bill come in, they go through my things 'til they come to wastepaper basket; then they stop and tell me to go away, never come back."

"Wastepaper? How come?" Molly asked.

Zack watched the slow shaking start in Dimitre's belly and then spread like an earthquake as chuckle transformed into guffaw. "Because, I locked up for two hours and had to piss in wastepaper basket!"

The thought of Bill Bennet searching through urine-soaked papers made them all laugh.

"Geez, mine was pretty boring then," Jerry said, wiping tears from his eyes. "I never even made it up to my office. I was late today because of a dentist appointment. I was met at the employee entrance with a box of my things and a dismissal slip. Never even saw Julie."

"So that leaves you, Zack-o," Jimmy said. "How'd they ax you?"

Zack told them about his morning, including Allen's ranting.

"Geez," Jerry said. "Well, that confirms it; I guess he found out somehow. Any idea how?"

"No, none."

Paul stood up and cleared his throat, all eyes on him.

Here it comes, Zack thought. Whatever it is, here it comes.

"Listen, Zack. There's something else that's really bothering me, and I have to clear the air here. You know that I don't give a rat's ass about your personal life. Hell, by the time Imagination hits the streets, you won't have a personal life. But since Creative Partnership is investing 4.3 million dollars to get your company going, we have a vested interest in its number-one employee. And that's you, pal."

"Sure, Paul." Zack sighed, having heard this speech before.

"You told her, didn't you?

Zack rolled over and sat up. "No, I didn't. I may have talked indirectly about it but never openly," Zack said.

"What does that mean?"

"It means that I did not tell her about Imagination, but we've had discussions about my leaving the company."

"Ah. Okay, so she knew something then, right?"

Zack felt his temperature rising. He was conscious of the eyes on him. Did they think he'd betrayed them? He wracked his brain, trying to think if he'd ever even said the word *imagination* around her, but he was sure he hadn't.

"I would never break any of your trust. I hope you all know that. I—"

"Look," Paul said, "I may not know technology from the contents of a pooper-scooper, but I do know people. Remember? That's *my* job."

Zack had heard this speech as well. Every time they'd met a potential investor, Paul had said that although a sound business plan helped grease the investment wheels, it was really the quality of the people behind the plan that convinced the money brokers in New York or Sandy Hill to invest. So far he'd been right.

Paul pointed a finger at him. "You, my friend, have your ass backward when it comes to your girlfriend."

"Hey," Jerry said, "if Zack says he didn't tell her, then that's good enough for me."

"Yeah. And me," Jimmy said.

Molly and Brett voiced their approval too.

"Zack is saint," Dimitre said. "If Saint Zack says he did not talk, he did not talk. End of story."

"Okay, so then who *did* talk, huh?" Paul asked. "How the hell did Henley find out about all of us? Seems to me, pal, that Mary Anne is the obvious choice here for the leak. We've got to know what she knows and do some damage control."

"Paul, it could be anyone," Dimitre countered. "KGB find out things all the time. Maybe investors talk, maybe lines tapped at work, maybe hack into personal computer. Who knows? Fact is, is over. Imagination is started. Good for us."

"Let's just concentrate on business and not my private life. Keep Mary Anne out of it," Zack added.

Paul shook his head. "Not when your personal life and your business life connect, my friend. And this is a major intersection. What does she know?"

"For Christ's sake, I told you. Nothing."

"You've been spending practically every waking hour away from the office thinking about Imagination. And you're telling me your girlfriend doesn't know shit about it? Give me a break."

As embarrassing as it was to be called out like this in front of everyone, Zack realized that if he was truly putting the DisplayTechnik mind-set behind him, he couldn't start out on Day One acting like Allen Henley. If he'd screwed up, then he needed to admit to it, apologize, and find a way to fix the problem.

"Like I said, I'm sure I told Mary Anne that I wasn't happy at DisplayTechnik. But I never—not even once—mentioned that we were going to start Imagination. And whenever I brought up the subject of leaving the company, she'd go into this cruise-control speech about how her father built it, how Allen felt about me, that it was a great opportunity for me. For us. In her wildest dreams, she couldn't understand how I could possibly think of leaving."

"So you did tell her you were leaving?" Paul asked.

"No, I did not. I just told her it was a thought that passed through my mind, nothing more."

"What did she say when you said you wanted to leave? Didn't she ask where you'd go? Seems to me that'd be a natural question."

That did sound like something she would have asked. He tried to remember for a moment. Did she ask that? What did he say?

"Well, if she asked, I'm pretty sure I would have said I didn't know. Just somewhere else."

"Pretty sure? Zack, this is important. You've got to be sure."

"I am sure. I know I didn't say I wanted to start my own company, and even if by some chance I did say I was thinking about starting another company, I certainly would not have talked about Imagination."

"I am having enough of this," Dimitre said. "It is over and done with. It is—"

"Yeah, come on, Paul," John said. "I think Zack's answered this."

"Well, there has to be something more."

"I'm telling you, that's it. Whenever the issue came up, we never got past Mary Anne's commercial about how wonderful our life was at DisplayTechnik."

"So then how did Henley find out about all of us?"

Zack said nothing.

"How did Allen Henley," Paul said slowly, taking a step toward him, "know every single player involved in Imagination? That can't be coincidence."

Zack surveyed the room. He'd wondered that too.

"Hold the phone!" Jerry said. "You think someone here leaked the info?"

"No," Zack said. "I didn't say that."

"You don't have to, buddy. I can *feel* it."

"I work very hard these months." Dimitre wrestled his way out of the love seat and stood up. "All here are making pledge to Imagination. To you. I am not believing you are thinking someone here could be like KGB spy. I am not believing this."

There was a murmur of consensus. Somebody muttered

"girlfriend," but Zack didn't catch who said it or what came after it.

Zack took a deep breath and made eye contact with everyone. Despite all the hard work so far and with so much more work to come, he knew that this was a defining moment.

"I repeat, I did not say that. We've sacrificed far too much to doubt one another now. I trust all of you completely. I didn't mean to imply it was someone in this room, and I'm sorry if I gave that impression. Sure, I wonder how the information got out, but I don't believe that anyone in this room leaked it. I would bet my life on it."

He paused and then added, "I don't know; maybe it was Mary Anne." There, he'd finally said it, even if he hoped with his whole being that it wasn't true. "I guess it does say a lot that she's not here with us. She must know by now what happened, and I really hoped she would come to our support—although in her defense, she is Allen's daughter, so it's awkward for her no matter which way she turns." Molly nodded knowingly. "And, yeah, I'm disappointed in her.

"Guys, to the best of my knowledge, I never, ever slipped and said anything about Imagination. Maybe Allen himself was able to put two and two together based on something I said. If that's the case, I'm sorry. And I'm disappointed that I didn't see this coming. Given who Allen is and how deep his contacts run in the Valley, I should have planned for this possibility."

Zack paused, making eye contact with everyone again. "To be honest, like Dimitre, I'm glad that the secret's out. I feel like I've been living a double life for the last six months. We knew the news would come out eventually, right? So it's a few months premature, but we've got the plan, we've got the technology, and as soon as Paul can arrange it, we've got the money. You heard him. That's 4.3 million coming our way just from his investment group. Four point three million! With another thirty on the way. Now that the cat's out of the bag, we can finally concentrate on making Imagination a reality. Right?"

Smiles began to appear all around.

"Um, actually ..." Paul began, "I wanted to talk to you all about the money situation."

"Paul, tell me there isn't a problem all of a sudden," Zack said. The one thing no one wanted to hear was that the financing was no longer in place.

"Well, it's not quite like that ..."

"What, then? For God's sake!" Zack exclaimed.

"Well, it's just that Dickens called this afternoon. He's been doing some reading, and he thinks the timing is hot and was thinking about adding another two million if we could step up our plans a little."

The apartment rang with whoops of joy.

"Oh my God!" Molly said. "Talk about good timing!"

Jimmy waved his hand in the air. "Wait, wait a second, there's still one thing that really gets me," he said.

Zack frowned at the young engineer. He'd hoped they'd settled this discussion.

"How come," Jimmy went on, "whenever we order pizza, you always forget to order sardines with cherries and pineapples? You know that's my favorite."

Zack's slice of half-finished crust was the first to ricochet off Jimmy's head.

"I hope you design better than you eat, Morgan," John Baker said. "Otherwise, we're in big trouble."

"Is actually very simple to know if you have good engineer or not," Dimitre piped up, grinning under his beard.

"I'm afraid to ask," Jerry said. "How?"

Zack rolled his eyes, as did the rest of the engineers, who were all too familiar with Dimitre's ensemble of anecdotes.

"Is very simple. You ask his wife if she is satisfied in bed. Then you know answer."

"Now what in tarnation does that have to do with his engineering skills?" Brett asked.

"Because, if engineer cannot complete one simple job in twenty minutes, how can you expect him to be completing big complex project on time?"

There were more groans, punctuated by a slice of pizza whizzing by Dimitre's head. The engineer ducked, and the slice hit a San Francisco '49er team poster that was taped onto the wall next to the television. The piece oozed its way through the offensive line.

"Aw, now who did that?" Jimmy asked. "That's sacred."

Zack was relieved to see the mood in the room lighten. This really was a time to celebrate. There'd been a lot of tense moments the last month or so as they'd begun to wrestle with the decision to take the plunge.

As the group dove into the remainder of the pizza, Zack went through a checklist of things to do. Moving into the new facility, getting all the permits lined up, refitting the building, ordering testing and construction equipment, finalizing the design on paper, and the big one—verifying the design with prototype samples. Then it was test and calibrate, design and redesign, and finally bringing in more people and organizing the company infrastructure. Hell, they'd even have to hire a cleaning staff to make sure the paper towels were restocked. The list went on and on. But in the back of his mind, one thought persisted.

Where *was* Mary Anne?

By the time everyone filed out several hours later, it was well past midnight. Zack looked down at the remaining pizza slices on the floor. The smell of the cardboard boxes, with grease pools in the collapsed corners, filled the living room. He turned his back on the mess. He'd clean up tomorrow. He was too tired emotionally and physically to deal with it.

Zack stretched and yawned. He patted his stomach, feeling the Parmesan cheese still settling inside. For the briefest moment, he considered going out for his nightly jog, but knew he'd never make it and strange noises from his stomach settled the argument.

He slid open the door to the second-floor balcony off his

bedroom. He breathed in the pleasant night air, opening the door wider to wash out the stuffiness and the pizza smell. As he stepped outside, the sprinklers replenished the grass of the island boulevard that separated the traffic on Stoneridge Road. It was just cool enough but not too cool, though he did wish he could have seen some stars. There was something about them that was always reassuring.

He went back inside, leaving the sliding door open, and crawled into bed without stripping off his jeans or T-shirt.

Before he fell asleep, his last thought was that he hadn't called Mary Anne. He hoped her absence meant she was just trying to feel her way through what had happened, much as everyone else was. They weren't engaged yet. And even if they were, would that matter? Would her loyalties be to her father, or to him?

He decided he didn't want to know the answers, at least not yet.

CHAPTER THREE

Dean McSorley—the last surviving, original senior partner of Travis, McSorley, and Davis—watched Allen Henley storm around his office. The recessed, dimmed ceiling lights allowed the nightlights of San Francisco to show off their colors through the expansive corner window, giving the office a theater-like quality. If Dean could have hit some cosmic mute button, Allen might have been rehearsing a scene from *Macbeth* instead of ranting against his protégé.

Ever since Dean had met Allen in college, Allen had always gotten whatever he wanted. It wasn't that he was spoiled or even terribly lucky. What he wanted, he got. Simple as that. If it meant working hard for it, so be it; if it fell into his lap, all the better. It didn't matter how he got it; it just mattered that he did.

The man had an "old colony" bearing about him. It was easy to imagine Allen commanding bright red-uniformed troops marching in straight long lines onto an open battlefield. Who cared if the enemy was camouflaged, hidden securely behind dense thicket and walls of fieldstones? Who cared if his troops were decimated by cannon fire? Just march onward for the glory of king and country—and Allen.

When Allen turned his back to him, Dean stole a glance down to the other end of the room. Bill Bennet perched on the edge of the leather couch. Mary Anne sat quietly in an armchair, hands folded in her lap, her short mop of brown hair dissolving into the mahogany paneling as though she were in the first stage of disappearing into the wall. She hadn't said a word since coming into the office, not even her customary cheerful, "Hello, Uncle Dean." She just sat staring out at the lights of Market Street below.

This had to be extremely difficult for her. And yet, he sensed a steely indifference. Maybe indifference was the wrong word. Resignation? Determination? Or maybe she just didn't want to be here?

And yet, her actions were what had brought them all to his office. Surely she had to realize that. He wondered how much Allen had told his daughter about what he planned to do to Zack. She was still young and perhaps a bit naïve, but it was hard to imagine she had no clue. Funny. He thought Zack and she were closer than that. Well, their relationship was over now, he'd bet on it. Too bad he didn't have a son of his own to go pick up the pieces.

Dean looked at his notes. Over the last few weeks, his office had been drawing up the complaint, thoroughly researching the minutest aspects of it. Tonight it was just a matter of putting on the finishing touches. Tomorrow he'd call the judge and have it signed.

When Allen finally ran out of steam, Dean said, "I'm going to say once again that these noncompete/infringement cases are not always easy to win, even with a signed, airtight agreement and evidence of intent."

"I don't care what you *think*," Allen snapped back. "What you *know* is this: Zack Penny and his penny-ante gang of thieves have stolen the intellectual property of DisplayTechnik. Period. They have also violated the noncompete contracts they signed and are starting up a company that is based upon *my* technology, *my* ideas, and *my* money."

Dean folded his hands in his lap. "You don't have to convince me that you're right. It's my job to play devil's advocate, to make sure you understand both the upside and downside. All I am saying is—"

"That you're going to nail these sons of bitches to the wall."

Dean studied Allen's reddening face and jutting jaw. "Of course," he said. "Nailing is the specialty of the firm."

The CEO's mouth twisted into a nasty smile. "I guess it's a good thing that you and I have a long-standing relationship; otherwise, you could just as easily be playing for the other side—if they had the money to pay your retainer."

"Knock off the lawyer digs," Dean said. "I'm a gun for hire, and you hired me." He looked to Bill for support, but he seemed to be doing his best to pretend he wasn't listening. The general counsel for DisplayTechnik had not said a word so far. He was gazing out the other corner window, apparently watching the lights of a cargo ship coming into the bay.

Allen snorted. "You lawyers could make a case that Judas betrayed Jesus because his stock-option plan wasn't as equitable as the rest of the disciples."

"Your humor is boundless."

"God damn it, listen to me!" Allen said. "This is not one of the dozens of minor cases we send your way every year. This is personal. Understood?"

Silence hung over the room. Even Bill looked up.

Dean frowned. He didn't like a lot of the things that Allen had asked him to do. But, then again, he wasn't paid to like them. DisplayTechnik had been Travis, McSorley, and Davis's most important client for a long while. Four years of private schooling and two years of college for each of his three daughters were directly financed by Allen's sometimes trivial, sometimes vengeful legal pursuits. This wasn't the first time that former DisplayTechnik employees were being sued for violations of one sort or another— nor, he was confident, would it be the last. Competition was too fierce in the Valley. Time was too precious, and the egos of the men running the companies were too big.

"Mary Anne," Dean said, "there's some coffee and food down the hall. Would you like some? Or better yet, how about if you order up some takeout? Your choice. I think we might be here a bit. You can use the phone in the other office."

Mary Anne got up and left. At a nod from Dean, Bill closed the door behind her.

"Am I understood?" Allen said. "Call whomever you need to, hire whomever you need to, do whatever you need to do to win this. I don't care what it costs, but you will win. Destroy that little asshole and all of his friends. I want them to curse the day they met him."

"That's a certainty, regardless of whatever legal counteractions they may attempt. Now, how much does Mary Anne know? She's the weak link here."

Allen turned away and looked out the window, his hands clasped behind his back. Dean could see the fingers of one hand fidgeting.

"This is her boyfriend we're talking about here," Dean continued, "and I was under the impression that they were very close, that it was serious between them. I can't imagine she knows the full extent of your plans. And just how far *are* you planning on taking this?"

"She knows what she needs to know. She's strong; she'll come through this all right. In the end, she'll see that this is the right course."

"I hope so, for her sake."

"I know my own daughter," Allen said.

"I hope so. For your sake. I'm guessing that we'll need to call in Fong to handle what my office can't. Or won't."

"Yes, yes, give our fat Asian friend a call. If we're going to draw blood from a stone, we'll need the right surgeon—that son of a bitch named Fong."

Dean cracked a smile, and for a moment, the two of them were back at Stanford together. He began to recite, "There once was a guy named Fong ..."

"Whose family came from Hong Kong ..." Allen chimed in.

"He was a shark who could swim with no restrictions ..."

"And do things without any sign of remorse or convictions ..."

Dean joined his old friend in the last line, "That son of a bitch named Fong!"

Bill stared at them, a pained look on his face.

"God, that brings back some memories," Dean said.

"Yes, it does. Give Sandy a call. We could use his computer skills, among other things."

Dean saw the light on his phone console wink out. "Mary Anne is coming back," he said. "Let's get back to the details of what will be added to the complaint. She can help us with that."

Around six o'clock in the morning, Zack and his new team of engineers met for breakfast at the Milpitas Denny's just off Highway 101. After coffee and French toast, the group drove to Santa Clara, the home of such notable high-technology heavyweights as Intel and Applied Materials. By a stroke of good luck, Zack and Paul had found an existing plant built by a near-field display start-up that had closed due to economic pressure. The 56,000-square-foot facility had over half the manufacturing equipment they needed already in place, saving them months of tooling up, not to mention reducing the time to obtain all the county permits that required the patience of Job.

While Zack watched, the three engineers and Brett were running around whooping and laughing like kids at a playground outfitted with all the latest toys and games. They started throwing balls of paper at each other, only calling a truce after Jimmy fell halfway down a flight of stairs. There was such an insane amount of space that each engineer claimed an area that was probably bigger than the biggest office of any Fortune 500 CEO.

"Holy crapola!" Jimmy exclaimed. "My office is bigger than my entire apartment!"

"Maybe you should move in here," Jerry Steiner said.

"Better keep that one under your hat," Brett said. "If Paul hears ya, he'll probably go recommending that to Zack."

"You do not need to worry about Paul, my friend," Dimitre

said. "Worry about me. I will kick your ass all the way to promise land!"

Dimitre let out a deep, resonant laugh that carried down the entire main hallway, which split the building into two equal halves, one for the manufacturing area and the other for offices.

Zack was leaning on the rail of the catwalk that surrounded the main hallway. It was good to hear the excitement and enthusiasm of his product team.

Even though they were on their own now, he wondered how long before they were all replaced at DisplayTechnik. Allen was probably already interviewing. He also wondered what bothered Allen more about all of this: that some of his key technologists, including a potential son-in-law, had abandoned the Henley dream, or that they were ready to search for their own?

Paul stood outside talking with Rob Kennedy, the property management representative, who'd decided to stay and chat up the moneyman of the new company. Perhaps Paul knew of other start-ups as well. There was a lot of real estate sitting idle or about to go idle if the winds blew the wrong way.

Paul let the man talk. He'd seemed exceptionally happy to tuck their certified check away in his briefcase. So happy, in fact, that Paul's inner suspicions immediately started to bubble. Something didn't feel right. Was he not telling them something about the building?

A blue sedan turned left into the parking lot. Paul expected the car to turn around and do a U-turn, but it drove slowly toward them. Guy must be lost or something. He couldn't be looking for work already. Paul smiled at the thought.

Rob followed his gaze. "Huh? Looks like you've got your first customer."

"Well, people just can't stay away from a good product, what can I say?"

The blue sedan pulled to a stop, and a young guy about twenty-five got out. He was wearing a poorly fitting sport coat and looked like he'd be a good security man. Maybe that's who he was. Paul couldn't remember for sure, but it seemed that the companies on this road might have some sort of cooperative security system.

"Hey," the man said. "You Paul Ryerson?"

"Yeah ..."

The man went to shake Paul's hand but dropped his keys. When he stood up, he slapped a folded set of papers that he'd pulled from his pocket against Paul's chest. Paul instinctively grabbed at the papers, and the man let go. Paul looked down at the papers folded in thirds, bound in a blue outer liner.

"You've been served," the man said over his shoulder, already heading for his car.

"What the fu—?" Paul opened the papers, and the word "SUMMONS" jumped out at him. Beneath that was, "DisplayTechnik v. Zack Penny & Paul Ryerson (DBA Creative Partnerships)." Looking up, he saw the surprised look of the realtor, who'd been so happily chatting away about other buildings he had available. Paul's faced burned from both embarrassment and the rage building up inside him.

"This ... this has to be a mistake," Paul said. "I mean, we haven't even started anything yet."

Rob looked uncomfortable, holding his briefcase in front of him. "I, uh ... man! Not a good way to begin your first day."

"No shit."

"This, um, this was a certified check, wasn't it?"

Paul, who was used to dealing with all types in the business world, had a hard time restraining himself and not knocking the idiot on his ass. "Yes, it's certified," he said with a bit more anger than he meant to. Rule number one in the business world: Never, ever burn your bridges. "Don't worry," he said in a softer tone, "we'll get this straightened out. Look, I better go and give this to the boss. It was great seeing you again, Rob. You take care, all right?"

Rob nodded and shook Paul's hand. "Best of luck."

Paul went inside and ducked into an office off the main entrance.

He quickly read through the summons and attached complaint. It had been signed just that morning. But the extent of the complaint was incredible. The depth and detail of the explanation of how Imagination/Creative Partnerships would be competing against DisplayTechnik sucked the air out of his lungs.

Their entire business plan was exposed: what they intended to do, who was involved, and how they were going to do it. Each point was countered with how this infringed on DisplayTechnik. It asserted Paul and Zack had lured away valued employees, who were now in violation of nondisclosure and noncompete clauses in their previous contracts with DisplayTechnik. It alluded to patent infringements and insinuated that these might become part of the ensuing action pending discovery. There was an entire section of technical details attached that Paul didn't understand, but the thrust of it was clear: Allen Henley knew a hell of a lot more than Zack was letting on.

God damn it! What the hell was Zack doing? Henley had obviously been slipped a shitload of confidential information. This complaint was way more specific than it should have been at this stage. God! Zack had just sat there and lied in front of the whole group when he said that he hadn't told the little bitch anything. Where the hell were the ethics he was always talking about? Didn't Zack understand how much they all had riding on this?

He flipped open his cell phone, scanned through the internal phone book, and dialed up Jeremy's number.

Zack left the engineers and walked toward the front of the building, looking for Paul in order to ask him about the time line for phone installation. He'd just turned the corner into the entranceway when Paul stepped out of an office and came striding toward him. Paul pulled up short and stood in front of him; the faint crow lines around his eyes seemed to jump off his face.

"What's up with you?" Zack said.

"We just received this!" Paul thrust the papers into his face.

Zack took a step back to snatch the documents Paul was waving. "What is it?"

"A fucking summons! Some jackoff served me out in the parking lot right in front of Kennedy. What the hell's going on?"

Zack just stared at Paul. The relief of being out from under Allen dissipated, and his knuckles began to throb.

"Remember our little conversation last night?" Paul said. "About how did Henley find out so much about us? And that—"

"I was there."

Zack quickly opened the documents. His eyes widened when he saw the foreboding seal of the Federal District Court of San Francisco. Scanning further, his eye caught the name "Travis, McSorley, and Davis," one of the Valley's top business law firms, which specialized in litigation involving intellectual property. Patent infringements, copyrights, trademarks, inventions, nondisclosures, trade secrets, and noncompete and nonsolicitation contracts were the fallout of corporate paranoia that warranted their high-priced advice. There was no way Imagination's per-hire corporate attorney could match up with them.

As Zack read through the complaint, a huge lump formed in his throat. Allen had promised to forever bar his employment in the Valley, but he'd expected him to make calls to other companies, or work to separate he and Mary Anne, or perhaps file some sort of complaint once they were operational and had an actual product to show. He'd expected an opening move with a pawn or a knight or something. But this ... this was like bringing the queen immediately into play, with no subtlety.

For some reason, the complaint named only Zack and Paul. Why was that? The other key engineers who'd left DisplayTechnik were listed but were not being directly sued.

"Well?" Paul said.

Zack didn't reply. He just stood there, staring at the sheets of paper. His mind spun. How? Why?

Snap out of it, he told himself. The "why" was easy. This was Allen Henley, after all. This was the man who invented the phrase

"Take no prisoners." The CEO of DisplayTechnik was known to go psychotic when confronted with in-your-face competition; he was a man with no sense of decorum or scale. In his keynote speech at a Semicon West Exhibition some years back, he'd angered the local Asian community by saying that Japanese efficiency had been sabotaged by their work ethic. He speculated that a hard-lined, kamikaze corporate culture was boilerplate material taken from the attack strategy of Pearl Harbor. He'd left the podium under a deluge of catcalls and whistles. He was never invited back as a speaker.

But it was the implications of the "how" that devastated Zack. How did Allen know so much? And how did he do this so fast?

"Well prepared in advance, wouldn't you say?" Paul said. "This was not something they just slapped together last night. It must have taken weeks, maybe a month or more to get all this ready. The detail of this summons, well, I don't have to tell you what it means, what that implies. Hell, my four-year-old son could figure that out."

How did they find out so soon? Zack asked himself. How could Mary Anne have done this? Someone else must have talked. He desperately hoped it was someone, anyone besides Mary Anne, but his instincts told him that wasn't true.

A sickening feeling spread through him. It was over between him and Mary Anne. He'd been so sure things could be saved, but not now, not after this. How could they?

"I guess this isn't totally unexpected," Zack said in a weak voice. He cleared his throat. "We knew Allen would flip out. Did you call Jeremy yet?"

"Yeah, I did. I left a message with his secretary. He was in a meeting, but I told her this was extremely urgent. I'm going to run over to Kinko's and fax this over to him so he'll have it before lunch."

Zack took a deep breath. "Guess we better go inform the others."

"No." Paul shook his head. "Big mistake. Let's wait a bit first."

"What?" Zack said, his throat catching again. "Why? We have to appear in court the day after tomorrow."

"We don't have to inform the team. After all, Henley's not after them; he's after the executive management of Imagination. And that's you and me."

"They have every right to know."

"Look, just wait a day or so. Let me take this complaint to Jeremy and let him give us our options. Before we rattle the troops—and believe me, this will scare the hell out of them—let's find out our options first. Okay?"

"Of course it'll spook them, but I think it's only fair that we tell them. They're not kids."

"What the hell does fair have to do with anything?" Paul scowled and ran his hand through his hair. "God. Do you think that this little summons was sent to us because it was the *fair* thing to do? For God's sake, wake up. Allen did this for effect and for effect only. He's a goddamn general who wants to shake up our troops and scare the living shit out of them. And if you tell the boys, you'll be playing right into his hands. You think he didn't know you'd do something like that?"

The front of the clean-room facility, showcased by a glass window that stretched down the entire hallway, revealed their reflections from the waist up. It reminded Zack of the mutinous ship computer HAL, who undermined the plans of the doomed astronauts with its lip-reading talents.

"Do you know what makes engineers work at a suicide pace in a start-up company?" Paul said. "The pursuit of the Silicon Valley dream, man, that's what. The dream of hitting pay dirt. The opportunity for your start-up to go public and then cash out millions in stock options. Buying them at ten cents and then selling them on the open market at one hundred dollars."

"What's your point?" Zack said.

"My point?" Paul said and then indignantly continued, "Here's my point. Do you know what's the fastest way to stop an engineer from working? From thinking creatively? Killing the dream, partner, killing the dream. And once the boys find this out, without us having a clear strategy to protect them, this is a dream breaker. And in Silicon Valley, that is plain suicide. Hell, it's genocide."

"I'm sorry, but it's wrong to conceal this from the others."

"I understand your principles, Zack. Believe me, I really respect you for it. But how can we create a company with integrity if the company itself doesn't exist at all? That's what we're fighting for here. Surely you can understand that."

"No. This isn't what I promised the guys. I told them I wouldn't be like Allen. I told them I'd be straight and open with them—always. What I know, they would know."

"You're wrong," Paul said, his face reddening. "Your most important promise was that you created a new opportunity for them. That they could quit their secure jobs—potentially putting their families at risk—because *you* promised them a new future. But if we aren't careful, there may not be a future. What would your boys and their precious families think then, huh?"

The silence of the huge, mostly empty facility suddenly seemed oppressive. Zack closed his eyes, took a deep breath, and then slowly let it out. He imagined the looks on Dimitre's and the others' faces when he told them that the dream had already been shattered. "For how long?"

"Just a few days. I'll meet with Jeremy tonight, do some planning before our court appearance. Come on, buddy, what do you say?"

Another image filled Zack's mind: Allen Henley that last day in his office, screaming, vowing vengeance. Zack had sworn he'd never be like him, and wasn't this giving in? Wasn't this what Allen wanted, divide and conquer? But Paul was right too. Allen knew that self-doubt would attack the others if they believed the dream could dissolve so quickly.

He heard footsteps approaching.

"Well, bud? Better make a decision fast. They're coming."

Zack looked at the four men coming down the hallway. Dimitre was beaming like the proverbial Cheshire cat; Jimmy was behind Jerry and kept trying to trip him but kept missing his foot.

"I'd better go with you when you see Jeremy."

"All right! I knew you'd make the right decision." Paul grabbed the summons from his hand and stuffed it inside his coat pocket.

"That's not what I meant," Zack said.

Dimitre and Brett stopped, pulling Jerry up short, and Jimmy ran into his back, bouncing off the larger man.

"So, what is going on?" Dimitre said.

"Guys, something's come up," Zack said.

Paul's eyes looked ready to pop.

"Just this morning, we were handed a summons."

"A summons?" Jimmy snorted. "What for? Parking violations?"

"No, this is serious. Allen's sent a summons, claiming that we're violating our noncompete clause."

"When is this happening?" Dimitre asked.

"We were just talking about it when you guys came up. Show them the summons, Paul."

Paul reluctantly handed over the summons, and the four of them muttered their disbelief as they scanned through it. When they were finished, their faces were white, like they'd just been told someone close to them had been murdered.

"Zack ... I, I am not understanding this. Are they saying they can be stopping Imagination? How is this possible in America? The land of the free and of dreams?" Dimitre asked.

"It's poss—"

"Zack, so we've got something to fight this with, right?" Jerry waved the papers around. "I mean, if we can't make our display panels, then what the hell did we leave DisplayTechnik for? What the hell ever happened to competition? They can't outlaw competition, right?"

Zack opened his mouth.

"Yeah!" Jimmy said. "Where the hell's the right for competition? This is America, for Christ's sake! There's laws against monopolies. So, what, we can't open a business now?"

"What about my Anna? How can I be taking care of her if they are taking away our jobs before we are getting them?" Dimitre said.

"This whole dang thing's nothing but a snake in the boot," Brett said. "I don't think any of us has saved up enough to tide us over."

"Holy shit. Yeah, how am I supposed to make rent?" Jimmy said.

They started peppering Zack with questions, talking on top of each other. It was a blur of noise. Their mouths were moving, but he couldn't make out anything except for Paul, who leaned in and whispered, "Nice going. *Great* idea."

Zack raised his hands for silence, but Paul jumped in. "Look, guys, I'm sorry; I didn't want to lay this on you until we had something solid to tell you. I wanted to wait so you wouldn't get all worked up like this. It's unfair, but, well, now you know. But don't worry. Zack and I are going to meet with our attorney and get this straightened out."

If Paul thought he was making himself look good, he was dead wrong.

"You were wanting to wait to tell us?" Dimitre asked. "Why?"

"It was discussion only," Zack said. "And to be honest, I thought about waiting to inform you too. Paul had a good point. Allen would want to panic us, right out of the gate. But then I got to thinking about all the times Allen withheld information from one group or the other so he—and he alone—controlled the flow of information. I also thought that not telling you meant I didn't trust you. And that's not the way I want to build this company."

Dimitre nodded in appreciation.

"Look," Zack said, "this was a huge surprise to Paul and me, to all of us. I'm especially sorry we even considered withholding this from you. Maybe that would have been better in some ways, but we're telling you now because we believe in you and because I believe that there's strength in numbers. The better informed you are, the better we can all work together to overcome this. I don't know about you guys, but I don't want to start our company out on the wrong foot."

Zack wasn't sure, but he thought he saw tears in Dimitre's eyes.

"We're going to fight this thing, and we're going to win it," Jerry said. "We're not going to let Allen push us around anymore. And I certainly don't want him dictating how we treat each other."

"Get over here!" Dimitre shouted.

A bearlike arm wrapped around Zack's neck and pulled him close. Dimitre hugged him around the middle, lifting him right off the floor, squeezing the air right out of him. The others pounded on his back.

Zack and Paul went off to meet with Jeremy, leaving the others behind to start gearing up. As soon as they were out of the building, Paul turned to him and said, "I don't need you to come with. Jeremy and I can handle things."

"What, are you still mad that I let the others know?"

"Yeah, I am, but not as mad as I was ten minutes ago. I think it's a mistake, but the damage is done, so there's nothing I can do. All that bonding and belief stuff, well, we'll see how far that really goes. I may disagree with you, but I sure hope you're right because we're going to really need those guys to bust their asses. Anyway, I'm serious. Jeremy and I can handle this."

"We're getting our butts sued by Allen, and you don't want me to go with you?" Zack said. "Remember, pal, my name's on the summons too."

"I understand what you're thinking, partner," Paul said. "But the water's already burst through this little dam, and it's heading for town. I'll do my best to slow it down. So do me a favor—do us both a favor, all right? Find the source of this leak." Paul looked intently into his eyes. "Find Mary Anne."

Zack felt his face flush; his mouth opened, but no words came out. There was nothing left to say, so he just watched Paul disappear into his car.

But Paul was right. It was time he confronted Mary Anne.

After Paul left, Zack found his cell phone and locked himself in his office. He sat down amid the boxes, computer cables, and scraps of paper, some of which had sketches of how he'd envisioned his office layout. He didn't have the heart to pick them up.

He placed the call but hung up before it could even ring. What could he possibly say to her? She had abandoned him. If she wanted an explanation, she could have called him and asked for it. The more he thought about it, the more absurd Paul's suggestion seemed. Why would Mary Anne admit to anything at this stage? Why would she reveal anything? Without a confession, there was no way of telling whether she had betrayed them or not, or how much she knew. Or how or what she knew fit into the details of the summons. He definitely knew he'd never told her who else was involved. And yet Allen had hit a bull's-eye with every shot.

Perhaps Allen had hired someone to break into his apartment and tap his phone or plant a bug or breach the security on his computers. God, could someone really have broken into the apartment?

Even though the hope of uncovering the depth of her involvement was slim, there was still the matter of their relationship. Did they still have one under the circumstances? He needed to know the answer to that, at the very least.

Over the next several hours, he left messages on her cell phone, but there was no response. Maybe her cell was dead or she didn't have time to check her messages, but he had a hard time believing she hadn't heard what happened. More likely she was angry because she couldn't understand his decision to leave DisplayTechnik. Maybe what she needed was some time to cool down.

Around two o'clock, Paul called with his first report from Jeremy.

"Our lawyer says it's going to be an uphill battle. So much for getting this thrown out."

Zack sat down, feeling like he was going to throw up. "What do you mean?"

"Look, we're still discussing tactics, but both of us agree that it's essential that you find that girlfriend of yours." Paul's voice was raspier than normal. "The more we know what she knows and told Allen, the better off we'll be. Have you found her yet?"

He knew he should have gone. He should be there to discuss tactics. He knew Allen far better than either of them. "No, I haven't," he said, "not yet."

"You tried her more than once, right?"

"Of course. I called her a half dozen times over the last couple hours. If she's really involved, what makes you think she's going to tell me anything?"

"Her telling you nothing will explain a lot."

Zack wasn't convinced about that.

"Do you even know where she is?" Paul said.

"No."

"You gonna find out?"

"Yes, of course—"

"That's good. And oh, by the way, none of this really matters unless Imagination can actually make the paper-thin roll-like-a-newspaper flat-panel display work like we promised our investors we could."

By the end of the day, Zack had given up trying to reach Mary Anne by phone. He'd thought about calling her friend Deirdre at work, but he knew Allen would have already imposed a communication blockade on all of the former employees. He could have asked Janet for help, but he didn't want to get her into trouble.

Visiting Mary Anne at home was an obvious solution, but it presented big problems. She lived with her parents, so the possibility of a nasty confrontation with Allen was very real. Still, it was his best shot, and he figured if he got there around six, when Mary Anne was likely to arrive, and left before eight, when workaholic Allen came home, he would be okay. If Mary Anne wasn't home, then surely her mother would know her whereabouts.

CHAPTER FOUR

It took nearly an hour and a half of crawl to make it from Santa Clara to the north end of San Francisco. He spent the time thinking what he'd say if he managed to find her: this was a great opportunity for him, didn't she know how much this meant to him, he needed the chance to try to make it on his own, and everything her father had alleged in the complaint was simply not true. He found himself debating Allen more than explaining his actions to Mary Anne. God. Why couldn't she just see what a great opportunity it was for both of them? Couldn't she be happy for him? Other girlfriends would flip for joy if their man had started a company with a thirty-million-dollar bankroll.

But he knew what she'd say about loyalty to the company, because he'd heard it many times before. Where was *her* loyalty when she turned him over to her father?! He stopped himself. He didn't know if that assumption was even true, and bringing it up would only lead to a shouting match. He just wanted a chance to explain his actions and to reassure her that he still loved her and wanted to be with her. Finding out if she had spied for her father was secondary at this point.

He drove along the Embarcadero, past Fisherman's Wharf, hoping to find some inspiration in the excitement of the people on the street. While stopped at the light, he saw a fire-eater on the corner performing for the tourists. He spit out a ball of flame to the delight of the crowd. Now wouldn't that be a handy skill to have when dealing with Allen?

He continued along the bay, past Fort Mason and past the marina with its bobbing sailboats and yachts, their masts a forest of swaying white trees. The Henley mansion stood in the shadow of the Golden Gate Bridge, which meant winding his way through the twisting maze of streets surrounding the national recreation area.

Zack parked across the street from the Henley home. It was 6:55 p.m. Tension throbbed in his lower back, the muscles at their tightest from the stress of this day. He suddenly realized that the car seat was pushed too far forward; he hadn't reset it after moving boxes and computers to Imagination's new headquarters. He pushed with his legs until he heard a click, the seat reaching its final position. Too far back. He pulled the side lever, rocking back and forth to obtain the right distance, and then used the bottom of his T-shirt to wipe his dripping forehead.

Sweating bullets because he was about to confront his girlfriend? This is ridiculous, he told himself. Get it over with.

He took a deep breath, flashed his teeth to the rearview mirror, and opened the driver door. As he crossed the street, a car whizzed past him, the driver honking the horn, yelling something out of his rolled-down window.

Zack turned, but the car had already disappeared over the hill. Normally, this exclusive residential area was very quiet. He looked up the short drive to a barred, double gate.

The Henley name was embossed on a gold plate affixed under the electronic buzzer. Although the buzzer rang to several boxes placed around the house, they were all wired to a security system that sat on the corner of Allen's desk, replete with a camera, which looked down on him right now, and which he hadn't looked up at. The system was closed circuit and not connected to any outside security facility. Allen didn't relish the idea of someone knowing his comings and goings.

A gray stone wall encircled the Henley manor. Zack chose his spot and pulled himself over the top. The wall was only five feet high, but he managed to scrape his jeans on the limestone surface. He landed not so quietly on the other side, twigs snapping like a crackling bonfire at a New England clambake. A strong gust of wind from an incoming storm blew his hair in all directions.

The Henley mansion was well out of earshot, set back several hundred feet from the main road, with several rocket-shaped spruce trees lining the long snaking driveway. The profile of the trees had a French countryside look, reminding him of the photos that he'd seen in Mary Anne's holiday photo album.

As he looked between the trees, the house lights came on; it was getting dark. A massive bay window protruded from the center of the house, the gold and purple stained glass diffusing the floodlights along the ground underneath the sill. A miniature hedgerow encircled the building; tendrils of ivy climbed the pockmarked, Tudor-style exterior walls.

Zack checked the driveway for Mary Anne's car. He couldn't see it. However, that didn't mean anything, since it could have been in the garage. He was tempted to sneak a peek but knew the garage door was alarmed. No need to make the situation worse. He chuckled at the thought. Wouldn't that just make Allen's day to come home and find him being put into the back of a police cruiser?

He decided the best thing to do was to walk up to the front door and ring the doorbell.

He waited for what seemed like an eternity before the door opened.

"Why, Zack, what a pleasant surprise!" Mary Anne's mother, Charlotte, said. "Good God, what have you been doing? Rolling around on your father's pig farm?"

"Chickens, actually. And it's my uncle's."

"What difference does it make?" Charlotte said. "You still look like you've been doing some dirty business." A slight smile played at her lips.

A sudden gust nearly pushed Zack inside, and he had to steady himself until it passed.

"You know, sometimes I can't believe we're living in California," Charlotte said. "Sun 'n' sand and all that state-promotion ballyhoo. It's been getting frightfully cool in the evening here. How warm is it where you live? Pleasanton, right?"

"Uh-huh."

"What's the temperature inland? Mid-seventies today?"

"Higher. Over eighty."

"My God. We're lucky if it hit sixty today in the city. It has to be dipping below fifty. Ridiculous weather—hard to believe that summer's just around the corner."

Zack attempted a smile. Coming from New England, he found it hard to sympathize about the cool weather in Northern California.

The wind whistled around the entranceway again.

"Well, come on in, you poor boy. Get inside before you freeze to death."

As Zack stepped into the entrance hallway, the high cathedral ceiling drew his gaze upward, and his eyes followed the main staircase to the second floor, searching for the lord of the manor. When he was satisfied Allen wasn't standing along the rail anywhere, he looked into the foyer, at the statue of a Confederate cavalry officer sitting on his horse, a long sword brandished straight forward, pointing the way to the charge.

Zack had always thought the statue was a metaphor for the Henley household. Though it looked impressive and massive, the bronze was thin-skinned, and the entire statue weighed less than three hundred pounds. Allen had commissioned a platoon of them in more or less the same pose that could be lifted by a couple of strong men and interchanged as events warranted. There was the Confederate general holding Charlotte's great grandfather's actual sword, a samurai for Japanese guests, a Napoleon lookalike on a rearing stallion, Admiral Nelson on a parade mount, Ulysses

S. Grant for New York and Washington visitors, and a General Washington, among others.

No matter which statue was on the marble base, Allen always had it face the stairway and away from the front door. Perhaps Allen thought the officer was saluting and wanted to be properly greeted every morning as he descended. But to Zack's way of thinking, the statue should have been facing the other way, leading the charge out the door instead of greeting visitors with its ass.

"Want something to put a little fire back into that pancake belly of yours?"

Zack could hear Charlotte's southern accent with a twist of Cajun coming through. He shrugged. "Sure."

He followed Charlotte into the living room off the foyer. As they passed the foyer's floor-to-ceiling mirror, Zack caught Charlotte giving herself a quick, self-esteem peek. He guessed that she was in her early sixties. Her bra straps dug into her sides, producing skin ripples that could be clearly seen through her sheer white blouse. In dress and bearing, she tried to present herself as being in her late thirties, which was absurd with a daughter in her late twenties.

Charlotte stopped abruptly and turned, her head oddly tilted. "How are your parents, by the way? Is your father still ill from his operation?"

Zack's father had gone in for a routine screening, and they'd detected the early stage of prostate cancer. They'd removed it more than a month ago, but he hadn't seen Charlotte since.

"He's much better, thanks. The doctors feel he'll make a full recovery." Zack was a little caught off guard by the small talk. He wasn't entirely sure what to expect from Charlotte, but he was pretty sure she had to know he'd been fired.

"Excellent. Please give him my regards, won't you?"

Charlotte picked up her drink and finished it in a single swallow. She walked over to the side table, which had an assortment of liquor—there were several bars throughout the home—and poured a couple of Glenfidderichs. She handed a glass to Zack.

"Tell me, Zack, how do you manage to stay so skinny?"

Zack swallowed quickly. "Excuse me?"

"How do you stay so slim?" Charlotte said. She held her fingers to her cheeks, appraising him, and then ran her long brick-red fingernail from her cheek down to the bottom of her lip before picking up her drink. "Is my husband making you run scared?"

Zack felt his face flush.

"Did you know that my granddaddy, God rest his soul, told me that practically everyone in the Confederate army lost twenty pounds? Lots of reasons, he said. There wasn't enough food to go around or them Yankees stole their supplies or they couldn't keep the food down 'cause they were running so scared all the time."

"Really?" he said, not quite sure what else to say. The southern accent, normally buried, was working overtime. He wondered if Charlotte found playacting really that amusing.

"Oh, yes, it's quite true. But you never, ever see skinny Confederates in those glorious oil paintings they have back in the South." She took another long sip of her drink. "My granddaddy said the North didn't win because they were better soldiers but merely because they were better fed. Then again, according to him, the North didn't win so much as the South lost."

All the small talk must have made her thirsty because she walked back to the side table to refill her drink without ever having sat down. Zack noticed her hand was trembling slightly.

"So, which one is it?" she asked.

"Which is what?"

"Please. Do try to keep up with the conversation, won't you? It's rude for a handsome young man such as yourself to let a woman like me babble on without hanging on her every word." She smiled slyly. "So, which is the reason why you're as skinny as a stick?" She took a sip of her drink, eyeing him all the while. "Is it because there ain't enough food to go around? No time to eat?"

Charlotte sat down in a chair. When she threw her arm over the wide back, it exposed a bit of cleavage.

"Where's Mary Anne?" Zack said. "Is she here?"

Charlotte toyed with her necklace. "Now, Zack, you still haven't told me. My Lord. I just breathe air, and I gain a pound. Even if I eat like a chipmunk all day long, it doesn't make a difference. I just want to know how come you're as thin as a washboard. *C'est vraiment incroyable.*"

"I don't know, must be heredity or something. Is Mary Anne here? Do you know where she is?"

"Heredity? That's a Yankee explanation."

Zack shrugged again. "Perhaps I'm just working too hard." He hoped she'd eventually tire of the game and just tell him where her daughter was.

"Maybe." Charlotte took another long draw of her drink, "But I work pretty hard too. Maybe not as hard as you do, but I keep myself pretty busy with my charity work. So I'm not so sure about *beaucoup de travail.* And if I do remember correctly, you have a pretty healthy appetite. So if you ain't starving and no one's stealing your food away, then it must be the last one."

"The last one what?"

"What my granddaddy said about those poor thin Confederate soldier boys. That you must be running scared." Her eyes narrowed for a moment. "Is that it, Zack? You running scared?"

"Of course not. There's nothing to be scared of."

"Nothing to be scared of? It seems to me, then, that you're dreadfully uninformed."

Zack frowned. "Okay, so you do know about the complaint then."

"Complaint?"

"The playing around isn't fun anymore."

"Playing around is always fun."

"Allen filed a complaint to keep my company from competing against him. It's totally without merit."

"Oh, is that why you're here? I thought you were here to see Mary Anne."

"I am. I'll see Allen in court."

"Will you now? That'll be quite the sight. But to be perfectly honest, I don't know anything about this complaint."

"Really."

"It's true; I have nothing to hide. There have been some … discussions around here about your commitment to the company and to our family, but I really don't know the details. Oh, Lord, Allen and Mary Anne can just go at it tooth and nail. I hate to admit it, but she has far more of her father in her than I think either you or I would like. That temper! Frankly, I'd been under the impression that whatever they were on about had been solved." She watched him as she shook the ice for the last drops of single malt. "I do know that Mary Anne stood up for you."

Zack imagined it: Mary Anne and Allen arguing furiously after dinner about him, with Allen questioning his loyalty and Mary Anne defending him—and Charlotte taking her drink and bottle up to her room, where she hid out until the storm passed. Mary Anne had said something in the middle of one of their own arguments about defending him—he remembered that now.

"Does that surprise you? That she stood up for you?"

Zack said nothing.

"Regardless, it seems you now find yourself in a real pickle. Better make up your mind whether that bugle you're hearing is calling a charge or a retreat."

"You know, I really don't have time for analogies," Zack said. "Can you please just tell me where Mary Anne is?"

Zack jumped slightly when he heard the front door close and a waft of air swept across his back.

Charlotte laughed at him. "My, my, you are running scared. Don't worry, that wasn't my dear husband. That was our butler, Carl, who went out for some cigarettes for me. I really should quit, but I hear that if you stop smoking, you balloon like a pig." She gave Zack a once-over. "You know, we really should clean you up."

"She's not here, is she?"

"What do you think?"

"I think that it's time for me to leave." Zack put his drink down on the table.

"Oh, don't go just yet. I'm enjoying our visit. Tell me about this little company you're starting. Fair's fair; I told you what I know about Mary Anne and her father."

"There's not much to tell just yet," Zack said. "We plan to make cutting-edge flat-display screens."

"But isn't that directly competing with my husband's company? I thought that's what you worked on at DisplayTechnik."

He figured it didn't hurt to tell her. Besides, they seemed to know everything anyway. "No," he said, "it's a totally different technology. It will revolutionize the industry and change the way people see movies and TV. Allen's flat-panel displays use conventional engineering methods, so there's an inherent limit to their design. That's why this complaint will be dismissed."

"Your words sound confident, but your tone doesn't."

"It's no secret that Allen's hired some big guns."

"Ah, see? We're right back to the military analogy. It's always a struggle. Is it really worth it? The aggravation? Seems to me if you've already been served a summons on your first day of business that someone up there ..."—she pointed to the ceiling—"is trying to tell you that maybe you shouldn't be doing it. Bad karma, or whatever it is they call it out here."

The door opened again, and again Zack jumped.

"That's just Carl, again, leaving for the evening. You don't have to be concerned about my husband. He won't be home for quite a while. Come to think of it, he might even be out of town."

"You don't know for sure?"

"I'm his wife, not his secretary."

Zack detected a mixture of scorn and bitterness.

"I don't keep track of Allen's business or social calendar. You should know that. Please, have another drink. They say that alcohol is good for the nerves."

"In moderation."

"Please?"

Zack shook his head. "Do you keep track of your daughter's whereabouts?"

Charlotte rose awkwardly out of the chair. As she walked around the coffee table, her heels caught on the red Turkish rug, and she stumbled. Zack caught her before she could fall, gripping both of her forearms. She leaned heavily against him, her face pressed on his chest. He felt his own face redden at her closeness and smelled, under the camouflage of her perfume, an unpleasant mixture of smoke and alcohol seeping from her pores.

"Thank you," Charlotte said, straightening up. "I can see why my daughter enjoyed the company of your arms so much."

Zack released her and took a step backward.

"I keep track of her as much as a mother can," she said on the way back to the bar. "I can tell you that she isn't here."

Zack cleared his throat. "Any idea where she is?"

"I'm not sure, exactly. But she might be with her father. Actually, I thought she was with you. But she's obviously not, is she?"

She either didn't know as much as he thought she did, or she was doing a good job of disguising what she did know.

"So when's she coming home?" Zack asked.

"I bet I could call Carl back, and he could whip us up something wonderful to eat," Charlotte said. "He always does. Care for a meal, soldier?"

Zack shook his head. This wasn't getting him anywhere, and he was tired of the game. He glanced toward the front door.

"I'm not surprised. As I said before, you lose your appetite when you're running scared."

Zack looked hard into Charlotte's eyes. He'd thought at one time that she genuinely liked him. She'd certainly said so on numerous occasions. Was everything about her an act? God, what had he ever seen in this family?

"Do you have any message for my daughter?" Charlotte said, tapping her fingers against her arm.

"Just tell her to call me, okay?" Zack said. "I deserve that much."

Charlotte gave an exaggerated salute. "Yes, sir," she said.

He turned for the front door.

"I don't know exactly what you've done," she said as she followed him. "To Allen, my daughter, or the business."

Zack opened the door, and she held it as he stepped out.

"I don't give a rat's ass about the business," she said, her voice rising above the wind. "But I will tell you one thing: my granddaddy told me that when the enemy is running away scared with his back turned to you, you don't stop and regroup."

Zack didn't look back; instead, he marched quickly down the pathway, the long line of spruce trees waving over him. He could hear Charlotte shouting now, her voice fighting the wind.

"You chase the enemy all the way back to his hole and drown him if he buries his head in the dirt. So watch yourself, boy. You aren't a match for Allen, and whatever you've done, I feel truly sorry for you."

CHAPTER FIVE

Julie knew what her staff and other employees said about her. She'd heard the whispers about her spending as much time on her back as she did getting on everyone else's. She didn't give a damn. What annoyed her was the rampant sexual typecasting in a male-dominated, business world. When a man, eager to be promoted above others, deliberately undermined his colleagues, he was called a "go-getter." Yet a woman who exercised similar intentions and options was branded a "backstabbing bitch." Such unfairnesses preyed on Julie's mind, especially when she lectured on the Bay Area's "Girl Power" circuit.

Her fingers dug into the deep shag of the carpet as her hip movements kept pace with Allen's thrusts, becoming more and more frantic as she neared a climax. She only hoped that she could time it with his; she'd never managed it with any of her other partners, only with him.

Yes, she slept with Allen Henley, and as often as possible, but she didn't do it for political or economic gain. The fact was she truly cared for him. It wasn't hard to respect a man who had so much confidence in himself. Drive and ambition, weren't these the very things women supposedly desired in their partners? Certainly she did.

Allen cried out when he achieved release, and she cried out a moment later, her legs' death grip around his back powered by the intensity of her pleasure. For a long moment, they lay frozen—like an Eskimo carving of two animals locked in battle.

"You were explosive tonight," Julie hissed into his ear. "I felt like you were never going to stop. Mmm … so much energy; I don't know how you manage to do it, working all the hours you do."

Allen untangled from her embrace and rolled onto his back. Julie squirmed against scratchy carpet fibers that had scrubbed her back raw from shoulders to hips.

"You always say that afterward," Allen said.

"I know. But tonight, you outdid yourself. Wow, I'm a little tender right now."

Allen made no sign of acknowledgment.

She looked up at the ceiling, which was painted in a style reminiscent of Michelangelo, except rather than pudgy Renaissance figures reaching out to the hand of God, or fleeing his wrath, there was a parade of cavemen, Bronze Age warriors, Romans and Celts, Chinese and Japanese warriors, redcoats, Confederates, and Teddy Roosevelt leading a charge up a hill through a phalanx of World War I, II, Korean, and Vietnam War vets. On the top of the hill was a businessman in a well-tailored suit, holding a cell phone in one hand and a PDA in the other. The fresco was titled *The Evolution of War.*

Allen's office felt as spacious as a stadium, and lying there in a state of undress made her feel all the more exposed. She glanced into the corners that she could see, trying to spot the security cameras, but they were too cleverly disguised. Allen never had told her where they were, but he always disabled them with a code from his desk before they started their lovemaking.

"So—" she said, clearing her throat, "how did your meeting go last night with McSorley?"

Allen shrugged. "How do all meetings with lawyers go? It went."

"How's Mary Anne doing?"

Allen rolled onto his side, facing her. His eyes narrowed. "What do you mean?"

"I mean, how did she take it? I'm sure that this hasn't been easy for her."

"Well, it hasn't been easy for me, either." Allen got up in a huff. As he started getting dressed, his knee collided with the wooden edge of a chair. "Damn it!"

"Relax," she said soothingly. She had to be careful, or Allen could easily slip into one of those ugly moods of his. "I only asked because she's not as … battle-hardened as yourself. It must play with her head to be helping with the lawsuit against her boyfriend's new company, especially when it deals with violating a noncompete against her father's company. That's some conflict of interest."

"Nonsense! First off, it's her *ex*-boyfriend. Second, my daughter knows very well what that ungrateful asshole did. When you see one of your allies is changing sides, you don't wait for him to join forces with your enemy to make the two of them stronger. You crush the traitor before he has a chance."

Julie kept her expression deadpan, though she detested that ridiculous Chinese mumbo jumbo. Allen took a seat in his chair and she walked over, standing in front of him, knowing her disheveled, just-been-had look enticed him.

"I'm sure that Mary Anne knows she's done the right thing." She looked into his eyes before bending down to pull up one of her black lace stockings. "We all know it was the right thing, but for her to betray Zack? After all, she and Zack were pretty tight."

"Sometimes you can respect your worst enemy—if he deserves to be respected after you crush him in battle. But you can never respect an ally, a trusted friend, whom you invite into your own home and who then attacks you while you're sleeping. There can never be respect for such a person."

She sat on the edge of the desk, placed a foot on his crotch, and started to massage gently. "Regardless, Mary Anne must have taken some convincing."

Allen smiled with pleasure. He took her hand and pulled her forward until she was kneeling in front of him. He removed her hair clips one by one, until her long dark hair fell down to her shoulders. He played with her hair, coiling it between his fingers, guiding strands through the separation of her breasts. The hair was just long enough to loop them back like a "J."

"What evidence has she offered? Is it going to be enough to stand up in court?"

Without warning, Allen slapped her. The side of her face went instantly numb.

"I've had enough of your questions about Mary Anne," he said. He grabbed a fistful of her hair and forced her to look up at him. "Do not mention her involvement with this situation again. Do you hear me?"

Julie tried to turn her head away, but his grip was too strong. Kneeling before him, half-naked, she felt helpless. She trembled at the thought of what he might do to her.

"I said, do you understand me?"

Julie nodded, trying not to show her fear.

"Good." He released her hair and stroked her cheek gently. "You know how fond I am of you."

He pushed her head down toward his lap. Julie immediately started to fumble with his belt.

"Besides," he went on, "Zack's traitorous actions will be exposed. The trusted ally is now the enemy. And now that he has revealed himself as a traitor, it's time to make him doubt that he has the stomach for the fight. You can win more battles by never fighting them. Even Mary Anne knows that. And so should you. Now, get down to business."

He groaned and threw his head back as she engulfed him.

When Mary Anne opened the front door of the Henley mansion and stepped inside, she glanced sideways at the full-length hallway mirror, a habit she'd learned from her mother. She brushed back the bangs from her face, revealing the small, upturned, elf-like nose that her father had poked fun of ever since she was a child.

Mary Anne peeked under the raised sword of the statue in

the foyer and saw her mother, looking stranded, halfway up the stairs. She had a drink in her right hand, the light catching both the crystal and the numerous rings on her fingers.

"A rather late night gallivanting about town?" Charlotte said. "Or were you doing more dirty business with your father?"

Mary Anne was certain that her mother knew nothing about their dealings with Dean McSorley. Her father was apparently not home yet. He'd mentioned something about staying late when she'd talked with him earlier in the day.

"I had some work to catch up on."

"I see." Charlotte wavered on the stairs, as though undecided whether to go up or come down.

Mary Anne set her purse on a side table. "What is it, Mother? You've obviously got something on your mind."

"Do you know what's confusing about watching someone running scared?"

"What?"

"I said, running scared."

"I heard. What on earth are you talking about?" She hated when her mother was in one of her disconnected states.

"What's confusing is not knowing whether they're running away from something that's already scared them or they're running toward something that will scare them even more."

"Who are you talking about? Me?"

"Don't you know?"

"I'm afraid not." Mary Anne stood at the bottom of the stairs, hands on her hips, jaw set.

"One of the things that Hitchcock used so effectively was to create a scene where the audience knew what was going to happen before the character did."

Mary Anne shook her head and turned for the den. "I think you should go to bed."

"You remind me of one of those characters."

Mary Anne stopped, feeling a chill, as if a ghost had just walked through her. She heard the clink of her mother's glass bumping into the handrail. When she looked back, her mother was slowly climbing the stairs.

Charlotte Henley was a complicated woman. Mary Anne had always felt closer to her father. Over time, the relationship with her mother had become more and more perfunctory, especially after she decided to work at DisplayTechnik. One of her previous boyfriends had majored in psychology. In one of his rare sweet moments, he'd said something that she often thought of: Mothers love their sons and slowly disapprove of their daughters, because sons remind a mother of her husband in his youth and daughters remind a mother of her own youth passing by.

Was her own youth passing her by? She was twenty-eight years old and still living at home.

"Mother, stop," she said. "What exactly do you know about what's happening?"

Charlotte paused near the top. "I think I should be the one asking that question," she said. "I am your mother."

"We're not going to play one of your games."

"It seems that's the only way I can get your attention anymore, child."

"Perhaps you should try communicating like an adult."

"Spare me your lectures. I don't care for them from Allen, and they're very unbecoming from my daughter."

"Do you have something to say to me or don't you?"

Mary Anne could see she was carefully weighing something. She didn't know how much Allen had told her mother, but it wouldn't be like him to tell her anything.

"Zack was here."

Mary Anne felt her stomach drop. "When?" she asked.

Charlotte smiled. "Tonight."

"Why?"

"Why do you think? Looking for you."

"What did you tell him?"

"Why don't you ask him?"

"Mother."

"Don't take that tone with me. Have you called him? It seems he hasn't heard from you."

"That's my responsibility, not yours. Did he have a message for me?"

Charlotte hesitated, and Mary Anne knew she was debating whether to play her only trump card. "He said for you to call him," Charlotte said, quickly adding, "I take it from your reaction that you have not done so yet."

"No, I haven't."

"Care to tell me why?"

"That's none of your concern, Mother."

The two of them stood staring at each other for a moment.

"I thought you cared for Zack," Charlotte said quietly. "I'd been under the impression that I'd be hearing wedding bells soon."

"Things are ... complicated at the moment."

"So I gather. Zack looked very distraught. In fact, he looked downright scared, and I told him so. But I haven't been able to figure whether he's more scared by you or by your father. Or by where he's certainly headed."

"And where's that?"

"What have you done, child?"

"Mother, that's really none of your concern. I know what I'm doing."

"Your voice doesn't sound so confident."

"Well, I am very sure."

"Your father is involved. And when he's involved, you should never be sure."

"Trust me, I've got the situation under control, and I know what I'm doing. Zack and Allen have to have it out for a bit, but when things calm down, everyone will see reason."

Charlotte laughed—not just a chuckle or the snide little snicker that so angered Mary Anne; she actually leaned her head back and laughed heartily. Her drink splashed over the shiny stairs, and she had to sit down before she fell down. She mopped at the puddle with the hem of her robe, still laughing.

"Oh, Mary Anne," she said through her tears, "you're still so blind when it comes to your father."

Mary Anne clenched her hands, digging her nails into her palms. "You're drunk. You don't even know what you're saying."

"And you're in trouble. But the difference is that in the morning, I'll be sober, and you'll still be in trouble."

Mary Anne turned on her heel and grabbed her keys and purse.

"Go on, leave!" Charlotte shouted down at her. "Everyone's leaving me tonight. If we had a dog, he'd be leaving too. But the funny thing is, I'm the only one with a roof over my head."

Mary Anne slammed the door behind her.

It was nearly midnight when Zack arrived at his Pleasanton apartment. His voice mail was flooded with messages. The new company didn't have its phone system installed yet—that was coming next week—and until then, Zack had to use his home or cell phone as his message board.

After leaving the Henley estate, Zack had gone back to Santa Clara and done some work with Dimitre, Jerry Steiner, and Jimmy Morgan. Clearly motivated by the new digs, the trio debated over one of the design proposals. Dimitre had complained loudly that a change would require reformulation of the polymers. Even though Dimitre was outgunned two to one, Zack's money was on Dimitre winning.

He had relaxed for a while, sliding back into the comfort of a technological debate rather than dealing with everything else that was going on. Eventually he left them to finish the argument, feeling the urge to get some fresh air. He drove around, following the southern perimeter of the bay, from Redwood City to San Jose to Oakland and to Berkeley—always amazed by the heaviness of the traffic even at a late hour—before finally returning home.

Although there were calls from vendors and even a job applicant who believed he wasn't long for DisplayTechnik, Paul had left the bulk of the messages.

"Zack. This is Paul. I just came out of a meeting with Jeremy. I'm at his office. I'll drop by Imagination after I leave here. Bye."

"Okay, I can see that you're not at Imagination. Nobody knows where you went. Where the hell are you? Call me on my cell phone."

"You weren't in Santa Clara. You're not at home. But I am. Call me."

"Going to bed now. Don't know where the hell you are. You better be lying dead somewhere off the San Mateo Bridge. I'll talk to you tomorrow at the office."

There were still no messages from Mary Anne.

Paul sounded really stressed in his message about Jeremy. Why couldn't he have at least given Zack a clue what they'd talked about? This was too much to deal with. His dream was slowly slipping out from under him. And on top of that, he was losing Mary Anne too. He caught himself. No, I can't think that way. That would give Allen exactly what he wants.

He wondered what Allen would do if he did throw in the towel? Would he back off and let the others have their dream? Paul could fund them, and Zack could pack up and leave the Valley.

For Pete's sake, listen to you! he chastised himself. You haven't even had your first court appearance, and you're already tucking your tail between your legs and running. Running scared, just like Charlotte said.

Well, he wasn't going to give Allen easy satisfaction. Someone had to stand up to the man. Besides, they had the truth on their side. They weren't competing with him; Allen was just blowing smoke and making things difficult just because he could.

God, he wished that Paul had told him what Jeremy had said.

He rolled off the bed and opened the balcony's sliding door. The sound of passing cars immediately became more noticeable. He breathed in the night air. He considered going for a midnight jog but thought better of it. He felt exhausted.

Leaving the door open, he lay back on the bed, stretching out like a starfish. He really missed the weekend camping trips with Dimitre. They'd trek up to Tahoe and hike around the trails, trying to figure out what plants were safe to eat. He smiled when he remembered the rash that had broken out all over Dimitre's face after he'd devoured some whitish-blue berries. They hadn't gone in six months or more. Now, they talked so little about life outside Imagination. Everything was company-related. The thought of camping at a clear lake against a backdrop of snowcapped mountains seemed so idyllic and peaceful. No lawyers in sight. No crazed mentor trying to destroy their dream. And, in the quiet of the night with the campfire popping, there was the inevitable talk about the women in their lives. Dimitre would complain about the idiosyncrasies of his wife, Anna, in an affectionate way, and Zack would talk about Mary Anne and how close they'd become. And, when the vodka bottle was nearly empty, they both boasted of starting their own company and being free, finally and totally free.

Live free or die. That was what he'd told her during their argument on Sunday. It was the motto of his home state.

He pounded the pillow next to him. God damn it, Paul, what the hell did Jeremy say?

CHAPTER SIX

There's nothing like driving in sunny California. Thankfully.

It had taken Zack nearly two hours to get to Santa Clara on what should have been an hour's commute at best. Traffic had come to a complete standstill, even to the point that people were getting out of their cars. When things started moving again and he got to the point where traffic picked back up to normal speed, there was no indication what had caused the stoppage.

Zack pulled up to his new parking space—they'd all picked their own—and noticed that Dimitre's car looked like it hadn't moved from the night before. It was parked at the same skewed angle. Last night Zack heard the three of them arguing shortly before he'd left for Mary Anne's house and then make plans for dinner. They must have left Dimitre's car, and undoubtedly argued on the way there, argued at dinner, and then argued all the way back. Zack smiled at the thought. When they got into one of their debates, it could last days. He could just picture them at dinner, arguing away, with Dimitre pausing just long enough to smile and be polite every time the waitress came by, and then getting back into it the moment she turned around.

Zack unlocked the door and stepped into the expansive and empty entryway. He wasn't sure yet what they'd do for decoration. He felt it should make some sort of statement. Nothing ostentatious, but he thought they really ought to have something more than that just-opened-for-business look. The stacked, empty cardboard boxes really didn't do it.

Zack whistled on his way to the lab, assuming Dimitre was still there. The echo came back to him, and he smiled, thinking that one day—hopefully very soon—this place would be bustling with people.

Sure enough, Dimitre was in the lab. He was hunkered over a black lab table, his white lab coat making him look like a small white whale.

"Good morning, Zack," Dimitre said without turning around. "How are we doing this fine morning?"

"How'd you know it was me?" Zack asked as he put on his lab coat. The odor of chemicals hung in the air, and he assumed Dimitre was working on his latest formulation.

"I recognize whistle."

"Ah."

"You sound cheerful this morning. Everything is going okay then?"

"Well, other than the commute, sure. So far, so good."

"Good. I am glad to be hearing it."

"Have you been here all night?"

"Yes." Dimitre still hadn't looked up. Zack stood carefully at his elbow. A petri dish sat beside him, and he was holding a circuit board of some sort close to his chest and using a jeweler's eyepiece, trying to attach something to it.

"When did the others leave?"

"Sometime around eleven, I think."

"Anyone win the argument?"

"No ..." He paused. "Not yet. I am still thinking I am right, but we will see. For his skinny little body, Jimmy can be like a bull. My Anna would say I could crush him by sitting on him and be done with arguing. He is like weasel, no?"

"I think you mean a ferret. Ferrets are the determined, skinny animals. Weasels are tricky and mean."

"Yes. Ferret, that is the one."

"So, what are you working on?"

"I am proving my point." He reached for a tiny soldering gun, and Zack could now see about three dozen tiny wires hanging off the small board Dimitre held in his hand. The gun was just out of reach, so Zack slid it over to him.

"Thank you." Dimitre nodded.

Zack noted his red, swollen eyes. "So, are you really married to Anna?"

"What are you meaning? Of course, I am married to my Anna."

"Just checking. Some weeks, you spend more nights at the office than at home. I'd think she must get tired of going to bed alone without her big Russian teddy bear."

"Ah! She must tell you that one."

"Actually, I made that up."

"My Anna. She sometimes calls me that."

"So, is this just a marriage of convenience or something?"

"I am never hearing of any marriage that is convenience."

Zack laughed. "No, you know. One of those sham marriages. Where two people pretend to be married but actually aren't."

Dimitre tightened a screw on a circuit board, the jeweler's eyepiece still in one eye. "Why would you do this?"

"Forget it; I was just trying to tease you."

Dimitre picked up another tiny screw and set it into place. "My Anna, she is a good woman." He flipped over the circuit board and scrutinized it. "I am very lucky. She is very supportive of me. She is knowing I work late. She is knowing I get lost in my work." Dimitre reached for the soldering gun and sealed a wire into place. "And I call her more than you know. She is my, how you say? My ... my confi—confi ... my good friend."

"Confidant?"

"Yes. Confidant. And we are meeting for lunch sometimes two or three times a week." Dimitre inspected his work and then took up another wire. "Well, sometimes we are meeting for dinner. And besides, she is having her own work. After boys go to bed, she is working on her novel. I come home, and sometimes it is I who is going to bed alone."

Dimitre set down the dish and looked straight ahead. "I am complaining about her sometimes; about her smoking or how she is swearing like sailor or about her reconnecting Playboy Channel or some such thing. But I am knowing I am very lucky. Besides, this is what good marriage is. Marriage is more than legal papers. Marriage is marriage of two minds and souls. If you can be finding someone who trusts you, someone who is supporting you because you are loving what you are doing; someone who is knowing your every fault and loving you all the same ... this is wonderful love. This is making all the good times all the better."

As his friend reveled in his relationship, Zack began to feel a pit of emptiness spread through him: this was what he was so dreadfully missing. Mary Anne didn't trust him. She didn't support him in what he was doing. She might know his faults, but she didn't love him in spite of them.

He walked over to the sink to rinse his hands. It was just an excuse to do something, anything, to distract himself from the conversation.

Dimitre looked over at him. "I am sorry. I was forgetting about you and Mary Anne. My Anna is saying I am good with things, but when it is coming to people, I am forever putting big feet in bigger mouth. Forgive me. I did not mean to—"

"Forget it," Zack said. "I know you didn't mean anything by it."

"Have you seen her yet? Has she called?"

"No and no."

"Ach! I am sorry. I am not understanding this. She and you were close, no?"

"Yeah." He shrugged. "I sure thought so anyway."

"Do you think it can be saved, this relationship between you?"

"I don't know. I thought it could be, but it's pretty difficult when I can't even talk to her to find out what the hell happened. I mean, I don't know what to think. Did she turn us in or didn't she? And if she did, then why? And like you said, relationships are about supporting the other person even if it means sacrificing something for yourself."

Dimitre carefully slid his work aside and leaned onto the black surface of the lab table. "Be careful what you are saying. Sacrifice in relationship is being two-way. So far, you are only looking at this as though she is being the one to sacrifice, that she needs to being support to you in your dream. It is not so easy. Would you be willing to sacrifice Imagination to support her?"

Zack just about fell over. "What? You've got to be kidding me."

Dimitre smiled sagely. "You see? You are expecting her to follow you, to give up whatever dreams she was having to let you follow yours. Is not so simple. Because then you are saying your dreams, your wishes, are being more important than hers. You cannot be expecting her to give up something if you are not also being willing. Relationship is balance. Together you seek what is being best for both of you, never just one."

Zack was momentarily speechless. Would he be willing to give up Imagination to have Mary Anne? Was that some sort of cruel joke of fate, like Sophie's choice?

"Ah, now I am seeing wheels spinning in your head. Is good."

"You can't be serious. You think I should give up Imagination for Mary Anne?"

"I am not saying that, but yes, is something you must think about. What is being more important to you? Who can answer this? Only you. Perhaps Mary Anne is not being the one for you. If she was, then I am thinking there would be no doubt. Maybe you will not have to, but are you willing?"

Zack could do little but blink. The very thought was unfathomable. Imagination was everything he'd worked for, everything he'd dreamed. Mary Anne was supposed to be the final piece of the puzzle, not a substitute for the dream.

"Well, what have you ever given up for Anna?" Zack said. "You seem to have everything: a wife who loves you and supports your crazy work habits, a job you love, two boys, a great house. Hell, even a dog and cat, for crying out loud."

"Do you think I am just falling into this? I am working on relationship for fifteen years. I give up secure position for Anna to come to America to study her writing and to be closer to her papa. I give up seeing my own family to live here. I give up lots of things, but I am gaining others. Is give-and-take and trusting that when you are giving, you will also be getting. Plus, remember each person looking out for other person and what is being best for them. When that is happening, then is magic."

Zack still couldn't believe that Dimitre was even suggesting this. But luckily he was spared from more torment because Jerry and Jimmy walked in. They lived close to each other and often shared rides.

"Okay, you Russian bear," Jerry said. "Jimmy and I have been talking it over, and we think we ought to at least give you the benefit of the doubt. We'll try it your way, but if it doesn't work, then we're going with our design."

"Then we are going with my plan. Now sit down and be weeping."

Jerry and Jimmy put on their lab coats, and along with Zack, they sat around the table.

"Is that what I think it is?" Jimmy asked.

"No, is not pizza with anchovies," Dimitre said, "or whatever your puny mind is coming up with."

"I was actually hoping it was a spy camera into Julie's office."

Dimitre let out a big laugh and slapped Jimmy on the shoulder. "No, is not being that either. Is prototype."

Zack leaned closer, taking a look at it. There was a circuit board with wires running across a small, circular framework. Dimitre took the petri dish and carefully turned it on its edge. He worked a small knife along the edge, and out slid a nearly transparent rubbery substance that had the barest silvery blue tint to it. It looked slightly more solid than Jell-O. Dimitre used some tongs and carefully lifted it, positioning it over the circular framework.

He connected a small battery and looked up, ready to throw the switch.

"You realize," Zack said, feeling goose bumps standing all along his arms and spreading up the back of his neck, "that if that doesn't work, these two will never let you live it down."

"Bah!" Dimitre threw the switch.

Nothing happened. Jerry and Jimmy burst into laughter, reaching over Dimitre to give each other a high five.

"Idiots," Dimitre said. "That was just to be starting power cycle and to warm up. I am not yet tuning it. Be watching and weeping."

Dimitre inserted a small screwdriver into a tiny dial. He turned it slightly, and the bluish hue deepened into a glowing sapphire.

"Holy shit!" Jimmy said. "Holy shit!"

"Holy Moses!" added Jerry.

"Shut up, am not done being through."

Dimitre turned the screwdriver a bit more, and the blue faded to green and then to a bright amber. Zack felt like jumping for joy but restrained himself as Dimitre continued to turn the dial and the yellow faded to orange and into a bright, brilliant scarlet and then turned to purple and back to blue. Jimmy, leaning over the dish, was visibly trembling.

Dimitre repeated the process from purple all the way back to blue and then back again to red, stopping along the way to enjoy the various hues.

Zack looked down and saw his hands were shaking too. That rubbery little blob could be rolled up as easily as a sheet of paper and could cover an entire wall in clear and brilliant resolution, or be set in the tiniest displays, making them even thinner and lighter. They'd all talked about it for months, debated it, imagined it, but now there it was, a glowing circle that captured the rainbow—along with the pot of gold on either end.

Dimitre leaned back, arms crossed, the biggest smile across his face. "Is okay now to be yelling eureka."

Zack and the others shouted, "Eureka!" and leaped on each other in a flurry of hugs, high fives, and dancing.

God almighty, Zack thought. They were going to be filthy rich.

CHAPTER SEVEN

That same afternoon, Paul Ryerson said in a strong, confident voice to his audience of potential second-round investors from the Bay Area, "Flat-panel display technology has undergone a revolution." He was standing in front of one of the clean rooms, an all-white area where the reclusive billionaire Howard Hughes would have felt right at home.

Paul stepped aside, allowing the investors to peer inside at the sophisticated deposition and etching equipment that the previous tenant had left behind. While they nodded and made approving sounds, Paul allowed himself a smile. He knew nothing about the technology they were staring at, absolutely nothing. He could barely log on to the Internet and had been a poor-to-average student of physics and chemistry in high school. Yet here he was, in the spotlight, asking investors for money to develop a new technology that he had literally no clue about. But as little as he knew about Imagination's technology, the investors before him knew even less. At least he had a script to go by. Paul's father, a former design engineer of General Electric, would have been proud.

"At Imagination, we are reinventing the basic concept of flat display," he went on. "Gone are the days when the so-called flat panel was a piece of solid glass. We are about to enter a new era. An era that will not only revolutionize the flat-panel industry but the very way in which we interact with media. No longer will we simply look *at* a display. In the era of Imagination, we'll live *in* the display."

Paul looked in satisfaction at their silence and slightly opened mouths, hanging on his every word. He wasn't sure, but he thought the Asian man might actually be salivating.

When he first rehearsed this pitch in front of Zack, his partner had almost gagged upon hearing its syrupy delivery. That kind of sarcasm was exactly why Paul gave these tours—and not Zack. Zack was the CEO and president, but he was first and foremost a technologist. He was also too damn honest sometimes. Perhaps that's why they formed a good team.

"Have you ever wondered why movie theaters are still popular and profitable, despite the significant inroads of DVDs and pay-per-views?" Paul went on. "In America—and I suspect in the wider world—we go to movie theaters to get a sense of something bigger than everyday life. We want to see a large screen, shot in seventy-millimeter film so that our favorite actress's face can be seen up close or to watch the climatic action-packed finale of our hero battling the forces of evil. Now imagine, if you will, the average living room in America made to look as real as a movie screen.

"At Imagination, we are developing state-of-the-art, ultrathin, flat-panel display technology with the brightness, speed, color purity, and viewing angle of a normal television set, yet unlike a conventional television stuck on a stand or screwed into a wall, we will be able to wallpaper an entire living room with the display—ceiling, everywhere. The picture will surround the viewer, giving the illusion of true 3-D. The boundary between reality and imagination will vanish."

Three investors raised their hands. Paul listened to their questions, all of which he had anticipated.

"The first prototype units will be sixty inches long, forty-two inches high, and less than 0.3 millimeters thick," Paul said. "Since the technology is digital, it can be hooked up directly to the Internet. And best of all, when we go into production manufacturing, the Imagination display will cost less than two thousand dollars, putting us immediately ahead of the competition and putting us on a near-level price with many of the high-definition units currently available.

"Once the American public starts to watch their favorite soap opera, sitcom, or movie on the superwide, flat-panel display, consumers won't be satisfied with the much smaller, bulkier television sets of today. After they experience the technology of Imagination, there will be no going back.

"Best of all, the second-generation displays, which will follow on the heels of the first by less than nine months, will be every bit the equal of high-definition units and will be even thinner—about 0.2 millimeters. Third generation will then follow, and these will be truly wallpaper-thin."

The bespectacled, rotund Asian, wearing a dark blue suit that was clearly too big at the shoulders, stepped to the front. His shoulder-length, silvery black hair was pulled back in a Samurai ponytail. As he was a last-minute addition to the tour, Paul couldn't remember his name.

"Speaking of your competition," the Asian said, "most of the flat-panel display technology is currently manufactured in Japan or Southeast Asia. How will you compete with much larger companies that have such a strong infrastructure and significant technical resources? To say nothing of far-cheaper labor than what you can find here in the Valley."

Paul opened a laptop he'd had waiting for just this question.

"The majority of the current flat-panel display market is geared toward laptop computers," he said. "Although great strides have been made over the last few years, including backlit illumination and supertwist nematic LCDs, this technology group is confined to displays using conventional thin-film transistor, LED or plasma technology.

"We are developing a display that will be approximately eighteen times larger in total area than the current laptop computer display and five times larger than a twenty-six-inch television screen. The display will equal, if not outperform, the clarity and contrast of a high-definition television set, yet be light enough for a child to hang it on your living room wall. The larger displays will eventually revolutionize the way that we look at life, the way that we look at ourselves, even the way we dream. And, as I said in the beginning of this tour, we realized that—"

"Excuse me, Mr. Ryerson," the Asian said.

"Yes?"

"How will you do this? How does this *supposedly* new technology work?"

"Well, in the beginning of the meeting, I explained that the basic technology is described in the information kits."

"Yes, but can you give us more specific details?"

"Well," Paul said, "it would be difficult for us to go too much further. I'm sure that the minute technical details wouldn't interest you."

"Yes, actually, they would," the Asian said. "Before you can convince me or others here to invest in your company, I need to have some confidence that your *supposedly* new technology has a real chance for success. Can you give us an exact idea on how you plan to achieve this?"

"I'm not about to disclose the secrets of our technology," Paul said. "However, as I said, the media kit that we've already distributed clearly shows the technology road map."

"Are your alleged designs patented?"

Paul shifted uncomfortably on his feet. This guy wasn't letting up. And the patent issue was touchy. Patents were intended to meet a literary rather than a technical standard. Constructed with ambiguity and generality by patent lawyers, they were often supported by freehand drawings that more resembled the assembly instructions of a plastic model airplane than complex technology, and were so convoluted that the inventor himself would be hard-pressed to recognize his own creation. Their worth was a subject frequently debated in Silicon Valley.

"Like all technologists," Paul replied, "we're in the process of protecting our intellectual property. Of course, sometimes if you file patents, all you do is inform your competitors how you do what you do. Then they just modify it slightly, and the patent is no longer valid."

"Is that what you did?"

"I don't understand."

"Take someone else's design, modify it slightly, and call it your own?"

The audience started to shift away, to distance themselves from the man in the frumpy blue suit. Paul felt the heat rise into his face. He—literally—could not afford to lose these people.

"I was saving this for later," he said, "but why don't you take a look at this?"

Paul swished the cover off Dimitre's prototype. The investors gathered around, staring at the jumble of wires and the oddly tinted gelatin.

"Obviously, this is a very early prototype—completed, in fact, just this morning. Look at the gelatin there; see how thin it is? It's about the thickness of three quarters stacked on top of each other. It's too thick for our final specs, but until the rest of our equipment arrives, it's the best we could do."

Paul used some small metal tongs and lifted another gelatin sheet that lay next to the prototype. "Notice how flexible this is." He set it on edge, bent it in half, and it flexed like silicon rubber. "Now, here's the best part." Paul picked up the small screwdriver and rotated it through the spectrum much as Dimitre had done earlier. The whispers slowly grew until they were all talking on top of one another.

"This is all interesting, I am sure," the top-heavy Asian said, "but before I put my hard-earned money behind it, I need to be certain this technology originated with your team."

The murmurs died away. As the other investors stared at the Asian, Paul could practically hear their unspoken question: What did this guy know that the rest of them didn't?

Paul's temples throbbed. Taking a controlled breath, he said,

"Why don't we go back to the conference room for any further questions? Plus, I have one last display to show you."

The investors began to follow Paul.

"You still didn't answer my question," the Asian persisted.

"I would answer if the question were appropriate."

"No matter. Earlier, you mentioned that the president, Mr. Zack Penny, and his team have ... ah, what did you call it? A fine pedigree?"

"Yes, that's absolutely right. If you look at your investor's kit, we have a profile of all the key members of the design team. Looking on page—"

"Yes, yes. I can read what's in your kit here. But what I can't understand is that your president and his entire team came from DisplayTechnik."

Paul glared at the man. "What's so difficult to understand about that?"

"Since the majority of knowledge and experience came from a single company, perhaps the technology base of Imagination also came from this same company?"

"That's not so unusual," Paul said. "Start-ups are often started by a team of people who know each other and are familiar with one another's work and—"

"Yes, yes. Familiarity is very important. But my concern is that these people are too familiar with DisplayTechnik's work."

"All right, just what is your point? What are you implying?"

"My concern is that you're asking us to put millions of dollars into a new company, one that may not even be legal. It's standard practice for most Silicon Valley companies to ask their employees to sign nondisclosure agreements, and many companies insist that key employees sign noncompete contracts, preventing them from joining a competitor."

"Yes, and employees switch companies all the time. I'm sure that we would all agree that we aren't here to discuss the finer points of Silicon Valley's moral policies and legal practices, but the future of Imagination."

"I believe that everyone here would want to know the morals and ethics of the senior managers of your company."

"I guess I don't understand the relevance of your comment," Paul said. "What I'm hearing sounds more like an accusation than a question."

As Paul was thinking how to shut this guy up, the one person whom this asshole should not talk to emerged from the doorway.

"Is it true?" the man said, pushing his way past Paul and cocking his head to one side so he could make eye-to-eye contact with the casually dressed Zack. "Is it true that you and your engineering team worked for DisplayTechnik?"

Zack stopped in front of him, and the crowd slowly encircled them.

Please, Zack, please don't say anything stupid, Paul thought.

"Of course, we came from DisplayTechnik. That's certainly not a secret or anything."

"And did you and your team sign nondisclosure agreements and noncompete contracts with DisplayTechnik?"

Zack looked curiously at the man for a moment, and then Paul could see the dawn of recognition. Zack crossed his arms. "Ah, okay. I know you. Paul, did you actually invite this man?"

"Well, he called the office the other night, asking about startups, and, well, here he is."

The Asian man was now glancing from Paul to Zack and looking suddenly nervous.

"Gentlemen," Zack said, "Imagination is not in competition with DisplayTechnik, or any other current flat-panel display company. We are not here to develop a cheaper laptop display or a longer-lasting, brighter cellular phone display. We're here to develop some new technology that will revolutionize not only the current entertainment center of every living room in America but in the world. To say we are competing with what currently exists is like saying clouds compete with sheep because they're both white and round."

Some of the crowd laughed, and the atmosphere relaxed slightly. The Asian wavered for a moment, but only for a moment.

"Is it possible your supposedly new technology could replace the existing displays for laptops and cell phones?"

Zack opened his mouth but shut it, obviously expecting a trap.

"Your silence is telling. Because if it could or would replace those existing technologies, then it most certainly is in direct competition."

"You're wrong," Zack said. "This is like ... this is like saying the sewing machine was in competition with the weaving loom. Or better yet, with hand sewing. Yes, they both work with fabric and the sewing machine largely replaced doing it by hand, but there is still a need for sewing by hand sometimes. Just, I suppose, as there will always be a need for other types of flat-display panels."

Paul jumped in before Zack could go any further.

"Okay, good analogy. And with that thought, let's venture into the meeting room so you can see a model of how our display technology will look on your living room's wall. Hanging there like a famous Picasso painting, full of bright colors spanning across five amazing feet, but with one key difference: this painting has life. This painting has, well ... imagination."

After the visitors left—but only after consuming enormous quantities of Napa Valley white wine and Monterey Jack cheese—Paul closed the door in Zack's office. He marched over and leaned heavily on Zack's desk.

"Who the fuck was that guy? I thought that John and Molly had prescreened all the potential second-round investors. I'm going to rake John's ass for exposing us to that asshole. For Christ's sake, Jeff Kincaid was here."

Zack nodded. Jeff Kincaid was one of the moneymen from New York who could transform the entrepreneurial spirit of Northern

California into the honeypot of New York's financial district. He had the horsepower to make dreams become true.

"So who was that Charlie Chan?" Paul asked, suddenly straightening up.

"His name's Sandy Fong," Zack said, reaching for a wedge of Monterey Jack. He got up from his chair and retrieved a half-full glass of Sauvignon resting on top of his bookcase.

"How do you know him?" Paul brushed his hands through his hair. "Why didn't you say something?"

Zack watched Paul take off his charcoal gray pinstriped-suit jacket. It was bizarre, really. Zack was the president, wearing jeans, and here stood Paul, ready for a banker's convention. Despite the contrast—in more ways than one—he felt they still made a good team.

"Well, one thing's for certain." Zack reached out and put a hand on Paul's shoulder to stop his pacing. "Sandy Fong is no investor."

"What is he? A spy?"

"There's a whimsical rhyme I once heard." Zack tilted his head to one side, a playful smile on his lips. "Want to hear it?"

"What?" Paul threw up his arms helplessly. "I don't find this very funny!"

"Humor me." Zack cleared his throat. "Okay, it goes something like this. There was a guy named Fong. His family was from Hong Kong. He was a shark who could swim ..." Zack paused to make sure he got it right. "With ... with no restrictions. And do things with no sign of remorse or convictions. That son of a bitch named Fong."

"How cute. Done reciting poetry now?"

"Relax. Have a seat."

"Relax? God damn it! We have a corporate spy come right in through our front door—apparently at our own invitation—our court appearance is tomorrow, and you're asking me to relax? Jesus!" Paul sat down in one of the two chairs in the office. "Look, I'm sorry, Zack. I'm ... I'm letting this get to me, and I know I shouldn't. Hell, I've been involved with enough start-ups; you'd think this would be old hat by now."

"How about a glass of '97 Sauvignon?" Zack said. "It's quite good."

Paul shook his head.

Zack took a sip. "Are you sure?"

Paul shook his head again. Zack had never known Paul to refuse a social drink. He wondered if there was something Paul hadn't disclosed to him about this court appearance—much the same way as Paul had wanted to wait to tell the design team about the summons.

"Last year, I had dinner at the Henleys'," Zack said. "Mary Anne was there, Allen and Charlotte, of course, and lots of Allen's old college buddies, mostly from Stanford and Berkeley. Among the alumni was Dean McSorley."

"That blood-sucking lawyer who's suing our ass?" Paul said.

"Yes, exactly. As usual, Allen dominated the dinner conversation. Charlotte was ripped—as usual. Both Mary Anne and I kept our heads down, plowing through the meal, hoping to leave the table early on the wings of any excuse. McSorley starts talking about a mutual friend of the group who wasn't there. Apparently, this guy had the balls of a charging bull. At Stanford, this mutual friend heard that the contract law professor kept the year's final exam answer sheet at his home and that some leggy coed was doing some extracurricular activities with the dear professor. So, this guy actually convinces the girl to leave the front door unlocked one night while she is upstairs with the professor, teaching him that penetration is nine-tenths of the law. Our guy sneaks in and calmly copies the exam. By hand."

"You're kidding me."

"Truth is stranger than fiction, my friend." Zack paused to take a sip of wine. "But then later, this guy takes up the professor's generous open-house policy by banging the coed himself. Of course, as these stories go, the girl dumps the poor professor, breaking his heart in the process. And, predictably, a few select students ace the exam, and the poor professor is none the wiser. After Allen tells this story, both he and Dean McSorley howl like intoxicated baboons. Then they start singing that crazy limerick thing. I wouldn't have remembered it so clearly, but they kept reciting it over and over and over until they got the words right."

"That son of a bitch named Fong," Paul said.

"Exactly."

"So what could Henley hope to accomplish by sending Fong here?"

Zack closed his eyes and leaned back in the chair. "What is of supreme importance in war, is to attack the enemy's strategy."

"What? More poetry?"

"More of how Allen thinks," Zack said, opening his eyes. "His philosophy."

"We need to go after that bastard. Sue him for all this shit."

"I don't know about that, but if we can get those prototypes going, we won't ever have to worry about Allen ever again. So, first things first."

"What?" Paul leaped from his chair and pounded his fist into the palm of his hand. "That bastard's got to pay! He has to!"

Zack wasn't in the mood to argue. "Well, I guess you better get going then. Meeting with Jeremy? Remember?"

"I remember; you don't need to remind me!"

"Relax already. Why are you so agitated? Is there something you're not telling me?"

Paul shook his head. "No, no. You're right; I need to relax."

Something in the way he said it left Zack feeling convinced.

"I told you Jeremy said this wasn't going to be a piece of cake, but that we looked pretty safe. I think the big-gun lawyer on the other side has him on edge, though. God knows it does me." Paul picked up his jacket and put it on. "Any messages for Jeremy?"

"Tell him to pull a magic rabbit out of his hat tomorrow, will ya?"

"Will do. It's okay, Zack. We'll be ready for Allen's little war."

Zack watched Paul leave. Ironic that he should bring up the

subject of war, because it was Allen's second rule of battle that had been lurking in the back of his mind: after attacking an enemy's strategy, disrupt his alliances.

CHAPTER EIGHT

"We got totally fucked," Paul was saying, throwing down a fistful of papers on Jeremy's coffee table, "totally and completely fucked."

Zack couldn't have agreed more. The scenes kept flashing in front of his eyes like a nightmare that refused to go away. God, he felt sick. He swallowed hard and took a deep breath to try to calm the impulse to retch that threatened to overtake him. He felt like an accident victim in the trauma ward of Jeremy's office. Except this was no accident. It was obviously carefully planned and orchestrated.

It had been his first court appearance—ever. The closest he'd come before was a summons for a speeding ticket he'd forgotten to pay, but he'd got out of that by simply mailing in the required fine. He hadn't known what to expect. Sure, he'd seen movies of court dramas on TV but knew that the reality was probably different than the reenactments. That much was certainly true. On TV, the good guys always won.

What bothered him most was that the judge never looked at him. Not once. It was like he wasn't even there while this unknown person was deciding his fate and the fate of his friends and their company. He just flipped through the papers in front of him, staring down most of the time, occasionally glancing up at the lawyers. But he never looked at Zack.

The three of them had waited patiently in a small anteroom

outside the courtroom until their case was called. They'd been there since before nine, had taken a break for lunch, and then returned to wait some more. Zack had wondered aloud if Allen had managed to get this put last on the docket in order to play with their minds.

"No, that sort of thing doesn't happen," Jeremy said and gave him that kindly smile of his. "Everything's on the docket, and they just come up when they come up."

Not long after that, they were called. Jeremy led the way to a courtroom. Zack had expected a grand setting with wood paneling and chandeliers and a high bench, a carved witness stand, and a jury box off to one side. There was none of that. Just a well-worn linoleum floor and some chairs behind two desks that faced a raised dais with its own desk. At least the desk was made out of wood, though not nearly so ornate as he'd imagined. If it hadn't been for the dais, he'd have thought they were in some sort of seventies'-vintage conference room.

Allen was already there, flanked at the table by his lawyers, Dean McSorley and Bill Bennet. Behind them several other attorneys stood. Zack felt chills as Allen watched him enter, with a smile full of arrogance and barely concealed fury.

"Hello, Zack," Allen said silkily.

It reminded him instantly of Anthony Hopkins's "Hello, Clarice," in *Silence of the Lambs.*

Something was wrong, something was terribly wrong. Forget all of Allen's Chinese warrior philosophy posturing, that wasn't it. There was something else hanging in the air—he could feel it.

Moments later, the judge came in. "All rise," shouted the bailiff, unnecessarily as everyone was already standing.

"Hi, Dean," the judge said, "how's the wife?"

Zack's feeling of dread continued to rise as the judge and Allen's lawyer chatted about everything from Dean's kids to the judge's latest record-setting score at the golf club.

"Well, I suppose we ought to settle down to work," the judge said. "So, what's the problem here, gentlemen?"

"The problem, your honor," Dean said, "is that the company formed by Mr. Penny and Mr. Ryerson is in direct violation of the employees' previous noncompete agreements."

"If I may, your honor," Jeremy said when Dean paused a moment to draw breath, "there are several key points—"

"I'm not through, your honor," Dean interrupted. "Regardless of the noncompete clauses that are viewed by *some* courts as not worth the paper they're printed on, we can demonstrate by clear and compelling evidence beyond any reasonable doubt that Mr. Penny not only appropriated the employees of DisplayTechnik but also DisplayTechnik's intellectual property, with which he intends to be in direct competition with his former company. If my associate may approach the bench?"

The judge nodded, and one of the lawyers behind Dean stepped forward with a box. In it were book-sized documents bound in blue. The junior lawyer first handed one to the judge and then set one on the table in front of Jeremy. Zack guessed it was at least two hundred pages thick.

"This will fully support our request for a temporary restraining order," Dean assured the court.

"What!" Paul exclaimed. "Restrain what?"

The judge pounded his gavel. "Restrain you, for a start, sir."

"Your honor, this is the first time we've heard anything about a TRO," Jeremy said, his voice quavering. "I haven't had any forewarning. I'm not prepared to address this today. My clients just moved into their new building a few days ago; the phones aren't even operational."

Dean gave a contemptuous snort. "My client can't be held responsible for other people's inability to join the human race. I've had no other recourse but to mail a copy of the TRO. Unfortunately, it appears it hasn't arrived yet at Imagination's headquarters, but I can't be held responsible for the post office, either."

"You should have mailed it to me at my office," Jeremy said. "I contacted you regarding my representing Imagination and—"

"A copy *was* sent to your office as soon as you notified us of your representation. I imagine yours should arrive today, or whenever the post office decides to get around to it."

"Gentlemen ..." the judge said in a firm tone.

"Your honor, if you would just take a look at these supporting exhibits," Dean said. He then proceeded to explain how Zack and the others had taken advantage of Allen Henley's goodwill, how Zack was groomed to be Henley's successor, even positioning himself to marry Allen's only daughter. But all Zack apparently intended to do was to hurt the Henley family and DisplayTechnik. DisplayTechnik was also formally charging the officers and employees of Imagination with competing directly against DisplayTechnik, in violation of their individual contracts. Zack was also charged with solicitation of key employees while they were still employed with DisplayTechnik.

But Dean didn't stop there.

They were also charged with misappropriation of trade secrets. Dean claimed that Zack and his engineers had taken key confidential information, which formed the intellectual groundwork for Imagination's products.

Zack's nauseous feeling began to give way to anger. This was ridiculous, he kept telling himself over and over. There was no resemblance in any form between DisplayTechnik's TFT LCD displays and what Imagination was working on. Everything Dean was saying was a lie.

He felt like he should jump in and say something, but Jeremy had warned him that he should restrain himself, that there would be no need for him to talk to the judge, and to let Jeremy do all the talking to prevent anything inappropriate from coming out.

Dean concluded with, "We are, therefore, requesting an immediate temporary restraining order."

"Your honor," Jeremy said, "I ... I would again press that we have not had time to put together any sort of rebuttal and—and respectfully request that you deny their temporary restraining order until such time as we can put together an adequate response."

The judge looked at the voluminous filing before him. He'd

been flipping through it the whole time that Dean and Jeremy had been speaking.

"Request denied, counsel. I'm going to grant the TRO for thirty days. DisplayTechnik is bringing serious charges, and I feel that there's enough here to merit a TRO. This will also give you an opportunity to put together a response, but in the meantime, the TRO will go into effect immediately."

Zack had his head in his hands, focusing on his breathing to keep from vomiting on the office rug.

"I should have said something. I should have jumped in and said something," he told Paul and Jeremy. "In two minutes, I could have explained how vastly different our designs are."

"No!" Paul and Jeremy said in unison.

"That would have been a very bad thing to do," Jeremy said. "If you'd done so without some sort of counseling in advance, you could have slipped up and accidentally said something incriminating and shot the case out from under us before it even started. McSorley was hoping you'd do just that."

There was some comfort in that, but not much.

"But I don't understand," Zack said. "How could the judge order a TRO without even hearing our side of the argument? What about due process and all that? He'd just been handed his copy too. Obviously, he didn't take the time to read the thing."

"This is pretty common with a restraining order," Jeremy said. "The theory goes that if you throw enough shit at the wall, something will eventually stick. Just provide a judge with an overwhelming tonnage of evidentiary documentation, and even the most conservative-minded judge would believe that there's a strain of truth somewhere in there. It's like what the spin doctors in Washington say: If you tell a lie long enough and hard enough, the lie will eventually become a fact."

"But this is ridiculous," Zack said. "Our designs aren't just generations ahead of anything that anyone else is doing; we've invented a vastly different technology. And so what if some of the guys followed me? Hell, they were fired the same day I quit. And even if they hadn't followed me, those guys were just as fed up with Allen as I was and would have quit soon anyway. I didn't need to solicit them to do anything."

"Well, see, now we're getting into a bit of a gray area," Jeremy said. "Real touch and go. It doesn't matter what anyone was feeling or what anyone's intentions were. If there was a noncompete clause, then they can make a case of that."

Zack felt that sick feeling rising up again.

"What are you saying?" Paul asked. "Are we screwed?"

"No, no, I didn't say that. I said they could make a case of it; I didn't say they'd win. I think I can use the idea that your people were fired, which could nullify the noncompete."

"Yes!" Paul said. "That's right. That wipes out their case entirely."

"No, I didn't say that either. They'll say this whole thing was planned with great foresight, that it was all done *while* working at DisplayTechnik. In that sense, they're right."

"Shit," Paul said.

"But what I'll counter with is that it doesn't matter where any supposed planning took place—you can't prosecute someone for their thoughts—what matters is what actually occurred. And what occurred is that Zack and his friends were fired."

"Actually, I quit," Zack said.

"Ah, shit," Paul said.

"Does that matter?" Zack asked.

"Let's not deal with that right now. What bothers me is that they have a great deal of technical information here. That indicates a good deal of planning on your part before you left, so they'll argue that end of things. Obviously, you can't claim you made all this up in the three days since you've left DisplayTechnik."

"So we're back to shit then."

It had been several hours since the court appearance. Zack was completely drained, and this discussion wasn't helping to revive him. They'd been on the phone immediately after the court ruling today with every law professor and scholar that either Paul or Jeremy knew, had played poker with, got silly drunk with, or were part of their wives' circle of friends. Everyone said that DisplayTechnik had given them a raw deal, but that what they were experiencing was hardly news in high tech—especially in Silicon Valley. From what Zack was told, the afternoon conversations backed up what Jeremy and Paul had uncovered last night.

A sudden thought occurred to him. "Paul, do the investors know what's going on?" Maybe they might have resources they hadn't tried yet.

"There hasn't been anything to tell them."

"You didn't mention we'd been issued a summons?"

"Jeez, no, Zack. We don't need to inform them of everything. Up until today, it was just a piece of paper."

"For God's sake, call them, would you? No arguments, please. They need to know. All right?"

"Yeah, sure. I'm really looking forward to it."

Zack sighed, rubbing his temples. His head was spinning. "Look, we may have already been over this at some point, but what's next?"

"When a court issues a TRO on behalf of the plaintiff," Jeremy said, "all of the rights belong to the plaintiff. It's like the legal system reverts back to the Stone Age. They can go immediately into an expedited discovery, which is what I'm sure they'll do next. The other side doesn't have an opportunity to dispute the claims. At the end of the filing, there's a list of DisplayTechnik employees they want to get declarations of one sort or another from."

Zack started to flip to the back pages of the document to find the list.

"I don't think they're just after statements, either," Jeremy said. "McSorley's tone indicated that this list of witnesses would be testifying against you and that you and others had conspired to leave DisplayTechnik, intent on stealing company documents to start your own competing company."

Zack couldn't find the list. Maybe there was an index or something. He turned back to the front.

"Something else bothers me," Jeremy said. "It was pretty obvious that the judge had received the amended complaint and adjunct documents several days ago. He'd already made a decision before we walked into court today. This was just for the sake of procedure."

"Are you serious?" Zack said, tightening his right hand into a fist.

Jeremy cleared his throat and looked at Paul.

"That's not all," Paul said.

"There's more?" Zack said. He found the appropriate page number on the index and started flipping to the back.

"While you were in the restroom, Paul and I were talking. The kicker is that US marshals will have permission to go into the Imagination facility and confiscate all documents and computer equipment as potential evidence."

"When?"

"We should hear shortly. Probably as early as tomorrow."

Paul and Jeremy waited for his reaction, but none came—at least, nothing outwardly. Two pieces of information had slammed into him simultaneously, and he was too stunned to move or speak.

Zack had finally found the list. At the very top was Mary Anne Henley.

CHAPTER NINE

Mary Anne always thought it a bit ironic that Chez B's, the preppie San Jose restaurant that she was having lunch in with Deirdre, advertised itself as low-calorie. They had more than twenty different types of salads, some of which were truly incredible—Mary Anne's personal favorite was the teriyaki chicken salad with a sesame seed dressing. Yet this same restaurant also offered gourmet desserts in addition to the usual standards of Boston cream pie, mile-high mud pie, and the like. The very successful restaurant owner deserved a medal of commendation from the chamber of commerce—tell the masses what they want to hear, but sell them what they really want to eat.

She and Deirdre were in the back of the restaurant, at a corner table dignified by a single rose sticking out of a brass urn with Arabic writing on the side. Deirdre was going on and on about her latest struggle to choose between the two men in her life. Mary Anne wasn't surprised. Deirdre was two years her junior and had the right assets to attract a number of suitors.

Mary Anne took a sip of water. She smiled when she remembered how Zack had called this place a "chick hangout," making a bad pun—that he'd had to explain—on a "chic hangout." She really did miss him. She missed the sleepovers: waking up in the middle of the night, shivering, realizing he'd hogged the bedcovers—again. That problem had been easy to rectify; a well-placed shove in his back regained her majority share. Zack was such a sound sleeper.

She wished she could call him, but her father had suggested a cooling-off period until things settled down. "Suggested" was perhaps not the right word, which sickened her because, despite her claims to her mother, things felt like they were rapidly slipping out of her control. She hadn't cared for the look on her father's face when he left for court this morning, like he was entirely too happy about something but was trying to conceal it. She would be so glad when all of this was over and Zack was back in the fold.

The kitchen door swung open and a burst of unintelligible noise flowed out, a mixture of at least two, maybe three, different foreign dialects in addition to English. How could they possibly understand one another? And yet everything always managed to come out wonderful.

Come out wonderful. That's what she hoped for Zack and her.

"Earth to Venus, woman," Deirdre said. "Are you there?"

"Huh? I'm sorry. I wasn't paying attention."

"Well, duh. So what do you think I should do about Craig and Barry?"

"Um ..."

"Oh, forget it. It'll take too long to explain it all again, and we have to head back soon. No rest for the drones, not even the daughter of the queen bee. Hey, speaking of the queen—or king—can I ask you a question?"

"Sure," Mary Anne said. She poked her fork at a nibble of shrimp that shouldn't have been part of her vegetable salad.

"What's the story with Zack?"

"What do you mean?" Mary Anne straightened in her chair. She'd figured the subject would come up at some point during lunch, but wasn't surprised her relationship with Zack was last on Deirdre's list.

"I mean," Deirdre said in a whisper, "what is it with all this cloak-and-dagger stuff, you know?"

"Huh? What cloak-and-dagger?"

"Well, like yesterday, Bill Bennet comes to me and asks me not to pass any phone calls from Zack to you. Then says I shouldn't even mention what he said to you."

"So? It's company policy to discourage ex-employees from contacting current employees, especially during business hours."

"Yeah, right, but not coming from the mouth of the general counsel himself."

"Well, Zack was an important employee, and I assume that Bill has taken a special interest in this situation—"

"I know all that. But then, this morning, your father comes by the office and tells me, 'You are forbidden to transfer any phone calls from Zack to Mary Anne.' Forbidden? I mean come on. That's a word that my dad used to tell me when I was, like, five or something. And speaking of my dad, I mentioned it to him because it was so cloak-and-daggery, and he says to stay out of it."

Mary Anne wasn't surprised Deirdre had gone to her father, who was a police detective in San Francisco. He'd been extremely grateful to Allen for helping Deirdre a year ago. She'd always been a heavy partier and managed to get herself into trouble with some drug use and second-degree theft. Because she and Deirdre were longtime friends, Allen had personally testified at the hearing and vouched for her, telling the judge he'd give her a position in Mary Anne's department at DisplayTechnik, where she could be monitored. Because of his testimony, the judge put Deirdre on two years' probation instead of giving her jail time, which would have hurt her father's career for sure. Even though she'd been friends with Deirdre since high school, she rarely saw Deidre's father and had been surprised when he'd come by the house at Allen's Christmas party last year.

Deirdre stopped eating the pine nuts that had spilled from her Monterey special sandwich. "Oh. And your dad also said that if Zack did call, that I should go directly to him and not to you. Isn't that, like, totally bizarre? I haven't spoken, like, you know, two words to your father and Bill Bennet in the three years that I've worked at DisplayTechnik, and now, in the space of twenty-four hours, they both come up to me. It was kind of creepy."

"Oh, I don't know." Mary Anne looked away. It *was* kind of creepy.

"Well, I do. Why doesn't the Metal Queen or one of her bitchy witches tell me not to transfer calls from Zack to you? Or why don't you tell me not to do it? After all, you're my boss, you know, and I'd do anything you asked me. So why would the CEO come by personally? It's almost as if ..."

"As if what?"

"Nothing," Deirdre said.

"Come on; what is it?"

Deirdre shook her head.

Mary Anne could tell that she wasn't going to go further. She knew perfectly well what Allen's strange behavior meant: her own father didn't trust her. Not even after all she had done for him, for the family, and for his blasted company. Why wouldn't he trust her? What was he afraid she was going to do? That look on his face this morning came back to her. Maybe he didn't trust her because he wasn't being honest himself. Was it that, or was it because she really couldn't be trusted? After all, she'd betrayed Zack.

"So, are you gonna tell me?" Deirdre was picking at the cuticle of one of her nails, a habit Mary Anne hated. "You know, about Zack?"

"What about him?"

"Like, are you guys through or something?"

Mary Anne was silent. She wasn't entirely sure herself. "I really don't know."

"What's he think about all this?"

"I really don't know. I haven't spoken with him since Sunday."

Deirdre's head popped up. "Oh, my God. It must be over then."

"What? What do you mean?"

"Come on, girl, think about it. Zack gets the axe Monday morning, and here it is Thursday and you never even talked with him about it? And you think Zack's going to take that? That's like major cruel. Has he tried to call you?"

"Well, yeah, a couple times."

"And you were dead?"

"My cell phone was off." That was pathetic, but it was the first thing that popped into her head.

"So, what's your excuse now?"

"I ... I really don't have one."

"No shit. So did your father tell you not to call him too? I hope he disconnected your phone or ran it over or something."

For someone who could be remarkably ditsy, Deirdre sometimes knew exactly how to cut to the heart of a matter. Deirdre was right. She had to call Zack. If she had any hope at all that the relationship could be saved, she had to call him. Doing so meant going against her father.

Well, dear Father, you were right. I guess I can't be trusted.

CHAPTER TEN

After he left Jeremy's office, Zack drove around for a while, still in shock over the court hearing. Everything they'd been planning and hoping for over the last nine months was in danger of being taken away. Was it really only yesterday that Dimitre had demonstrated his prototype? Seeing that little blob of plastic glow had made their dream a reality.

Zack had envisioned himself the leader of a flourishing company, growing exponentially—a company that treated its employees with honor and respect. Not like DisplayTechnik. He'd always wanted a company that had incredible benefits programs, one that truly shared the wealth with the people who helped create it in the first place, rather than hoarding it at the top and doling it out in small, insignificant increments. He'd seen himself as a benevolent shepherd, taking care of his employees, becoming the envy of and the model for other companies to follow. And with the incredible, almost unimaginable, amount of money at his disposal, he knew it was possible.

He'd seen himself making a company-wide announcement that work was suspended early and that everyone was going to the Giants' game. He'd even planned to surprise Dimitre by having him sing the national anthem, something—as an immigrant—he'd always dreamed of doing. He could see the tears in his eyes as he sang, belting out the anthem in his full, rich voice. He'd certainly sung it often enough on their camping trips after some vodka. He'd seen himself surprising Jimmy with a new car instead of the beater he always drove—or perhaps more to Jimmy's liking, a full-size cutout of Julie Reynolds for his office. He envisioned sending Jerry, his wife, and his five kids to Disneyland for two weeks, all expenses paid. The sky was the limit when your new company went from zero to multibillion in a two-year span.

But the dream was in limbo, and it was quickly slipping through his fingers.

The judge's words haunted him: "Request denied, counsel. I am hereby granting the temporary restraining order for thirty days. Mr. Penny, Mr. Ryerson, you and your company are restrained from pursuing, in any form, flat-panel research until this matter can be resolved."

Just like that. No argument, no debate, just wham. End of story. That judge had no idea what he had done, the lives he was playing with. Or maybe he didn't care.

If it was only thirty days, why did it feel like it was all over? A nagging feeling was spreading in Zack's stomach: if Allen had so easily manipulated this judge into granting a TRO, you could bet he had something else planned. This wasn't over by any stretch.

Jeremy's response had given little comfort. "The other side files a complaint," he explained, "we're given time to respond, but in the meantime, things are shut down to make sure the plaintiff's rights aren't compromised. We'll have our day in court to prove the charges wrong. In the meantime, we have to abide by the law, or it'll seriously hurt our case."

This was due process? Come on! What about *their* rights?

Zack hit the steering wheel so hard that he swerved toward the other lane, catching it just in time before he crossed the line.

When Zack pulled up at Imagination, there were three cars in the lot, meaning the entire staff was there, with the exception of Brett, who'd already gone back to Dallas to start the marketing. He'd called before court this morning and told them how excited his contacts were about the initial breakthrough. Now, Zack would have to call him back and tell him to hold off.

As he walked into the lobby, Dimitre waved at him from the end of the hall. "Dimitre, we need to talk about what happened today," he said.

"This is not sounding good."

"It's not. Can you get the other guys together? I need to check my messages, and then we can talk. Let's meet in the lab."

Dimitre nodded and went off to find the others; Zack headed to his office.

Zack's father had worked weekends in the Vermont sugar bush to supplement the family's income. His father said that despite the long hours, he enjoyed taking the horse's cart around the forest path, which was marked by red kerchiefs tied to the branches. There was a certain satisfaction, he used to say, wading knee-deep in the snow to reach a maple tree, and discovering a clear liquid, which wasn't there a week earlier, pooling at the bottom of a bucket. If you let nature take its course, then a small miracle could happen, a drop at a time.

Zack prayed his father was right.

He sat down at his desk and dialed up his voice mail. At the prompt, he pushed one and recognized the phone number immediately. He was glad he was sitting down because it was as close to an out-of-body experience as he'd ever had.

Mary Anne had left him a voice-mail message.

She spoke so softly that it was difficult to make out all the words.

"Hi, Zack, it's me ... I know that you're not home right now and going through your thing, which is why I'm leaving you this voice mail. I know that it must sound a little, well, you know, not the right thing to do, but so be it. Live free or die, right?"

Zack flinched. It seemed like ages since they'd had that conversation.

"I ... I can't really begin to explain or understand everything that's going on between you and Allen, but I want you to know I'm really sorry that things didn't work out. Believe me, I really wanted to talk with you Sunday night, but I just couldn't get out of my own way. That must be a Henley trait or something."

There was the sound of the phone receiver falling on a hard surface. "Sorry, uh … this isn't going very well. Gotta stop now. Bye."

Zack hit the "one" button at least ten times and replayed Mary Anne's confused message over and over before finally pressing "two" to save it. Right at the end, he thought he could hear tears. Or was it just nervousness? It sure sounded like she wanted to say something else but didn't. Or couldn't. And every time he heard her address her father or refer to him by his first name, the word choice sounded awkward and out of place, although he surmised it had something to do with working in the same company.

Thank God she'd finally called. It really did feel good to hear her voice. He'd been through so much and been in denial over a lot—including missing her.

Abruptly, the warm feeling dissipated. He'd imagined her calling so many times, wondering what she'd say when they finally talked again. He'd wanted her to say she was sorry or say she'd been kidnapped or had somehow managed not to know any of what had happened. But this afternoon, when he saw her name on the top of the witness list, he knew she'd lied to him.

He pounded his fist on his desk, knocking over a jar of drafting pencils. Damn it! Why had she waited four frigging days to call him? She knew that her father had fired him. She knew everything, and apparently knew a lot more than he'd thought she did. Had she called just to torture him?

Jimmy walked past the open door and gave him a friendly salute. Normally the engineer, whose red hair behaved like Medusa's, made Zack smile, but he could only nod grimly and Jimmy walked away, frowning. He gathered up the pencils and gripped them like he was sizing a serving of spaghetti. Zack spread them out onto the green ink blotter and looked at his hands. The black lead had tattooed his palms. He knew deep in his heart that he still cared for Mary

Anne, which was so insanely stupid. How could he possibly have feelings for someone who had betrayed him? He willed himself to ignore what was coming from the right side of his brain, the creative, caring, loving side. It would only lead to more heartache and pain, and he couldn't deal with that now.

Grabbing a tissue, he wiped his hands clean. Out the window, the sun revealed a spider dropping down in erratic jerks, its silk scaffold looking fragile in the light. Without warning, a small burst of wind spun the spider around, its tiny body banging several times against the window. However—to Zack's amazement—the scaffold remained intact, and a few moments later, the spider continued its descent.

Zach watched the spider for some time before turning around and heading to the lab.

CHAPTER ELEVEN

Zack took a seat at one of the stools in front of the black lab table that had become their conference table. The other three all wore looks of concern—he was sure Dimitre had passed on the fact that bad news was coming—but it was the trust in their eyes that got to him.

"As you know, we had our first go in court today," he said. "It didn't go well. In fact, it went about as bad as it could go. But Jeremy believes this is all going to be over in thirty days."

"So what exactly happened?" Jerry asked.

"DisplayTechnik—"

"You mean Allen," Jimmy said.

"Yeah," Zack corrected himself. "They—or he—formally charged us with competing directly against the company. They claimed we violated the noncompete contracts that we signed when we were hired, and I was specifically charged with soliciting you while you were still employed at DisplayTechnik. So the judge granted them a thirty-day restraining order that prevents us from operating while the courts determine if there is any evidence of what they asserted and whether our displays will be in competition with DisplayTechnik's."

"Well, then is solved," Dimitre said, slapping his thigh. "We are replacing DisplayTechnik's displays, not competing them. We are the next generation."

"True," Zack said. Gotta keep this upbeat, he thought. "While nothing is ever 100 percent, Jeremy is pretty sure that we should come out of this clean."

"So, what's the bad news then?" Jimmy asked.

Under the table, Zack squeezed his hands until the knuckles popped. The sound reverberated around the room. They all knew that popping his knuckles like that was a sure sign of stress on his part. When he'd started at DisplayTechnik, he'd been dubbed "Bubble-wrap Boy."

"Uh-oh," Dimitre said. "This is being bad."

"Well, it's not good," Zack said, mad at himself for betraying his nervousness. "They are also claiming we took confidential information—trade secrets—that formed the intellectual groundwork for Imagination's products."

"Oh, bullshit!" Jerry threw his arms up in the air. "We worked independently! We worked after hours. DisplayTechnik never even asked us to work on anything remotely similar to light-emitting polymers!"

"Yeah!" Jimmy said. "All they ever wanted us to do was to improve the design of the current FPDs and figure ways to drive down manufacturing costs."

Dimitre was silent. Zack knew that meant he was absorbing and digesting the information.

"Look, I know all this," Zack said. "Jeremy knows all this. But the fact is, the judge made a very unfounded and broad decision that puts us in a major bind."

"Shit! Zack, I can't afford this," Jerry said. "I can't wait thirty days for a paycheck. What if this doesn't work out? How are my kids gonna eat? I gotta know now if I need to be looking for work. It's a tight market out there."

"I already spoke to Paul about that, and we're going to make sure everyone's covered. Don't worry. Even if I have to cover you out of my own pocket, I'll do so. Okay?"

Jerry didn't look convinced. "Why am I feeling there is more than is being said?"

"Because I'm not done yet," Zack told him. "Here's the deal.

The temporary restraining order gives Allen a lot of rights, one of which is the right to shut us down temporarily while they ascertain whether we've violated anything."

"You are already saying this. What, precisely, is this meaning?"

"There's no easy way to say this, but here goes: the federal marshals are showing up tomorrow to put us under lock and key."

"Holy shit!" Jerry exclaimed.

"Jeremy said this is when the courts revert to the Stone Age and it gives Allen a big club. He said they now move into 'expedited discovery,' and all of the rights belong to the plaintiff."

"So why the feds?" Jimmy asked.

Zack hadn't really gotten into that with Jeremy, and he was caught off guard. "Well, as I understand it, they're coming to lock things up. You know, seal it off like a crime scene or something."

The three engineers exchanged looks.

"I don't think that's what it is," Jimmy said.

Dimitre sat, arms crossed, shaking his head.

"Huh? What do you mean?" Zack said.

"Is meaning they are coming to take things. They are like KGB now. Here to confiscate."

"No, I—"

"Zack, wake up!" Jerry growled. "What do you think expedited discovery is all about? I've been through one ugly divorce already. Discovery is when the other side finds out what you have and whether any of that will help their case."

"What?" Zack's mind started to spin. Jeremy hadn't said anything about this. Or had he just assumed that Zack knew what he'd been talking about?

"No, I don't think that's what it is. Jeremy was saying this has more to do with the other side interviewing key witnesses. They had a list of people they want to interview. All you guys were on it."

"Zack, come on," Jerry said. "I know you put in hundred-hour workweeks and all that, but for crying out loud, you must watch *some* TV, right? Every court show talks about how the two sides get together and discuss their respective cases, interviewing the other side. That's how they find out if they really have a case or not, and then they'll also be prepared to mount a defense against whatever you plan to throw at them. Trust me, I learned this stuff the hard way. That's how I kept my first two kids; my wife was a total nutcase, and when the other side found out what things I was going to present, my ex balked and we never went to trial. Discovery means they have access to our files. Our computers, our plans, everything."

Zack leaned on the table. He felt dizzy. Is this what Jeremy had meant? Oh, my God. *Everything* they had would be exposed?

When he fell silent, the other three jumped in, all at once, talking over one another, not even waiting for responses.

Think. Breathe. Take one step at a time. We have to get through this.

"Zack?"

Dimitre's voice filtered through the noise. His hand was on Zack's shoulder, and he was shaking him gently.

"Are you being okay?"

Zack managed to nod his head. Had he blacked out for a second?

"Fire me," Dimitre whispered.

That didn't make any sense at all. "What?"

"I am saying fire me," Dimitre hissed at him.

Zack could see the blue streaks in the Russian's gray eyes, eyes that matched the gray streaks in his beard. The eyes were burning, trying to force a message into his addled brain. "Fire me, you dummkopf," he said.

Zack sat upright.

"Yes, you are stupid, silly dummkopf," Dimitre said more loudly.

Jimmy and Jerry stopped their shouting match, both turning to see what was going on.

"*Dummkopf* is meaning stupid person. and you are idiot. You are ruining us all with this dumbass plan of yours. We follow you from DisplayTechnik, but now you are leading us to ruin."

Zack could only gawk at him.

Dimitre put his back to the others so they couldn't read his lips. "Fire me," he mouthed silently. Then aloud he said, "I hate you, you stupid American. I come to this country to find new way, and this is where I am going? To poorhouse? To losing job? To KGB raids? No! You ruin me. I hate you."

Before Zack could defend himself, Dimitre attacked, slapping him across the face, knocking him off his stool and then pinning him to the floor.

As Jerry and Jimmy dove into the fray, Dimitre shouted Russian expletives.

Finally it dawned on Zack what the man was after. If he was fired, Dimitre could take his computer and leave. He could be blamed for sabotaging, stealing, or hiding their proprietary files. Unlike DisplayTechnik, Imagination had no policy as yet against such actions, and certainly no policies about firing employees.

Zack was amazed at the cleverness of Dimitre's plan. Jeremy would be pissed, but it was perfect. Zack could play innocent. He hadn't stopped him because he was so mad at Dimitre for insulting and assaulting him that he just didn't think to stop him from stealing his company's secrets. And Jimmy and Jerry didn't know what was happening, so they wouldn't be at fault, either. The feds wouldn't find anything because Dimitre could easily transfer all of it to his own computer, purge the rest of the system, and then simply walk out. Because he would no longer be a member of Imagination, the feds couldn't search his files. If it worked, it could buy them time that they desperately needed.

Zack had immediate second thoughts. Dimitre was still named in the lawsuit, and the feds would interview him whether he was a member of Imagination or not. They still risked exposure, and if they were caught, hiding things would only make it look worse.

"Enough!" he shouted. "All of you, get off! Get off me!"

The three of them stopped wrestling and stood up.

"Dimitre, I am not going to fire you," Zack said as he rose to his feet. "We can't hide things. That would only make things worse. We have to believe that taking the high ground here will see us through. If we show them we have nothing to hide and that we truly are not competing with DisplayTechnik, that we're the next generation, then they'll have to release the temporary restraining order and we can get back to work. We can't fall apart like this. We have to stick together. We have to believe that we're right and stick with the system."

Dimitre put a hand on his shoulder apologetically.

"Yeah," Jerry said, "but the system screws people every now and then. I know. I've seen it—anyone who's ever been through any divorce can tell you that. Hell, that's why men have become nothing more than wallets for their ex-wives while being shut out of their kids' lives. The system isn't perfect, Zack. You have to face that. I think Dimitre had the right idea. We can trust each other, but we can't trust the system. At least not blindly."

"I don't want to compromise our principles on this," Zack said. "I don't want to try to win the case with lies and deceit. And if we hide things, it's only going to make it worse. They'll find out."

"I agree," Jerry said. "But we're fools, and damned ones at that, if we go into this believing in a system that's flawed."

Dimitre nodded. "I am thinking, too, that this is not a good time for principles, my friend."

Zack looked at the two of them and then at Jimmy. "What do you think?"

Jimmy shrugged. "I guess I don't know. I don't have the benefit of having gone through things like Jerry has, and I'd like to think doing the right thing will get us through. But Jerry has a point that we can't walk blindly. Hey, I'm about six hundred years younger than you guys, but even I know that real life doesn't always work the way it should."

"How about this?" Jerry said. "We give the feds what they ask for, but we make sure we keep copies of everything we give them.

That way, we can verify what they've taken and have records of everything."

Zack thought a moment. "I don't see anything wrong with that. We aren't hiding anything; we're just keeping copies. We'll move our base of operation to our homes, and we can continue work from our home offices."

"Good!" Dimitre clapped his hands together. "I am liking this. We are team again."

Zack smiled. "All right, then, let's get to work. Make sure you copy everything."

Inside his office, Dimitre fumbled in his lab coat pocket and extracted his cell phone from beneath his keys and scraps of paper. He quickly brought up his wife's number and punched the call button.

"Ah, Anna, my love," he said in his native tongue. "It's the KGB calling. Would you kindly prepare our house for dinner guests?" He paused a moment, listening to the silence on the other end, and then added, "I'll be home in about two or three hours after I straighten things up here a bit."

He shut the phone and slipped it back in his pocket.

Chapter Twelve

Friday morning, Zack was surprised at how good it felt heading to work. Even the crawl over the Sunol grade seemed a bit lighter this morning, although that didn't explain his mood, nor did the good night's sleep he'd had. He felt good because yesterday while copying the hard drive, he'd come to the conclusion that as bad as the day had been, he knew he was on the right path. In thirty days, they would be done with Allen. Once the judge saw their designs and realized how vastly different—not to mention superior—they were, he'd have to let them continue to operate. And even if this judge ruled against them, his decision would be overturned on appeal. The last time he looked, they were still living in a country where entrepreneurship was not only encouraged but blessed and sanctioned by society.

When he arrived at the plant at 6:30 a.m., he was surprised to see US marshals already there. He felt his good mood dissipate a little until he took a deep breath, reminding himself that this was all just part of the process to be rid of Allen. The parking lot was blocked off by yellow tape, and he had to drive about a hundred yards to find a spot to pull off the road.

The marshals had already set up a perimeter, with two sawhorses acting as the gate. Inside the perimeter, there were several cars and two $19.95 specials on loan from U-Haul, along with about a dozen officers leaning against their cars or milling about. A small crowd of bystanders had gathered outside the perimeter, attracted by the demise of yet another American dream.

Although it seemed counterintuitive to the likes of Wall Street, a start-up failure was worn as a badge of honor in Silicon Valley, a place that recognized the biggest success stories were often built on previous disasters. *Silicon Valley Business* and other weekly journals, as well as the local papers, reported the wild successes and spectacular failures with equal zeal. In fact, judging from the fervor with which they pursued the divergent story lines and the reaction of their eager readership, it was hard to say which made better copy.

As Zack approached the crowd, he saw people sipping Peet's coffee and holding bags from the baker just around the corner. Most had probably stopped on their way to work.

"Real bummer," said a guy wearing white khakis.

"Yeah, sure is," said the woman behind him. "Who is this company, anyway?"

"Don't know, just another Silicon Valley start-up that bit the dust," white khakis replied.

"We're called Imagination," Zack said, and all eyes turned toward him.

"Never heard of ya," a guy with a reversed Giants cap said.

"Guess you never will now," white khakis quipped. "So, what did you guys do?"

"Yeah, why the feds?" the woman asked. "You the next Enron or something?"

"Bad boys, bad boys," someone down the line sang.

"Whatcha gonna do when they come for you?" several others chimed in.

Everyone laughed. Even Zack smiled.

"No, no," said the guy in khakis. "I meant what *do* you guys do? As in your line of business."

"Once all this blows over, we're going to make the next generation of FPDs—flat-panel displays."

"Oh, yeah ... I heard about you guys," said a man wearing a

headset. "You were the ones that were going to compete head-to-head with DisplayTechnik."

"That explains the feds," backward ball cap said. "Shee-it! They gotta own parts of everything in the Valley."

"Man," the man in khakis said to Zack, "you guys got some serious nerves to go head-to-head against Henley."

"Well, we—"

"I think you mean you gotta be seriously stupid," reversed baseball cap said. "No offense, dude, but that's just like going after the government."

There were murmurs of agreement.

"Worse," said someone down the line. "At least the government follows rules."

The murmurs got louder.

Someone clapped Zack on the back. "Don't let us stand in your way, buddy," the man said. "You better get in there. And don't let 'em take all the pencils. You might need 'em ... and a tin can to sell them out of."

Zack didn't laugh at the joke.

The crowd parted, and he made his way to the barrier. A couple of marshals stepped forward and then moved the barricade when he identified himself. As he stepped through, there was a smattering of applause and some cheers of "Go get 'em!" and a "Woo-hoo! All right!"

As Zack turned and waved to the crowd, he saw a van with "Silicon Valley Business News" painted on the side pull up behind his car. A reporter and a camera crew jumped out and immediately waded into the spectators. Media was to be expected, but that didn't mean he had to like it. One of the marshals led him over to the man in charge, who was standing by the front door.

"You Penny or Ryerson or someone else?"

"I'm Zack Penny."

"US Marshal David Jones." He flashed his ID and badge and then took a folded paper from his windbreaker pocket and shook it open. "By order of Judge David A. Rafkin," he read, "you are hereby ordered to cease and desist all activities associated with normal operations of the business. The restraining order will remain in effect for thirty days or until such time as it is lifted by order of the Marin County Court. The U.S.—"

"Wait a second. What do you mean until 'such time'? I thought it was lifted in thirty days, end of story. When we left court yesterday, it was supposed to be for thirty—"

"Look, pal, I'm not a lawyer; I just execute the damn things. I'm not even allowed to advise you in any way or you could sue me for giving you false legal advice, so I'm not saying anything, got it? You want advice? Ask your attorney."

Zack was quiet while the marshal read the rest of the document. Jeremy had said it was for thirty days, didn't he? Hell, he was there himself. He knew the order was for thirty days. He imagined the court stenographer lying and saying she'd recorded something differently from what Zack *knew* he'd heard.

Stop it, he told himself. That's ridiculous. "Such time" could just as easily mean that the judge could lift the order in advance of the thirty days, couldn't it? Of course; that's what it was. Sheesh.

"Look," Zack said, "I'm not an attorney, and for all I know, you could be reading me something you took off a Hollywood script. How about if we hold off on this 'til my attorney shows up? He said he'd be here by seven o'clock, and it's almost that now."

"Sure. No problem. How about if you open the doors so we can get started?"

"Umm ..." The polite side of Zack wanted to say yes, but the logical side told him to put the brakes on. "If it's all the same, I'd just as soon wait on that too."

"Technically speaking, we could break the door down, but we can wait a bit."

Zack couldn't tell if the marshal was serious or not. "How about I run over to the bakery and get everyone some bagels or something and some coffee instead?"

"Sure. But US marshals like muffins, not doughnuts."

Jeremy and Paul walked up under escort, and Zack was happy

to hand the reins over to them. Then over their shoulders, he saw Bill Bennet standing at the makeshift gate and showing his papers to the marshal on duty.

"Jeremy!" Zack said, pointing at Bill. "What the hell's he doing here?"

"He's here as part of the discovery process. He'll be overseeing what's removed to catalog it, and also to lay claim to anything that they might want to declare is DisplayTechnik's property."

Zack frowned. The US marshals were one thing—they were just strangers, part of the system—but the idea of Bill Bennet fingering and touching their private things seemed over the line.

"Is that standard procedure?" he asked.

"Sure. I'd insist on being there if it was the other way around."

"Look, if you see the guys before I do, make sure you explain that to them, okay? They're not going to like this. I know *I* sure don't like this."

He turned around and nearly collided with Bill.

"Jesus!" Bill said, tucking the papers to his chest. "You gotta stop doing that."

Zack was determined not to let it show that it bothered him that Bill was here, even if it killed him. "Hi, Bill," he said, fighting to keep the strain from coming through in his voice. "I'm getting coffee for people—can I get you something?"

"No. I'm fine, thanks," Bill said, walking past him.

Zack was tempted to call out after him to ask if he'd caught the Giants' game but decided not to. Bill wouldn't get it anyway. He made his way back to the crowd.

"They kick you out already?" someone asked.

"No, no, I figure I'll play nice and get some coffee for everyone. This could take a bit."

"All right! I like mine with cream," said the guy in khakis, a smile on his face.

"Yeah, you getting doughnuts?" said the guy with the earphones.

"Excuse me, are you Mr. Zack Penny?" a woman's voice called out.

When he turned to look, he saw the reporter push through the crowd toward him.

"Yes, I'm Zack Penny."

"I'm Elizabeth Fonteneau, *Silicon Valley Business News* and KPIX. Can I ask you a few questions?"

This wasn't the way he'd hoped to make his first appearance on television or in the *SVBN*. At least he wasn't charged with murder. "Um, sure. But I'm running an errand right now. How about you give me ten minutes, and then we can go somewhere private."

"Sure, we can wait." Her smile was dazzling.

Zack came back from the bakery with a couple dozen muffins and a pot of coffee on loan from the bakery. Elizabeth Fonteneau was directing a shot of the crowd—which had at least doubled, if not tripled, with the arrival of the TV crew—and also of the exterior of Imagination. She caught sight of him and tapped the cameraman on the shoulder. The two of them followed him through the crowd and into the main lobby of Imagination. A US marshal was coming down the hall with a box stuffed full of papers, a computer keyboard balanced on top.

"Oh, damn!" Elizabeth said. "We're missing it. Tom, you—"

"Nope, nope, I got it," the cameraman said, zooming in on the marshal.

"You probably want a good visual for a backdrop," Zack said. "The windows outside the clean room are the best place for that."

"No, no," Elizabeth said. "I'd like to do it in your office."

Zack shrugged. After he set down the box of muffins at the engineering station and stopped so Tom could get a few shots of the marshals as they sorted through papers and unplugged the newly installed equipment, Elizabeth and Tom followed him to his office.

Elizabeth took a seat opposite him and pulled out a notebook and microphone. The sky-blue suit she wore complemented her eyes perfectly. She flipped her long straight chestnut hair out of the way as she found her place in her notebook.

The door burst open.

"Zack, could I see you for a moment?"Paul said. "Maybe about ten?"

Tom swung the camera around to focus on Paul, who started to lift a hand to fend him off but then apparently thought better of it.

"Uh, sure. Elizabeth Fonteneau, this is my partner, Paul Ryerson."

She stood up, but Paul quickly disappeared out the door after a quick "hi."

"I'm sorry," Zack said. "Would you mind waiting for a bit? Ten minutes, tops. I'd say wander around if you like, but I'd like you to stay here, out of the way of the marshals. After that, I'll be happy to take you—"

"It's okay," Elizabeth said. "We'll stay here. I can make a call or two." She smiled at him again.

Zack excused himself and followed Paul down the hall to an office that had been serving as Paul's temporary office. Jeremy was already there and looking a bit pale.

"What's going on?" Zack said as soon as Paul shut the door.

"Just a quick strategy meeting," Paul said. "So, just what are you planning on telling the reporter?"

"Is that what this is about? You don't trust me to talk to a reporter?"

"No, of course not," Paul said. "Just be careful what you say, that's all."

"Well, it's not quite that simple," said Jeremy. "With everything else happening, we haven't had time to go over how to deal with the press as a company officer. You're no longer an employee of a company; you're the head of it. Where a court might be lenient when it comes to an employee saying something rash, it takes the word of the CEO much more seriously."

"So don't say anything at all negative about DisplayTechnik," Paul said.

"Not even remotely negative," Jeremy added.

"What, hide out?"

"No, not hide out," Paul said. "Just don't say anything, you know, to make matters worse."

"Basically, don't criticize," Jeremy said.

"And don't get into anything personal or anything about the new technology," Paul said.

"Well, maybe you can hint at it," Jeremy said. "I'm sure you'd like to say something about it. But when it comes to the situation, stick to your own personal feelings. Say how *you* feel and how this affects *you*. What *you* believe. You can't be criticized—"

"Or sued for libel—"

"For just saying what you feel and believe. After all, you're entitled to your opinion."

"But don't try to turn the press into your own personal pulpit until you're more experienced at it."

"I'd concur."

Zack smiled at the pep talk. "Anything else, coach? Or should I say, coaches?"

"No, that's about it on that issue."

"'On that issue'? Is there something else?"

Jeremy and Paul looked at each other, replaying some debate they must have had earlier. Jeremy took a deep breath and turned to Zack.

"Well, it bothered me that the wording of the TRO was thirty days or until the court says otherwise."

"Yeah, I caught that too."

"It could be nothing. A simple wording change. But usually they read that they're in effect a maximum of thirty days. After that, the other side has to renew it or it'll expire. I talked with Bill briefly, and he said that McSorley handled all that. Anyway, I'm sure it's nothing."

"Whew," Zack said. "Okay, good, you had me going there for a minute."

"No, no. Just my job to point out worst-case scenarios."

Tired of standing, Zack took a seat on a box of files that Paul hadn't had a chance to unpack yet. "You know, while we're on the subject, this whole TRO thing seems overblown and ridiculous."

"Zack, we've already covered this ground," Paul said.

"Bear with me a second. I read through that monster of a TRO, and there isn't one bit of truth to it. Allen doesn't have a leg to stand on. But what I really don't understand are his tactics here. Allen may be an egotistical bastard, but he's extremely intelligent. You guys told me that it's practically impossible to prove a noncompete case in Silicon Valley, right?"

Paul frowned at him. "Yeah, so?"

"Well, every single day in California, people are jumping ship to join a different crew. So how can Allen charge us with recruiting the same boys he's just fired? That's lunacy. We can't be charged with recruiting them away if he's already fired them. Why didn't he just wait until we'd quit on our own? Then he could legitimately say they were coerced away."

Jeremy edged forward in his chair. "McSorley will argue that you'd coerced people like Dimitre and Jerry to leave DisplayTechnik, and did so long before they were fired. He will also argue that Allen then fired all of you to protect his company's best interests. And he would be right."

"Well, that's encouraging. Whose side are you on, anyway?"

Jeremy leaned back in Paul's chair, rubbing his forehead. "It's not a question of taking sides, Zack. I'm just pointing out how the other side would make their legal argument."

"I know. But you're missing the point. This isn't just about legal tactics. I worked with Allen for years. I know the man. The fact is, Allen can't bear the thought of anyone having a dream of his or her own. So instead of doing the smart thing and letting the other guys resign with me, he fired them. Where he's really blown his case is this whole cock-and-bull story about the misappropriation of trade secrets. Have you ever seen a more ridiculous bluff? I don't know how to prove it yet without disclosing our designs, but our technology isn't anything like DisplayTechnik's. Maybe we can get Judge Rafkin to hear our ideas behind closed doors. Then he'll know just how absurd this TRO is."

"I'm not so certain that Rafkin would listen anyway," Jeremy said.

Jeremy looked at Paul, and Zack felt an unease spread in his stomach. Now what?

"This was actually something that I wanted to bring up this morning," Jeremy said. "Did you know that a lottery is used to appoint a judge to a case?"

"No, I didn't."

"Now, this may not mean anything, but I have a law clerk friend over at the district court. He called me from home after you left to tell me there's a rumor floating around that Allen specifically got Rafkin assigned to our case."

"So?"

"So what he's saying," Paul added, "is that Allen can cook our legal system and that Rafkin's on the take."

"We've been over that ..." Jeremy protested.

"It's a goddamned conspiracy!" Paul exclaimed.

Jeremy shook his head. "My friend here has no hard evidence to support that allegation. But I do know this: in normal TRO proceedings, the plaintiff must post a bond in case the accusations turn out to be false. This policy discourages any Wild West free-for-alls. In our particular case, the normal bond should have been set for at least one hundred thousand dollars. But Judge Rafkin assigned only ten thousand dollars, out of which Allen only needed to put down 10 percent."

"That doesn't mean there's a conspiracy," Zack said. "Couldn't Rafkin have just been feeling generous or something? Allen has had a lot of business go through the courts. Maybe he figured he was good for it."

"This whole thing doesn't smell right," Paul said. "It's too slick.

DisplayTechnik needed to put up just one measly thousand dollars to guarantee our temporary restraining order? Come on! Henley probably tips more than that for lunch."

"Why all the gloom and doom?" Zack said. "We just do our homework, and all of this goes away. We already know that the noncompete will never stand up in the state of California and that the employee solicitation and trade secret charges hold as much water as Death Valley. In thirty days, this whole thing blows over, and we go back to being Imagination. End of story."

"Maybe, Zack, maybe," Paul said. "Let's hope so. But in the meantime, this legal defense isn't cheap. In order for Jeremy to prepare, he'll need some serious help here. This is going to cost us a bundle. What, Jeremy, one hundred thousand dollars to prepare?"

Jeremy nodded, avoiding Zack's eyes.

"We have twenty days to respond to the court on the TRO," Paul said. "Given the weight of that TRO, Henley's lawyers are going to do some fancy dancing in court to ensure it sticks."

"I don't care if Henley himself comes to court dressed like a ballerina wearing a pink tutu; we've got the truth on our side. All Allen can do is delay us; he can't stop us. And once we prove these charges have no foundation, we can go ahead and sue Henley's butt. Let's see how Allen can soft-pedal out of that."

"Jesus, Zack," Paul said, his voice sounding very tired, "we don't have any money to sue DisplayTechnik. We're lucky that Jeremy's such a good friend; otherwise, I'm not even sure we could fight this TRO thing."

"What? But yesterday you were the one hungry to go after him." All last night Zack had comforted himself with visions of suing Henley for interference, harassment, and all sorts of things. He'd envisioned the US marshals pulling up to Henley's mansion and sniffing through Allen's personal belongings. "We have to go after him. Someone like Allen has to be taught a lesson. That's how you stop bullies: you face them head-on. We are going to go after him! It's our moral responsibility."

"Zack," Paul said, "you're not listening. We ain't got the money to go toe-to-toe with Henley in court."

Zack hadn't considered that. With the millions of dollars they'd already been given, the ten or twenty thousand he'd estimated needed to go after Allen had seemed insignificant.

"Well … go talk with our investors. You were the one who put this financial deal together. Go ask John and Molly for help. When you explain that these charges are all trumped up, I'm positive that the investors will back us. Besides, they'll more than recoup any legal fees with what we wring out of Allen. What did they say when you called them to let them know what was going on?"

Paul sighed. "I didn't call them yet. I was—"

"What? How could you not call them?"

"—at Jeremy's 'til late last night, and I just didn't. I don't have enough to tell them, anyway. Believe me, I already know their mood, and they're nervous. We're a brand-new company and—"

"That didn't stop them from investing millions of dollars to get us going."

"Yeah, you're right. But they invested in our technology, not in lawyers' fees."

Zack shook his head. Investors could be such a fickle lot, and this was more than just money now. "Look, just remember that we're on the high road here. We'll win this thing; I know it."

Paul yawned, shaking his head.

For a moment, Zack felt like he was a kid explaining his belief in Santa Claus to an older schoolmate who scoffed at the notion. For all his good points, Paul didn't put much stock in moral absolutes.

"And for God's sake, call the investors, will you? We need to be open and up-front with them. The last thing we need is for them to bail on us because we didn't communicate with them. Okay?"

Paul nodded.

"Hey, besides, Jeremy here can work pro bono on this case. Right?" Zack gave Jeremy a wink. "After we get our product to market, he can make more money than he ever dreamed of."

"Zack, didn't you hear *anything* Jeremy said? Allen got a favorable judge assigned to the case. This thing is fixed. Done deal."

Jeremy held up a hand. "Whoa, let's not go there. Nothing is fixed, and a judge isn't going to jeopardize his position simply to—"

"Oh, for God's sake!" Paul yelled. "Listen to you two! You both live in a fantasy world. Zack with his high-and-moral road, and you not believing that the justice system could be fixed! Wake up! This is the real world. People can be bought. People change allegiances. People—"

"I didn't say—" Jeremy tried to speak.

"Oh, just forget it," Paul said. "We're not even going to agree to disagree, so let's just move on. Tell him the other piece of news."

Jeremy grimaced. "The TRO is a bit more extensive than what I thought yesterday in court. It also encompasses your homes in the search for information. I just got off the phone with McSorley, since Bill didn't know anything. He added the language, and the judge agreed to it because you guys had been working from your homes for months before any of this came to light."

"Oh, crap," Zack said.

"Why'd you say that?" Paul asked.

Zack looked at them and shrugged. "Well, it's not all that big a deal, I guess. I just had the guys make copies of their hard drives so we could continue working during the thirty days—"

"I wouldn't recommend doing that," Jeremy said. "A temporary restraining order means just that. You have to stop. You can't be working on things; it's in violation of the order."

"I … I thought it meant we just couldn't actually be implementing things, you know, start up the manufacturing process."

"No, no. This means you have to stop. Period."

"Oh, that's ridiculous. What, do we have to stop thinking about things too? A judge can't stop that."

"Of course not. That's not what I'm saying. But for all practical purposes, Imagination is shut down."

That was ridiculous, utterly ridiculous. "So, you're saying we can't even keep copies of things? We have to be able to do that at least."

Jeremy looked at Paul.

"Stop it!" Zack said. "You keep looking at him as though he has all the answers. I'm here too. I make decisions. Just because he holds the money, doesn't mean I don't have any say."

"I'm sorry, Zack. I didn't mean to offend. It's just that Paul and I already did a lot of talking after you left, and we wondered how you and the other guys would take all this. I guess on the surface, I don't see anything wrong with keeping copies. In fact, maybe that's wise considering what we're up against, but you need to declare them and DisplayTechnik will need to be the ones to verify that they're *only* copies and not that you're handing them things that have had deletions. Otherwise, you can hand them all sorts of ludicrous things and claim that was the extent of your files. *Everything* has to be handed over, and then they will hand things back to you after they've gone through them. This includes the copies you made. I'll tell Bill about it."

Jeremy looked very intently at Zack. "The worst thing you can do is to hide things. I sure hope none of your engineers did anything like that."

Zack felt a rush of fear. What if Dimitre or one of the others did something really stupid last night? It could ruin all of them. And now he was beginning to doubt the system could get them out of this. Especially if there was any truth at all to what Paul said. Though he believed in taking the high road, he was well aware that others didn't share his beliefs—especially Allen.

"I told them to just make copies of things. I told them not to hide anything."

"Good," Jeremy said.

Paul shook his head; it was clear to Zack that he had voted to hide things and let DisplayTechnik bear the burden of proof.

"That should be fine then," Jeremy said. "Just make sure they cooperate fully. Any noncooperation, and it'll look guilty."

Zack got up and started walking back to his office. On the way, he passed the lab windows and saw Jerry inside with the marshals and Bill Bennet. They were standing over a piece of equipment, taking notes. When he arrived at his office, Elizabeth was standing by the window, looking out at the crowd.

"Looking kind of unruly for mere onlookers, aren't they?" she remarked.

Tom had the camera back at his eye and was filming away. "Yeah," he said out of the corner of his mouth, "wonder what's going on?"

"What are you talking about?" Zack said.

Elizabeth turned to him and said, "The crowd, they're … acting funny."

Zack immediately saw what she meant. Instead of facing the goings-on at Imagination, they were focused on someone in their midst. Arms were waving, and people were shouting.

When he caught sight of a familiar burly figure, Zack bolted for the door. "I'll be back!" he yelled over his shoulder. He ran down the hall, through the lobby, and hit the door full tilt. As he ducked under the police tape at the edge of the parking lot, he heard someone say, "Well, a buddy of mine from DisplayTechnik told me you guys stole some technology from them to make really flat panels."

"Is bullshit! Your friend is knowing nothing!"

"Jesus, what's your problem, buddy?" the reversed baseball cap said.

"I am not your buddy. What are you doing here at my company? Go now; leave!"

"Dimitre!" Zack cried as he pushed toward his chief engineer. The preoccupied Russian didn't seem to hear him.

"Yeah, then how come the marshals?" the guy in the baseball cap went on. "If you didn't steal their flat-panel stuff, how come they're here?"

"Only thing flat will be your face!"

Dimitre raised his hand, but Zack dove for him before it could come crashing down.

Dimitre toppled backward and fell to the ground. He popped up surprisingly quickly for such a large man, like he'd landed on a trampoline. His nostrils flared like an enraged bull's.

"Dimitre, knock it off!" Zack said, as he tried to reach past him for the loudmouth in the Giants cap.

"You stupid person with the brain of a yak!" Dimitre shouted. "We do nothing wrong!"

"You're a stupid commie screwup!" the guy in the baseball cap said. "Why don't you go back to Siberia?"

"Why don't you go home and take your wife out of the barn? I hear she gives good ride for ten cents a minute."

The guy lunged at Dimitre, but the crowd blocked his path. Zack dragged and pushed Dimitre toward the front door. Jimmy met them on the other side of the police tape and helped steer Dimitre into the lobby. Bill Bennet, notebook in hand, looked on from one of the windows.

"Jeez, Dimitre, what the hell was that all about?" Zack said.

"When I arrive, I do not like to see them there. I hear them saying bad things about us and things they are knowing nothing about. I tell them to go away, and they say we stole things and that we are criminals."

"Yeah, that's about where I came in." Zack looked up to see Elizabeth and Tom at the end of the hall. He wondered just how much of the episode they'd filmed. "Look," Zack said, "we can't start falling to pieces. The press is here, and we need to keep it together in front of the marshals. Okay? Speaking of which, something else has come up."

"What?" Dimitre and Jimmy said simultaneously.

"That stuff we talked about last night?"

They looked at him blankly.

"You know, steps we decided to take? Jeremy says it's really bad if we've changed or deleted anything. The marshals are going to search our houses as well."

Jimmy hissed, "Shit."

"This is all wrong." Dimitre shook his head. "This is America."

"Damn it, I don't want these guys going through my stuff at home," Jimmy said.

"You didn't hide things, did you?"

"No." Jimmy's face flushed. "It's just ... you know. I have an issue about privacy. I'm antigovernment as it is, and this is like the fucking Nazis, man."

"You're right, it is. But we need to be clean, or it'll hurt us in the end. Look, let me go deal with the press, and you guys find Jerry to tell him what's up, but do it quietly. He was down in the lab showing the marshals what was what. Oh, and Dimitre, Bill Bennet's here, so be nice."

"What?" Dimitre exclaimed. "What is supreme idiot doing here? He has no business—"

"It's part of the procedure," Zack said, motioning with his hand for Dimitre to keep his voice down. "I can explain later, but basically a representative of the company has the right to be here to go through things. If you can't keep it together, then go sit in your office or something. Until they escort us to our homes, just hang around in case they have any questions."

Jimmy walked Dimitre down the hall, his skinny arm around the Russian's broad shoulders. Dimitre was mumbling foul-sounding Ukrainian oaths.

"Miss Fonteneau?" Zack said, trying his best to smile. "How about that interview now?"

―――――――――

Zack spent the better part of an hour with the reporter. It actually felt pretty good. He was able to talk in vague terms about their plans and goals, and hoped that in the end he'd strengthened their case. To make sure he didn't slip up, the whole time he pretended that Allen was sitting in a chair right behind her. He managed to work in some key differences between their technology and the technology of his former employer and how vastly different they were. He hoped Judge Rafkin watched *SVBN's* show. He also spoke about his outlook on business and how he'd planned a company that was truly different from "the others" out there.

Who knows? Maybe he'd get some sympathy.

After the interview, he took her around the plant. Unfortunately, the place was mostly stripped bare by then. Equipment that couldn't be moved was tagged with special seals. One of the moving vans had already left, and the other was nearly full. It had taken them days to move in, and had they not been interrupted, it would have taken them several weeks to be truly settled. But it had only taken a few hours to undo everything.

Elizabeth was about to leave when US Marshal Jones stepped up to him, followed by Jeremy and Paul.

"We're going to need to go to each of your homes once we finish up here," the marshal said, "which should be by about ten thirty. When we're done, we'll stop in at the Bakers' bank office. Do any of you maintain a safety deposit box or other off-site storage? If so, then we'll need to go to those locations as well."

Zack felt Elizabeth's bright blue eyes on him. "I have a safe deposit box, but the key is at home."

"That's fine."

There was a moment of awkward silence. Zack didn't know if he was supposed to say anything else. "Um, so do you just want to follow me back to my house?"

"Actually, we'll be starting at ..." Jones pulled out a piece of paper. "Dimitre Koz ... Koslov's house. We'll then proceed to Mr. Ryerson's, then Mr. Morgan's, Mr. Davis's, the Bakers', then Mr. Steiner's, and finally yours."

"You know, if it's all the same to you, could we take care of Jerry's—uh, Mr. Steiner's first? And then go the Bakers' bank later in the afternoon?"

The marshal eyed him closely. "Why?"

"Well, it's just that your schedule puts you at the bank in the middle of the lunch hour, which is really busy for the bank, and I'm sure that Molly and John don't want a crowd of marshals there in the middle of it."

"Uh-huh." The marshal stood erect now, his hands clasped behind his back. "And what's your reasoning with Mr. Steiner?"

"Well, he has kids, and it sounds like your schedule would put us there about the time they get home. They'd be ... underfoot, if you know what I mean." Did he have to spell it out for this guy? Zack had caught sight of a wedding ring earlier and just assumed he had kids as well.

"Uh-huh." Jones paused a moment and then said, "Request denied." He turned away.

"Wait a second," Zack said, walking after him. "Look, no one's trying to hide anything if that's what you're thinking."

"That's fortunate for you, son."

"It's just that ... you know, Jerry has kids. I'm sure he doesn't want his kids to see US marshals going through their things. That could be really, I don't know, frightening."

The marshal stopped. "I'm not unsympathetic, but the fact of the matter is that I was given an explicit order by the court in terms of how to handle this search for information, and I'm not going to deviate from it."

"Wait a second, the court—"

"Any inconvenience is regrettable, but that's also par for the course. Now if you'll excuse me."

"Look, can't you—"

"And be very careful," the marshal said. "You should know your houses are currently under surveillance until we arrive."

Zack stopped in his tracks. God, this really was Nazi tactics.

Zack watched the *SBVN* van in his rearview mirror. Lured by the possibility of another confrontation, or maybe hoping to get video of someone's door being broken down, Elizabeth had decided to follow them on their rounds. He hoped she'd get caught by a light, but so far, no such luck. She'd probably tell Tom to run it anyway.

Molly and John had politely waved away his apologies for the timing. They said they knew it couldn't be helped. He only wished he was as unflappable as they were when he reached their age. Nothing ever seemed to faze them.

The invasion of the Koslovs' had been memorable.

Anna showed up at the door in her robe, an infant on her hip, a cigarette dangling from her lips, with smoke pouring out of the house like it was a dragon's den. She'd launched into an avalanche of Ukrainian aimed at Dimitre. After about fifteen seconds, she'd swung her body out of the way and allowed them inside, still ranting away at Dimitre.

Actually, it all went pretty smoothly until the marshals tried to remove the home computer. That was when Anna really got mad. Between her volleys, Dimitre did his best to translate for the marshals in his own broken English. He explained that the computer was not his; it was his wife's.

"She is writer. She says you cannot take the computer because it is hers and not mine. It is … how you say, for her work. It is … it is her …"

"Livelihood?" Zack interjected.

"Yes. She is making money from it."

"You take that," Anna said, "and I'm calling the biggest goddamn attorney you ever saw to sue your ass to high heaven." She again launched into Dimitre in Ukrainian, and although he did his best to defend himself, it was clearly a losing battle.

The marshals conferred. After some discussion, they turned to Bill Bennet.

"I'm dubious about this woman's claim," he told them.

"You son of a bitch," Anna said. "Dimitre's job is his own, but you better not interfere with mine."

"I have a court order to search for evidence pertaining to his involvement with—"

"If you take it, then how am I supposed to do work? Are you going to pay for me to rent a computer and any downtime I've lost? Inconvenience?"

Bill appeared to reconsider. He said they wouldn't take the computer, but would make a total copy of the hard disk instead.

Anna launched into them again. "You have no goddamn business even looking at my computer! Your warrant doesn't apply to me."

"Look, lady," Marshal Jones said, "you can either do it the easy way or have the equipment seized. This seems like a fair—"

"The hell you will," she said. "Those are my private writings. I'll sit here and go through them with you."

"We don't have time for that," Bill said.

Anna clenched her fists. "Then you better make time. There are all sorts of copyright issues at hand here."

But neither Jones nor Bill would relent. Jones waved in his technician and they started to make a complete copy of the hard disk, while Bennet started explaining the rights granted under the search warrant.

In the end, Dimitre had to take his wife out of the room while they did their business. As Zack watched over the tech's shoulder, he felt his energy slipping. He prayed Dimitre hadn't screwed up and hidden something on his wife's computer.

Zack left Dimitre at his house. He could still see him standing in his doorway, slowly raising a hand in good-bye.

At Jimmy's place there was drama too. Debbie, his girlfriend, ran out of the apartment in tears when they started going through her underwear drawer. Zack could only say how sorry he was and leave Jimmy to comfort her.

Zack had spoken with Brett in Dallas by cell phone and arranged to call a locksmith to open the door for the search. It had been a short one. Brett wasn't involved with any of the planning of Imagination and didn't have a home computer. His laptop would be taken from him the next time he landed in California. Still, they removed several boxes of files that had to do with Brett's sales while still with DisplayTechnik. Bennet complained these things should have been turned in until Zack reminded him that Brett had been fired and that no one returned work from home once they'd been fired.

"Well, it's still company policy," Bennet had muttered.

Molly had left the bank to meet the marshals at their home. She had a small file folder with some papers and cheerfully invited them in. There were some glasses with iced tea laid out on the drainboard that she offered them. They didn't maintain a home office, having decided early in their marriage to leave work at work. The file, she explained, was something the marshals had overlooked at the bank that she thought they might want to have. Bill took a look at it and decided it wasn't necessary.

The two quick stops in a row had given Zack hope that they could get in and out of Jerry's home before his kids arrived, but they were taking a very roundabout route. He wondered if Allen had arranged this on purpose. There was probably something in Sun Tzu that talked about embarrassing your enemies to take the fight out of them.

By the time they arrived, it was nearly three. Two US marshals' cars, the moving van, Zack's and Jerry's cars, and the *SVBN* van all pulled up in front of the house.

Jerry met his wife at the door, and he quietly ushered the marshals inside. Zack waited outside with Jerry's wife, Sally. He didn't know her very well, and the awkwardness of the situation wasn't conducive to conversation. Elizabeth stepped up, and the two of them chatted easily, with Sally saying how much she enjoyed watching her on KPIX and was sorry that she'd left the morning show. They quickly fell into talking about each other's hair, and Zack was amazed at how two women who were complete strangers could talk so easily to one another.

When Elizabeth asked for an interview shot, Sally politely declined, and the two of them went right back to chatting, moving into restaurants, Sally's kids, and how fun it must be for Elizabeth to have an endless wardrobe provided to her by one of the local boutiques in exchange for her wearing their latest designs on the air.

It was then that Zack noticed groups of kids making their way home from school. Sally excused herself to go inside. She hadn't been inside for more than a few seconds when Zack caught sight of Tommy, Jerry's middle son. Sally must have spotted him before she went in.

He was a cute little boy of seven, his brown hair tousled by his walk home, his jacket askew due to the backpack that looked like it outweighed him. He wore a '49er's jersey and was kicking at the heels of one of his friends who was a step in front of him. His friend turned to take a playful swing at him, but Tommy ducked out of the way and outmaneuvered him, using a tree to slip around and get back on the sidewalk now three lengths in front of his friend.

He stopped dead in his tracks when he saw the strange cars and vans parked out front. Strange men were carrying things out of his home in boxes and putting them in the back of the van and in the cars.

Before Zack could go over to him to try to explain what was going on, Jerry came out of the house, followed by Sally. Tears brimmed in her eyes but stubbornly refused to fall. Jerry met his son at the end of the stone path. He put a hand on Tommy's shoulder. Zack couldn't make out what was being said, but he could see the worried look on Tommy's face. While Jerry talked, the boy looked from his dad to his mom to Zack to the men carrying things out of his house.

The full weight of being in charge hit Zack hard. Any actions that he took would have huge impacts on Jerry's family and this little boy, who stood in his own driveway while people he didn't know took things from his dad. And a TV crew was there to record it all, and his friends and their parents would see it as breaking news that evening. Would Tommy be teased tomorrow at school, accused of being the son of a criminal, or simply shunned by all, judged guilty for something he had nothing to do with?

If every CEO who had ever stolen money, set up fictitious companies, or destroyed retirement funds of innocent strangers were made to stand in the driveways of the people they had harmed …

"Hey, Zack, you remember Tommy, don't you?" Jerry said,

waving him over. His tone told Zack that he ought to be upbeat too.

"Sure do," Zack said. "He's a Niners fan, just like me. How you doing, Tommy?"

"Hi, Mr. Zack," Tommy said quietly.

Sally slipped the backpack off the boy's shoulders. "You hungry, Tommy? How 'bout we get you some pretzels or something? We have about two or three hours till dinner. I was thinking of ordering pizza since these guys might be here a while."

"Pizza? Hey, can we get sausage this time? Last time we got pepperoni because Alex *had* to have it ..."

Sally steered him toward the side entrance to the kitchen.

Zack sat down on the low retaining wall that bordered the driveway. "Jerry, I don't know what to say."

Jerry sat down next to him, his arms crossed. "Don't worry about Tommy. He's a good kid. And he's smart. We'll explain it all tonight—how some people sometimes think you've done something bad and it's just not true. He'll be fine, and so will the others. We're raising our kids to be a part of the real world, as scary as that is."

"I'm sorry he had to see this, though. I tried—"

"Jimmy told me," Jerry said. "Every dad wants to be a superhero to his kids, but eventually they figure out that he's not. If you can stay big in their hearts, that's all you can really ask for."

Zack nodded.

"I know you can't control everything, but just be careful," Jerry said. "There's more riding on you than you know."

CHAPTER THIRTEEN

Zack stopped briefly at his apartment to let the marshals inside and then took one of them down to the bank to open his safe deposit box. There were some disks inside, along with some technical drawings and formulas, and the personal items were put back.

When they returned to the apartment, the search was far from over. Bill Bennet was standing in his living room checking things off before the marshals toted them out. He wondered what they thought of his less-than-perfect housekeeping and just as quickly realized he didn't give a damn. His closets and dresser drawers had been opened and searched, his office was completely ransacked, and its contents were removed with the exception of the furniture. Even his kitchen garbage was upended and searched.

Zack sat patiently on the floor inside the entryway watching as they took out box after box. He knew for sure that some of what they were removing had nothing to do with Imagination. Jeremy had explained that they'd go through it all at a neutral place and then promptly return whatever they found to be harmless. The lawyer estimated they'd have their computers back within five to seven working days once the hard drives had all been thoroughly searched.

Just how thorough were the marshals, and what would have happened if they *had* hidden something? Did they scope the hard drives checking for deleted data or simply go through the files? The

FBI could recover something from a completely wiped hard drive by going over it with a super microscope that could read the tiny magnetic signatures that still remained.

Zack followed the last of the marshals out and watched as the van drove away. It was after six o'clock. They'd been at it for nearly twelve hours. He was ready to collapse on the sofa; his evening jog was not going to happen. The automatic sprinklers were jetting, providing relief to the islands of grass like putting greens on a desert golf course.

It had been hell watching the lives of his team being so thoroughly violated. The more he thought about it, the more he was sure that Allen had coordinated every aspect of it, including the timing.

As he started back up the steps of the apartment complex, he saw movement behind the staircase.

"Hello, Zack."

Stepping out of the shadows was the last person he expected to see. And the only person he really longed to see. Mary Anne was beautiful; there was no getting around that. He longed to take her in his arms, he wanted to yell at her, he wanted to kiss her, he wanted to just hold her and be held by her. He wanted to know, to finally know, what had happened.

"Hello yourself," he said.

"I'm sorry to surprise you like this; I just couldn't show myself when ..."

"When the marshals were here?" Zack said. Or was it because Bill was here and you didn't want word getting back to Daddy? He didn't ask the question, but his eyes narrowed. "Exactly how long have you been here?"

"Not very. A few minutes."

"Long enough to watch the marshals storm into my home and take everything that's sacred and precious to me? Long enough to watch Allen destroy something good that we're trying to—"

"Maybe I should just leave," Mary Anne said, taking a step backward.

Maybe you should.

Zack looked beyond her and saw two kids in the parking lot, running barefoot toward a Volvo that had a Frisbee on its roof. They were laughing as they retrieved their toy, but hushed the moment they saw Zack. He realized he must have been scowling.

"Stay," he told her. "We need to talk. We *really* need to talk. Look, I'm … I'm just a little tense at the moment." This used to be when she'd come over and rub his neck and shoulders. He shook off the memory.

Mary Anne's face was partially lit by the sun that was nearly below the roof of the apartment complex. Her arms were folded across her yellow jacket, hiding a necklace of oddly shaped metal beads that looked like spent bullets salvaged from a shooting gallery.

Stepping forward, she said, "I know you're tense. I … I'm sure my sudden appearance didn't help."

"Come on, let's go up," he said, leading her through the open front door. "Have a seat. The good news is they didn't take the couch."

Mary Anne glanced at the two-person love seat but chose the brown La-Z-Boy chair in front of the television. Zack went into the kitchen and watched her through the rectangular opening in the wall that, oddly, made him think he was watching her on live television. The sight of her trim figure still had an effect on him, though he tried to ignore it. He saw her touch the flowery embroidered wool cushions that his grandmother had knitted for him. They were her favorites. Normally whenever she came to his place, she snuggled her face against them.

"Do you want something to drink?" Zack opened up the refrigerator, stocked with typical bachelor fare of half-eaten fried chicken, lumpy porridge that used to be milk, a head of lettuce whose color resembled the parched California hills, and a six-pack of beer from Seattle's Red Hook microbrewery. "What do you know? They left the beer. There is a God after all." He grabbed an Extra Special Bitter Ale.

"Nothing for me, thank you."

Zack shut the fridge door and went to a cabinet drawer to get the bottle opener. He rummaged through the tangled knives and forks, but there was no opener. Where was it? He was sure that he put the opener in the drawer. This was ridiculous. He always put it here. God, did the marshals take that as well?

Come on, stupid, you know that's ridiculous. He scanned the countertop, seeing a trail of pizza crusts leading to dirty plates stacked in the sink. He gripped the bottle cap and tried turning it, the serrated edges digging into his fingers. Nothing. He turned harder—still nothing. He looked up at Mary Anne, sitting quietly, staring straight ahead at the bare white wall. God, he could really use a beer right now. Where was that damn opener? He went to the drawer one more time, and sure enough, sitting in plain view on top of the heap of utensils, was the opener.

I am losing it.

Zack took a deep swig and walked into the living room.

"I guess we might as well dive right in," he said, collapsing on the green love seat. "So, why are you here?"

"I want to see you. It's natural, isn't it?"

Zack took another swig of beer. "Yeah, sure, it's natural," he said. "But not five days after I got fired. Not after all the crap that I've gone through. Not after, what? Thirty messages that you didn't bother to return?"

Mary Anne made a face but said nothing,

"I mean, I called you at work. I even went looking for you at your home. Or, don't tell me, you didn't get any of my messages, right?"

Silence. She looked out the window, turned in profile, teasing him with her cute, elf-like nose.

"Did you know about all this?"

"Pardon?" she said, softly.

"Come on, Mary Anne, don't play games. Did you know Allen was going to sic the Keystone Cops on us? Storm into Imagination, strip us dry, and then go house-to-house and do a strip search on my team and me?"

"I knew about the temporary restraining order," Mary Anne said. "But I didn't know the full extent of what was planned. I only found out a few hours ago from Deirdre—apparently one of your engineers' girlfriends called up everyone she knew at the company to complain."

"Who'd she call?"

"I don't know, Deidre didn't say, but you know how fast news can spread."

"Sure, especially bad news. But what happened to the grapevine this week? Did someone chop it down right after your father fired my ass on Monday?"

"I don't know."

"Stop saying 'I don't know,' for Christ's sake. Five days passed by before you called me back. Five days!"

"Maybe I should go. This isn't healthy for either of us."

"Seems healthy for me," Zack said. "My head's buzzing with questions. Did you know that Paul's been a big worrywart all week? In fact, I sometimes think he's my surrogate mother. The very moment Allen kicks me out of DisplayTechnik, Paul starts quizzing me about you. He starts questioning our relationship: how much did I tell you about the new company, how did I compromise our position? But you know me and my principles. I stuck by you. I actually defended you!"

"Save your sermons. Don't start in about morals. You should have told me."

"What did you say?"

"You heard me. You should have told me about Imagination. How can you preach about morals and principles when you're hiding things?"

"I had—"

"I thought we loved each other. We'd talked about sharing our lives together."

"And if I had told you, you wouldn't have gone running straight to your daddy with it?"

"That doesn't change the fact that you didn't trust me. How do you think that makes me feel?"

"Every time I brought up anything even remotely connected to my leaving the company, you blocked me out. You made it perfectly clear that I *owed* a great debt to your father, a debt that could never be repaid."

"Well, you do! You owe him—"

"I'm not finished. You didn't listen to me then, just like you're not listening to me now. You're always so sure you have all the answers, but you're wrong."

"I think you're talking about yourself. Did you give any thought to the position your abandoning the company put me in?"

"Yes, I did, and that's precisely why I didn't tell you everything. I did it to protect you."

"So, you didn't believe I'd keep your secret."

"You invade my office like a common thief, and I should trust you?"

"What do you mean I invaded your office?"

He'd wanted her to confess on her own without an accusation, but he couldn't hold back. "It's the only logical conclusion," Zack said, choosing his words very carefully. "The kind of information that's been gathered against us points to Allen having an inside source. And by a process of elimination, that points to you."

Mary Anne stared at her hands for a long moment and then said, "Yes, I did look through your things."

"While I was asleep?"

She nodded.

Up until that moment, Zack still harbored the tiniest shred of doubt, thinking that perhaps Allen had hired a PI to break into his apartment. Now, there was no going back to the way things were. Not ever.

"I really didn't want to believe you were capable of something like that," he said. "I wanted to think Allen had hired someone to search my things, or that maybe they'd hacked a way past my firewall. So much for trust."

"You have no idea what you're talking about. You have no idea what I went through or what I am up against. You're so concerned about yourself that you didn't even stop to think about the consequences of your actions."

"Look what happened from your actions," Zack said, raising his voice. "My company was shut down. I'm being sued. I could even go to jail. You've proved where your allegiance is. God! Paul *was* right about you."

"And what exactly did he say about me?"

When Zack didn't answer, she said, "Okay, fine, don't tell me. More secrets. Like your plan to sneak behind my father's back, rallying your little engineers around your own flag."

"You sound just like your father, turning everything into a personal Pearl Harbor. No one was sneaking around his back."

"Then what would you call it?"

"We worked after hours, on our own time, not his. It had nothing to do with him."

"After all he's done for you and the others? For someone who thinks so highly of his morals, it seems to me that you're the one who's taken a page out of Pearl Harbor. You don't attack someone first and then declare war afterward."

It was scary—and sad. Paul was right about her: she would always be a Henley first. "Is that what you truly believe?"

Mary Anne crossed her arms over her chest. "When my father first became suspicious, I didn't want to believe it. I defended you because you're always talking about loyalty and honor."

"If you'd really listened, you'd know I believe loyalty is earned."

"Loyalty means sticking with someone."

"But not sticking with a corrupt leader."

"So now my father's corrupt?"

"You can't seriously think he's not."

"My father has his issues, but in his heart, he's still a good man. You're the one who's stealing his ideas and his employees."

Zack leaned forward on the love seat. "Is that what you honestly believe?"

Mary Anne flicked her bangs to one side, returning his stare. "What did you mean earlier, when you said you didn't want to put me in a compromising situation?"

"I was leaving the company, and so were the others. We all knew what your father was capable of, even if you claim you don't. I'm talking about his Sun Tzu, 'kill 'em all and let God sort 'em out' approach to business. That put anyone connected to us at grave risk of being fired, sued, or in your case, disowned. Until it was all out in the open, it was better for you not to know anything. 'Plausible deniability' is the legal term."

"Zack, can't you see all that means is you didn't trust me?"

"I did, but I felt I had to protect you from the consequences."

"It doesn't matter what noble rationalization you put on it; the heart of the matter is that you didn't believe I could keep your secret, because of who I am."

Boiled down like that, it was hard to deny. Sure, he was worried she wouldn't share his goal, or that she'd run and tell her daddy before they were ready. But on top of that, he knew how much she seemed to love and respect her father, and he couldn't bear to tell her to her face how much he had come to despise the man.

"I'll tell you what the heart of the matter is," she went on. "You're nothing but a hypocrite. Always talking about taking the high road, then stealing my father's engineers and ideas."

The unfairness of the accusation burned into Zack's very soul. The love of his life had become a stranger to him. She'd betrayed them all to a man who hid his thefts behind phalanxes of lawyers and mountains of money, a man without conscience or restraint, a man who didn't deserve any part of her loyalty.

"Why are you sighing like that?" she said angrily. "Am I boring you?"

"Look, we're not getting anywhere, are we? Maybe we should just call it a night."

"I have a much better idea," Mary Anne said as she rose from the chair. "Why don't we call it over and leave it at that?"

She walked out the door, without looking back.

———————

Twenty minutes later, Zack threw on his blue Adidas track pants and a '49ers' T-shirt and set out for a jog. Normally, it took thirty minutes, but tonight, he crossed Freeway 680 and ran up into the hills bordering the west side of Pleasanton. Ignoring the private property signs of the gated community, he sprinted past the unattended security post.

"I hated the bastard when I worked for him," Zack muttered as he ran. "I hated how he treated people. That sanctimonious, pompous, arrogant asshole made his own daughter his slave."

He started to laugh uncontrollably. She'd actually chosen her father over him. Her father! His jogging became erratic; he weaved down the street like a drunk running on a listing ship.

A woman walking her dog in the opposite direction regarded his approach with concern.

As he leaned against a post to catch his breath, she yanked hard on the leash. Her poor dog yelped, and she hurried away, shaking her head.

Charlotte was right, he thought. I'm running scared, scared out of my frigging mind.

———————

Jimmy scrunched down into his chair, trying to find a comfortable position. He and the other two Imagination engineers sat in the main lounge of the Marriott Hotel in Santa Clara, one of their many hangouts. It wasn't their usual Friday night spot, and Jimmy wasn't clear why Dimitre had wanted to meet here. Personally, he liked O'Toole's and its old brewpub atmosphere much better: dark paneled walls, a massive bar along one wall, and half-walls that broke the remaining floor space into smaller enclaves. The Marriott featured deep, grainy-patterned armchairs; the ergonomics prevented them from easily reaching the small round glass table that held their drinks and a bowl of unsalted, roasted peanuts.

Even so, after their experiences with the marshals today, it felt good to get out. He wondered if Zack was going to show.

Dimitre downed his Guinness. He immediately waved for another one from the waitress in a short skirt. Between sips of red wine, Jerry Steiner was cleaning his eyeglasses—as he often did when things got uncomfortable. Jimmy was having his usual Pepsi, chewing on the straw, his eyes darting between his two senior colleagues.

Dimitre held his right hand in the air, forming the letter "C" with his thumb and index finger. "Do you know how far my fingers are spread?"

Jimmy shook his head.

"Russian men say that it is twelve inches. Most women say is six inches."

Jimmy chuckled.

"Christ, you have sex on the brain," Jerry said. "What's your point?" His left leg was bouncing up and down; the vibrating was making the peanut dish migrate toward the edge of the table.

"I wonder how much is reality and how much is fantasy," Dimitre said.

Jerry shifted in his chair. "Fantasy about what?"

"Fantasy of Imagination."

"What are you talking about?" Jerry's leg was still imitating a jackhammer.

Dimitre glowered at him, grabbed the peanut dish, and brought it back to the center of the table. Jerry stopped shaking.

"First we are being told we violate our noncompetes. Zack and Paul were thinking this was not even possibility when we are first forming Imagination."

"Well, none of us did," Jimmy said. "Hey, we all talked about it. We all believed that the company was so different there was no way that they could nail us on noncompetes."

"Yes, this is true, my little friend. But then they never saw the TRO coming, either."

"Well, who the hell could?" Jimmy grabbed some peanuts out of the dish and popped a few in his mouth. Yuck. They were soft, spongy. He didn't spit them out, so swallowed with an effort, and dumped the rest back.

"Sounds to me like it's a problem with the attorney, not our leaders," Jerry said.

"Yes, this is very true. But I am thinking Zack is bearing some of the blame as well. He should be anticipating this action from Henley."

Jimmy shrugged his shoulders. He drained his Pepsi.

"What do you think?" Dimitre asked Jerry.

"I think there's a lot of things that Zack has to worry about," he said. "I trust him completely. That's why I left Henley."

"Dimitre, I thought you were Zack's greatest fan," Jimmy said.

"I am." The Russian picked up the frosted glass of chocolate-colored beer. The head sloshed over, leaving a dark puddle on the glass table.

"Well, if you have problems with the way he runs things, go speak to him," Jimmy said. "You know Zack. He'll do his best to bend over backward—twice—to make things right with you."

Dimitre nodded. Everyone knew this to be true.

"They went into our bedroom and made our children cry. My Anna ... Never mind. It is being long time before I am forgetting this. Long time."

The three of them sat in silence. Images from the marshals' raid flashed through Jimmy's mind, and from the silence and the looks on the other two men, he could tell they too were remembering the invasions of their homes.

Dimitre finished the last two-thirds of his beer in one long draft and then signaled the waitress for another. "I am thinking we just need to keep our ears open and be watching Zack and Paul—especially Paul. I do not have good feeling about him."

Jerry shrugged. "Well, he did bring in the big investors from New York and Houston."

"Yes, yes, I know." Dimitre waved the comment away. "But he is just moneyman; he is not caring about us or our technology. He is just wanting to make money. And I believe he does not care how he gets it."

Dimitre excused himself and headed for the restroom. Jimmy frowned as he watched him go. He found that kind of talk worrying. He was the youngest of the principal engineers; only twenty-six years old, he graduated from UCLA at the top of his electrical engineering class. He'd decided to move to Northern California because Zack and Dimitre had greatly impressed him when he interviewed for the job. He swallowed an ice cube and glanced across the table at Jerry, who sat staring at some far-off point.

Jimmy knew all this had to be affecting him a great deal, but he didn't show it. Jerry was fifteen years older and always had a serious expression on his face. An intense guy, his mind was always going. Where Dimitre was brilliantly creative, Jerry was a great conceptual thinker, seeing the end of the problem at the same time he saw the beginning. It was the steps in between that sometimes gave him problems. Jerry was a devoted family man and had joined the start-up because he needed a big financial hurrah to cover his kids' college educations. He'd made no secret about his motivation.

A few minutes later, Dimitre returned, his yellow-stained teeth in full view. "Do you know the story about people's brains?" He leaned over, snagged a few peanuts, and popped them in his mouth before sitting down.

Jimmy heard the seat groan under the weight.

"A man asks storekeeper, 'How much is costing for chemist's brain?' The storekeeper answers, 'Is ten bucks per pound.' 'Okay,' man says, 'then, how much is costing for an engineer's brain?' The storekeeper answers, 'Is twenty per pound.' 'Okay, is fine,' says the man, 'then, how much is costing for a financial person's brain?' The storekeeper rubs chin and says, 'Is one hundred dollars per pound.' The man is being very upset. 'This is being crazy. How come financial brain is costing so much more?' The storekeeper says, 'Do you know how many financial people I am having to kill to collect one pound of brain?'"

Jimmy howled.

"Good one, yes?" Dimitre said, giving Jerry a nudge. Then he slapped his hand on the table to catch the attention of the waitress. He ordered another drink, this time a double shot of Italian grappa.

CHAPTER FOURTEEN

Alone in the dark of the den, Charlotte sat just outside the foyer, holding a tumbler of scotch. She knew she really should be getting to bed. The stereo had exhausted its last CD a long time ago. Still, there was an oddly superior feeling, a certain smugness to be sitting there in the shadows with no one telling her to stop drinking or to go upstairs and to stop bothering them.

She made an effort to stand but fell back when she heard a car pulling up. It was Mary Anne. She'd become quite good at recognizing the sounds of her family's cars. She tried to take a strengthening sip of her scotch but found only ice in her glass. Well, no matter. Plenty more where that came from.

She got up and wobbled along the shadows to the bar behind Allen's desk, where she'd filled Zack's glass three days earlier. It seemed longer than that. She was determined to press Mary Anne about what was going on between them. It had been weighing heavily on her mind since Zack left.

Charlotte steadied herself against the bar. Mary Anne simply didn't know enough about her father. Ever since she was tiny, she'd had him up on a pedestal. He might as well have been out in the foyer too. Along with Teddy Roosevelt and Genghis Khan. She was surprised that Allen hadn't made a statue in his own image, with a massive codpiece and astride a rather obvious stallion. She giggled and poured a hefty splash of single malt into her glass.

The door opened and slammed hard. Charlotte clutched the bottle to her chest as she turned, suddenly fearing the worst. She saw something black hit the statue. She couldn't see what it was, but it fell to the marbled floor with a thud.

Expecting to see Allen violent and out of control, she clutched at the neck of her dressing gown and backed deeper into the shadows, trying to disappear. When Mary Anne came into view, she stopped. Her daughter scooped up whatever she'd thrown at the statue and began to beat it against the metal horse's hide. She was crying and cursing.

Tears sprang to Charlotte's eyes. She wanted to go to her but knew her presence would only make things worse. Because they'd grown so apart over the years, she could do nothing to help.

Mary Anne finally exhausted herself, kicked at the contents that had fallen from her purse, and then stumbled up the stairs.

Charlotte moved to the foyer doorway and caught sight of Mary Anne disappearing around the landing. Another tear rolled down her cheek. When she wiped it away, she was surprised to discover that neither drink nor bottle was in her hand. She knew she had completely wasted her own life, and she couldn't let her daughter do the same.

CHAPTER FIFTEEN

Paul looked at his watch. In three hours, he was supposed to meet with the Imagination team over at the Bakers. They would demand answers. He couldn't put it off any longer. When he reached for the phone, his fingers were shaking and he jerked his hand back. Instead of making the first of the dreaded calls, he pulled a soft pack of Marlboros from his desk drawer. It was a bit crumpled, having competed with files, pens, and other items for elbow room the past eight months.

Without a thought, he lit a slightly bent cigarette and leaned back in the chair, slowly exhaling the smoke in a long plume. He sucked in another puff, watching the bluish gray mass rise slowly to the ceiling, dissipating until little of it remained.

Zack had insisted he notify their investors about the TRO before the meeting. He ran a hand through his hair, pushing it back from his forehead, and angrily stubbed out the cigarette. Zack just didn't get it. Investors were told what they wanted to hear, and any bad news was downplayed or recast as good news.

Paul figured he'd come up with a way around the problem when the time came to call. The problem was, he hadn't come up with anything, and that damn phone just sat there, staring at him.

Each investor was different, and he had no idea how any of them would react, with the exception of Bruckmeyer, who had flat out told him he didn't want to be kept informed about developments. Bruckmeyer had put up 5.5 million and said his target return was

20 percent. If it exceeded that, then he would add to his initial investment by a factor of ten. If not, then he would cut his losses and take it off on his taxes. He really didn't care. He just wanted an update in six months' time—earlier if it was going well. Paul had no intention of calling him.

The others were much more tricky. He'd considered saying he'd misspoken when he'd said they'd actually started work. That he wasn't aware they were still waiting for special equipment. That wasn't dishonest. They *were* waiting for equipment. He'd just omit that they didn't have a place to put it once it arrived.

He tried to shake another cigarette out of the pack. When none came out easily, he ripped off the top, spilling cigarettes all over the desk. Two of the six were bent at forty-five-degree angles, which was probably why none had come out. The bent ones were salvageable, as long as he broke them off south of the bend. He gently tore one in two at the midpoint and then lit it and leaned back. Success.

He had five investors to call. There were seven total, but he was one of them and Bruckmeyer was already dealt with. He looked at his watch. Another fifteen minutes had slid by. At this rate, it would be well into tomorrow before he was through.

Enough. Get this over with.

He picked up the phone and punched in the number for Dickens, the financial linchpin.

"Hello, Mr. Dickens, sir?" he said. "It's Paul Ryerson." He hoped his voice didn't betray the nervousness he felt. He crushed out the cigarette, not wanting anything to distract him. "I was calling to give you an update on Imagination."

"Good, good. Let's have it."

"Well, I wanted to let you know that we've already managed to get our first prototype working about two months ahead of schedule."

"Hey, that's terrific."

"It's not a true prototype, more of a preliminary prototype, a test for the basic polymer formulations more than anything. Dimitre, our lead scientist, assures me that the formula is a go based on all computer models and stress-factor projections." He followed up with a barrage of terminology lifted from the Imagination brochure. Technical jargon prevented egocentric investors from asking too many questions because they didn't want to appear dumb.

Sure enough, there was dead silence on the other end.

"Good, good. Glad to hear it. But what do you mean it's a 'preliminary prototype'? Isn't that what a prototype is, a preliminary model?"

Perfect. Exactly the response he'd hoped for. "What I mean is, this is not something display-case worthy, meaning it doesn't look pretty with all the wires going every which way."

"Oh, okay, now I see where you're going with this."

"This is just a rough draft of a rough draft," Paul said, trying to infuse some levity into his tone. He quickly lit another cigarette. "We'll have Jimmy Morgan put together rock-solid packaging for it once we have a full model. You should see it. It's the damnedest thing. It's like a thin slice of Jell-O glowing every color of the rainbow."

"That does sound interesting. Well, keep up the good work. Anything else?"

Paul took a quick drag on the cigarette, letting the smoke seep out of his mouth as he spoke. "No, sir, that's everything."

Chapter Sixteen

Allen tapped his fingers on his highly polished, Philippine mahogany desk. Sandy Fong was late. It was already midafternoon. He stood up and looked out the floor-to-ceiling windows, then down onto the parking lot and grounds of the DisplayTechnik campus. The greenery and trees were islands in a black sea; a jogging path led back into a small wood that was a mixture of firs, palms, oaks, and flowering dogwoods, designed to be a soothing respite for his workers.

Perhaps this was how the Creator felt, he mused.

Hell, he *was* practically a deity in Silicon Valley—even the *Business News* reporter had said so.

A smile played across his lips. If he was a god, he was definitely Old Testament. Something Zack Penny was soon to discover. The wrath of Allen Henley had begun to build more than six weeks ago, after he had uncovered the conspirators and their plans. They were like scurrying ants—unaware of the breadth and depth of his reach, or of the giant bootheel preparing to crush them. That they had the gall to think they could actually fool him made him livid. In this very room, at the start of the campaign against the traitors, he had told Bennet and McSorley, "I want blood, and I don't mean a trickle from a fingertip. I want severed arteries. I want to remind every hotshot out there that to go against me means total destruction!"

Once he'd managed to get Judge Rafkin assigned to the case, he knew the TRO was a done deal. Rafkin owed him, big-time. Allen smiled again. Unlike the *other* God's gifts, his were always repaid, with interest. Rafkin would do his bidding, extending the TRO another month, another year, whatever it took to bury Zack alive. His financial backers would see their money shoveled down a legal black hole. It was all part of a carefully orchestrated campaign, and in war, there was no such thing as a low blow. Everything was fair game. He'd had the goods on Zack and the others for weeks before he'd duped Mary Anne into agreeing to search his office. He'd sent her in because he knew in advance what she'd find and what that discovery would do to their relationship.

Payback was a bitch.

Sandy Fong, a benevolent look on his face, sauntered into Allen's office without knocking. The expression was pure camouflage; he was one of the most treacherous men that Allen had ever met. He held a duffel bag with a Chateau Sportif logo on the side.

Fong worked with the investment crowd of Sandy Hill, a venture-capital epicenter of Silicon Valley. It was said that a third of all venture funds came from the inconspicuous area located a stone's throw from Stanford University in Palo Alto.

"It's about time," Allen said. "I'd just about given up."

"There were unforeseen complications. I'm here now."

"Let's get down to it," Allen said, sweeping aside the knickknacks on his desk, which included various awards for community involvement. Julie organized all the PR and photo ops; he just showed up, made the speech, and took the credit.

Sandy put the duffel bag on the desk, unzipped the cover, and began to empty out the contents, stacking dozens of labeled CDs into separate piles.

"Any problems?" Allen said.

"Nothing serious," Sandy said. "There were copies of everything, so there was twice as much material to go through, and I am still checking the copies against the originals."

"Who made copies? The marshals?"

"No, the Imagination guys duped their hard discs before turning them over to the feds. Apparently Zack's conscience got the better of him, and he made them turn the copies over as well."

"He chickened out, you mean. Did they change anything?"

"I'm still trying to determine that, but so far I haven't found anything."

"Are you sure you got all of it?"

"Hey, whatever was in the van, we got, okay? All the PCs' info, scans of every drawing, document files—a shitload of raw data." Sandy pulled a notebook from his shirt pocket. "I've organized it into financial data, business plan information, patent searches, portfolios, chemical formulations, and engineering schematics. We also got—"

"What was the last thing?"

"Uh … engineering schematics."

"No, no, before that."

Sandy squinted at the page. "Chemical formulations. Mostly about polymers."

Allen's eyes narrowed. "Where did you find that?"

Sandy thumbed through his notebook. "Some were on Zack Penny's PC, but the majority of them came from Koslov's computer."

"What kind of polymer formulations?" Allen asked.

"How the hell should I know? I'm not a damn chemist. Check the files yourself; I have the entire database catalogued. Here's the notebook."

Allen began scanning through the pages, looking at the various subdirectories. There were lots of companies listed, including well-known chemical firms, technical consultants, financial advisors, and investor profiles. There were project-planning schedules, as well as an incredible variety of technical publications and Internet search printouts. There were hundreds of Word documents. And amidst all this information, an acronym was repeated over and over—OLED. Which Allen knew was short for organic light-emitting display. OLED was everywhere.

He knew the concept had promise, but up until now, there were far too many technical hurdles to overcome. Replacing glass with plastic required a significant breakthrough in polymer science. But if it could be done …

"Geez, man, you're practically jumping up and down," Sandy said. "What's so exciting?"

Allen didn't answer. Instead, he thumbed through the notebook again, going back and forth until the pages began breaking free of the binding.

Sandy sat down on the couch, leaning against the arm, his legs sprawled out like he was lounging at a Roman feast.

Out of the corner of his eye, Allen saw him watching with amusement. Fine, let the fool smirk. He had no idea he'd just held a king's ransom in his hands.

Every so often, Allen barked out a demand, and Sandy sprang forth to retrieve the requested CD or tape backup from the pile of computer paraphernalia. Allen shoved disk after disk into the computer, eyes darting back and forth across the screen.

"You know, of all the stinking jobs that you've asked me to do," Sandy said, "this one was the easiest. I just had to walk into—"

"Shut up," Allen said.

"Fine. Listen, you've got your toys to play with. Maybe I should just get out of here?" Sandy stood up and took a step toward the door.

Allen ignored him.

The Chinese-American hesitated a moment and then shook his head and left.

It was several hours before Allen noticed that he was gone. And several hours after that before he was finished.

CHAPTER SEVENTEEN

John and Molly Baker lived in a four-bedroom, split-level home on a hilltop in San Ramon, the next town north of Pleasanton. John was a vice president at Bank of America. When Zack had walked in to open an account, John had offered him a big, rough hand. Zack had thought it odd that a banker would have calluses like that, but soon found out it was from John's other passion: he was a master carpenter. He'd personally built the monstrous, dual-level patio deck that surveyed Freeway 680 and the valley below. Since their house was on a steep hillside, the patio took up most of their backyard.

Zack, Paul, the Bakers, the three engineers, Brett, and Jeremy were gathered on the sundeck for the crucial Saturday afternoon meeting.

"It was God dang amazing," Brett said. "There were two federal marshals waiting *on the walkway* between the plane and the airport. And this after I'd called to let them know when I was coming in and all. I was expecting to meet them on the other side of security. Embarrassed the hell out of me to be standing there while everyone else was getting off, and two plainclothes cops are going through my stuff like I'm a terrorist or a drug dealer."

"This thing is total bullshit!" Dimitre said. Deep perspiration rings had already formed under the arms of his purple T-shirt. "Allen's thugs steal our PCs, drawings, and documentation. They break into our homes. This kind of police action is illegal in

America, no? You call *this* the land of the free? Are we not being innocent before guilty?"

The sun made beads of sweat pop out on Zack's forehead. He adjusted his Red Sox baseball cap, one of the few remaining mementos of home back East. "Brett, you weren't there yesterday when I tried to explain how this TRO doesn't follow the normal court proceedings. Jeremy, maybe you can do a better job of it?"

The lawyer scooted to the edge of the built-in bench that lined the railing. "It's one of those quirky things about the law," he said. "If a judge thinks there's enough evidence to support a claim, then he can immediately impose a restraining order until the two parties settle the issue in court. There's no discovery phase, meaning that there's none of the buildup you normally think of before you go to court. It's not at all like what you see in the movies. All the plaintiff needs to do is convince a judge that there may be a realistic basis for the complaint, and the judge issues a restraining order for a limited time as a matter of protection."

"Protection for who?" Dimitre said. "Bad guys?"

"That's why the TRO has a limited time frame," Jeremy said. "In our case, the TRO was set at thirty days. In the meantime, we have twenty days to respond to it, whereupon the judge will hear arguments whether a preliminary injunction is in order. A preliminary injunction is a court order made in the early stages of a lawsuit or petition that stops the parties from doing whatever act is in dispute, thereby maintaining the status quo until there is a final judgment after trial."

"This here preliminary injunction," Brett said, "sounds like it could stop us dead in our tracks, and then some."

"That's not going to happen," Paul said. "We're going to slam-dunk this bogus TRO within the thirty-day limit. Once we present our case, there'll be no need to go further. This thing will all blow over in a month, max."

"Listen," Zack said to all, "this situation sucks, and I hate it as much as you do. We all knew when we formed Imagination that it was a risk. We expected Allen to be pissed off and to make trouble;

that's why we did our homework to make sure we weren't violating the noncompete contracts we'd signed with DisplayTechnik. So it's okay, no matter what it looks like now. Believe me."

No one said anything. The only sound came from the traffic in the valley below.

"Remember," he went on, "Allen's whole case proceeds from the lie that Imagination's technology is similar to his, and he's lying about our using *his* technology to create it. Dimitre produced the first-ever, functional OLED right before your eyes. When someone builds a foundation of lies like this, it has to fall apart. And when it does, we're going to wipe Allen's puny, Etch-A-Sketch displays right off the face of the Earth."

That brought smiles to the faces of the engineers.

"Not to worry, people," Paul said. "Noncompete contracts are very hard to enforce in California. Every day there's a new spin-off in Silicon Valley made up of engineers from their former companies. Hell, if the courts had to enforce noncompetes, the entire Valley would be up to their asses in litigation. Right, Jeremy?"

Jeremy nodded. "The only time a noncompete contract has any weight is when there's a company buyout and the seller goes down the street and sets up shop to compete against the company he just sold to. Other than that, the noncompete just doesn't hold water."

"If that's the case," Jerry said, "then why did Henley come after us?"

"Because he's a dickhead!" Jimmy stomped his foot on the bench.

That made everyone laugh.

"What about the other charge?" John asked, shooting a concerned glance at Molly. "I mean, that you guys stole DisplayTechnik trade secrets?"

Zack smiled at the couple. They had done a lot for the fledgling company. They'd introduced Zack and Paul to first-round and potential second-round investors, as well as brokering a big line of credit at their bank. They had a personal and professional stake in all this.

"Actually, John," Zack said, "as weak as the noncompete contract violation is, the other charge is even weaker. Like I said, it's built on lies, so Allen actually has to *prove* that we've taken confidential information that his competitors wouldn't have access to. How could we have stolen it when we know we originated the technology ourselves? The misappropriation of trade secrets charge has zero credibility."

"All right," Brett said, "I know I'm just riding the merry-go-round here, but I still don't get it. If Allen knows all this won't work no matter which way he goes, *why* is he doing this?"

"I told you. Because he's a dickhead," Jimmy said.

"No," Paul said. "Because he's a dickhead with an ego."

"Sorry. I ain't buying neither of those," Brett said.

"So he did it because he wants to wear us down financially," Paul said, "or he thinks he can scare us, or—"

Zack put a hand on Paul's shoulder. "Let me do this." Paul looked like he wanted to keep going but nodded and sat down.

"I think Allen's acting this way," Zack said, "because he can't help himself. He doesn't know any other way to operate. He has to attack because it's not in his nature to forgive, or to let people have their freedom, or to give credit where credit is due. If he did, we'd still be working for him, wouldn't we? He wants something he can't have. He wants our dream. A dream that didn't include him, a dream that didn't benefit him. And we didn't even consult him. How dare we?

"I will not let Allen Henley destroy Imagination. Let him exercise his ego for thirty days—so what? After that, they have to give all our stuff back, and we'll be back on track."

Jimmy shook his head. "Look, I'm onboard with everything else you said, but it's just total bull that we can't be working. Thirty days? That's a lifetime in Silicon Valley. You know the Germans and Japanese are onto OLEDs; I read they figure they'll be ready for a prototype in forty-five days."

"Yeah, I just saw the same thing," Jerry said. "But it's a different type of display, still using rigid formats, still using—"

"But in another six months, they could be onto what we're onto!" Jimmy said.

"I very much doubt that," Paul said.

Zack thought about stepping in and putting a stop to the debate, but the smirk on Paul's face intrigued him.

"Jimmy," Paul said, "would you mind giving me a hand with something?"

The abrupt change of subject seemed to confuse the young engineer for a second. Then he shrugged and followed Paul off the patio deck.

The two returned a few minutes later carrying two large Army-issue duffel bags. Barely containing his grin, Jimmy carefully set a duffel bag down, bent over, and pulled out a brand-new laptop, which he handed to Jerry.

Jerry looked baffled and then started to laugh. "Well, at least we can be working, even if it's from scratch! It'll at least keep me busy so I don't pester Sally."

"Not quite, man." Jimmy dug into the other duffel and extracted big three-ring binders filled with drawings and specifications. "Guess what Paul made copies of? Just in case any investors needed more information."

"Oh my God, Paul," Jerry said. "What a stroke of luck."

"I made them to not only hand off to investors but also because I believe in keeping backups of everything. It's part of being a moneyman. You always think in duplicates."

Dimitre shook his head in amazement. "Paul, you would be making good Communist. In Ukraine is old saying, when handling cooperating with KGB, give them everything in house. Just don't tell them about your other house."

Then the Russian turned to Zack, an apologetic look on his face. "My friend, I have confession to make. When I am hearing that marshals are coming, I am not trusting you. I want to believe that doing right thing will win in the end, but I know that good guys are not always winning. I know much more of this than any of you. Me and my Anna left Ukraine because they think we are spies. They think because I go to America for study or for conference that I am meeting spies. They come and search our home, break furniture, destroy walls, accuse us of hiding things. They tap phone. They accuse Anna of being political radical, and she is jailed for six months. All this happens before the wall in Germany is coming down."

Tears brimmed in Dimitre's eyes as he continued. "When wall does come down, my Anna and others are released in big push toward freedom. We realize is our chance to get out, and so we leave immediately. Anna's father and mother are already being in United States because her father is ill. We use this as added excuse to get out. Soviet Union is saying okay for people to leave because everything falling apart, so we get visas and then apply for citizenship. But it is meaning we leave behind our home, our friends, Anna's sister and brother, and my brothers and my papa. Mama already die years before, working long hours at factory, and then freezing while waiting for bread and catch death of cold."

Dimitre heaved a sigh that seemed to shake his whole body. "My papa die during the unrest, when there was no food and riots and looting and shooting. My brothers try to get to him but cannot leave their houses because police are shutting down city. I am not trusting police anymore. When Anna and I come to America, we make many plans, even though we believe we are living in paradise, because we are never being vulnerable again. We are learning our lesson once already, and it is hard lesson."

Zack nodded. After their experiences yesterday, he doubted he would ever fully trust the system again. He could only imagine what it must have been like under the Communists. No wonder Anna had reacted so badly.

"When you tell us marshals are coming, I call my Anna. I give her code words, and she is immediately going to work. She takes files and computer disks and copies all of them, hiding them in secret location."

Zack couldn't believe what he was hearing. How could Dimitre not trust him? After all the months of planning and sleepless nights—and that was only about Imagination. What about the camping trips, the baseball and football games, the dinners and nights out? He told himself that it was the system that Dimitre didn't trust, but it still stung.

"Did you change *any* of your formulations after you made copies?" he asked the Russian.

"I am telling you, I make backups. No time to make changes. I gave them what they ask for, but I am making more backups. The KGB have formulas."

Zack knew it must have been painful for Dimitre to hand over copies of his hard-earned formulas to the police after what he'd been through. The question was, had he handed over everything? For now, he'd have to take him at his word.

"So, the way Anna was behaving yesterday was all an act?" Zack said. "Because if it was, she deserves an Oscar. If she'd already protected the data, why bother?"

Dimitre smiled. "Is no act. My Anna *was* upset. You leave before she is really getting mad. I get kids and dog out of house, and we drive around till it is dark. No one is safe in there."

"Well, what was she mad about then?"

"Because she was telling truth. That *was* her computer. She is writer, and now they are taking everything away. Plus she does not want them to see what she is writing."

"What's she writing?" Jimmy said. "Some sort of subversive column or something?"

"When we first come to America, she look for work as writer. But not many want to talk to her because she is immigrant. She has very good English, good skills, and good imagination, but they don't want to talk to her without writing credits. But my Anna is very creative person, like a fire inside her. So she start to write … how you say it? Bra tearers? No, bra rippers?"

"You mean bodice rippers?" Molly said.

"Yes, that is it."

"What the heck are you talking about?" Jimmy said.

"They're the racy romance novels you see in grocery stores," she said. "The ones where the woman on the cover always has half her dress torn off."

"Well, that's not so bad," Jerry said. "I've heard a lot of famous writers started that way."

"Yes, but my Anna also writes advice column for men's magazines on what women like. She is embarrassed about them. She uses pen name to hide."

"Which ones?" Jimmy asked.

Dimitre wagged a finger at the younger man. "Oh, no. I cannot say. If I do, my Anna will have to shoot you."

"Don't you mean she'd have to shoot *you*?"

"No, no, no. My Anna loves this Russian bear too much. Where you think she is getting ideas for novels?"

Everyone laughed at that.

"I don't know about you guys," Jerry said, "but I'm ready to go back to work. Time to catch up to the other rats in the maze." He picked up his new laptop and switched it on.

Jimmy and Dimitre each pulled a new computer out of the duffel bag.

"I should probably go," Jeremy said. "I don't want to see or hear anything that would compromise my position as an officer of the court."

"Wait a second," Zack said. "Are you saying we shouldn't be doing this?"

All eyes turned to Jeremy.

"As I told you before, the court can't stop any of you from thinking about Imagination or making future plans. It's only stopped the business end of things, preventing you from selling your product. I'd say do what you need to do and whatever keeps you sane. You guys didn't steal anything, and that alone will prove our case. Frankly, I just want to sneak out of here before the rest of the afternoon slips away. Got chores to do at home, you know."

"More likely a three o'clock tee time," Jimmy quipped.

After Jeremy left, Zack said, "We have Paul's copies and notebooks, and we also have Dimitre's backup computer files. I turned in my original and my copies, so I guess we've got at least a week of transcription before we can get rolling again."

"Or a month," Jerry said.

"No way," Paul told them. He pulled some CDs from the bottom of one of the duffels. After checking the labels, he started handing them out like Christmas presents. "We'll lose three days at most. I never got to finish my story earlier. Right before we moved into the new building, I asked you guys to back up everything you had, and I left the copies at my neighbor's house for safekeeping, in case we had a fire or something."

"You mean you didn't turn these in?" Zack said, looking at the CD he'd been given. "Why didn't you tell me that?"

Paul shrugged. "Because I knew you'd flip out if you knew that I'd kept really important stuff from the marshals. Why do you think I've been so calm through all this?"

"Dammit, you should have told me."

"Are you kidding? You wear everything on your sleeve, and if you'd known, you'd have blabbed in a heartbeat. You were the one telling all of us to do exactly as the marshals said."

Zack could feel anger bubbling up. Again, he wasn't being trusted. Paul had deliberately hidden something important from him. Worse, they were breaking the law. Not disclosing it was in direct violation of the court order. Even though it was just copies of what they'd already turned in, it still felt like they were being dishonest.

"I am thinking we will not lose even three days' time," Dimitre said. "I never quite finish *my* story, either. We start talking about Anna. When all of you leave that night at Imagination after making backups, I also make copies of your work as well and of your files in cabinets. Copy machine is probably still sweating."

The deck rang with howls of laughter. Zack looked around at all the happy faces. Either they were oblivious to the legal downsides of their actions, or they didn't give a damn. After the merriment died down, they all stared at him, waiting for some kind of official response. He took a deep breath and said, "Looks like we're back in business."

Paul gave Zack a playful punch in the arm. "All right, chief!" he said.

Jimmy jumped off the bench and started handing out high fives. Jerry Steiner used the white patio side table as a kettledrum, and Dimitre jumped up and started thumping poor Brett on the back, nearly flooring the poor guy.

Right or wrong, they'd decided as a group to move forward. And that felt pretty good. Zack was sure that would never have happened at DisplayTechnik. The design team enthusiastically set up their new office on the Bakers' sundeck, stringing extension cords scavenged from the garden shed and garage. It seemed like forever since he'd seen them so excited. Still, as he was handed a brand-new computer, he couldn't help but feel uneasy.

As he waited for the laptop to load, Zack closed his eyes and leaned his head against the high railing, feeling the heat of the sun-warmed wood seep through his baseball cap. He shut his eyes and tried to clear his head.

Then a strange thing happened. He had a waking dream or vision. One second he was resting on the deck, and the next he was playing tennis with Allen and actually winning the match. He looked across the net and saw Allen's calm face, unfazed by the lopsided score. He readied himself for the legendary Henley temper, but it didn't come. Instead, a wry smile crept across Allen's face as he prepared to serve. Halfway through his motion, Allen stopped. A moment later, an umpire in a long black robe appeared from nowhere and told Zack that he was disqualified from the match. Zack looked across the net and saw Allen laughing his head off.

Zack snapped his eyes open and jerked forward, almost dumping the computer off his lap. He had to grab it to stop it from sliding. Papers were flying in the air. The west wind had whipped up, scattering the loose documents lying on the sundeck. Jimmy Morgan leaped at the papers, snatching them out of the air like an butterfly collector. Dimitre stomped on a few papers and swatted another one with his hand when it landed on the bench next to him. A single sheet flirted precariously close to the edge of the deck railing. Paul moved forward just in time to save it. It was a long way down into the valley.

They had just learned a valuable lesson on how to run a business on the Bakers' patio deck.

Bring lots of bricks.

Chapter Eighteen

Mary Anne banged the air tank against the back of her Taurus, leaving a small ding. Damn it. She was wet and tired from the dive in the bay but not so tired that she couldn't lift a single tank into her car. It was more from distraction than tiredness, although she hadn't slept well last night. She'd drifted off sometime after three but then tossed so much under her fluffy comforter that when she woke up a couple of hours later, she found herself wrapped in a suffocatingly tight cocoon. Staring at the dark ceiling, she started replaying the argument with Zack for the hundredth time. Her heart began to pound, and she knew she'd never be able to get back to sleep. After a light breakfast, she'd decided to go for a dive in the bay. It was an excuse to try out the new fins she'd bought in anticipation of her annual trip to the Cayman Islands, her favorite dive spot even though it was becoming more and more trendy—and crowded.

The bay was hardly a prime dive spot. The water was consistently cold, although not quite cold enough for a dry suit, and the visibility could sometimes be poor. But she'd laid claim to a little spot off Golden Gate Park that had easy access, and there were some interesting underwater rock formations, remnants of the sheer cliffs on which the Golden Gate Bridge sat, that were home to anemones, starfish, and even some octopus, which she loved.

Today, the dive had done little to settle her unease. She leaned over and squeezed the water out of her hair, removed the upper portion of her wet suit, and then leaned against the trunk to start sliding out the bottom.

Once again, the argument from the previous night rolled through her mind like a highlight reel. She was damned no matter which way she turned. If she supported Allen, she betrayed Zack; if she supported Zack, she turned her back on her own family. She was sick of the tightrope act.

And if the history of similar clashes in the Valley meant anything, they would ultimately come to some sort of agreement. No one wanted to fight these things out in court, except of course the lawyers. If it went that route, her relationship with Zack would certainly be over. A year of bitter legal wrangling would finish off even Romeo and Juliet.

━━━━━━━━━━

As Mary Anne stepped through the front door, lugging her wet suit, flippers, and mask, a voice out of nowhere said, "You had a bad night." She looked around and couldn't see her mother anywhere.

"M-mother?"

Mary Anne jerked as Charlotte stepped out from behind the horse-and-rider statue.

"I'm sorry, dear. I didn't mean to frighten you."

"You scared me to death!" Mary Anne stomped past her mother and started up the stairs.

"You didn't let me finish," Charlotte said, following her. "You were tossing all night. I could hear you down the hall. Did you have a bad dream?"

Mary Anne ignored her, continuing to climb to the top of the stairs. She crossed the hall and ducked into the safety of her room. Dropping the wet suit and mask in the bottom of her closet, she grabbed her robe. She thought about turning on the tub for a hot bath but collapsed onto her bed and the burgundy comforter, suddenly too exhausted.

There was a light tapping on her door, and her mother stuck her head in. "May I come in?"

Mary Anne shrugged, and her mother slipped inside. Charlotte went to the window and opened the heavy burgundy drapes. Saturday afternoon sunlight poured in, the light transforming the wide, dark wooden beams into something that belonged in a cathedral. Mary Anne wasn't sure what her mother wanted. She hoped if she remained very still, her mother would just go away. She closed her eyes as she felt the bed sag on her left side.

"You didn't answer my question," her mother said. "Did you have a bad dream?"

Mary Anne felt no compunction to respond. She resented her mother's attempts to pry into her life. Charlotte was emotionally absent for nearly all of her childhood. She'd hear other kids at school talking about their home lives, which sounded warm and soothing, or she'd see comforting mothers on television, and she'd wondered why couldn't her own mother be like that? Instead, she came home to a parent who was either pretending she was a caring soul by volunteering at charity functions, or locked away in her room with her favorite companion of the month—one month, it would be whiskey, the next, schnapps, the next, a sampling of Napa Valley's finest. The house always felt empty and tomb-like, whether her mother was present or not.

She'd often wished her mother had been physically absent as well—at least that would have explained the emotional disconnect. When Mary Anne played with her dolls after school, she imagined they were mother and daughter. The mother would have cookies or tea waiting for daughter when she came home from school. In other fantasies, the mother couldn't be there because she was a dedicated doctor, off to the wilds of Africa to save the impoverished from treatable diseases. The imaginary little girl was sad but knew her mom was important to so many others besides herself. They would send long letters to each other or talk over crackling phone lines, and the little girl would tearfully say how much she missed her and how much she loved her and asked when would she see her again? Would she be there for her band concert? Or her birthday?

When the real tears began to fall, Mary Anne would stop

and put away the dolls and throw herself into her homework. But the next afternoon, the dolls would come out again, the fantasy renewed.

It wasn't until she became a teenager that her mother began making attempts to bond with her. By then, Mary Anne had become suspicious of her motives. She often wondered if her mother made these attempts out of guilt or loneliness. By age fifteen, Mary Anne was old enough to see her parents' marriage was a sham. She dreaded the prospect of leaving home for good, certain they would divorce the moment she did. By her late teens, she had drifted far from her mother, in part as a self-defense mechanism in case they did separate. But her parents stayed together through her college, although, granted, she'd only gone to UC Berkeley across the bay.

That wasn't to say that the three of them didn't have some happy moments. A truly enjoyable dinner, a vacation that they all enjoyed, though often for very different reasons, and an occasional heart-to-heart. These moments were rare but sufficient to make them still feel like a family. Her father talked a good game about loyalty and supporting one another, and whether from those lectures or a lack of other options, she stood by them. They weren't perfect, but they were the only family she had.

She felt the bed sag on her right side and realized she must have drifted off momentarily. Her mother had gotten up and opened the other set of curtains.

"I can remember when I used to be able to sleep in," Charlotte said, sighing. "If your grandmother hadn't dragged me out of bed, I could have slept till two o'clock in the afternoon. But now, I wake up before it's even light out, and I can't do a damn thing about it. *C'est terrible.* What's the point of letting Southern Comfort whisk you far away if you can't take advantage of its frequent miles plan?"

Mary Anne had heard this many times before. She rolled over so that her back was once again to her mother.

"God is cruel. The more you sin, the more time he allots for redemption."

That was another frequent lament. She was never quite sure, though, what sins required her mother to do penance.

"Zack and I had an interesting chat the other night," Charlotte said.

Mary Anne made a face. "What about? Why didn't you tell me?"

"I didn't tell you," Charlotte said, resettling herself on the side of the bed, "because I assumed you two would get together the next day. As you usually do, my dear. Assumptions, assumptions."

"You have something to say to me, don't you?"

"Why do you think that?"

Any drowsiness Mary Anne felt was now gone. She pulled herself to a sitting position against the headboard. "Tell me."

Charlotte reached out and stroked the bangs away from Mary Anne's forehead.

"Stop it!" Mary Anne said, turning her face away.

"You know I hate your father's business. The deception, the late nights, the behind-closed-doors sessions, the lies, and the cover-ups. I resent the fact that he forced me to take a percentage of company stock; it's not publicly traded, so why should my hands be tainted? But most of all, I detest the way he uses the people around him."

Mary Anne turned back, surprised by her mother's apparent honesty.

"Oh, come now," Charlotte said. "Don't tell me you haven't heard the sordid stories about your father. Surely your friend Deidre must have passed them on. That's why I was so against you joining his company in the first place. But that's water over the dam." Her hand fluttered in the air, waving away the thought. "I haven't had any influence in this blasted household for years."

Mary Anne remembered many arguments on the subject. Charlotte had wanted her to find her own way in the world, but neither she nor Allen paid any attention to her. Her father had lofty ambitions for her, wanted her to take over the company, but she quickly realized she wasn't cut out for executive decisions. She opted for a lesser role in the accounting department, content to watch over the finances.

"Well, I might not be able to influence things around here, but I do know that you care deeply for Zack. I know that you love him."

Where was she going with this?

A smile played at the corners of Charlotte's lips. "It's obvious to anyone who sees the two of you together—anyone but your father. If it doesn't have at least five zeros behind it, I don't think he even knows it exists. And I also know Zack loves you. I never knew how much until I saw him Tuesday night. That kind of love is miraculous and shouldn't be discarded without a great deal of thought."

"Why are you telling me this now?"

"Because I saw you come in last night and saw that shell-shocked look on your face like you'd lost a part of yourself. I saw it even though it was buried under a layer of hurt and anger. I recognized that look because I wore it myself once."

Was she still drunk? Still hungover? She'd never shared exploits of her youth before. For the first time, Mary Anne imagined her mother caught up in some doomed love affair.

"Anyway, that's when I realized I'd made a terrible mistake by not telling you. Youth is a terrible thing to let slip away."

Mary Anne assumed she meant love, not youth.

"Before you know it, you find yourself in a marriage that you didn't intend to get into, a mother to a daughter before you were fully ready—a wonderful daughter to be sure, but one whom you weren't quite ready for. And so you spend your years wishing for what was or what could have been rather than living in the moment, and time slips by regardless of whether you are paying attention or not.

"I don't want to see you take the path that I did. The other night, after Zack left, I found myself starting to come to grips with my own choices, my mistakes. I am still wrestling with them. Last night, I knew I had to say something."

Her eyes were suddenly full of tears. "I don't want to see you trapped in a loveless marriage. I want you to be happy, even if it's too late for me."

"Mother, you and Allen aren't loveless ..." Even as she said it, she knew how feeble it sounded. Her mother looked at her and didn't need to say anything.

"There's something else," Charlotte said. "I do care for Zack. I really do. But in the back of my mind, probably poisoned from living with your father for all these years, I always wondered if he had an ulterior motive for going out with you. Have you never wondered why your father's golden boy was dating you?"

"That's an absurd question."

"Is it? Your father always told me that naïveté was your biggest weakness. Perhaps that's why you still live at home at twenty-eight."

"I don't understand. What has this got to do with Zack?" Mary Anne said.

"Because when I saw Zack a few nights ago, I saw a boy who was terribly scared, a frightened little boy, really. I could tell that your father had spooked him—badly. I have seen enough of your father's business casualties to recognize the symptoms."

Charlotte looked at her intently. "Do you have anything you want to or need to tell me? Anything at all?"

Mary Anne looked out the window at wisps of clouds passing by.

"I think it's high time I took my head out of the sand when it comes to your father's company—and my only daughter," Charlotte declared. "And perhaps it's time I helped you and Zack put this behind you. You two belong together. I realize that your father has driven a wedge between the two of you. I'm not sure what Zack has done to deserve your father's wrath, but I know in my heart, that your father is the cause of everything."

"How can you be so certain?"

Mary Anne looked up into her mother's clear blue eyes, void of puffiness or redness. She'd forgotten just how blue they were. Would it make any difference if she told her mother why she had betrayed Zack? Or was it all now just pointless? "You don't live with a man for thirty years without discovering a few closets and the skeletons hidden within them," Charlotte said. "Your father has gone too far—even for him. And maybe, just maybe, it's about time that you and I really talked. We haven't really done that for what seems a lifetime."

Mary Anne bit her lip.

CHAPTER NINETEEN

It was past midnight when Anna poked her head into the home office. The door was hard to push. It was the only room in their house that never had the drapes drawn—not because they loved the perennial California sunshine but because Dimitre insisted that the window stay open. The room stank of smoke, and she was surprised he could work in here as much as he disliked the smell. She smiled at Dimitre's back, hunched over the desk. He was surrounded by papers, weathered textbooks, and overstuffed binders—this in addition to her own piles of papers. The office looked like a back room of a bar, where they cooked the books before the tax auditor arrived.

"Are you planning to stay up all night?" she asked in their native Ukrainian.

Dimitre made a grumbling noise. He was madly scribbling on a piece of paper. She couldn't see his face, but his right hand was whipping back and forth.

"Dimitre? Are you coming to bed?"

He nodded, but didn't look up. Anna rolled her eyes. She tried to close the door, but it stuck partway. Dimitre had agreed to let her smoke in the office as long as she lined the bottom of the door with damp towels. She kicked them aside and shut the door.

Starting this new company with Zack was supposed to make her husband happy, she thought. He'd always hated working for Allen and dreamed of a new start. Now he had his new start, and despite the initial setbacks, she had never seen him more full of enthusiasm and energy. But this afternoon, when he'd come home from his meeting at the Bakers', she had noticed a change, a seriousness that wasn't there before. It had continued through a mostly silent dinner before he retreated to the office. After their many years, she knew when to leave him alone.

Anna went to bed thinking about her university days in Moscow. When she met Dimitre at the Moscow Institute, they were both in the same English class. While Dimitre took the language course to improve his technical writing skills, Anna was there because she planned to become a professional translator. Dimitre said he was drawn to her because of her blond hair and the sprinkle of freckles on her nose—but Anna knew better. Quite simply, Dimitre was failing the course and badly needed a tutor. Eventually, they fell in love, got married, and then fled together to America. But one of her best friends, a cautious girl named Katya, told her why she would never go to the West. It wasn't due to money, she said, or differences of culture or ideology. She simply said the grass wasn't always greener on the other side.

For her part, Anna was still glad they'd made the decision. They'd left the terror of the Cold War behind them, settling briefly in Chicago and then moving westward to Santa Rosa, a community north of San Francisco. Then Allen Henley acquired Dimitre's considerable skills. Not having any debt, they could afford a comfortable three-bedroom bungalow in the Wine Country, as the locals called it. She loved it there. In between the pockets of the rolling hills, there were fields and fields of grapes, the vines twisting around skinny sticks, all sheltered by fishing nets to keep away the ever-hungry birds.

Anna rolled over to the other side of the bed. She reached over to her husband's pillow, feeling for the pocket that his head normally filled. She thought of the many times she, too, had come to bed far later than she should have, caught up in her own creative process. She sighed, turned over, and closed her eyes, listening to Dimitre's soft muttering through the wall until she heard nothing more.

Chapter Twenty

Zack woke up from a dead sleep, screaming and gripping his right calf like someone had just hammered a nail into it. "Jesus Christ!" he cried.

He squeezed the muscle as hard as he could, but that didn't stop the pain. It was dark all around. and he didn't know what to do or where he was. A second or two ago. he'd been on the Bakers' back porch and it had been sunny.

He'd been dreaming. He sat up in his bed and kicked the blanket to the floor. He pulled his toes toward him, straightening out the arch of his foot. He pulled harder and harder, gritting his teeth, until finally, mercifully, he began to feel the ache start to dissipate. The numbers on the bedside clock read 1:11. What an odd time to wake up, he thought. He'd had a friend once who believed in numerology, especially numbers in triplicate like that. He wondered what three ones signified.

An overwhelming sense of dread stole over him. With an effort, he shook it off. When he tested his toes, the cramp tried to return. He straightened them out immediately and worked on the calf some more. It had been stupid to run so far last night, but he'd wanted to exhaust himself so he'd sleep soundly for a change. Now, he was paying for it.

He eased himself back under the covers. He had to get up in about five hours for a 10:00 a.m. meeting with Paul and Jeremy. The upcoming court appearances and investor meetings required considerable preparation, especially given the bizarre events of the past week. Who said that Sunday was a day of rest?

Zack put his hands behind his head, staring at the dark ceiling. Despite yesterday's rah-rah speech, he knew that his young company was in serious trouble. It's not every day that a start-up gets a court complaint on its very first day of business, receives a temporary restraining order on the third day, and gets its operation shut down on the fourth day. And that was just the first week. Allen certainly had more in store for them; it wasn't like the man was going to take a vacation from being a bastard.

He rolled onto his side, hugging the pillow in lieu of a warm body. Just what *could* happen next week? Another goon squad turned loose? He couldn't imagine an already unfriendly judge looking kindly on their attempts to go around his order. But Jeremy seemed okay with it. Maybe they'd just keep working until caught, but how many times could they afford to buy new laptops?

God, maybe *he* should just stop working. The judge could be mad at the others, but at least the CEO wouldn't be involved. Was that good leadership, or merely a cop-out because he was so worried about getting caught? After he returned home from the Bakers', he'd been half tempted to run the laptop down to the garbage bin, but then he remembered it would be deemed public property once it was thrown out. He'd dismissed the whole notion·and berated himself for being so stupid and fearful. *Running scared.*

Thinking about Charlotte naturally led to thoughts of Mary Anne. Despite the insanity, he wished she were with him. He ached for it. He'd seen himself the proud co-owner of Imagination, taking the accolades of the upper echelon of Silicon Valley, accepting awards for innovation, maybe even the cover of *Time* or *Newsweek*. He knew Imagination could be *that* big. And all through it, he'd always pictured Mary Anne by his side. He'd never expected her to quit DisplayTechnik and come to work for Imagination, but when he fantasized about the days ahead, he saw himself coming home tired and exhausted to Mary Anne.

Zack let go of the pillow and rolled onto his back. He had a lot of reasons for forming his own business. The desire for success, the drive to be better, the need to prove to himself that he could do it, and the desire for money and fame were all mixed in there, though he normally didn't focus on those aspects any more than he focused on the need to prove himself to disbelieving friends and family back East. But he was doing this in part because he wanted to stick it to Allen. It would so burn the man to see him on the cover of some trade journal, triumphantly raising an award with one hand, the other arm around Mary Anne, her smile beaming up at him. He had seen Allen screw over more employees than he cared to remember—and not at all the same way he screwed Julie. He trampled through Silicon Valley like a mythical giant, with no regard for the people he crushed or the lives he ruined.

Nine months ago, the giant's victim had been Brett. He had done nothing wrong other than lose the potential deal with HP. A sure thing had gone sour for some inexplicable reason; in sales, things just happened that way sometimes. Allen had flipped out, positive that Brett had somehow betrayed the company for personal gain. He'd wanted to fire Brett, but before he did that, he'd called around to bad-mouth him to competitors and friendly corporations alike, which meant Brett would have a hard time finding a new job anywhere post-DisplayTechnik. Zack had joined with several others to defend Brett to Allen, and because of their combined stance, Allen had backed off. In the end, to try to smooth things over, Brett had returned a bonus he'd received from another sales effort.

That had been the wrong thing to do. Allen had taken Brett's gesture as an admission of guilt and waved it in front of all of Brett's supporters. But the bottom line was that Allen couldn't prove anything against him and couldn't legitimately fire a person who was under contract without paying out a good deal of money. Instead, Allen pulled Brett off the more-lucrative contracts and gave him the smaller ones, effectively removing the bonuses that Brett stood to receive and hurting his future résumé when his contract expired. Brett had later confided that he ended up losing about 40 percent of his annual income.

That episode was really the start for Imagination. Zack had seen how Allen would go out of his way to destroy someone's life and knew there was no way he could continue to work for such a person. He regretted not talking to Mary Anne in detail about it, but Allen's behavior had forced the entire office to take sides. He'd assumed she knew everything that was going on, but maybe she didn't. He'd taken her silence on the matter as simply not wanting to talk about work and the awful feeling that went with it. Or was she waiting for him to talk about it when he was ready? Brett was, after all, his friend, not hers.

Zack shook his head. It didn't matter now, did it? She was a goddamn witness for Allen. After their argument Friday night, there didn't seem to be any pathway to reconciliation.

He used the corner of the sheet to wipe his brow and then got up and got a drink of water from the bathroom. Betrayal had such an evil ring to it. He leaned on the sink and stared into the dark mirror. He knew what to expect from Allen by now, but Mary Anne ... she'd totally blindsided him.

Chapter Twenty-One

Charlotte took a sip of her Diet Coke, the ice cubes clinking loudly. She was in a chair by her daughter's bedside, dressed in a white nightgown with a matching robe. Their conversation had continued, with only occasional breaks, into the wee hours of the morning. Charlotte had enjoyed the time immensely. She'd forgotten what a skillful debater her daughter could be. Allen had never come home. He'd called around six to say, somewhat absentmindedly, that he'd be working very late in San Jose and didn't know when he'd be back. She'd been relieved to hear it, though she knew he was lying as usual. No matter. It left more alone time with her daughter. "Why did you ever believe Zack betrayed your father?" she said.

Mary Anne sat up in bed, a fortification of blankets and pillows surrounding her. An antique lamp, with flowery petals in the glass shade, cast a soft light in the otherwise dark room. There was the occasional banging noise from an outside shutter, the ocean wind trying to burrow inside.

"At first, I didn't believe him," Mary Anne said. "How could I? I loved Zack and knew what he stood for—or so I thought. I couldn't imagine him stealing company secrets. I mean, it sounded so ludicrous at first, but Allen kept supplying me with details."

Charlotte had heard some of these arguments from the safety of her room. "What sort of details?"

"Oh, he knew lots of things. The new company's name, the lease they intended to acquire, the key investors, their bank. He painted such an explicit picture that it was hard not to ... to ..."

"To buy it?"

"I guess so," she said. "Then he showed me an internal e-mail message from Dimitre to Zack. The message was short, but I'll never forget the words. The subject line was 'our discussion,' and the message said, 'Hey, Zack, okay—formula works. Time to use our Imagination and see where it can take us. Hopefully stinking rich and away from SOB.' Dimitre is one of Allen's most important engineers."

Charlotte nodded. She'd heard about Dimitre a number of times. The man sounded brilliant. She had only met him briefly at Christmas parties and such, and she didn't feel comfortable talking with him because of his heavy accent.

"It was such a brief message that I really didn't know what to make of it," Mary Anne went on. "It could have meant anything, and I told Allen that. But then he showed me Zack's reply to Dimitre. It said, 'Use your imagination and stop.' By themselves, the messages were totally innocuous, even incoherent. Allen said that Zack's brevity was intended to discourage Dimitre from communicating plans of a breakout. He didn't want to leave a trail of any sort."

"And *that* convinced you?"

Mary Anne shook her head. "No, of course not. Allen showed me letters from the Santa Clara municipal office. The name Imagination appeared everywhere, and Zack and Paul Ryerson were listed as the principal directors of the new company. I asked him where he got the incriminating documents. They seemed like they would be confidential."

"What did he say?"

"He said something about it being public information and then laughed. You know, in that flippant way of his."

Charlotte nodded. She knew it all too well.

"He told me that I could never confront Zack with any of it. He said that would compromise the situation and potentially harm the company. He still had to do some further checking. He said it was very important that I didn't ask Zack about any of this. He asked me to promise."

"Good heavens. I take it you refused to promise him any such thing."

"Well, I told him that I thought that the best way to clear this up was just to ask Zack directly. Then Zack would tell me that the entire episode was a big misunderstanding, and we could all just forget the whole thing."

"That seems the sensible thing to do."

Mary Anne bowed her head, the lamplight catching the hair that was stuck to the pillow behind her.

"My Lord, you never asked him, did you?" Charlotte said.

Mary Anne refused to look at her.

"Incredible. *Incroyable.*"

"I know it sounds ridiculous now, but at the time, it sort of made sense in a warped way. I didn't want to be caught in the middle, and I realized that if the whole thing was a farce, then nothing would happen. Zack would still be working at DisplayTechnik; everything would stay the same. But if it were true, then something would have to break. Allen told me that whatever was going to happen would happen soon, so why chance an ugly confrontation? What was there to gain, really?"

"You were still seeing Zack at the time?" Charlotte rubbed her eyes, fighting a growing tiredness. "That must've been extremely awkward."

"Yes, but not as much as you think. You see, the whole time, I really didn't believe that Zack was going to do what Allen said he was going to do. I guess I didn't want to. I just pretended that things were normal."

Charlotte looked at her daughter. "And your father didn't mind that you were still staying with Zack?"

"Oh, he was extremely unhappy. When I told him I wasn't going to stop seeing Zack, he pressed me to stop, and the harder he pressed, the more I resisted. In the end, I guess he just gave up."

"Good old Allen. A consummate actor to the end. He really missed his calling."

"Huh?"

"Come on, Mary Anne, wake up. If your father thought for even a moment that Zack was going to steal his secrets and stab him in the back, do you honestly believe that he would want you, his only daughter, to be anywhere near a traitor?"

Mary Anne shrugged defensively. "I don't know what Allen was thinking."

"You don't know, or didn't want to know?"

Mary Anne didn't answer. Charlotte was tempted to press her on the point of Allen using his own daughter as a weapon, but decided not to. "So, what were *you* thinking?"

Mary Anne pulled her knees up, crossed her arms, and laid them across her knees, pillowing her head. She looked past Charlotte, at the shelf behind her. Charlotte had seen Mary Anne looking over there before and couldn't figure out what held her attention.

"So, what were you thinking?" Charlotte repeated.

"I guess I wanted to try and get into Zack's head. What did he think about DisplayTechnik? Where did he see his future? Where did he see us in six months or a year? We talked about how good Allen has been to him, how quickly he'd advanced in the company, being the youngest technical director and all. I wanted to make sure that he wasn't lying, and then if I found out that he was, I wanted to try and bring him back to his senses."

"Why was that your responsibility? Who were you to decide for Zack what was best for him? When you love someone, you support them in whatever *they* choose to do, not what you want or think is best for them."

Charlotte stopped. Her wisdom about love and support was mainly based on what one shouldn't do. She didn't want to give Mary Anne an opportunity to point out that fact. "So you were spying on Zack for your father?"

"I was not spying!"

"Did what you found out get back to your father?"

Mary Anne stared at the foot of her bed. "Maybe we should stop this conversation," she said.

"Maybe if you and I had a real conversation before ..." Charlotte let her voice trail off. Then she sighed. "What convinced you in the end that he was a traitor?"

"Stuff in Zack's office," she said.

"And Zack gave you ... permission to go through his office?"

"Well, not exactly but ... I was only in there a few minutes," Mary Anne said. "He was sleeping, and I was nervous about being in there. But I did have his key chain. It was lying next to the bed, and I knew that it had the small key for the filing cabinet."

Charlotte frowned. Allen had turned their daughter into a sneak thief, and she hadn't done anything to stop it. How far had they all fallen? "Go on," she said.

"I ... I found all sorts of Imagination files. There were files on a new company's location and business plans for displays. I didn't have much time to look through them; I was too scared he'd wake up. I didn't need to, though. Ugh, it makes me sick to my stomach to talk about this. But it did prove Allen was right. Zack was set on betraying us. I wouldn't have believed it otherwise."

Charlotte stared at her daughter. "I never really believed it," she said, voicing her thoughts without really meaning to do so.

"Believed what?"

"How much you're like your father."

"I am not. Well, sure, we share some characteristics, but every—"

"I mean how quickly you and Allen can justify whatever action you take. The excuse always justifies the means or the end, no matter how despicable."

"Despicable? How can you say that?"

"What would you call breaking and entering—or spying?"

"Hardly. I was merely looking at what Zack should have shown me all along if he'd been honest with me. And even if it was spying, sometimes it's needed to protect your interests. Isn't that what countries do in the name of national security?"

"See what I mean?"

Mary Anne looked taken aback, obviously realizing the truth in what Charlotte had just said. Charlotte hoped she could come to terms with it before it was too late.

"Is that all your father asked you to do?"

Mary Anne shook her head, turning her gaze back to the shelf over Charlotte's shoulder.

"What else?"

"A couple weeks ago, Allen asked if he did bring formal charges against Zack, would I testify that I saw those Imagination files?"

Charlotte wished to God she wasn't hearing what she was hearing. She stood up, unable to sit still a moment longer. "Perhaps I was wrong," she said. "Perhaps I was wrong about this whole thing, and especially about wishing you two back together again." Charlotte cinched her robe tight around her waist. "I'm not sure Zack deserves that."

Mary Anne's face turned white as a sheet.

Charlotte spun on her heel and left.

CHAPTER TWENTY-TWO

Paul watched Jeremy pour fresh coffee from Java Connection paper cups into three ceramic mugs. One of the advantages of a strip mall office, so Jeremy claimed, was that he had a coffee shop on one side and the Thai Palace on the other. Breakfast, lunch, and dinner were a couple of steps from his door.

"What *exactly* do the investors know?" Zack asked as he picked up a sticky Java Connection pastry.

"As much as they need to," Paul said. He put down his own coffee cup, reached into his breast pocket, extracted a Marlboro, and rolled the filter between his thumb and index finger.

Zack raised an eyebrow at him. "When did you start smoking again?"

"I haven't," Paul said.

"What do you call that?"

"It brings me back to my happy place."

As Jeremy stood up, his polo shirt came untucked from his jeans. "Well, as long as you don't light it up. I don't want the stink in my office."

"Right, right," Paul said, the sarcasm fairly dripping, "wouldn't want to lose the springtime-fresh smell of the barbeque pork, would we?"

"Okay, okay." Zack waved his hand, sending a spray of crumbs onto his cream-colored T-shirt. "We've all been under a little stress this week—God knows we could all use some extra shut-eye—but let's try to stay constructive. Again, Paul, what do the investors know?"

Paul took a sip of coffee and then said, "I told them we've run into some roadblocks but that we were handling them. Has the crew been able to put together a new prototype? It's really important to have a full-size model for the second-round investors, not that little blob with wires hanging every which way."

"Dimitre's running simulations—wait, what? How can you be thinking about second-round investors when we have all this hanging over our heads?"

"Because we have to think beyond the thirty days, Zack. We all know the TRO will blow over, so we need to continue to be thinking beyond Allen's grandstanding."

Paul watched Zack over the rim of his mug, which concealed his smile. He was only too happy to turn the focus on Allen.

"I guess you're right," Zack said. "We do need to be thinking past this."

"So," Jeremy said, "the investors know about the TRO?"

Damn it. He'd been so focused on Zack that he hadn't counted on Jeremy nailing him on specifics. Damn lawyers.

"Not exactly," he said. "I told them we'd encountered some bumps in the road, but that was to be expected with a product this innovative. I kept the conversations focused on our successes. Like the early prototype."

"You *didn't* tell them about the TRO?" Zack said. "Jesus, Paul! You said you were handling it."

"I did handle it. And the more I thought about telling them about the TRO, the more I knew it was a mistake. You've got to trust me on this. The investors are really my call."

Zack stood up.

Shit, Paul thought. Here comes the canned lecture on the principle of the thing and all the rest.

"Aside from the fact that you told me you would tell them and didn't," Zack began, "what I'd like to know is who *did* tell Dickens about the TRO?"

"What?" Paul sat up so quickly that he slopped coffee down his front. He pulled the crotch of his slacks away from his skin and reached for a napkin. "Shit! Dickens? What?"

"Dickens called me early this morning. I assumed he was calling because he'd already talked to you."

Paul's face began to flush, remembering his lie to Dickens that things were fine. He'd probably learned about the TRO from a contact in the Valley, and now he didn't trust Paul anymore, so he'd called Zack to confirm what he'd heard. And Zack had done just that. Goddamn it, the whole thing was a setup because Zack already knew he hadn't filled in Dickens on their legal problems.

Paul suddenly felt lightheaded as he realized what this meant: Dickens, their main financer, was going to pull up stakes. He really had intended to tell Dickens about the injunction, eventually, when the timing was right.

"So what did he say?" Paul asked, dreading the answer.

"He said he was coming in tomorrow instead of later in the week. Wanted to make sure we could pick him up at the airport."

Paul didn't think his stomach could sink any lower, but it did. Oh, shit, it was all over. He stood up and ran a trembling hand through his hair. "Wonderful. Just wonderful. Did he say why he was coming?"

"No ... that's why I wanted to know what the investors knew."

"Huh?"

"I said, that's why I wanted to know what exactly the investors know. I get a call from Dickens, and he said he was coming in Monday morning to talk to us. It caught me by surprise, so I just said, okay, we'll meet you at the airport. He said fine, that he was looking forward to seeing me again. I was surprised he called me. He normally deals with you."

Paul sank back into his chair. Maybe there was a small chance that Dickens didn't know about the TRO after all, but he doubted it. "Why did he call you rather than me?"

"He said he did try to call you but got your voice mail, and since he was coming in on such short notice, he thought he'd try me rather than trust his message to a machine."

"Well, I guess we're in for it now," Paul said.

"No, I don't think so, not yet anyway. When Dickens gets here, you can explain your lack of communication any way you want, but we're going to tell him the truth. What else didn't you tell him and the others? The seizure of equipment in Santa Clara? The closure of the plant? The original summons?"

Paul shook his head. He'd already been caught in one lie—no sense digging in even deeper.

Zack put the coffee cup on the corner of Jeremy's desk. "Our first-round investors are from New York City and Houston, not Pluto. There is such a thing as a telephone. When you told me you would inform the investors of the current events, I believed you."

"I did. I called them and gave them the big picture but just haven't filled them in on all the details."

"When Dickens shows up tomorrow and asks to see our new facility in Santa Clara, how are you going to explain the padlock and chains around the front door? Some new kind of management technique to keep the employees from leaving work too early?"

"Now, that's not a bad idea." Paul smiled but dropped it quickly when he saw the look on Zack's face. "Look, I know these guys. They don't want all the details. I trust you on the engineering side; you need to trust me on the financial side. This is not the kind of news that should be discussed on the phone."

"Well, I guess now you'll have the chance to tell one of them in person, won't you? You would have made a great doctor. Wait until the patient is dead before telling the family that, oops, sorry, things may be worse than originally thought. What were you thinking?"

Paul figured Zack would never approve of what he had in mind but decided to go with it anyway. "It occurred to me that every building in the Santa Clara industrial park looks the same."

Jeremy held up his hands. "Listen, maybe it's better that I don't hear what you're about to say," he told them. "Know what I mean?

I'll leave you for a bit. Just give me a holler when we can talk about the TRO and our legal tactics."

As Jeremy walked toward the door, Zack extended his arm to block his exit. "No, no, it's okay, Jeremy. Stay. Nothing's going on here that you shouldn't be privy to. Right, Paul?"

"Look," Paul said, "I say we find out why Dickens is here. If he knows, then okay, we go with that. If not, then there's really no harm delaying the news to him and the other investors for thirty days when this TRO thing blows over. This is just some excess testosterone that Allen is oozing, so why cause the investors any undue stress and concern? I can just take them around to a different unit. In fact, there's a unit across the parking lot that's just about our size. We just tell them that there has been some delay with the equipment and utilities. So rather than move the boys in right away, we decided to wait a month before moving in. No big deal. We show them the completion schedules—you know, the GANTT charts. Hell, the first critical milestone date isn't for six months, and we already have Dimitre's prototype. You should have seen those second-rounders. They were nuts over the thing. Just think how our principals are going to react when they see it."

Zack walked over to Jeremy's desk and sat down on his chair. "We are not going to start off Imagination, barely into its first week of existence, by lying to our principal investors."

"Who's lying? I'm just saying we delay telling them the news for thirty days. And you're a fine one to talk about lying when you lied to your own girlfriend for months."

"Our first-round investors have invested millions of dollars in this project. They put their trust in us. It's important that they hear the truth. At all times."

"Wrong. You're not thinking like an investor. Our principals— with the exception of yours truly—weren't stretching their finances to invest millions of dollars. It'd be like you investing a hundred bucks. Okay, maybe a thousand. Sure, you don't want to lose it, but if you did, you wouldn't sweat over it. Besides, we're protecting them by not telling them the whole story. It's our duty to take care of them. Remember, pal, I put up money too. You know, if anyone should be upset, it should be me."

"You?"

"Yes. I put up a big chunk of my own personal money—nearly half of it, in fact. Everyone else may have invested more money, but to them, it's just peanuts. To be honest, I feel a little used."

"What are you talking about?"

"You should have given me better warning what Henley was capable of doing, that there was even the slightest chance he would pursue enforcing the noncompete clauses. I trusted you. I believed in your idea. So spare me your Boy Scout's code of honor. What's most important is that the moneymen understand we have things under control."

"You knew exactly what kind of a person Allen was, and we did talk about it," Zack corrected him. "But if we lose credibility with our primary investors, the show's over."

Paul stared at his younger partner. Zack was president and CEO of Imagination. Ultimately, what they did or didn't do was Zack's decision, and that was killing Paul. After putting up 3.4 million dollars of his own capital, he should have insisted on having the deciding vote. In fact, he had even less voting power than the New York investors, and that fact worried him considerably. Even though he was the anointed babysitter, there was no guarantee the moneymen wouldn't pull the financial rug from under them. Their investment was indexed on the corporation meeting certain benchmarks. Granted, there was a "no confidence" clause, but the only thing that really mattered was the benchmarks.

"Look," Zack said, "it's obvious we don't agree on this. The important thing is that Dickens is showing up tomorrow. We can't take him to the plant, and he's probably going to ask questions. So I say we be up-front with him, tell him about the TRO, let him know what's happening. Who knows? He may be able to offer some advice. But we'll also be sure to show him the prototype and let him know we're a little ahead of schedule. Agreed?"

Paul nodded his assent. Not that he had much choice. Zack and Jeremy started going over plans to counter the TRO, but Paul wasn't listening. All he heard was the sound of chains locking away his future forever.

CHAPTER TWENTY-THREE

Dean loved Sunday mornings because he had the house to himself. His wife, Marjorie, usually took off for golf, a sport that Dean tolerated but didn't excel at, so he played only casually. Two of his three daughters were away at college; the third was always out with friends. He often took the paper out onto the deck to enjoy the view of the San Mateo Bridge, or would sink into his pillowy recliner and watch the ESPN buildup to a morning of football. After that, he'd putter around the house.

This morning, he intended to open the Sun Tzu book he'd picked up. He'd decided to read it in the hope that it might help him understand—and perhaps even manipulate—Allen's psychology.

It was possible that Marjorie would return in the late afternoon and want to take in a show, but she was just as likely to be gone all day. There were times when she'd call and say she wouldn't be home for dinner and then show up unexpectedly. She hoped to catch him in an affair, but she never would. Dean wasn't interested in affairs, although he was reasonably certain that her suspicion arose from her own guilt over what she spent her Sunday afternoons doing. She claimed she was out shopping, but she rarely came home with anything, at least nothing that ever showed up on credit card bills. And she always used credit cards.

Dean didn't know for certain if Marjorie was unfaithful. He supposed the truly unfortunate thing was that he wasn't terribly interested in finding out. The only time he had felt an emotional pull was when he briefly suspected that Allen had been dallying with Marjorie, but it turned out that Julie Reynolds was the one keeping him busy on Sundays. Marjorie and Dean still made love occasionally—when they did, he noticed she was always home early the next Sunday—but the passion had left the marriage long ago. He guessed they were either drifting toward divorce, or that they would eventually reconcile. It didn't really matter to him, either way.

He had just gotten comfortable with his Sunday paper when the doorbell rang. He pushed up from his chair and walked to the foyer. Allen stood on his doorstep with a duffel bag at his feet and an armload of files. Dean knew what the exuberant look on his face meant: there was no turning him away. He stepped aside and let Henley enter.

Allen swept aside the Caribbean vacation brochures from the glass table in the breakfast patio to make room for the duffel bag and then plopped down in a wicker chair. A vase filled with dried flowers wobbled but maintained its upright position.

"Where's Marjorie?" Henley said.

"Sunday is golf day," Dean said. "She's gone with her girlfriends to Pebble Beach."

"Pebble Beach? That's impressive. Driving all the way down to Carmel must mean she has a real devotion to the game. Then again, Pebble Beach is a great place to meet someone. Celebrities, if you're into that sort of thing."

It appeared Allen had his own suspicions about Marjorie's plans, but then again, it would be like him to suspect nuns. "Coffee?" Dean offered.

"Please."

Dean poured coffee from a pot that had shut off an hour ago. "As I recall," he said as he put the mugs in the microwave—he knew Allen hated reheated coffee—"you don't play golf."

"You're right, I don't. Hate the game. Tennis is much more athletic and demanding. But I do entertain a lot of business guests from Japan, and they surely do love their golf. I just arrange for them to play with the local pro and then meet up with them for dinner. Pebble Beach has a nice clubhouse and restaurant there. I highly recommend the prime rib."

Dean brought the mugs to the table. He noticed the duffel bag's prominent position on the table. It was obvious that Allen wanted him to ask what it contained, so he could reveal the big secret bubbling inside him. That was Allen's way. Because Dean had power and knowledge that he didn't, it made him feel inferior and dependent, which was unacceptable. Allen needed to be the one in control at all times. It would have been funny if it hadn't been so sad.

"Well, you certainly seem to be in a good mood this morning." Dean blew on his coffee. It was still too hot, but he took a defiant sip.

"Yes, I am quite happy, thank you. It's a gorgeous day out, isn't it?" Allen's glance darted to the duffel bag.

Dean smiled politely but ignored the invitation. "Yes, quite. Almost unseasonably warm," he said.

Allen continued to stare pointedly at the duffel bag, but Dean still didn't take the bait.

Apparently unable to contain his rising irritation, Allen got up and stalked around the kitchen, his hands clasped behind his back. "You should get rid of this island-style oven," he said.

"Marjorie loves it," Dean said. "Why do you care?"

"I used to have one. I was always banging into the damn thing. Who would put an oven right in the middle of a fucking room? I ended up gutting my whole kitchen. You should too. Let me call someone who can do it for you at a good price."

"Yeah, Marjorie would love that. Come home from golf and find her kitchen ripped apart. So what brings you here anyway? It is Sunday, after all."

"Can't old friends just see each other?"

Dean had wearied of the dance. Time to end it. "All right, what's in the goddamned bag?" he said. "Gold bars? Severed heads?"

"Much better than gold," Allen said, beaming. "It's polymers."

"Polymers? You're joking. You brought over a duffel full of plastic? I think they have recycling centers for that."

"Not funny. Polymers are a special type of plastic, comprised of conjugate pairs of molecules, such as hydrogen and carbon. They may well be the future of display technology."

Dean felt a yawn coming on and didn't manage to suppress it.

Allen glowered at him and then said, "At least thirty Japanese companies are working on new concept designs. And that doesn't include what's going on in Korea. On the other hand, there are only a handful of US companies and an equally small number of European companies making that kind of R and D investment."

Dean nodded, trying to look interested.

"The fundamental principles of flat-panel display technology were developed in the United States and Europe, but the Japanese poured a tremendous amount of money into scaling up the manufacturing process. They were able to produce displays more quickly and cheaply than practically anyone else. Now that manufacturing is being done offshore in places like Malaysia, Singapore, and the Philippines, it's even harder for US companies to compete—the companies that had pioneered the technology to begin with."

Dean picked up his coffee and settled back, waiting for the Sun Tzu to kick in.

"So," Allen said, "global competition doesn't always come down to who's the smartest or who has the cleverest technology. It comes down to who has the financial resources to eke out small successes, small improvements. The Asians are very good at that, improving on what's been done. Although Americans can do that, we're happiest if we can innovate and leap ahead of the competitors. That's what makes Silicon Valley so great. We're the real dreamers, we still have that pioneer spirit, and now we're the new pioneers of the West."

Dean considered pointing out that Allen was British-born but opted against it.

"This duffel bag holds the secrets of pure innovation. Dean, the displays of the future will not be made out of glass but out of thin plastics—polymers. Polymers illuminate when an electrical charge is applied to them. With the right formulation, red, green, and blue illumination can be created. And voila! What you have is an inexpensive, fully functional color television screen that can be rolled out like pizza dough. Imagine having a television screen that covers your entire den wall. Even better, why not all the walls? Maybe the floor and the ceiling too. If you have the right formulation, you can have a television screen that is lighter, brighter, cheaper, and a hundred times bigger. Think of the possibilities in the commercial sector, aerospace, factory automation, communication, and entertainment.

"Find the right formulation. Figure out how to keep the production yields high. Figure out how to maintain enough brightness and contrast. And most important, figure out how to extend the lifetime of the product to a reasonable level, like a CRT tube. Lifetime is the key, because no one wants to replace a TV every three months. Solve the lifetime, and then, my friend, the entire world will come courting—on their knees."

Dean still didn't know what was in the mystery duffel, and Allen was lurching around like he was intoxicated.

"I want you to get hold of the patent group," Allen said. "Who's the senior partner there? Tweedle?"

"Twindle. Joseph Twindle."

"Right, right. Twindle. Set up a meeting with Twindle for tonight. In the city. Chinatown. That restaurant where they serve the best Peking duck. Oh Christ, I've forgotten its name." Allen snapped his fingers, trying to remember.

Dean's eldest daughter popped into the kitchen but did a quick turnaround when she saw the look on Allen's face. Allen openly leered at her pert bottom, practically smacking his lips. Dean felt his face flush with anger, but he let it go.

"The Golden Palace," Dean said. "It's called the Golden Palace."

"Yes, yes, that's the ticket. Great place. They have a banquet room in the back. Good place to talk."

"It's Sunday, for cryin' out loud, Allen."

"I don't care if it's Gay Pride Day. Considering the amount of money I stake your firm every year, I expect you to do as I ask."

There was no point in debating the issue. The hours were billable. "I'll try to set it up for tonight, but I can't guarantee Twindle's schedule. What's the agenda?"

"I want a full-court patent search. Start here in the United States, then Japan, Europe. Then let's push forward with a patent submittal of our own. Establish prior art. You know the drill. Also call Sandy and tell him to get his fat ass over to the restaurant. Make the dinner at seven; schedule Sandy for ten."

"And if Sandy asks what this is about, what do I tell him?"

"Tell him I want to use his special talents to do a little historical art for me. He'll know what I mean."

And so did Dean. A patent wouldn't be issued if the invention in question had already been described by someone else in a published document—or was available in the public domain. The term used was *prior art*. It was difficult to date an electronic Word file with reasonable confidence, but hard-copy printouts were another matter. There were people in the Valley who stockpiled white bond paper, arranged chronologically in neat little stacks: a stack for 1973 and another stack for 1982, and so on. For the right price, you could get paper of any vintage. Ink formulations and the delivery method had evolved over the years as well, especially with the advent of the laser and ink-jet printers. The days of the daisy wheel were long gone, but in their garages, these same enterprising folks had row after row of obsolete printers and typewriters.

Contrary to popular belief, a patent didn't really protect the inventor. Many companies didn't submit patents for fear of showing their hand to competitors. In large corporations, it was a common practice for research engineers to take out patents on their designs. Although owned by the corporation, the inventors regarded patents as professional perks. Companies also used patents to raise their intellectual property value. Although patents were still filed to protect new designs from forgery, large corporations routinely violated them, or skirted them so closely that it took a team of lawyers to arbitrate the issue.

In the grander scheme of things, patent theft came down to measurable risks and gains. The big guy stomps on the little guy until he gives up. Or the little guy tries to trip the big guy and hopes his money doesn't run out. Even if a company were legally right, it could still lose if the other side was willing to sling enough mud until hell froze over.

This was the type of business that was putting Dean's daughters through the best colleges in the country. It wasn't a question of morality, or who was right or wrong. If the law allowed corporations to hire law firms to test the boundaries of intellectual property, then he was a willing accomplice, even for a noteworthy prick like Allen Henley.

When Sandy Fong arrived at the Golden Palace, he found Allen probing his teeth with a toothpick, while a pair of busboys cleared the large lazy Susan from the banquet room table. One had long frizzy hair, which he kept sweeping off his face with a repetitive motion, like a cow's tail shooing away flies. The other busboy had short hair, straight as nails. Sandy noted the bits of food falling onto the floor as they shifted the plates. Food that merged with similar debris already ground into the carpet. The restaurant wasn't noted for its ambiance; instead, it was the quality of the food that drew a predominantly Asian clientele.

"Sandy, my friend, glad you could make it," Allen said.

"No problem."

Sandy surveyed the dishes being carried away. He recognized moo shu pork, General Tso's chicken, and Peking duck. It was past ten o'clock at night, but the sight of the food made him start to salivate. He could smell the black bean sauce and barbecued pork permeating the restaurant. Allen's tablecloth had prominent stains on three sides. It seemed he'd just missed Allen's dinner guests.

"Have a seat," Allen said, pointing at the chair opposite.

"I'm surprised you called me so soon," Sandy said. "After I dropped off the stuff on Saturday, I figured you would have needed some time to analyze it."

"I'm a quick student," Allen said.

"Does this meeting have anything to do with those polymer formulations?"

"Why do you say that?"

"Yesterday, you were pretty gung ho about those formulations from Koslov's PC."

The sharp scent of plum sauce flooded Sandy's nose. He tried to think of something other than the rumbling in his stomach.

"I need you to do a little historical art for me," Allen said, lowering his voice. "I want to plant some information on polymer formulations into the public domain." Allen laced his fingers together and leaned forward. "Specifically, I want a paper that explores the application for display technology."

"You mean that OLED stuff that kept turning up in the files that I gave you?" Sandy said. "My notebook had lots of references to it."

"No, no, no. I don't want you to mention OLED at all. I want this paper to be put in the public domain before OLED was OLED. Do you understand?"

"Of course. You want it to predate the first appearance of that terminology. What kind of publication or conference are you interested in?"

Allen rubbed his chin for a moment. "Something about material science," he said.

Then—without warning—Allen turned to the busboys and yelled in nearly perfect Mandarin. The tone was harsh, and the owner of the restaurant scrambled out of the kitchen to see what was the matter. Without a word, he slapped the short-haired busboy across the forehead. The boy with the long hair hurried to a side bar and brought out a new white tablecloth that had plenty of starch.

"I'm very sorry, Mr. Henry," the owner said. "Very sorry."

Allen said something dismissive, his words causing the proprietor to bow profusely. With every bow, Allen flung another obscenity at the cowering busboys.

Ever since their days in college, Allen had amazed Sandy. His command of the complex dialects of Chinese—not to mention Japanese, German, and a smattering of French—was impressive. But the way he assumed command in other languages and how people reacted to his commands was really remarkable. Native speakers reacted as though he were a member of their ruling elite.

"How about the American Association of Chemical Engineers?" Sandy offered. "They are a big society, with conferences every year. I know some of the people."

"That sounds possible, but I don't want to submit a technical paper. There's always some nerd who attends every conference lecture and can recite, from memory, who gave what paper when and about what."

"We could include the paper as a late submission. Too late for publication in the conference journal."

"It's still too risky," Allen said. "Even a late submission would be presented at the conference. No, let's use a poster session. Even better, let's make it a late submission to a poster session. You would have to be a real hard-on to remember every poster session."

A fresh pot of tea with a single cup arrived for Sandy and a tumbler of scotch with ice for Allen, as well as complimentary bowls of coconut ice cream and fortune cookies.

"So, what's this OLED thing about anyway?" Sandy asked.

"You don't need to know. Just start to gather all the conference abstracts and proceedings from the Society for the last twenty years. I'll choose the year to insert our precious gem; you worry about how to get our poster session late submission logged into the Society's archives."

"All the proceedings for the last twenty years? That's a lot of material. Who are you going to get to author this polymer formulation paper?"

"Someone who'll never remember this paper—even if he were still alive."

Sandy laughed. Allen was referring to a research scientist who'd worked for DisplayTechnik until his death a decade ago. His name was Knowles, but Allen referred to him as "Special K." They'd used Mr. Knowles posthumously before. A quiet man who'd kept to himself, he'd had no family, no real friends outside of work, and the misfortune of dying from cancer at a relatively young age. He was the perfect choice to author a buried technical paper on polymer formulations, whose origin, Sandy guessed, came from inside that duffel bag.

Sandy lifted the teapot and poured the jasmine tea into his cup. Despite his careful attention, the tea dripped down the side of the blue pot, creating a big damp spot on the fresh linen cloth. Sandy pushed the dish with fortune cookies over the stain.

Allen downed his scotch and reached for a fortune cookie, breaking it open to extract the pink paper from the shell.

"Tell me something I don't fucking know," he said with a laugh.

Sandy took the pink slip from Allen, fingers fumbling with the sliver of paper. He squinted to read it.

Your destiny is to be famous.

CHAPTER TWENTY-FOUR

Driving to work, Mary Anne was caught in the usual stop-and-go of Monday traffic. She turned up the radio. As she listened to NPR's *Morning Edition*, her mind wandered back to the argument she'd had with her mother over breakfast. It was so recent, she could replay it in painfully exact detail. As had happened in their earlier conversation, nothing had been resolved, the same issues rehashed.

Charlotte had still been in her dressing gown, white tissues sticking out of her oversize, kimono-style cuffs. She'd tried to camouflage the dark circles under her eyes with hastily applied makeup—Mary Anne couldn't even recall the last time she'd seen her mother without makeup, regardless of the time, day or night. But makeup couldn't hide the redness of her eyes. She looked like she hadn't slept well, and Mary Anne wondered if she'd been up plotting her next attack. "I refuse to believe Zack would do what he's been accused of," she'd said.

"Of course he could do it." Mary Anne had crossed her arms across the brass buttons of her Chanel jacket. "That's the whole basis for the lawsuit. Zack took company files and then solicited the engineers and that marketing guy. And that's why they were all fired."

"And you believe that?"

"Of course. Wouldn't *you* fire them? He tried to walk away with vital employees."

"And you honestly believe that—knowing Zack the way you do?"

Mary Anne had nodded.

"Amazing." Charlotte had pulled a tissue out of her cuff and blown her nose. After a moment, she said, "Why didn't you ask Zack outright?"

"I told you. Allen told me not to confront Zack because he wanted to protect me and didn't want me to get in the middle of it. He also said he didn't want the legal case compromised."

Charlotte had stared at her for a long moment. Too long. Mary Anne realized her mother was trying to be dramatic. She had felt like reaching across the small table and slapping it out of her. Instead, she looked down at the breakfast table. The orange juice glasses, the coffee cups, the white melon with strawberries, the stack of toast, all remained untouched—only the napkins had been unfolded.

Finally Charlotte had said, "Are you trying to tell your mother that you wouldn't ask your boyfriend such an obvious question because your arrogant father told you not to? Do you really expect me to believe that drivel?"

Mary Anne hadn't answered right away, but not for the sake of drama. In the bright light of a Monday morning—long after the fact and long after the passionate late-night argument with her father, when it had all made sense at the time—not asking Zack directly about Imagination did seem like a foolish thing. Why hadn't she asked him straight out? Had she been afraid of his answer?

Charlotte blew her nose again. "Blast this cold! Who gets a cold in May, for God's sake? Well, are you going to answer me?

"I don't care whether you believe me or not. I didn't ask him because Allen asked me not to. Now, back off!"

"I've spent a good deal of my life blaming your father for what I've become. I blame him now for how he's changed you. I've even blamed him for our lack of closeness." Charlotte cleared her throat. "But for once, don't look to your father for the cause. Look at yourself."

That had really hurt. Mary Anne felt anger boiling up inside her, and she was no longer able to contain it.

"All right, fine! Zack betrayed me!" Mary Anne said. "There! Are you satisfied? He hid the truth about his new company. He hid the truth about his dreams. He couldn't even confide in me. I gave him lots of opportunities to tell me, but he never did. So why else wouldn't he tell me unless he was planning to betray Allen? Why else?"

"God, I can't believe I've raised such a naïve daughter! Did it ever occur to you that Zack wanted to protect you? Didn't you just tell me that your father's trumped-up reason was because he wanted to *protect* you? Isn't it possible that Zack wanted the same for you?"

At that point in the conversation, she'd gotten up and walked away, unable to hear any more. But rerunning the conversation in her mind, it suddenly hit her—maybe her mother was right. Mary Anne slammed on the brakes and whipped over to the curb of Mission Boulevard.

A horn blared, and a red-faced commuter in a Lincoln Town Car shot past her waving his fist. Mary Anne pulled out her cell phone from her handbag and pressed the speed dial.

"Hi!" a pert young voice answered.

"Deirdre. It's me. I'm going to be late—probably a few hours."

"Sure, babe. But, hey, do you know what's going on around here?" she said, almost in a whisper.

"What are you talking about?"

"There's been, like, massive meetings ever since first light. A major geek parade. Engineers and scientists sitting on the stairs, all waiting to see your father. Everything's all, like, you know, hush-hush-like and behind closed doors. What's up?"

"No idea," Mary Anne said, her mind racing with the possibilities. She had to find Zack.

Chapter Twenty-Five

As Zack drove back from the San Francisco airport, he kept glancing into the rearview mirror. The three men in the back all had white hair; all were dressed in very expensive, tailored suits. They looked comfortable, as there was plenty of room on the seat. He had rented a big Cadillac four-door for the occasion, foregoing his Toyota Cressida or Paul's Z28.

Zack had the air conditioner howling at full pitch, but sweat was still oozing under his arms. Paul was in the front passenger seat. He kept combing his hair back with his hand, like he had OCD. Zack hadn't slept well. There was no way of telling what the investors knew, but he figured it wasn't a good sign when they suddenly showed up like this. Damn Paul! He should have never withheld the bad news.

By the time they arrived at the Bakers', poured drinks, and were sitting on the deck, the sun was getting quite warm. The suit jackets came off, ties were loosened, top shirt buttons were undone. Jeremy arrived shortly after, and idle chitchat ensued. Molly and John were still at the bank, their two young sons in school. Zack felt a queasy tightness in his stomach that refused to go away.

In the end, it was the goatee-bearded Dickens who broke the ice and asked for an update.

Zack dutifully explained the past few days, talking factually about the TRO, the day at court, the seizure of the PCs, and the shutdown of the Santa Clara facility. Paul or Jeremy added an occasional sentence or two, but he did most of the talking, somehow managing to keep his voice calm and steady.

He was winding down when Dickens pivoted stiffly in his chair. "Paul, you called me Saturday morning. Did this whole TRO thing somehow slip your mind?"

Paul blanched and opened his mouth, but nothing came out.

Zack had been expecting the question. "If I could just answer for my CFO," he interjected, "we didn't have a lot of information to pass on, other than the TRO had put a temporary halt to things. We were hoping to gather more information before we talked." Zack cringed inwardly. It sounded like the kind of tripe that Paul served up, but he also hated seeing his friend take all the heat.

"Yes, that's true," Paul said. "At the time, we just really didn't have much to go on. We studied the situation on Sunday, and now we know better what we're up against. Since you were coming out for a visit anyway, we figured we'd wait until you arrived to fill you in."

"Fair enough," Dickens said. "So, after the thirty days, then what?"

"Excuse me?"

"Let's say we go through this little dance for thirty days, or twenty-six days, or whatever it is now, and then what? Business as usual?"

"Yes, sir," Paul said.

Dickens kept his eyes on Zack. "And there are no other loopholes or snags that can drag this out longer?"

Zack watched Dickens take a long sip of ice water, the tall glass sweating in the sun.

"While nothing is a given," he replied, "we don't believe Allen has a strong case against us because what we're doing is so radically different from his technology. The long and short of it is, we're confident that it'll be dropped or dismissed."

Dickens turned to Jeremy. "What if the judge decides an injunction is in order at your next hearing?"

"Then the TRO will be replaced by a more permanent injunction until we can either settle with DisplayTechnik or go to court for a verdict."

"How long could that be?"

"That's hard to say. I would venture that—"

"It doesn't matter," Paul said, jumping in. "There's no need to be concerned with an injunction, because the entire TRO is fraudulent! There isn't an ounce of credibility to the claim. We all know this."

"Yes, yes, I understand all that," Dickens said with obvious impatience. To Jeremy he said, "If a case *could* be made for a preliminary injunction, how long could this Henley keep our jockstraps in contraction?"

Paul opened his mouth to speak again, but Dickens raised his hand for silence.

"It depends on whether we can settle things before it gets to court and—" Jeremy said.

"Let's assume worst case and we go to trial."

"Well ..." Jeremy reached back and gently massaged the nape of his neck. "Could be six months ... could be eight." He shrugged. "Maybe more."

Dickens stroked his white goatee, looking at the three of them, one after another.

Zack held his breath. He knew if they were held up for six months or more, things could get ugly for his fledgling company. They had a two-year lease for their building, which they were paying monthly. Also, Imagination had ordered several million dollars' worth of equipment for pilot production. Within the next several months, there would be a lot of capital equipment queued at loading docks with no place to call home, for which they'd be charged storage fees.

There were other logistical issues, but the most critical problem was the lost time. In six months, they had to demonstrate proof of concept to convince second-round investors to continue research and development funding, and get ready for production scale-up. And that was when the really big bucks got invested.

A glass door to the house slid back, and Molly Baker stepped onto the deck, shielding her eyes from the glare with a cupped hand. She was wearing fluffy yellow slippers that matched the color of her hair. It was just past three o'clock, but she had arranged flexible hours with the bank so that she could be home before her two boys arrived from school.

"Hello, everyone," Molly said. "Hope I'm not interrupting anything too serious."

Dickens stood up at once, a big smile on his face, his perfect white teeth in full view. "Molly! Wonderful to see you," he said. "No interruption at all. Besides, we're the ones invading your lovely home."

Taking his lead, Zack stood up, along with everyone else.

"Matt, it's great to see you again."

Zack looked at Paul. They'd never heard Dickens's first name used before in casual conversation. They always just called him "sir."

Dickens embraced Molly, her narrow shoulders lost in the investor's thick arms.

Zack caught sight of a tattoo on Dickens's upper arm under his short-sleeve white shirt. Was he in the military service? Aside from having memorized Dickens's very impressive financial pedigree, Zack realized he didn't know much else about his principal investor.

After the hug, Dickens held both her hands in his. There was no mistake that she was very glad to see him too.

"So, how are Paulette and the kids?" Molly said.

"Oh, she's fine, just fine, but her legs are giving her problems these days. She can't do the long walks that she loves, but we still manage to get around at the summer home. And the kids are doing great, though I worry about them more now than when they used to run around in diapers."

Molly's laugh sounded completely relaxed and genuine. "That's only natural."

"Well, I better go get some snacks ready for the boys," Molly said. "Just give a yell if you need anything." She excused herself and slid the glass door shut behind her.

Everyone sat down again, the deck chairs squeaking in unison.

"You know, Zack," Dickens said, "one of the main reasons I invested in your company was because John and Molly believed in you. They're wonderful people."

"I know that, sir," Zack said.

"It's not the only reason, of course, but it was one of the reasons, and an important one."

"Yes, sir."

"So, to avoid any embarrassment between the families of the Bakers and the Dickens, I suggest we do everything possible to nip this unsightly thing in the bud. Don't you agree?"

Zack nodded, feeling a flood of relief. "I couldn't agree with you more."

"Good, good," Dickens said, his hand stroking his goatee again. "So, pretend I'm the judge and tell me again why this TRO is a bunch of horsepucky. I want to know all the details." Dickens snapped his fingers at Paul. "And you, get me a real drink. Enough of this eternal springwater crap; I'm not going to live forever. A vodka with lemon. And something stronger for my friends as well."

For more than an hour, Zack, Paul, and Jeremy dove into the minutest details of the temporary restraining order. When they were finished, the investors all concluded that they had a very good argument on their side.

"You know, perhaps it would be a good idea to bring in a few of my lawyers," Dickens said. "It looks to me like we're undergunned. No offense, Jeremy."

"None taken, sir," Jeremy said, sounding relieved. "We *are* undergunned. Do you know if your people are licensed to practice law in California?"

"Don't know," Dickens said, "but I'm sure it can all be worked out. Don't worry. I'll make a few calls."

The news that they were bringing in high-powered attorneys from New York would wipe the smirks off the faces of Allen and his legal retinue. Zack knew they weren't out of the woods, not by any stretch, but between Dickens's white hairs of experience and the clarity and honesty of Jeremy's legal arguments, maybe they could pull this off and give the bastard a run for his money.

"Say, Zack," Dickens said, "isn't your girlfriend the daughter of this Henley fellow?"

Zack shifted on his patio cushion, feeling the sticky plastic seat cover suctioning at the back of his thigh. He shot a quick glance at Paul, wondering how much personal background he had given the man. Or maybe this was something Molly had let drop.

"That's right," Zack said. "Her name's Mary Anne. She works in the accounting department for DisplayTechnik."

"My, my, there must be spoilage in the state of Denmark."

"Excuse me?" Zack said.

"There must be considerable unease between you and your girlfriend given the current situation," Dickens said.

"Yes, I'm afraid so."

The glass door slid open again, sparing Zack from having to go into details. Molly stepped out with a pained look on her face. "Zack, I'm sorry to interrupt, but there's a gentleman out front who says he needs to speak with you urgently," she said. "Maybe he's an engineer? He didn't say what it's about, just that it was urgent."

A young man in his early twenties followed her through the open patio door and, looking from face to face, said, "Zack Penny?"

Zack didn't recognize him. Was he a job applicant? And how did an applicant get the Bakers' address? "Yes, I'm Zack Penny," he said, rising from his seat. "Can I help you?"

"Zack Penny of Pleasanton Estates, 35 Springhouse Road?"

Zack frowned. "What of it?"

The young man tossed a document at Zack, and he instinctively caught it.

"You've been served by the district attorney of Santa Clara County. Have a nice day."

With that, the man turned and walked out the patio door, brushing past Molly Baker, whose face had gone ashen.

Zack tore open the envelope and pulled out a document, eyes widening as he saw the official seal of the Santa Clara County notary. The intense sunlight washed out most of the writing.

"What is it?" Paul asked in a low voice.

Zack squinted at the papers.

"May I?" Jeremy said, snatching the documents away. He scanned through the pages quickly, his eyes darting back and forth. When he was finished, he said, "Very bad news, I'm afraid. The district attorney's office has issued a criminal complaint against Zack for theft of trade secrets from DisplayTechnik. We have twenty days to respond."

"A criminal charge?" Paul said in astonishment. "Henley filed a criminal charge? That arrogant, backstabbing snake!"

Zack sat down heavily. His eyes refused to focus. It was one thing to be sued in a civil court. The penalties were usually monetary. But a criminal case could mean jail time and the end of one's livelihood. Just the word "criminal" made him feel sick. Criminals were thieves, rapists, and murderers. Zack looked around and saw the bowed heads. All the optimism had been washed away.

Molly came over to Zack. "Zack, I'm so sorry. I didn't know who he was. He seemed so polite. I never imagined he was a ... a ..."

"Don't worry. He would have found me anyway, sooner or later. He was just doing his job."

"What are you? Fucking nuts or something?" Paul said. "How can you be so calm?"

Zack shot Paul a warning glance. "I'm not calm," he said. "I'm just trying to figure out what the hell is going on. How can Allen bring charges against me for developing my own ideas? It doesn't make any sense."

The patio door slid back again. Zack looked up and realized

that the visit by the process server was not his biggest surprise of the day.

Mary Anne walked onto the deck. "Hello Zack," she said.

Dickens leaned over to Paul and whispered, none too quietly, "And this I assume is the girlfriend?"

CHAPTER TWENTY-SIX

Dimitre had been holed up in Anna's office—now their shared office—almost two full days, with his bloodshot eyes glued to the screen of his new laptop. Anna's chair seemed to have fused with his backside after so many hours. The desk was too low for him, and his legs were painfully crammed beneath it. Many dozens of cigarette stubs littered the three ashtrays, and the smell of smoke mixed with stale vodka had seeped into the pale blue carpet.

He was running another simulation program to test the reliability of the new display. He had been forced to make some minor changes to the polymer formulation because his most recent calculations indicated it was unstable, behaving like a fluorescent light just before it dies. He hadn't told Zack or the others because he'd thought he'd solved the problem almost as soon as he'd discovered it.

But now, as he stared at the results of the program, he knew something was terribly wrong.

Dimitre leaned an inch closer to the laptop, crowding the screen that was streaming with data. There was decay in the electrical field intensity. That couldn't be. It couldn't. But there it was—the significance of the numbers leaped out at him. He rubbed his face with both hands and then rubbed his eyes, surprised at how badly his fingers trembled.

The implications of the simulation results were catastrophic.

Under the burden of carrying electrons, the polymer material would start to disassociate within a few months. That meant that the display would slowly lose intensity, and it could not be recovered by simply changing to a fresh battery. Over the years, the world's best material scientists had battled lifetime and efficiency issues of large displays. No one would buy a flat-panel television if you had to replace the screen every few months—no matter how paper-thin it was. He shook his head. He thought that he and Zack had solved this problem.

How could he have missed this? Could it have been a typo, bad input in the original tests? Had he been in such a rush to assure Zack of the formula's success that he'd completely overlooked something?

Sweat trickled down the bridge of his nose, sliding to the right when it hit his old ice hockey scar. Dimitre canceled the simulation program and started all over again, doing his best to ignore the pressure that was building inside of him. He would find the mistake in the simulation. It couldn't be the polymer formula itself. It just couldn't.

One thing was certain: he was not about to tell Zack any of this. Not until he was sure he'd solved the problem.

CHAPTER TWENTY-SEVEN

"What the hell are you doing here?" Paul shouted. "And how the hell did you know where to find us?"

Mary Anne crossed her arms as Paul's eyes bored into her. They had only met once—last summer, by accident—when she bumped into him as she came out of Zack's apartment. She remembered the creepy feeling he gave her, especially when she saw those pale blue eyes and faint blond eyebrows. She'd felt his eyes on her all the way across the parking lot. "I didn't *know*," she said, "I guessed. My friend, Deirdre, knows Jimmy Morgan's girlfriend, and she said you met here last weekend. So I took a chance that you were meeting here again."

"People should learn to keep their mouths shut." Paul's jaw tightened. "How'd you get in? Breaking and entering? You do have quite a talent for it."

Mary Anne felt her eyes start to tear up.

"Paul, that's enough," Zack said.

Mary Anne saw the three white-haired strangers standing behind Zack and Paul. Another man stood off to the side, mid-thirties, with a small gut shaped like a wineskin. She didn't recognize him, either. "Look, I'm sorry if I've interrupted something. Perhaps I should just leave."

Mary Anne took a step toward Molly and then stopped and turned back. "Zack, I don't mind waiting until you're finished. My car is parked across the street. Come talk to me when you're available. Please?" She glanced at Zack, but her eyes were drawn to Paul, whose face was so red it looked like it had been spray-painted.

"I gotta admit," Paul said, hands on his hips. "You Henleys have got nerve. You first offer to be a witness for your father against your own boyfriend, and then you barge in here, unannounced, and demand Zack's attention. I'm surprised that you don't have your hand out, asking for a donation to pay for your father's legal fees."

Jeremy moved away from the deck railing and moved close to Paul. "Paul, play it cool," Jeremy said in a low voice. "Perhaps she just doesn't know."

"Know what?" Mary Anne said.

Zack stepped in front of Paul. "Allen just filed a criminal complaint against me."

She felt the blood drain from her face. "What? What for?"

"He claims I stole trade secrets from DisplayTechnik. Evidently the district attorney wants to prosecute."

"That … oh, that can't be true! He couldn't—"

"Couldn't what?" Paul said. "Screw us? Spoken like a true whore."

"Shut up, Paul," Jeremy said. "Just shut up."

"Shut up? After what this bitch and her father did to us? You've got to be kidding! Maybe *we* ought to file a criminal complaint. She just committed breaking and entering. We all saw it."

Jeremy put a hand on Paul's arm and said, "I suggest you go, Mary Anne. Now."

Her mind was racing. Trade secrets, proprietary drawings. The drawings she'd seen in Zack's home office. Her father had said she would testify in civil court, but only if it was absolutely necessary. That's what he'd promised her. He'd said he'd wanted her name on the witness list to scare Zack into submission. He'd never mentioned anything about a criminal charge. She would have never agreed to any of it if she'd known that.

"Zack, I … Please. I'll be waiting in my car." With tears brimming, Mary Anne ran from the sundeck, nearly colliding into Molly, who was standing at the sliding door.

Chapter Twenty-Eight

Allen put the cordless phone back on its cradle. He took out a cigar and rolled the brown leaves between his palms. He had quit smoking years ago because the habit hurt his tennis game, but he still kept the Havana specials in his office desk drawer, a reward for accomplishing something extraordinary.

Company sales were on target, and although profit margins could have been better, all in all, he couldn't complain—at least to himself. Armed with the same information, he took a different tack with his troops, accusing them of slacking and demanding they do better—or else. What made today special were the results of the closed-door meetings with his advanced technology group and the marketing staff. This little shit start-up had inspired him. Lately, he had been slacking a bit himself. He'd missed having something big, something groundbreaking, to sink his teeth into. Now, he'd found it.

The phone rang. It was Louise. "Miss Reynolds here to see you."

The door swung open, and Julie sashayed into his office. He had called her after the last of the strategy meetings had ended. He needed to explain his ingenious strategy—or at least a portion of it—to someone who could understand the brilliance of his actions. He needed someone who would applaud his vision and support him unconditionally. Allen understood all too well that his own wife could never be that person. It wasn't that he didn't trust Charlotte. He did trust her. However, her open disdain for his business and business practices infuriated him, especially since she owned significant shares in the company.

Allen watched his sounding board take a seat. She was wearing a red plaid skirt and white blouse, with a frilly something modestly covering the cleavage between her lovely breasts. He'd noticed it before, but Julie really did look like the Charlotte that Allen remembered from his youth—at least before Jack Daniel's became his wife's closest friend. Their personalities weren't that different, either. Julie was just younger, and therefore a little less cynical and more malleable. In Julie, he not only had a younger version of his wife, but one who would listen with admiration and rapt attention—not question him or look down her nose at the business side of his life. She was the perfect ego boost, exactly what a wife—or mistress—should be.

Allen swept the cigar leaves to the carpet and then picked up the duffel bag and set it on his desk. He opened the long, golden zipper. "Today has been a very good day," he said.

"I'm glad," Julie said. She crossed her legs, wriggling off her left shoe. She teased her toe in and out of the shoe's black leather mouth. "So, what's in the bag?" she said.

"Utopia." He rounded the front of the desk so he could sit on it and command her full attention. "The field of display technology is changing, rapidly. In a few years, we'll look back and be amazed that we ever actually had these clunky things weighing down our desks."

Julie crossed her legs. The plaid skirt rose up to mid-thigh. "You've said all this before. The movement toward flat-panel display technology—lighter, flatter screens, like in our laptop computers and such."

"Yes, yes. I have talked about these things. And we're currently working in parallel on a variety of innovative display technologies, like plasma, FEDs, electroluminescent LCDs, and reflective LCDs. But none of these designs are a quantum leap in technology, at least not in terms of true affordability and performance. The issues are always the same: price, contrast, brightness, color, FCC standards, and viewing angle. Despite all the advances of technology and software programming, it's hard to beat the old reliable cathode ray tube on the main points."

Allen gently laid both hands on the duffle like it was the Ark of the Covenant.

"This bag holds the keys to change all that. A true paradigm shift. And we are going to exploit it to the hilt. Patent the technology, license it to our competitors, and radically change the playing field. It's going to be brilliant." He grinned at the pun, though Julie didn't seem to get it.

She leaned forward to try to peek into the open duffel bag. "And which of our research groups figured out this wonderful stuff? Who's your next *wunderkind*?"

Allen laughed. "That's the truly brilliant part. That's what makes this whole thing so ironic, so delicious. Don't you get it?"

Julie shook her head.

"When I found out about Zack's desire to spread his entrepreneurial wings, I assumed he would take his little prick and stick it in one of the holes already dug by our various research teams. I thought he was going to start up a rival company to make competing displays, something prettier or with a slightly improved resolution. I figured he'd be working with one of the so-called 'cutting-edge' displays, like the plasma screens. That made sense because he was in charge of new technology. Which particular hole he crawled into, I didn't really care. I only wanted to make sure I squashed him like a bug.

"I never imagined that Zack and that nutcase engineer Koslov would be clever enough to make the quantum leap. But then, I suppose I should have. After all, Zack was my protégé. I taught him everything he knows."

Julie leaned forward in the narrow black chair. "So … so are you saying that there *isn't* a basis for the lawsuit?"

If she'd been in arm's reach, he would have slapped her across the face. "That doesn't concern you, understand?" he said. He took a deep breath and slowly let it out. As much as he enjoyed screwing Julie, as much as he enjoyed having someone to listen to his brilliant plans, the fact of the matter was that Julie wasn't his wife. There really wasn't that bond of trust and blood.

He truly missed having Mary Anne solidly in his camp. She was still mired in those foolish romantic notions of hers, notions that he was confident she would eventually see through. In the meantime, she was robbing him of a true confidant, a like-minded spirit. Children could be so disappointing. Just like wives. Everything starts with hopes and dreams of what it will all be like, and then they go their own path—up to a point. He knew Mary Anne would come around. He didn't raise a fool for a daughter.

"Of course, there's a basis for the lawsuit," Allen said in a much softer tone. "Zack stole my engineers—that still stands. Dimitre and the others worked for me. They dutifully received their paychecks, all the while planning to undermine me. Now they're attempting to destroy this company by making displays that will make everything we do obsolete."

"Aren't you fighting an uphill battle then? Didn't he take precautions to protect all this? After all, he's not stupid."

"Of course, Zack's not stupid. He's brilliant. I made sure of that." Allen laughed, recapturing the euphoria of the moment. "The problem with Zack is that he slavishly follows the rules and believes in the system, which makes him weak. It means that he misses the whole point of engagement. Which is to win. So he'll fail to win because he believes in something outside himself. True strength comes from within, from self-belief. I don't believe in the system, I believe in winning."

"No, I mean Zack must have acted to protect himself. And if he did, then how can you win the lawsuit?"

"Don't worry. The details have all been taken care of. Besides, our Zack won't have time to be concerned over the loss of his precious technology. He'll be spending too much time worrying about his new life in jail."

Julie seemed at a sudden loss for words. Allen realized he

was bored with the exchange. He hadn't derived nearly as much pleasure from it as he'd thought he would. Time for something else. Reaching out to grope Julie's breasts, he gazed into her wide brown eyes and saw the tiny creases at the corners.

Allen frowned. He hadn't ever noticed that before.

CHAPTER TWENTY-NINE

After Mary Anne left, an awkward silence hung over the Bakers' sundeck. Zack looked at Paul's red face and then at Jeremy and Molly, who sadly shook their heads.

Dickens, mellowed by vodka and jet lag, broke the tension and matter-of-factly said, "So, that's the girlfriend. Hmm. She's pretty."

Zack got up and without a word went after her.

He could hear Paul shouting at his back. "Idiot" and "fool" were part of the verbal volley. He had to admit chasing after Mary Anne seemed like a stupid thing to do. But he couldn't help himself. Why had she shown up? And of all moments to choose, why now? And the way she reacted when she heard about the criminal charge, it was more than just surprise.

She was sitting in a dusty blue Ford Taurus, parked across the street. The keys were in the ignition, her hands on the steering wheel. Zack was taken aback. Tears streaked her cheeks. Mary Anne hated to cry, especially in public. He knocked lightly on the driver's window.

She rolled down the window, leaning her head back against the headrest. Another tear welled up and slid down her cheek. "Zack, I'm really sorry what's happened." She sniffed. "Getting charged by the police is horrible. I didn't know anything about it, I swear."

Zack wanted to believe her. "Paul was out of line back there," he said.

She shook her head, rummaging in her purse for a tissue. "It's okay. I can imagine how he feels, how you must feel."

"Can you? Can you really understand what's going on here?"

"I thought you were going to steal Allen's designs and technology and then set up shop to compete against him."

"I'd have to be an idiot to do that. It'd be suicide to start a new company to compete head-to-head against your father. Of course, given the current circumstances, it looks like its suicide anyway."

"Suicide? What do you mean?"

"Nothing. Forget it."

"So you're not competing against my father?"

"Of course not. Our company, or should I say what's left of our company, is branching out into a new display technology. It is unlike anything that DisplayTechnik is doing."

"Then you should have trusted me. I might have been able to stop all this. Now it's out of control."

"Mary Anne, I do trust you. But you have to understand that this technology is unlike anything that your father or anyone else is doing. It's completely revolutionary. A lot of people would be very interested in it—including your father. So I thought it was better until I was completely free and clear of DisplayTechnik before telling you anything about it. You would have wanted me to tell your father about the ideas. But, Mary Anne, they were *my* ideas. They were Dimitre's ideas. We wanted our own place to claim for our own, to hope and dream and build and create, where everyone was treated differently. Remember?"

"Yes, I remember."

"Is it so hard to understand that I loved you but hated your father? You're your own person. And I really believed that once you saw what we were doing, you'd believe in it too."

"Loved? Past tense?"

"After all this, honestly my feelings are a bit confused."

"I know. It just sounded so final, that's all." She blew her nose. "My parents are right. I can be so naïve sometimes. Well, not anymore." She looked up into his eyes. "I just wish we'd been able to be honest with each other from the start. This all could have turned out so differently."

"It still can. I haven't given up hope. Not yet anyway." Zack tried a smile, but it felt fake so he quickly changed the subject. "Why did you come here?"

"I needed to explain something to you. I needed to ..."

"I'm all ears."

"The drawings," she said, almost in a whisper.

"What?"

"Proprietary drawings."

Zack waited for more. "I still don't get it."

"I'm really sorry. Listen, I've got something awful to tell you, and I have to say it while I still have my nerve." She took a deep breath and then said, "I already told you I went into your home office. I saw all kinds of drawings and documents with the name Imagination written all over them. I didn't understand them, of course. And I saw lots of reports between yourself and other engineers, like Dimitre, Jerry Steiner, Jimmy Morgan, and others."

"Go on."

"I also saw many DisplayTechnik drawings on your desk and elsewhere. 'Confidential' was stamped all over the drawings."

"So?" He felt his back tense up. "I take work home all the time. Everyone does."

"God, I can't believe what I did. I wrote down all the drawing numbers of both companies. Which, of course, I didn't understand and—"

"And gave them to Allen." Of course, she did. Christ, more ammunition, as if he needed it. Well, at least now he knew exactly what Mary Anne was going to testify about.

"I didn't take any of your drawings. I would never do that." Mary Anne pressed her hands to her face.

"Jesus," he said, "two seconds ago, you were talking about honesty. You broke into my home office. Nothing dishonest there. You waited until after we'd made love, then crept into my office and took inventory for your daddy. Did you have a little spy camera in your cosmetic bag or just shoot the photos with your phone?"

"Please don't think of me that way. Please. I'm going to tell my father I was wrong; I'm going to tell him I'll never testify."

Zack snorted. "Paul was right, you really are a two-timing bitch." He slammed his balled fist down on the top of the Taurus so hard that Mary Anne jumped. "Well, at least now I don't have to wonder if your father will succeed in sending me to prison. You confirmed my reservation at San Quentin. But hey, on the bright side, San Quentin's awfully close to the city. You won't have to drive very far to visit me."

Zack slammed the car roof again, this time hard enough to leave a dent. He turned away, heading to the Bakers'. "Have a good life," he barked over his shoulder, "because you just destroyed mine."

CHAPTER THIRTY

Anna's freelance writing gave her a lot of leeway with her work time, and she often crammed it in late at night. Today, she was in the kitchen, writing on a tablet that she'd later type into her computer. The tablet obscured most of the faces of Hulk Hogan and the Rock, their magnificence displayed on the yellow place mat. Both she and Dimitre were big fans of the WWE.

Anna looked down the hall at the door to the den. It was now after four in the afternoon. Zack had called last night, telling Dimitre not to come in today because the big-shot New York investors were in town. That was good because her husband had been in a horrible mood. She had hoped he'd take the day off, but he stayed in there, muttering to himself.

Sometime later, she was surprised to hear the door open, and she glanced up. It was nearly dinnertime. Dimitre walked stiffly into the kitchen. She'd gotten busy herself and had lost track of time.

Dimitre rubbed his eyes. He opened the fridge and bent down to investigate. He stroked his beard as he searched the shelves. He closed the fridge.

"Before you ask what's for dinner," Anna said in her native Ukranian, "tell me what's wrong."

"I'm not hungry. I just needed a mental break. Watching figures on the screen can be a bit boring."

"If you're bored, why don't you sit down and talk to me?" Dimitre grunted.

"Look, you either tell me, or I'll call Zack and tell him that he's made a big mistake hiring you as his technical genius."

Dimitre's eyes opened wide; he looked like he'd seen a ghost. Anna had unexpectedly hit a nerve. He dropped onto the kitchen chair, the chair feet grinding against the linoleum floor. He slouched down, spreading his legs wide under the table until his socks touched Anna's bare feet. His feet were ice-cold.

"Anna, I've made a big mistake," he said, head in hands, the curly hair sticking up through his fingers. "A big mistake."

"I see. And what is this big mistake?"

"It's the polymer formula. The wonderful formula that I told everyone works. The miracle material that so many scientists could not make work, but I, the great Dimitre Koslov, had finally found the answer."

"You did discover the formula. You even showed me the prototype. It's pure genius."

"Unfortunately, my formula will make a display that doesn't last much longer than it takes to drink a bottle of vodka."

"I don't understand. I saw the prototype the day after you—"

"I'm being facetious. But in truth, it doesn't last anywhere near as long as it must. Let me explain." Dimitre launched into a technical discussion that Anna barely followed, but she knew he needed to get it out, to hear himself talk. When Dimitre finished, Anna looked at him calmly. "What does Zack think of this?"

Dimitre lowered his eyes, a low, gurgling sound coming from his belly.

Anna caught her breath. "My God. You haven't told him?"

Dimitre wouldn't look at her.

"Dimitre! How could—"

"Zack always said, don't give me a problem without having the solution. I haven't yet come up with a solution."

"Yes, but—"

"I don't need the lecture right now. I feel terrible. Zack has had far too many problems to start this company. Even now he's meeting with the investors, something I wouldn't want to do no matter how much money they gave me. And now, after everything, I have to tell him that the entire foundation for the company is flawed, that we have nothing? That is asking too much. I feel terrible."

She grabbed her husband's big hands that were balled into fists, feeling the thick black mat of hair. She had married an ape. She cupped them long enough until, slowly, he opened his hands to allow hers to slide inside. She studied his brown eyes, smiling at him. His eyes were very watery, and that was not like him. Despite his thick eyebrows, she could still see an old scar on the bridge of his nose from when he played ice hockey back in Moscow. Her teddy bear had been as graceful as a dancer on the ice. She had always thought that ironic because Dimitre was by far the worst dancer of any of her boyfriends.

"You have to tell him," she said. "He's your friend. You simply must."

Dimitre sighed in the way that he always did to signify that he knew she was right. "I know … But it is not that simple."

He clenched his jaw, shaking his head. "There is a great deal more going on that you're not aware of. I don't trust this Paul fellow. He doesn't have the scruples that Zack does, and Paul has been having some influence on him. Now I don't feel I can trust Zack like I once used to." Dimitre sighed. "I don't know where all of this is heading. I …" His voice faltered, and he let go of her hand and looked away.

Anna gave him a moment or two before asking, "There's something else, isn't there?"

"Anna, I feel like I've made a big mistake getting into Zack's company. I feel like I've jeopardized our future. And everything was riding on this formula of mine. I don't know if it can be fixed. I believe it can, I hope it can, but what if it can't?"

"If you believe it can be fixed, then I know you'll find a way. I have every confidence in you."

Dimitre smiled at her and took her hand in a way that made

her feel warm all over. "Thank you, my love. But what if it can't? If there's no more Imagination, what then? There's also a part of me that is very angry. I wouldn't be following this stupid dream if Zack hadn't filled my head with thoughts of grandeur of going our own way. I had security. It was not the best place to work, but I liked it. And we had security. Now, we can't go back to DisplayTechnik; Allen would never have us. He's bent on destroying all of us, not just Zack. Where will we go then? This is not like when we were at university. We have two boys to look after now."

There was silence between them for a few moments. Then he said, "What do you think that I should do?"

Anna looked at her husband. She always told him that she was smarter than him. But right now, she had no answers for him. "I don't know. Perhaps you'll solve the problem, and all this worry will be for nothing. If not, then I believe a solution will present itself. And if it doesn't, then somehow we'll make our own solution. We always have."

CHAPTER THIRTY-ONE

L ate Monday afternoon, Allen drove his silver Porsche 911 over the Bay Bridge that linked Oakland to San Francisco. Although the Golden Gate received much more attention, the Bay Bridge was a true marvel of modern engineering. Eight-and-a-quarter-miles long and more than four times the size of the Brooklyn Bridge, it was ahead of its time, the designers foreseeing a vast number of cars traveling between the two cities, so they made room for the magnificent span to carry five lanes of traffic going in each direction stacked on top of one another.

Despite the innovation, it was often a two-story car park. It was a vivid example of the need not only to foresee future demands but to exceed them.

Since it was only just after five o'clock and the crush of cars had not fully started yet, the traffic was moving along fairly well. With the black vinyl top down, Allen drove his car fast, zigzagging across all five lanes, envisioning his own plans for the future. He foresaw massive displays in every living room across America, all with the logo of DisplayTechnik proudly in one corner. They'd license the technology and gladly share it with their competitors—all for a piece of the action, so that with every display sold, a portion of the profit would find its way back to DisplayTechnik.

The CEO of Imagination, despite his company's name, simply did not think far enough ahead. From what he'd read so far, Zack had planned only to exploit the display, leaving the highly profitable applications for existing companies to work out. How simpleminded to want to share the wealth. To truly take advantage of a six-sided, three-dimensional display, you'd need new cameras to film in six directions, not to mention a vast array of software to feed the displays, accompanying hardware, and delivery systems. And that was just the tip of the iceberg.

Allen exited onto Eighth Avenue and eventually parked in the underground lot of the law office of Travis, McSorley, & Davis, located on the upscale side of Market Street. He stepped into the glass-encased elevator and pressed the twenty-third-floor button with the tip of his black umbrella. As he silently rose above the street, he looked out. The view of San Francisco was truly spectacular. It never ceased to amaze him how city planners could have conceived of building a city over such incredible hills at such steep angles. He could make out a train of cars slowly navigating the crazy S-turns of Lombard Street. He shook his head. Engineers were merely cattle, as he had often explained to Julie, and unless they had the right leader, they would only focus on the tail waving just in front of them. No imagination.

How that word just sprang to mind.

When the elevator door opened, he stepped out and turned left and saw a gorgeous young woman walking toward him. She had striking high cheekbones, glasses on her forehead, and a stack full of files in her arms. She smiled at him. Before Allen could say anything, she was past him. The scent of Chanel Number Five wafted over and around him, as though her essence had just passed through him. Inhaling deeply, he turned and stared at the woman, feeling a familiar stirring in his trousers as he watched her hips, their sway accentuated by high heels.

"Do you need any help with that?" he called after her.

The young woman didn't turn around. Instead, she shook her head and waved her free hand.

Allen thought of going after her. She was wearing one of those back-slit skirts that gave hints of what lay beneath. He noted which office cubicle she disappeared into, in the same area as the rest of Dean's legal staff.

That was encouraging. If she worked for Dean, he could finagle an introduction. He continued down the wide corridor, the sounds of a busy office surrounding him, the happy little lawyers all excitedly fattening their checking accounts as they fed off the businesses of the Bay Area.

Travis, McSorley, and Davis took up the entire top floor of the office building. Dean's office was in the southwest corner, the command center for the firm's intellectual property department. Allen waltzed into the spacious office with the same brashness as Julie Reynolds had entered his office a few hours earlier.

The senior partner was sitting behind his white, peanut-shaped desk, a computer on either side of him.

"Did you hire a new assistant?"

"What?"

"Who's that lovely girl I met coming off the elevator? She has these amazing cheeks that are so inviting."

"Oh. You must mean Terri. She's a new paralegal."

Allen sank into a deep pillowed chair that was across from the narrowest portion of Dean's desk. He clasped his hands in front of him and said, "Let's start off with the thieving little shit. Did you contact Grimes from the Bank of America?

The lawyer nodded.

"Is he going to play ball?"

"A little complicated."

"What is that supposed to mean?"

"It means that, legally speaking, it's hard to enforce."

"Is there a way, goddamit?"

"There's a way."

Allen grunted. "Well, then do it. I don't how you brilliantly manage to force him into compliance. Impress me with results." Allen made a sour face. "Damn straight that Grimes should help, given all the money deals that I've thrown his way. That ought to make Zack and his New York friends take notice. Let them dip into their own stinking pockets."

Allen got up and walked toward a small vestibule off to one side of the office. "How about Kennedy? Did you make contact with him?"

"Yes."

"And?" Allen picked up an ivory elephant from a teak table located in the vestibule. There was a whole row of them on the table, each in a slightly different pose. He held the sculpture in his hand, testing its weight with the same regard that he would given to a package of meat from the local butcher over on Van Ness.

Dean got up from behind his desk and walked quickly toward Allen, his hands clenched in front of him, his face set. Allen played with the elephant, using it to do an arm curl. He watched with amusement as Dean stood there nervously. It made him want to chuck the bibelot against the nearest wall.

"Are you going to answer?" he pressed. "What did Kennedy say?"

Allen put the albino elephant back on the display counter. The figure wobbled slightly and then was still. Dean immediately seemed to relax.

"Although Kennedy's annoyed that there's a padlock and chain around his building," the lawyer said, walking back to his desk, "he's willing to wait for the outcome of the TRO before taking any action."

Allen scowled. "What the hell is wrong with him? Doesn't he know that having chains around prime industrial park estates will pollute the real estate market? There's a bloody quarantine around the entire facility."

"Zack paid six months' rent in advance. That's why Kennedy isn't nervous."

"He will be. Did you check into that sister property near the Great America Park? It's available, right?"

Dean flipped through a pile of papers and extracted a folder. He thumbed through some pages until he found the flyer. "Apparently yes," Dean said, scratching his head. "An optical disk-drive company filed for chapter eleven almost four months ago. The facility is apparently 50 percent larger than Imagination's."

"Wonderful. Tell Kennedy that I'll pick up the lease on that one right now. Let him name his own deposit, plus all the usual benefits, if he starts the eviction process immediately."

Dean's eyebrows lifted.

Allen pointed a finger at him. "But just make sure that Kennedy realizes that when he files for the eviction, he does not give Imagination one penny back. I want to make that clear. If he returns any money to those bastards, then the entire deal is off. Got it?"

Dean scribbled some notes on a yellow legal pad. "Listen, Allen, maybe we should get Henderson involved with this. Real estate isn't really my forte."

"You're my point man," Allen said. "I don't care who you delegate it to, but I want you to deal with this traitorous little bug for me."

Dean set down his pencil. "You're spending a lot of money on a bug."

"Why do you care? It's just more money for your daughters' college funds."

"I understand this full-court press against Zack. However, it seems like you're wasting a lot of money to lease a building for no other purpose than to get Kennedy to evict Zack a little sooner."

Allen sat up straight and looked into Dean's eyes. "How I destroy Zack is none of your concern. Your only concern is to see that it gets done."

"Of course."

Allen got up from the chair. "I need a break," he said. "You worry too much. Besides, you're wrong about wasting money on that building near Great America Park. I do have plans for it."

He walked out without shutting the door behind him.

Twenty-four minutes later, he returned. He walked to Dean's sofa and sat down, bringing with him the faint odor of Chanel.

"As I mentioned to you yesterday, I'm working on some historical documentation," Allen said, his arm thrown over the back of the sofa, a grin playing at the corners of his mouth. "This will clearly establish the prior art claims, which will both sabotage and undermine any and all claims that Zack has to the originality of his designs. The documentation will be a combination of DisplayTechnik's archives and a paper that had been submitted at a previous conference some years ago. It will be done in such a way that no one will be able to say with absolute certainty that they hadn't seen it before. I'll know about this prior art because I received a copy of it from the original author, who was in my employ.

"But of course, until Zack made a move to make his own company, I'd forgotten all about it because there were so many other projects happening, and this had all been mere speculation by one of our previous wunderkinds. Little did I know that Zack was planning to use my own company's innovations against me. But when I learned what Zack was up to, I had to act." His right hand smacked into his left palm. "How dare he make plans to destroy me? How dare he make plans to lure away key engineers? Engineers that I'd trusted, provided for, some of whom I had personally recruited, giving them their first break in the Valley. I was shocked." Allen got up from the couch and stood in the office corner with his toes nearly touching the wall-to-ceiling windows on either side of him. Looking down onto Market Street, Allen seemed to be standing on a pinnacle suspended in air.

There was no doubt, Dean thought, the man was truly a maestro. Little wonder that he was touted as one of the most charismatic figures in Silicon Valley. And yet, despite Allen's best efforts to draw him in emotionally, he realized he didn't have the stomach for it. It started yesterday, a strange feeling creeping over him. They'd destroyed other companies using far worse tactics. Why did this latest campaign feel so different from the rest?

"At first," Allen continued in a low voice, "I refused to believe it. How could I? After all, Zack was my handpicked protégé, and I refused to believe that he could so underhandedly stab me in the back. If it were true, it meant someone in my inner circle had betrayed me, someone I'd trusted, someone I'd ... I'd seen as a son." Allen's voice faltered and faded away as he rocked on his heels, still staring out the window.

Dean didn't think the pause was merely for effect; there was some truth to it.

As a senior in high school, Dean had dated the daughter of an abusive alcoholic. Dean and Nicole would be snuggled on the couch when her already-drunk father staggered home to drink another couple of beers before passing out in his well-worn easy chair, snoring over the movie they'd been watching. The man had taken a shine to Dean, sharing in semi-drunken moments what he considered "secrets." How he overinflated the prices at his gas station, overcharged customers for car repairs, hid money from the IRS by simply taking cash right out of the till and then never reporting it. They wouldn't know and couldn't prove anything because they only knew how much he bought from his distributor, not the price he sold it for. He'd smile and look at Dean with watery drunken eyes, giggling at his own cleverness.

But Dean had seen another side to the man and heard from Nicole about the man's cruelty toward her, her sister, and her mother—who herself had fully retreated into her own drunken stupor. There was a part of Dean that wanted to rescue Nicole, and there was another part of him that was intrigued by her father. Dean had come from a relatively poor family, and the way Nicole's father threw his money around was beguiling.

His education saved him, literally. Dean had briefly considered marrying Nicole after they graduated from high school, but the acceptance letter from Stanford changed all that. He realized he had broader prospects in front of him, and he broke it off with

Nicole a month before the senior prom to go with someone else—who'd heard of his acceptance to Stanford and made her intentions obvious. The breakup hadn't gone well with Nicole or her family. She'd called him in tears, desperate to repair the relationship. Over her sobs, he heard her father in the background say, "I'll fix that son of a bitch." Soon after, his tires had been slashed, brake fluid emptied, sugar put in his gas tank. The attacks on his car only stopped when he moved four hours away by plane to Stanford, and even so, for his entire freshman year, he chose to ride a bicycle.

It was some years later that he met Marjorie. She'd been attracted to the handsome, confident law student. She was a psychology major, and in their quiet moments of afterglow, she'd sometimes probe into his past relationships. He usually didn't like to talk about such things, but she'd been a terrific listener. She told him that as an abuser, Nicole's father couldn't handle the fact that Dean had betrayed his trust. Abusers like him could only see the world in black and white: you either loved him or you hated him, you were either for him or against him. In his mental state, he literally could not see Dean in any way other than friend or mortal enemy, confidant or Judas.

"So I began some low-level probes into Zack's activities," Allen was saying. "I even approached my daughter, who was outraged that I could even suggest the idea. But then I showed her the fruits of my investigations—e-mails, receipts, and corporate filings. Then, during one of her overnight stays at his apartment, she accidentally saw proprietary drawings—stolen from DisplayTechnik—and she finally had to admit that I was right.

"Thus, I found out that Zack had been taking proprietary secrets from DisplayTechnik and claiming them for his own. He enlisted the help of that damned Ukrainian and the others to cover his tracks. And then, when everything was exposed through the seizure of material, I knew for certain that Zack had used my very own formula as the basis for his own. Oh, Dimitre had tweaked it a little, but it was obvious to me that they'd obtained the ideas from DisplayTechnik's own archives."

Dean sat silently, which Allen mistook for rapt attention, and launched back into his diatribe, which Dean only half listened to.

Something was wrong.

In this full-court press against Zack Penny and Imagination, some cardinal rule had been violated. It wasn't just that they were bending the legal rules; they'd done that numerous times before. Nor was it a rule of business ethics, because in business there were no rules—or ethics.

Allen had already won. He already had the TRO, and he was in the process of completely destroying Zack and his team. He had the magic goodies in his duffel bag, setting the wheels in motion to legally establish DisplayTechnik as the originator of this intellectual prize.

Looking at Allen, Dean realized he had found his way back to an abusive relationship. The feeling of this being wrong had nothing to do with the details of this case. It had more to do with the manner in which Allen spun the story—the tone of his voice, the menacingly arrogant smile that followed every pause. Allen was preaching the new display technology as if it were his private vision, his own creation.

Allen didn't act this way because he was arrogant, although he certainly was; he didn't act this way because he was filthy rich, which he also was; nor did he act this way because he wanted to provide a confident façade to his employees, although he did. No, Allen acted this way because he had such utter contempt for the world that he assumed that anyone who had a good idea would be too stupid to understand how to leverage it.

That's how dictators thought. That's how Nicole's father had thought. Allen couldn't let Zack go, because it meant that Zack didn't slavishly follow him. Marjorie was right. Allen couldn't let Zack be successful because he couldn't see Zack as anything other than the enemy now.

There was a thud.

Dean looked up and saw Allen standing over the albino elephant, the figurine lying sideways on the thick carpet. Allen smiled at him contemptuously and made no move to pick it up.

He had to be stopped, Dean told himself.

The very thought shocked the hell out of him.

Dean rose from his chair and retrieved the elephant. He couldn't see any cracks in the delicate tusks or trunk. As he put the elephant back in its place, Allen resumed his oration.

Dean retreated behind his desk and listened to the maestro's lecture with rehearsed attentiveness.

CHAPTER THIRTY-TWO

Zack sat with Paul, Jeremy, and John and Molly Baker on the back deck, enjoying the cool evening breeze. The three New York investors had left about an hour after John had arrived, retiring to the Hilton in nearby Pleasanton after canceling their previous reservation in Santa Clara. Apparently the three-hour time difference had finally caught up with them. Once the investors left, the group filled John in about the criminal charges.

Zack let Paul and Jeremy do the talking. Despite the warm California day, his hands felt cold, as though icicles were shooting through his knuckles. No one had asked about his private conversation with Mary Anne. He had already decided not to disclose Mary Anne's confession to anyone, even if they asked. He supposed he should have been bothered by that thought—but he wasn't.

Jeremy had no criminal law experience; hence, they had to find a second lawyer. Before he left, Dickens had offered to help with the criminal defense in addition to supporting Jeremy with the civil suit. Considering the shit storm that Dickens and the others had to absorb, Zack thought they had taken it all remarkably well. Almost too well. Then again, he didn't know what the three wise men were thinking, and he wondered what they would say when they got to the hotel. An exit strategy? Given the situation, who could blame them for wanting to back out? Zack felt sick at the thought. If they did, Imagination wouldn't have any money left, and he'd be abandoned to defend a criminal case on his own meager savings. He'd last less than a week.

"You know, I think it's pretty damn convenient that Zack gets served just as the boys from New York arrive," Paul said. "I wonder who got tipped off?"

"I don't buy it," Zack said. "The only people who knew when the investors were arriving are the people on this sundeck and the principal engineers."

"Well, it's still one hell of a coincidence."

"What are you implying, Paul?" John said. "That one of us gave it up to Allen and the D.A.?"

"You got to admit, it has the same taste as when we got the civil complaint on our first day."

"I don't think anyone here would do that," Molly said firmly. "And I don't think Dimitre or Jimmy or Jerry would say anything either. They're entirely too loyal to Zack."

"Yeah, but Jimmy's girlfriend apparently tipped off Mary Anne as to where we met," Paul said.

"Okay, okay." Zack waved his hand. "Enough of this. I can just imagine Allen grinning like a Cheshire cat, hoping we'll tear down our loyalties to each other."

"Maybe it's something else," Paul said, in a suddenly hushed voice. "Maybe our phones are tapped. The sundeck as well. Electronic surveillance in our homes."

"Don't you think that's a bit paranoid?" John said.

"I don't think it's paranoid at all," Paul said. "Look at the facts. The TRO, the search on our homes, the plant being shut down, and now this criminal charge."

"Don't worry, we'll have our day in court," Jeremy said.

Paul rolled his eyes. "Yeah, that'll save us."

Jeremy rose out of his patio chair. The wind picked up, tossing his combed hair over onto the wrong side. He brushed the long strands of hair back into place. "If you'll excuse me, I'm going to go make a few phone calls inside." The glass door slammed shut.

"We should get this place swept," Paul went on. "Be sure that it's clean. I know some guys."

Zack raised his eyebrows. Where does one find "guys" like that? Clearly, there were things about his partner he didn't know. He was about to say something more when the inevitable question came.

"So, are you going to tell us?" Paul said, waving for everyone to follow him over to the backyard fence line. The group obeyed, suddenly infected with his paranoia.

"Tell you what?" Zack said.

"Oh, for Christ's sake. You know everyone here is too polite to ask. What the hell did you and Mary Anne talk about outside?"

"It's personal."

"You're kidding, right? Let's do a recap, shall we? Your girlfriend waltzes into our meeting just after Allen gives you a criminal complaint. And then, you run after her like her ass was a candied apple and you were a starving mule."

Zack saw Molly look away. "I think you can skip the tasteless remarks," he said.

"She knew all along about the criminal charge, didn't she?"

Zack took a deep breath. He really didn't want to talk about this and considered telling Paul to lay off. But he couldn't think of a way to distract the focus.

"Well?" Paul pursued.

"I don't know. I'd like to think that she didn't. If she did, I don't think she believed Allen would go forward with it."

"That's double-talk if there ever was any. I bet she even helped dear old dad prepare the case against you."

Paul was right. She had. He couldn't protect her anymore. Their relationship was over. Zack explained the conversation, all the while staring down into the valley below. When he was finished, he saw Molly's eyes were teary. At least someone understood a little of what he was going through.

"How much does this change things?" Paul said.

"Well, if Mary Anne was telling the truth and she just recorded some document numbers, then not too much," Zack said. "After all, I did take work home with me. Hell, everyone did. I think that's believable. The problem is, it doesn't look good. It does look like I was stealing secrets."

"Well, no wonder he was so well-prepared," Paul said. "He knew all about our business plan, our investors, our bank, our financial state of affairs. And now, thanks to the TRO, he has all of *our* proprietary drawings and hardware and all the rest. Even the polymer formulations."

"Yes, but thanks to the US marshals, it's all safely under lock and key," Zack said. "And as far as protecting our idea goes, they're better than a patent."

"Why's that?" Molly asked.

"Because they have guns."

Chapter Thirty-Three

Allen looked up as the kitchen door of the Golden Palace swung open, releasing a torrent of smells and sounds. High-pitched voices going up and down the musical scale could be heard above the clanging of pots, woks, and stacked dishes. Even though the smell was pleasant, it had a heavy body that quickly permeated anything it came in contact with.

There was a shout, deeper in tone than the others were. A few moments later, a busboy came out of the kitchen and put two cups and a teapot on the table where Allen and Sandy were seated. He went back to his station, wiping his hands on a dirty apron.

Despite being British, Allen hated tea. For one thing, the color bothered him. During afternoon tea back on the Isle, a boyhood friend had once remarked that it looked like piss, and ever since, he had a hard time not remembering that comment. Also, the sight of leaves collecting at the cup bottom annoyed him. He liked things to be clean. Had the Chinese never heard of tea bags?

Allen snapped his fingers at the bartender and in moments had his scotch. "What have you got for me?" he asked Sandy.

Sandy fumbled with the clasp of his old leather briefcase. The release button was stuck. He couldn't budge the button, and his finger continued to slide off the worn metallic edge. He grabbed a spoon to try to extract the locking mechanism. Allen watched him with amusement. Sandy worked carefully, his fondness for the old briefcase evident. Tiny sweat beads populated his wide forehead; he was aware of Allen's scrutiny.

"Why don't you take that piece of junk and toss it in the bay? Get yourself a real briefcase from Louis Vuitton."

Allen watched him continue to struggle with the case. He'd worked with the man in many different situations and had always found his single-mindedness amazing. He'd be the only person still hanging up clothes on a clothesline as a tornado raced toward him.

Click. The locking mechanism finally gave way. Sandy smiled triumphantly and pulled out a bunch of papers. He pushed the untouched teapot to one side and set photocopies of program summaries of various American Society of Chemical Engineers' Conferences in front of Allen.

"I haven't got all of them yet," Sandy confessed. "I've located nine of the past twelve years. Before then, it gets a little sketchy. I've only managed to find five others. You know, you'd kind of think that engineers would do a better job of keeping organized records."

Allen scanned through each program summary, studying the topics, and placed them in two separate piles: possibilities and non-possibilities.

"From what I can tell," Sandy said, "one program's missing entirely, from seven years ago. Apparently, the firm that the ASCE hired to record the sessions disappeared, and their records are MIA."

Allen looked up. "You don't say."

"Yep."

"Well, that's tempting, but I think it's a mistake. We need to be absolutely sure of where we're inserting this. The last thing we want is to claim it was inserted only to have someone turn up with full transcripts of every panel discussion and poster session."

Sandy nodded. "That's just as well. I was running into a lot of dead-ends with that one."

Allen continued to read. After ten minutes, he was finished.

"Two or three of the conferences look like good candidates. That one in Carmel nine years ago looks especially promising. Some of the poster sessions dealt with polymers of one sort or another."

Allen pulled a disk out of his jacket pocket and handed it to Sandy.

"I've written the poster submission. Start working on the presentation. Give me a call tomorrow when you get more conferences for me to look at. But for the time being, let's plan to go with the Carmel conference."

Sandy gathered up the papers in the non-possibilities pile. "You know, you still haven't told me what's so damn special about this polymer stuff."

Allen winked. "There was a guy named Fong. His family was originally from Hong Kong. He was a shark who could swim with no restrictions. And do things without any sign of remorse or convictions.

"Screw you, Allen," Sandy said.

"Been tried, my friend. Been tried. Didn't turn out all that well." Allen chuckled, got up, and threw a twenty-dollar bill on the table. He clapped an appreciative hand on Sandy's shoulder and gave it a squeeze. "This is a promising start. Have a good night. Don't let the cockroaches bite—especially in this place. I hear they have rabies."

━━━━━━━━━━━━━━

Charlotte Henley heard the car in the drive and then heard the car door slam. When she opened the front door, she saw Mary Anne coming around the bend in the sidewalk. The poor girl's eyes were so red and swollen it looked like she'd been sobbing, the black mascara accentuating the paths of the tears. Charlotte opened her arms and Mary Anne rushed forward, breaking into deep, shuddering sobs. Charlotte embraced her daughter, gently at first and then more firmly. They stood there for some time, Charlotte trying to remember the last time she'd held Mary Anne like this. After a few moments, she guided her inside, quietly telling Carl en route to take the night off, and he left without a word. They moved to the couch in the den, where she held Mary Anne for a few more minutes until her sobs subsided.

"I ... I have to confront Allen," Mary Anne said. "I have to make him tell the truth."

Charlotte stroked the back of her daughter's head. Mary Anne had such lovely, silky hair, just like she used to. "And what is the truth?" she said.

"What you were trying to tell me over the weekend—that this temporary restraining order is nothing but a fabrication. Zack's not in direct competition with him. He has to stop this insanity." Mary Anne sat up suddenly. "Did you know that Zack received a criminal summons today?"

"For what?"

"Stealing trade secrets from DisplayTechnik."

"I see."

"You don't exactly seem surprised." Mary Anne stood up.

Charlotte shook her head. "Nothing Allen does surprises me anymore."

Mary Anne walked into the grand hallway. Charlotte watched her march past the mounted Confederate soldier, hearing her shoes clap on the marble floor. She got up and followed her to the kitchen.

Mary Anne was leaning against the walnut cabinet by the kitchen's main door, a Diet Pepsi in her hand and a determined look on her face. Charlotte went to the sink and filled a copper kettle and then put it on the gas stove. There was an immediate whoosh as the flame tickled the side of the kettle.

"I need to convince him to drop the charges against Zack," Mary Anne said. "And the restraining order too. He has no right to do what he's doing."

"I'm confused. You spent the weekend defending your father. And now all of a sudden, he has no right. But before ... he did?"

"Before he did because that was when I thought that Zack was stealing Allen's people and designs."

"He did that. *N'est-ce pas?*"

"No, wrong. He didn't take the engineers; they followed him."

"That's semantics," Charlotte said, eyeing her daughter. "Just like falling in love or being in love."

"Mother! All weekend *you* defended Zack, and now you're being difficult just to be difficult." Mary Anne slammed the can down, soda splashing over the counter and then oozing out in a bubbling eruption. "Look, Zack hasn't done anything wrong!"

"But, certainly, you have."

"What?"

"You heard me. What you and Zack had was special. How could you help your father set up Zack? That is incredible. Even though you've told me, I still find it impossible to believe."

Mary Anne reached for a tissue on the table and wiped under her eyes. When she tossed the used tissue on the side plate, Charlotte saw it was smeared with black streaks.

"Live free or die," Mary Anne said, trying to sound defiant.

"Pardon?"

"Live free or die. It's the state motto for New Hampshire, where Zack grew up. A week from last Sunday—"

The kettle started screaming. Charlotte took the kettle off the burner and filled two mugs with peppermint tea. She handed a mug to Mary Anne.

"Go on," Charlotte said, sitting down at the table.

Mary Anne raised the mug to her lips but then put it back on the table. "We had this terrible argument about living free or dying with Allen's company. A really stupid conversation. I don't know what got us started. Maybe I started it, I don't know. I was word fencing with Zack, trying to see if he was going to betray Allen."

Charlotte couldn't help but smile. There was some of her in Mary Anne after all. "You mean, knowing his Boy Scout ethics, you wanted to see if you could get it out of him?"

"Now that I think back on it, it was quite insane, wasn't it? I always poked fun at him, but I guess his views were genuine. I don't know why I wanted to tear him down. Why couldn't I have just trusted him?"

"Because of your father. Don't you see? Allen set you up. When he first got an inkling that Zack might be leaving, he felt betrayed. So the natural step for him was to hurt Zack back—and a hundred times as badly as he had been hurt. So he dragged you into it because he knows you're like Pandora. He made you curious, made you wonder if Zack really would do it, knowing full well it would eat away at you until you couldn't take it. Because that's how he raised you. Mary Anne, you don't know how to trust. You don't know how to forgive. You never learned it, and by God, I've forgotten it."

Mary Anne looked at her

"I know one parent isn't supposed to say bad things about the other—unless it's true. This is all happening because he's molded us not to trust anyone. We've taken on his characteristics." Charlotte sighed. "It's a weakness of being a woman. We tend to emulate the men we're with more than they emulate us."

Mary Anne sniffed derisively. "That's real modern of you."

"Well, it must be true. Look at us. We're always on the defensive. We don't even trust each other, and we're mother and daughter. So how could you ever possibly trust Zack?"

Mary Anne stared straight ahead. "And now, I've become a witness against him. God, I could end up putting him in jail for something that he didn't do."

Gently, Charlotte reached over and took one of her hands. "My dear, your father would never count solely upon your testimony to put Zack in jail. He has something else; I'm sure of it."

Mary Anne smiled at her through her tears. "Yes, I suppose you're right. We weak women just can't be trusted, can we?"

"Now who's old-fashioned?"

"Yes, but I was joking." Mary Anne gave a little sniffle. "I'll let him have it this evening when he gets home. I'll tell him he's perpetrated this enormous lie about Zack long enough and that he must stop this entire lunacy right now."

"Mary Anne," Charlotte said slowly, "your father will not stop anything."

"Yes, he will! When I tell him what I know," Mary Anne said, speaking faster, "what I feel, then he'll change his mind. I know he will."

Charlotte took a sip of her tea. The peppermint scent filled her nose, making her want to sneeze. She took another sip and then put the mug down. "Don't continue to be a fool. I thought we were finally getting somewhere. You and I both know your father. He will not change his mind. He will merely say that *you* don't know all the details. Then he'll tell you that it's already in motion and it's up to the courts to decide, and that if you're right, then the courts will vindicate Zack. If not, then Zack will get what he deserves. That you need to trust the system."

"Then I'll go to the district attorney's office and tell them that the criminal charges against Zack must be dropped."

"Sometimes your foolishness astounds me. Listen to yourself! What credibility do you possibly have? You already signed a written declaration that supported your father's claims. Plus, you don't have any proof that can help Zack."

Mary Anne straightened up. There was a quiet defiance in her body language, even in defeat.

"Well, I have to do something. I can't sit by and let Allen destroy Zack's life. I've got to try to help him."

Charlotte admired the determination she saw in her daughter. "I think it's time that you and I started to trust each other again. Wouldn't you agree?"

Mary Anne looked at her for a long moment before answering, "Yes."

"Then I want you to trust me on this matter. Do not confront your father about this. Promise me."

Mary Anne just continued to look at her, obviously weighing things carefully. "I won't promise," she said. "But I won't talk to him tonight about it. I'll agree to that much."

"I guess that will have to do. Let me go do some thinking. Between the two of us, I believe we can fix this mess. I truly do."

Charlotte ran a hand across her daughter's shoulders and then left her. She started up to her room, stopping for a moment at the top of the stairs to listen for sounds from the kitchen. Mary Anne didn't emerge, and Charlotte guessed she was fixing herself something to eat. She hurried to her room and shut the door. She picked up a small address book and flipped through it until she found the correct phone number and then dialed it quickly before she could change her mind. Her heart throbbed, waiting for him to come on the line.

"Charlotte, how are you?"

"I'm fine, thank you."

"If you're looking for Allen, he just left a few minutes ago."

"Yes, I know. Your receptionist told me. Dean, are you free tomorrow night by any chance?"

Chapter Thirty-Four

True to his word, Paul escorted Nigel, his electronic surveillance buddy, onto the Bakers' deck early Tuesday morning. Nigel wore a San Francisco Giants baseball cap backward, with a headset strapped on. Zack watched him tiptoe around the sundeck, gracefully avoiding electrical cords and cables. Next on his hit list was the house itself, along with its phones, followed by the backyard garden and fence that staked the plunge line to the valley.

"Are you really believing this is necessary?" Dimitre asked him, a bushy eyebrow raised at Nigel.

"Paul doesn't like how Allen seems to know more about us than he should. And neither do I."

"Well, is good then."

Zack had caught himself about to say that Paul didn't like how the process server showed up with the criminal complaint, but then he remembered he hadn't told the engineering team about that yet. He planned to fill them in sometime today, but right now, he was enjoying the escape that the engineering process offered, and trying not to feel guilty. So far, no one had asked how the meeting with the investors had gone—that, at least, was a bit of good news—but he didn't really feel like talking about it. Yep, they'd missed a real party yesterday.

Zack caught sight of Paul again, who was standing by the glass door and waving him over. Jeremy was pacing behind him, and from the heated look on Paul's face, Zack guessed they'd been arguing. Zack took a step toward the house, but Dimitre caught his arm.

"Zack, I must talk with you about something."

"Uh ... not right now; let's do it later. Okay?"

"No, is really important. How about two of us going to get coffee? What do you say?"

Zack was distracted by Jeremy's walking disgustedly away and Paul practically jumping up and down for him to come into the house.

Dimitre's face was screwed up in an anxious way. Now what? God, there was always something, some new fire that needed to be put out. Somehow, when he envisioned himself a CEO, he never pictured himself as having to handle these sorts of problems. His daydreams always entailed meeting reporters and making statements to shareholders about the company's progress and congratulating his engineers on their latest brilliant innovation. They had never been about restraining orders and criminal charges.

"Sure, okay," he told the Russian, "but it'll have to wait a bit."

Dimitre opened his mouth, but Zack stepped past him and navigated over the cables to the back door. For the second time that morning, he felt guilty. So much for always having time for his best friend.

The Bakers' living room was even more cluttered than the back deck, wall-to-wall with cushions, bags, and knickknacks. He nearly fell over a pair of bright orange bags that were filled with rice and dried corn, evidence of Molly's latest buying spree in Cancun, where she'd bought up the entire shop. He followed Paul and Jeremy into the Bakers' home office, located off the living room.

Paul was the last to enter the office, swinging the door shut behind him. "About an hour ago, I got served this eviction notice for our Santa Clara facility."

"Wha—? Here?" Zack said.

"Yep. Seems like everybody and their third cousins know we're here."

"Why are they evicting us?" Zack said. "And why didn't you tell me immediately?"

"Oh, you tell him," Paul said to Jeremy. He sank into an old cloth-covered armchair with wooden arms.

"Well, before we talked to you," Jeremy said, "I wanted to find out a bit more about it. So while you were outside with the boys, I called a buddy of mine who works at the law firm of Litchfield and Crumm. They represent Jason Kennedy, who's the principal property manager of our building. Anyhow, my buddy tells me that we have three days to leave the facility; otherwise, his firm's going to file an unlawful proceedings detainer."

"Leave the facility? You've got to be kidding? They want to throw us out? Just like that?"

"Just like that."

"Based upon what?"

"My buddy says it's linked to the TRO."

Zack stared at Jeremy. "But … how can they do this?"

"To be honest, this thing blew me away," Jeremy said. "You paid a healthy six months' rent in advance, so I would have thought that they'd wait for the outcome of the TRO before deciding anything. I mean, they have guaranteed income for the next six months. But then I looked through the terms of your lease, which was attached to the eviction notice." Jeremy shook his head solemnly. "You guys really should have had me look at it before you signed it. I mean, there's a difference between saving some legal fees and being stupid."

Zack had never heard Jeremy take a tone like that. This was getting to everyone. Zack glanced at Paul. Leaving Jeremy out of the loop had been Paul's idea; he said he'd looked over plenty of lease agreements before.

Jeremy said, "There's a clause in there that states that a breach could occur if there are activities that may defame the landlord or the property management company, or somehow devalue the property."

"So?" Zack and Paul said in unison.

"Well, putting padlock and chains on your building with yellow police tape around it could easily be construed as defaming the property management company. It looks like they're in bed with criminals. We could lose all the advance payments."

"Maybe it's time we defamed Henley's ugly face," Paul said through gritted teeth.

That was one of the dumbest things he'd heard Paul say in a long time—and that was saying a lot. Zack took the empty wastepaper basket and overturned it for a chair. He didn't like the way all their voices had been rising. "What else did your buddy say?" Zack asked Jeremy in a calm voice.

"Not too much else, really. It's not his case. He just did some quick checking for me as a favor. We used to play poker together when we were undergrads. However, he did say that one of the senior partners was taking a personal interest in the case. He thought that was kind of odd."

"Odd, my ass," Paul said. "That SOB Henley has orchestrated this whole fucking mess."

"What happens next?" Zack said.

"We have 'til Friday. If we can't settle it by then, they'll file to evict us. I assume it won't be settled, so we should get a notice on Monday to appear at a hearing in maybe fifteen or thirty days."

"Marvelous," Paul said. "It's going to be a busy month."

"In the municipal courts, cases involving eviction from property have a high priority. Court dockets tend to get cleared in a hurry."

"Well, well. Aren't we fucking blessed?" Paul said. "Glad to see the system's working so well."

Paul flopped backward into the armchair, making particles of dust rise in the air.

"Listen, guys," Jeremy said, "you're my friends, but ... this is just getting way out of my league. We're getting attacked on too many sides. With the new eviction, Henley trying to put Zack in jail, and us still having to fight the original TRO, I'm not sure if I can handle everything."

"Hey, don't panic," Zack said. "You're getting some help from the New York sharks, remember?"

———————

Dimitre watched Zack disappear into the house. He shook his head, feeling very much the second-class citizen. He had been agonizing over the formula since Saturday, finally giving up and resigning himself to telling Zack that there was a serious problem. This was no small admission on his part. Dimitre never liked to admit that he was wrong because he rarely was. He wasn't egotistical; it's just that he always believed that he should be able to defend whatever decision he made, especially because he only made decisions after a long process of clear and logical thinking. Besides, with Anna in his life, he always needed a ready answer for whatever he did.

Dimitre walked over to Jimmy and Jerry, but quickly bored of watching them work and went to his own station, where he brought up the test program's results. He still hoped to find the solution without having to talk to Zack about it. Vanity, perhaps, but also the dread of piling more on Zack than the man could bear.

As he scrolled through the rows of numbers, he wished for a moment he was back at his old workstation at DisplayTechnik, if for no other reason than to have a faster computer. Something he'd never told Zack, or even Anna, was that he'd used DisplayTechnik's computers to run the initial test. No one would be able to deduce anything from the test unless they knew specifically what it was he was testing. For all anyone knew, he could have been figuring out his taxes for the year 2042, which some people actually did for fun.

It didn't violate any clauses of his contract because he'd done it after hours. But now, as he sat there watching the numbers, he wondered if the numbers came out differently because the tiny laptop simply did not have the power of the supercomputer. What if there were variables that were unaccounted for because the laptop simply didn't have the computing power to handle the stream of data? Dimitre had thought of this on the first day he'd encountered the problem but had dismissed it. It was simple math; a calculator was a calculator. It just took the little machine a little longer. But still, what if?

Another paranoia was creeping in too. What if DisplayTechnik's big computer had been wrong? It was an older model, though it had been constantly upgraded. What if, in all those upgrades, some wires had gotten crossed? The human element. Or even more paranoid, what if someone at DisplayTechnik had set them up for failure? Was it possible they watched the systems that closely? He didn't think so. The calculator program of the supercomputer was just that—a calculator. And even if they did monitor the calculator, it would mean that they would have to know why he was entering the numbers that he did, and that would involve reading his mind. And he was relatively sure they couldn't do that.

He closed the laptop. He would go talk to Zack. There was never anything Paul had to say that Zack would not be happy to escape from. Although considering the news he was about to break, even Paul would be a welcome tonic.

When he opened the door, he heard angry voices coming from down the hall. He navigated his way quietly toward the office and heard Paul say something about being "fucking blessed." He walked quietly down the hallway and stood just outside the door.

"You're my friends," someone said, "but ... this is just getting way out of my league. We're getting attacked on too many sides. With the new eviction, Henley trying to put Zack in jail, and us still having to fight the original TRO, I'm not sure if I can handle everything."

"Hey, don't panic," he heard Zack respond lightly. "You're getting some help from the New York sharks, remember?"

Dimitre felt his heartbeat pick up. Zack? Going to jail? Eviction?

"Yes, I know. And that's a good thing, because we're going to need some serious legal firepower to fight this war. I hope your investors are ready for a siege."

Dimitre heard a deep intake of breath before Jeremy continued, "Quite frankly, I have never seen anything quite like this before."

An eviction? But they'd just moved in. Hadn't Zack said they were set up there for six months? And why would Zack go to jail? Dimitre had stumbled onto something he wouldn't have believed a few days ago: Zack had not been honest with them. He felt a surge of anger. What else hadn't he and the other engineers heard? He'd told Anna he was worried about leaving DisplayTechnik. He had sacrificed all of their security to follow Zack's dream. Dimitre didn't need the same freedoms that Zack did. Hell, he had lived most of his life in the Soviet Union; Allen was a prince by their standards. A pompous ass, but still there were other things much worse. Now, Zack was acting just like Allen. Hiding things, lying, and all the rest.

Dimitre leaned against the wall, utterly stunned, and then jerked up straight when the doorframe creaked.

In a moment of panic, he quickly knocked on the door, announcing his presence. "Zack?" he said, opening the door and sticking his head in.

"Hey, buddy," Zack said, quickly standing. "What's up?"

Dimitre hesitated. He looked first at Zack and then at Paul, who was also rising to his feet. "I, uh ... I am wanting your opinion on the ... robot-handling interface with the evaporator."

"Sure. I'll be just a few more minutes here, then come join you on the patio deck. Okay?"

Dimitre wanted desperately to ask him what was going on but also felt he couldn't take the disappointment if Zack didn't tell him. So he merely nodded and left, sure his face had given him away.

Walking back onto the deck, an uneasy feeling settled in his stomach with all the subtlety of an anchor through a plate-glass window.

Zack looked at the other two, his ears burning.

"That guy has a screw loose," Paul said, brushing back his hair. "I really wonder about him."

"He's one of the smartest polymer scientists in the world," Zack said.

"Yeah, well maybe, but he's still a lunatic." Paul glanced at Jeremy, who was closest to the door. "For Christ's sake, shut the goddamn door."

Paul lowered his voice. "Do you think he heard us?"

"He didn't give that impression," Jeremy said, returning to his seat. "What would it matter if he did?"

"Oh, I don't know," Paul sneered, "maybe he might be a bit concerned when you started to panic about needing heavier legal artillery? Or the three days before we're kicked out?"

"Okay, okay," Zack said. "Let's cool down a few degrees. I don't think Dimitre heard us. If he did, it wouldn't be like him not to ask what the hell was going on. I think he just happened to walk in at a bad time."

"How do you know?" Paul said.

"Because I can read minds!" Zack shot back. "I *don't* know. But it doesn't do us any good to speculate, and more importantly, it doesn't solve the problems that we're facing." Zack took a deep breath. "Look. I'm going to go see what Dimitre wanted, and after that, let's talk again."

Zack walked out of the home office. He'd promised his friend Dimitre that they'd always take the high moral ground together. Always. That's what they'd promised each other—no corporate politics, no bullshit, and no lies. But he realized that right now, he was too tired. He couldn't bear to give his team one more piece of bad news, especially since there wasn't anything anyone could do about it at the moment. He'd talk to them later when he knew more, or maybe by then he'd have something positive to give them.

When he stepped outside, the morning sunlight disoriented

him enough so that he bumped into Paul's buddy, who was on one knee, packing up his gear. The back of his Cal-Tech T-shirt was soaked.

"Find anything?"

The guy shook his head, forming a zero with his thumb and index finger. Looking around, Zack located Dimitre and Jerry Steiner huddled over Jimmy's workstation. Jimmy's head was barely visible, his red hair poking up between the shoulders of the two men. Jerry looked up and motioned Zack over. Dimitre remained hunched over, staring intently at something on the screen.

Back to work, Zack thought. What they *should* be doing.

CHAPTER THIRTY-FIVE

For the first time in more than a week, Mary Anne sat at the breakfast table with her mother and father. Carl the butler had nearly poured tea into Allen's black coffee mug. That was the closest thing possible to a mishap.

Mary Anne watched Allen work his way through breakfast. Every bit of sausage was chewed thoroughly, as if it were the last meal he would ever enjoy. He drank his coffee greedily, pouring the liquid deep into the back of his throat. She desperately wanted to talk to him, but she felt uncomfortable in her father's presence. If Allen noticed her unease, he did a good job of disguising it.

When she finally worked up the courage to speak, Charlotte broke in with some tidbit on the weather. Mary Anne tried a second time, but her mother interrupted again. Indifferent, Allen continued to speed-read through the *Mercury News*, the *New York Times*, and the *Wall Street Journal*, with a final glance at the *USA Today*'s sports section. It was one of his few frivolous pleasures. Then he glanced at his watch, got up from the table, muttered a "good-bye," and left.

"I thought we agreed that you wouldn't say anything to your father," Charlotte said.

"I didn't," she said, an indignant expression on her face. Her mother's eyes were bloodshot. It was far too early in the morning for her to be up and about. When Mary Anne was small, the family had always shared breakfast together. These days, that was a rare event.

"Only because I didn't let you," Charlotte said, stifling a yawn.

"I know what I said last night, but I made a terrible mistake by not asking Zack outright if he was starting a new company. If I don't ask Allen, then I'll just be repeating the same mistake."

"You're wrong. You'll be making a new mistake. The last time I saw Zack, I told him about your great granddaddy's views on the Civil War. Confederate soldiers, boys really, younger than Zack, were losing their lives like flies in a frog pond."

"What does that have to do with me confronting Allen?"

"Everything. Your father's chasing poor Zack all the way to his hole. And he isn't going to let up—not for you, not for me, not for anyone. If you ask your father to stop, it will only make things worse, because there's nothing more intoxicating to him than fear. Your fear. Zack's fear. If you talk with your father, you'll only give him his second wind."

Mary Anne shook her head at her mother. Everyone in this family is nuts, she thought.

CHAPTER THIRTY-SIX

Zack, along with Paul and Jeremy, had agreed to meet Dickens and the other investors Tuesday afternoon in a reserved meeting room of the Hilton Hotel in Pleasanton. Dickens had said he'd spend the morning consulting and the early afternoon with his Manhattan legal team.

At four o'clock, Zack led his two colleagues up the hotel escalator to the second floor. The pungent, unmistakable odor of vinegar wafted in from the restaurant, reminding him of his father buying fat, oil-drenched french fries in the Vermont sugar bush. He could almost taste them. As he tucked in his shirt, he noticed how loose his jeans hung on his hips, even though the belt was tightened to the last notch. He reckoned that wasn't a good sign.

The white-haired investors were waiting for them, sitting on the curved outside of a continuous, C-shaped conference table. Tall, perspiring pitchers of water sat on each segment of the conference table. A good idea, Zack thought, feeling an irritation in the back of his throat—except that there weren't any drinking glasses. He, Paul, and Jeremy took their seats, side by side, directly across from Dickens and his colleagues.

Dickens leaned forward, his hands folded in front on the table. Here in the conference room, he looked much more grave and businesslike than he had sipping vodka in the sunlight on the Bakers' back porch. Dickens glanced at his two colleagues, flanked on either side of him, and then turned his attention to Zack.

"I just spent the last few hours speaking to my legal friends back in New York. In fact, we all did. The conversation led us down paths that we didn't know existed."

Zack felt his heart begin to pound.

"In fact, one of Ted's general attorneys," Dickens nodded to the man to his left, "has had several dealings with Santa Clara County. He even knows this Judge Rafkin quite well; seems they were in the same year at Harvard. We discovered that your Judge Rafkin is on holiday. Gone windsurfing or something, which seems awfully athletic, considering this judge can barely touch his toes—so I've been told. But no matter, for the moment, he's out of the picture."

Dickens touched his silvery goatee. "We also have some unfortunate news to report," he said. "This whole sorry mess of a TRO is going to be extended another sixty days."

"That can't be!" Paul said, standing up. "We haven't even formally responded to the original fucking TRO yet!"

A scowl creased Dickens's face. Zack tugged on the elbow of Paul's suit jacket. Reluctantly, Paul sat down.

"Well, that may be, son, but this pigeon's already out of the coop and heading south fast."

Sixty days. Zack was sure the moneymen were going to back out, even before he told them about the eviction notice. He kneaded his knuckles to stop his hands from trembling uncontrollably.

Surprisingly, of everyone in the room, Dickens looked the calmest.

"But this is impossible," Paul said. "We all heard the judge tell us we had twenty days to formally respond to the TRO. After that, we'd get our day in court to block any attempt at an injunction."

"You may get your day in court," Dickens said, "but it'll be three months before you'll see the inside of one."

"Jeremy, can they do this?" Zack said. "Can they just extend the TRO without consulting us?"

"I've never heard of this before," Jeremy said. "But I suppose it could be possible. I mean, I told you the entire TRO process is a throwback to the Spanish Inquisition."

"We're not in fucking Spain!" Paul said, slamming the table with his open palm. "This is Silicon Valley, America's dream factory, for Christ's sake! You don't burn people's dreams at the stake without a trial!"

Zack wiped away the sweat forming on his brow. "Do you have an explanation for this?" he asked.

Dickens whispered something to his colleague on his right.

"What did your New York friends say?" Zack said, panic rising.

Dickens leaned over to his colleague on his left.

"How could something like this happen?" Zack could feel his throat tighten, and he fought to clear it. He could have really used a drink of water.

"I don't know," Dickens said.

"Then, how do you know that this TRO extension gossip is even real?" Paul said, his voice rising an octave. "Aren't we supposed to get something more formal? We still do that in this country, don't we? Or is due process gone as well?"

"You'll get a notification," Dickens said. "You'll get one just prior to the expiration of the original thirty-day TRO. However, I don't agree with Jeremy that our legal system is reverting back to a witch hunt. I'm certain that there's a very valid reason for the TRO to be extended; we just don't know what it is yet. But obviously, something potentially serious has been uncovered."

Zack swallowed.

"This is bullshit," Paul said. "Utter bullshit."

"I agree, Mr. Ryerson. But that doesn't help us to remove Mr. Henley's boot from our ass."

It was the first time Zack had heard Dickens use that kind of language.

"Some of my friends back in Manhattan have been giving me an crash course on your former boss," Dickens said. "I must admit that I regret not having done more homework on the man prior to beginning our little venture. A costly one at that.

"It seems your Mr. Henley is something of an icon in these

parts. My friends tell me he likes to play rough, that he plays for keeps. Well, in New York, we've been known to play rough as well. Actually, I think that the concept was invented in New York City."

Dickens's Manhattan colleagues chuckled. Zack smiled politely but wasn't sure where Dickens was going with this.

"But unfortunately, we're not in New York," Dickens said. "Instead, we're here in California. It's hard to talk with people when the sun has baked their brains to the consistency of my granddaughter's pabulum. Who do we trust? Back in New York, it's easy. We know everybody. But here, we don't have as many influential friends."

Meaning they didn't have *any* influential friends.

"We can always find allies. It'll take some time, mind you, but we can get them. There may be a lot of high-tech masturbation on the West Coast, but NASDAQ and Dow Jones still tell them which hand to use."

Zack felt a smile creep across his face. Was he hearing all this right?

"I will tell you boys that when I agreed to help finance this little venture, I wasn't expecting to be sinking in mud before the ship even left the dock. Hell, we haven't done anything yet other than create that fancy doodad of yours that turns colors. Right now, we don't even have access to our factory. The only thing we do have is a lot of slick, baby-faced lawyers trying to get a piece of our collective asses. Is there anything else that I should be aware of?"

Oh shit, Zack thought. He'd been concentrating so intently on what Dickens was saying that the speech he'd carefully rehearsed on the drive to the hotel had completely disappeared.

"Well, actually … there is something that just came to our attention. We may have a problem with the building." Zack groaned inwardly. His rehearsed speech had been much better.

"Go on," Dickens said. "And don't spare the details."

"It seems that we may get evicted from our building," Zack said.

"Apparently, the marshals locking up the building doesn't sit too well with them."

"I see," Dickens said, pausing. "Well, since we've got to wait it out another two more months, perhaps that isn't such a bad thing."

Zack could only blink. *It isn't?*

"I assume we have a lease?"

"Yes, sir, but—"

"We paid a deposit, right?"

"More than that. We paid six months in advance to get a good deal, but there's a clause about defaming the landlord and—"

"Son, who do you think invented those clauses about defaming? Until New York City got established, Webster didn't even list the word 'defame' in the dictionary." Dickens waved it all away. "Not to worry, just a bunch of lawyer scare tactics. Once we get my New York legal friends involved, we'll set the record straight. That's angel cake. Anything else?"

Zack felt like saying, "Should there be?" Instead, he just shook his head and then looked away. He was fighting back tears. He couldn't think of a time when he'd ever been more grateful, and a feeling like he was back in New England, living in the safety of his parents' home, came over him. A few minutes ago, everything seemed lost. He'd come here today believing he'd be ecstatic if Dickens didn't run screaming from the room. Now, a new sense of hope filled him as he realized that they just might be able to get through this okay after all. It was a glimmer of hope, a mere wavering spark, but that was all he needed.

"Well, there is one thing." Jeremy cleared his throat and continued, "We haven't been deposed yet."

Dickens sat up straight. "Is that unusual?"

"Very unusual. Normally when the court issues a TRO, the other side is granted a turbo discovery. But none of us have been interviewed by any of Henley's lawyers, nor has there even been a request to do so. Frankly, I don't know what they're waiting for considering they've done everything else at a record pace."

"I do," Dickens said. "I told you boys that hardball was invented in New York. Henley can play party games and charades with the legal system; he can try to play pin the tail on my ass, if that's to his liking. But these are just stalling tactics. He's trying to drag this thing out and make us bleed. He knows he can't win legally, but he's hoping to wear you boys out. But he isn't going to wear me out. And I'll tell you why. I've built three companies from scratch while Allen Henley was still trying to figure out what college to go to. He's got nothing. On the other hand, we've got this super-duper polymer formula for making paper-thin televisions. Right?"

Zack and Paul nodded like bobblehead dolls, incredulous at this turn in their fortune.

"Absolutely!" Zack said. *We just might do this. We just might do this.*

CHAPTER THIRTY-SEVEN

The next afternoon Allen spat pistachio shells into the trash can next to Dean's feet as he read through a preliminary draft of the latest filing. Instead of saying something, Dean nudged the trash can away from his desk, hoping that Allen would get the message.

He didn't.

He continued to spit the shells where the trash can had been, speckling the yellow rug with beige half shells. Dean got up and dropped the trash can directly beside his client with a loud "thump."

"Ah. Thank you, much better," Allen muttered and went back to reading.

Dean sat back down and watched Allen crack the shells open with his teeth. The sharp nose, the triangular jaw, and the hazel eyes gave him the look of a bored bird of prey, killing time until it was time to hunt again. Only the close-cropped beard spoiled the image. If Allen was a raptor, what did that make him? A jackal feeding off of what was left from the kill? He supposed most people would argue that jackals chased eagles away from their kills, so a lawyer would have to be more like a crow or some other opportunistic animal that cleaned out the eagle's nest when it wasn't looking.

He supposed Zack could be considered one of those smaller birds. Banded together, even small birds could harass an eagle until it eventually dropped its prey. Unfortunately for Zack, he didn't know this particular eagle. Allen wouldn't ever let go, or if he did, he'd be all too happy to drop a fish in exchange for one small bird. Or a band of them, one at a time.

Dean's mind returned to the image of cleaning out Allen's nest when he wasn't looking. Was that some sort of Freudian slip? For the second time in as many days, he felt a slight twinge of guilt. Dean looked at the small clock on his desk. It was four twenty-nine. That gave him an hour before he needed to leave the office, affording him a full half hour to get to Ghirardelli Square. It was fifteen minutes more than he needed, but he was not about to be late.

He swallowed the lump in his throat, noticing the dry feeling in his mouth. Thoughts of the evening ahead came unbidden, and he tried to think of something else, feeling very transparent at the moment.

A jackal, that's what he was. Much more noble than a pesky crow, and certainly more dignified than a vulture. And the idea that he could chase Allen from his prey suited him just fine.

As Dean hunched over his desk, pretending to look over a copy of the same document that Allen had, he slyly glanced up. A few days ago, he would never have believed himself capable of a secret meeting with a client's wife. Well, he certainly wouldn't have met any other client's wife, but perhaps for Charlotte, he would still have made an exception.

How quickly a person's entire life can change. Just yesterday, he'd made the decision to stop Allen and his wanton destruction of Zack and his fledgling company. And then, barely half an hour later, Charlotte had called saying she wanted to meet tonight.

"Dean, are you free tomorrow night by any chance?" Those words had rung in his ears all day. He'd been so caught off guard that when he first heard them, he'd been immediately suspicious, stupidly wondering how Allen could have possibly pieced together his betrayal so quickly when he'd merely thought it but a few minutes before.

"I might be," he'd said, putting out a feeler that, even as he said it, he knew to be totally ridiculous. Of course, no one knew what he'd been thinking. Unless Allen had suspected him for some time. *Know your enemy* and all that Sun Tzu sorcery.

"Do you think you could be sure?" After replaying the conversation time and again in his head, he was sure that there'd been a smile behind Charlotte's question.

"I suppose it depends on what I need to be free for."

There was a pause. "It's something of a private matter, really. Besides, I was ... I was just thinking the other day that I don't see you enough and that it'd be nice to get together sometime for a social drink or two, perhaps over at McCormick and Kuleto's in Ghirardelli Square. Say around six?"

There was another pause, and Dean had been about to ask her for further details when he heard all he needed to know: "Allen won't be there."

Dean had often wondered over the years whether Charlotte knew of his terrible crush on her when Allen and she had first started dating. When they eventually married, he respected that, and she had always been the wife of his client, even though the crush lingered as a slow simmer. Hearing those words and their tone, he wondered once again whether he'd hidden his feelings as well as he'd thought he had.

"You don't say," he'd said, hoping he hadn't paused too long.

"Yes, and, well, I ask that you not tell him that we're meeting."

"All right," he'd said, trying to sound matter-of-fact.

"Promise?" Again, there was that smile in her tone.

"Sure. I promise."

His mind, though, was reeling with questions, the foremost being, "Should I bring Marjorie?" but he didn't have a clue how to ask it without sounding like he was implying something that might not be there.

"What's Marjorie doing tomorrow night?"

Was it a Henley trait to read minds? "Uh, well, let me think. You know, actually, I think Tuesdays are her bridge nights." What luck! Or did she already know this and was implying he not tell her either? "She gets together with some friends of hers—"

"That's fine. It'll just be the two of us then. That'll be nice." That southern-belle voice of hers had turned very sultry when she said "nice," with just the slightest pause before it. "Tomorrow at six?"

He'd hung up, completely and utterly dumbfounded—and not entirely sure he'd actually said, "Yes, I'm looking forward to it. I'll see you then."

Was he reading too much into the situation? His training as a lawyer told him not to let his emotions affect his thinking; he would simply have to wait to find out. But at the same time, he was looking forward to this evening's encounter more than any court case he had ever tried in his life.

Perhaps it was Fate taking a hand? Marjorie had come back from some women's conference years ago spewing, as she always did, whatever facile wisdom had been imparted. She usually did this for a week or two afterward. He often wondered if this was merely to prove to him that she'd actually attended, especially since the effects wore off in short order and were hardly "life-changing." But for days and days after this one overnight seminar, she'd been going on and on about the doors opening for you when you were on the right path.

These doors were clearly being thrown open.

In the early days of their relationship, Marjorie and he had often discussed each other's views of a higher power. Marjorie had been sure that there was a higher power, though she hesitated to call it "God," since she was a former Catholic and now hated the church, and admitting that there was a God might mean the church was right after all. Was it at all possible that there was some higher power somewhere "out there" guiding him now? After all, he'd only just decided to help Zack when the woman he'd been in love with during college was calling him out of the blue for a date. Was this a reward for right behavior? It seemed a trifle bizarre to be reminiscing about Marjorie's theological opinions when his mind was filling with graphic images of violating their marriage vows. It was equally bizarre to think that a higher power could be guiding him into something like that. But wasn't this what lovers were always talking about? Their joined destiny?

And perhaps it was the strangest thing of all that he was in a room with her husband—his biggest client—while daring to entertain all sorts of fantasies about what the evening might present.

Nervousness and excitement warred with one another inside him. He picked up a pen and began doodling to hide it. Allen didn't even glance in his direction. Fortunately, Allen was not one to notice Dean's best suit jacket hung on a hanger by the door, nor that his shoes had recently been polished. Even if he had, Allen would merely assume that he was trying to make his own move on the young paralegal and steal her out from under him.

Dean looked at the clock again. Four thirty-one. Only two minutes had passed?

Annoying. It was truly a magical clock, though. By billing in ten-minute segments and always rounding up, an attorney could charge for one hundred minutes in a normal hour, as long as he limited himself to six-minute increments per case—theoretically, of course, because no one ever worked on a case for six minutes before setting it aside. Still, there were numerous times throughout the day when he might glance through two or three different cases in an hour's time, which, magically, extended an hour by another ten or twenty minutes. He did some quick calculations on a notepad, content to have something to distract himself from Charlotte.

If he managed just thirty minutes of rounded-up time per day, that was one hundred fifty minutes per week, or two point five hours. Multiply that by fifty-two weeks in a year, and that came to one hundred thirty hours. If he multiplied that by his going fee of five hundred dollars an hour, that came to sixty-five thousand for the year. Phantom minutes alone easily paid for his personal secretary and part of the salary of one of his interns. Maybe he ought to give one of them a raise. Or maybe he ought to be a bit more careful.

He wondered why clients never caught on. Maybe it was because, like Allen, they were too engrossed with their own affairs and arrogantly assumed that an attorney focused solely on their case to the exclusion of others.

"Nice work," Allen said suddenly. "In fact, excellent work; I only made two minor corrections." He closed the file and tossed it onto the edge of his desk. It teetered for a moment but didn't fall. Dean snatched it before it could spill all over the floor.

Allen dug inside his jacket and extracted a disk. "Here, take this. It has one of DisplayTechnik's technical papers that was presented several years ago at the American Society of Chemical Engineers—actually at a poster session. It talks about the future of polymer formulations, laying the foundation for the next revolution of the FPD industry. It refers to using polymers as the replacement for glass in displays such as television and the building blocks to dope polymers to accept the flow of holes and electrons."

Dean stood up and took the disk from Allen's outstretched hand.

"It's added ammunition for your brief," Allen said, smiling. "Actually, more like a howitzer. We state that DisplayTechnik had developed this new technology many years ago. We developed the formulas. We have prior art. And we have witnesses that will testify that Zack stole proprietary documents from DisplayTechnik."

"You've been busy."

"At your rates, I'd better be! I did all the spadework for you. Take a quick look at it, but then write it up in legalese and submit it to Rafkin's clerk tomorrow."

"Tomorrow?" Dean felt a wave of panic. He couldn't imagine adding this to his brief in anything less than three hours, which would mean he'd miss Charlotte. He didn't know her cell phone number, or if she even had one. "Don't you mean Thursday?"

"Afraid of a little overtime? But yes, you're quite right. After all, we wouldn't want Zack's hired shark to get a look at it beforehand, would we?"

Dean nodded and popped the disk in his computer. The paper

was riddled with technical jargon. Make that four hours to go over this—and that was his time alone and just for starters. Plus, he'd need to consult with members from his technical team. It would be nice to simply attach it as an exhibit, but this key piece of evidence would need to be carefully scrutinized, and he'd need to be able to argue effectively from it.

Allen got up from the chair and walked to the window, standing with his hands behind him and seeming to float in midair in the corner of glass. Dean, tapping the arrow key from time to time for effect, watched the man's back rather than the screen.

He still had time to change his mind about everything. The decision to find a way to stop Allen's legal pursuit could have grave consequences. It could cost him his partnership, his license, his career. And the fantasized dalliance with Charlotte—if that liaison ever came to pass, it was a toss-up which of his actions would have the more catastrophic outcome.

A passage from the Sun Tzu book came back to him: "Know the enemy and know yourself; in a hundred battles you will never be in peril. When you are ignorant of the enemy but know yourself, your chances of winning or losing are equal. If ignorant of both your enemy and yourself, you are certain in every battle to be in peril."

In any event, he was safe for tonight. Although he had his fantasies about Charlotte, he wasn't sure if that was what she was after, and she did love to flirt. For all he knew, she wanted legal advice for one of her charities. He was merely going through the motions with the TRO until he figured out how to put a stop to it. In fact, he wasn't entirely confident that anything *could* be done because of how far along it was. He smiled inwardly. Perhaps a door would open.

"Ready to do battle tomorrow morning?"

"Huh?" Dean said.

"Ready to do battle at seven?"

"Battle? What battle? I told you that the hearing's not until Thursday."

"For Christ's sake. We have a tennis court reserved tomorrow morning, don't you remember? Be sure to bring your 'A' game. You're going to need it."

"Sure, Allen, sure," Dean said, rubbing the back of his neck. He could feel sweat popping out on his forehead.

Allen looked at him with a puzzled expression. "What is with you?"

Dean again felt very transparent, and a rush of heat shot to his face. "It's nothing. Long hours and all, plus this blasted paper doesn't make sense to anyone who doesn't hold a master's degree in this shit."

"I haven't seen you this frustrated since the last time I aced you three times in a row."

"I'm not frustrated! I just—"

"Jesus, counselor, would you go get yourself laid? Leave the bloody brief 'til morning. Go on home and find Marjorie. I'm through here anyway."

Chapter Thirty-Eight

The three wise men decided to pack up and head back to New York, taking the red-eye back to La Guardia. They'd debated whether Zack should fly back with them to start the ball rolling with the legal team back East, but in the end, decided against the idea. By the end of the meeting, Zack was on top of the world, and his enthusiasm must have been contagious because when they parted ways, it was with genuine smiles. Dickens promised that he'd meet with his people the very next day to get the ball rolling and would be in touch with Zack sometime tomorrow morning. By the end of the week, he'd dispatch a full legal team as well as one of his very own corporate pit bulls.

"Don't you worry." Dickens took Zack's hand in a firm grip and laid his other hand on his shoulder as he said, "That sorry son of a bitch is going to wish he'd never started this little shoving match."

Zack felt like hugging the man but restrained himself.

Dickens moved down the line of start-up execs like he was passing out congratulations at a wedding. "Jeremy, you've done a fine job so far, all things considered," he said, shaking hands. "Fine job. Just tidy things up a bit if they need it. Our boys will want things neat and clean so they can start the dissection as soon as possible. Let us know how things go at Thursday's hearing."

"Yes, sir, will do."

"And Paul?" Dickens sized him up before taking his hand. "For God's sake, switch to decaf, would you?"

Paul's face flushed. "No guarantees on that one, sir."

Dean left entirely too early for his rendezvous and arrived at Ghirardelli Square with twenty minutes to spare. He drove down to Marina Park, slowly circled back, and still had ten minutes to wait. He headed over to the Embarcadero and came back, finding a parking space within a block of the Square. A rare find within walking distance of Fisherman's Wharf. He decided it was a good omen.

More than a century ago, Ghirardelli Square was the original site of the Ghirardelli family's chocolate, cocoa, mustard, and box factory. The building had originally been built sometime in the 1850s and was home to the Pioneer Woolen Mill until Italian chocolate king Domingo Ghirardelli took over the structure in 1893 and built it into an empire with the help of his sons. Then in the 1960s, the family decided to relocate the factory out of town. Unwilling to let such historic buildings be destroyed, the people of San Francisco banded together to save the complex of crenellated, white-trimmed brick buildings that had survived the great 1906 earthquake, due in no small part, to the fact that they were made of brick when most of the rest of the city was built primarily of wood.

In what was the first successful adaptive land reuse project in the United States, they refurbished the buildings into specialty shops, bakeries, and internationally famous restaurants, including, of course, a shop devoted to the namesake chocolates, which still housed some of the vintage chocolate-making machinery. Below the square was a small, green park where the cable cars stopped at the foot of Hyde Street one block from the Square. The park was a focal point for tourists, who were eager to see the turnaround point of the trolley, the city's most recognized icon.

As Dean passed the mermaid fountain in the courtyard, where

former employees used to take their breaks or eat lunch under fruit trees, he fished a quarter from his pocket and flipped it in for luck.

The view from Ghirardelli Square was always incredible, but he liked it best when the sun sank slowly toward the Golden Gate Bridge, painting the sky with gold and ever-deepening shades of warm purple.

McCormick and Kuleto's was famous for its seafood and its ambience. Dean could smell the crab cakes as he walked up, and his mouth watered in anticipation. Outside the door, he checked his watch. It was ten to six. Even though he'd been with Charlotte countless times at various social and business events, Allen had always been present, hovering close by. Dean had never been alone with her. He nervously wondered if he'd know what to say without Allen around.

Well, it was stupid to wait on the doorstep. He'd be embarrassed as hell if she walked up behind him right now while he was hesitating like a high-school sophomore.

He opened the door and walked inside. Though the crowds were unbearable during the height of the tourist season, he loved the ambience here: the elongated painted-glass ceiling lights, the great sweep of the rail separating the upper and lower dining areas, the old fireplace like a small brick yurt by the bar, the mounted fish and old photographs on the wall, and the amazing panoramic view of the bay through the wall of windows. He glanced out and saw the distant lights of a cargo ship sitting on the blue horizon of the San Francisco Bay, moving slowly to his left, toward the towers of the Golden Gate Bridge

When Dean saw Charlotte sitting at the bar, the sight took his breath away. She was framed by the golden sunset; a white shawl was thrown about her shoulders, slipping off just slightly as her crossed legs swung out to greet him. She smiled, leaning on one elbow, and tilted her head to one side as his eyes surveyed her figure until his eyes met hers, blue eyes matching a dress topped off with white lace around the neckline.

It was suicide to be thinking this way, but there she was, alone, with no Allen in sight.

As he sat down next to her, she reached out and squeezed one of his hands. "I'm so glad that you could make it." She gave him a light kiss on the cheek. "I know how busy you are."

Was it just his imagination, or was she still leaning into his personal space? "I can always make time."

What a stupid, clichéd thing to say. He felt himself blushing lightly and waved the bartender over. He knew that if he even thought about blushing in front of her, he'd soon be a deep crimson.

"You're being modest. Being a senior law partner and all, you must be pulled in so many different directions."

"I survive. What can I get you?"

"How about a scotch and soda on the rocks with a twist of lime?"

"Make that two," Dean said to the bartender, who nodded and left.

"This was my idea. I'm supposed to be buying you a drink."

"Oh no. I'd never let a beautiful lady buy me drinks."

"I see." She cupped her chin in her hand, definitely leaning toward him as she turned the full effect of her eyes on him. "And do beautiful ladies often offer to buy you drinks?"

Dean smiled, looking in her eyes. "None so charming," he said, noticing that his voice was a bit deeper than usual.

She chuckled and placed a hand on his arm. "Well now, aren't you the silver-tongued devil?"

It was amazing how quickly the banter of flirting came back to him. He'd been something of a ladies' man when he first went to college and before he'd met Marjorie, which, unfortunately, was before he'd met Charlotte. *This* was what he truly missed in his marriage. The dating and the flirting. The whole idea of the chase, the pursuit. The hunt. That long, slow, careful dance culminating in union.

Their drinks arrived, and they clinked their glasses together. "Cheers," Dean said.

"To ... possibilities," she said.

Dean smiled and nodded. "I like that. To possibilities." They clinked glasses again and then took a drink.

Dean would have loved to pin her down on what exactly she meant by "possibilities," but he was content to let the evening unfold as it would. They chatted amicably for a few minutes about the perfect weather they'd been having lately and the other usual chitchat until Dean asked, "So, how's the charity work going?" Showing women he was interested in them and getting them to talk about themselves had always worked for him in the past.

"It's going well, thanks. We're trying to get a building permit for some renovations down at the shelter, the mission had one of its best fund-raising seasons ever, and I was able to get Nike to donate one thousand shoes for underprivileged kids."

Dean smiled. It still worked.

"Although I'm pulling back a little from it, actually." Charlotte took another sip before setting the glass on the bar. "I feel like I've devoted a bit too much time to it of late and that I've been neglecting more important matters. After all, you can only spread so much jam over so much toast."

"Boy, I can relate to that."

"I bet you can."

Dean finished his drink and noticed that Charlotte's glass was nearly empty. He caught the eye of the bartender and waved two fingers over their glasses.

"So, how about you?" she asked. "How goes the war?"

Dean figured Allen's name would probably come up at some point, but when it did, it was like a brick to the head. It felt extremely odd to be talking about him when Dean was here alone with the man's wife. "The war?"

"Yes, to use an Allen phrase, the war with poor ol' Zack. Has he been chased back to his hole yet?"

"Let's just say that the guns are being loaded," he said, not really wanting to talk about it.

"Oh really? What's the latest?"

Dean looked at her and hesitated, his antennae up. Perhaps it was the habit of protecting his client confidentiality, but there was just something about the way she was probing. He supposed, though, that it wouldn't be like Allen to talk to Charlotte about it over dinner.

"Well, we have the hearing coming up a day after tomorrow." Dean shifted uneasily on the barstool. He really hadn't come here to talk about this. If that's all she wanted, couldn't they have done this over the phone? "I guess the outcome of that will tell us where the next phase will head."

Charlotte nodded. From her expression, it seemed she'd hoped for more.

The bartender set the new glasses down and removed the old ones with one hand and wiped a wet spot off the bar with the other. Charlotte smiled and thanked him.

"So, what should we drink to this time?" Dean asked, suddenly unsure of where the evening was going. He hated toasts anyway.

Charlotte smiled wryly. "How about to poor ol' Zack? Our valiant enemy?"

Dean chuckled. He hadn't expected that either. "*Nos morituri te salutamus?*"

Charlotte looked at him quizzically. "What's that?"

"It's what the gladiators used to say at the Coliseum before doing battle. 'We who are about to die, salute you.'"

She laughed. "Clever. Although it doesn't bode very well for poor ol' Zack. I was never good at Latin. About the only Latin I know is *pro bono*, and I used to think that was Latin for a gigolo."

Dean laughed loudly. "That's a term for when lawyers take on cases for free."

Charlotte looked at him, a twinkle in her eye. "Yes, I know that now. Although others would say that it's still a professional boning, whether it's free or not."

Dean smiled. Maybe there was hope after all.

"Okay then," Charlotte said, *"nos moritur ..."*

"Nos morituri te salutamus!"

"That's the ticket." They laughed and clinked glasses.

With this talk of Allen and Zack, Dean's libido was slowly slipping away, but he wasn't about to go down without a fight. He just couldn't think of a way to steer the conversation in the desired direction. With a different woman, the professional-boning line would have been an opening; with Charlotte, that approach seemed too crass.

She took a long drink and then set the glass down on the bar. "I'm curious. What *do* you think of poor ol' Zack?" she asked softly.

Damn. "I think he's a decent enough young man. It's ... unfortunate that things turned out the way they did. From everything I understand, he had a lot of promise. You know, I've been curious. How's Mary Anne taking all this? I can't imagine one of my daughters being in a similar situation, yet Allen never mentions her."

"It's been rather difficult. She's taking it hard, of course, but she's finally dealing with the consequences of her actions. I think that's been the hardest lesson for her to learn. She's had the world handed to her, and I think she thought that somehow she could stage-manage all of this. Of course, that line of thinking didn't take into account who her adversaries were."

Dean nodded and sighed. There was that name again. And that blasted phrase from Sun Tzu once again sprang to mind: "Know the enemy and know yourself; in a hundred battles you will never be in peril." Mary Anne apparently did not really know her enemies. She'd gone to war with idealistic visions, thinking she could manipulate the situation due to her relationships with them, but had failed to realize that such men are not easily tamed.

And maybe his own problem was that he didn't know himself anymore. He'd been so long in Allen's shadow that he no longer cast his own. He'd been involved with the law for three decades now, and what did he have to show for it? Allen had quickly become his main client, and the dreams Dean had had when he'd first gotten into law had quickly disappeared. He'd started law with visions of defending corporations and protecting intellectual properties, but somewhere along the line, he stopped defending and started attacking. He'd become so good at defending Allen that the transition to destroying another company's defense had been easy. Before he knew it, Allen and his company dominated his entire life, business and social. He was an inmate in a prison of his own making.

"Can I tell you a secret?" Charlotte said quietly, interrupting his thoughts. "Mary Anne was actually thinking of confronting Allen, telling him to call it off."

Dean looked at her, amazed. "She was?" Maybe Mary Anne had more fight in her than he'd given her credit for. A futile and foolish move, but a brave one nonetheless.

"Yes. Can you believe it? I always knew Allen enjoyed the Asian mind-set, but I never knew Mary Anne was so attracted to it."

"How do you mean?"

"A kamikaze. It would have been suicidal of her, don't you think?"

Dean saw now with clarity the reason for the date. Charlotte wasn't interested in him romantically. Mary Anne had sent her mother to approach Dean in an attempt to probe him for information. Charlotte leaned on the bar facing him, her hand close to his arm. He glanced at her, the last remnants of his libido sliding away. The diamond on her finger glittered blue in the track lighting over the bar.

Oh to hell with it; who was he kidding? He probably wouldn't have gone through with it anyway, even if it were openly offered. He'd taken a vow, and that still meant something to him. Charlotte was a comforting sexual fantasy, but unless things dramatically changed, she would remain just that.

"Don't you think?" she asked.

"Don't I think what?" Those blue eyes were still extremely

attractive, but now for a very different reason. They had the wonderful compassion of a lover, a wife, a confessor, and a friend, all wrapped into one. They were the eyes Marjorie used to have for him.

"Don't you think it would have been suicide for Mary Anne to confront her father?"

He looked away, slowly shaking his head. "You have no idea." He cleared his throat. "Suicide would be putting it lightly."

"That's what I figured too," she said.

Dean downed the rest of his drink, waving at the bartender for another round for himself; Charlotte declined.

"As vigorously as Allen pursues Zack," he said, "I don't think it'd bother him at all to go after his own daughter too. I just ..." He shook his head, realizing his eyes were getting a bit misty. Must be all the scotch. "I just don't get that kind of thinking. I mean, I've helped Allen with a lot of deals—*a lot* of them—but this one ... this one is just ... I don't know." He shook his head again, wanting to say that all of this was troubling him deeply on a level he wasn't used to exploring. Something told him, though, that she knew exactly what he was talking about. "I probably shouldn't be saying this to you."

"No, no, it's all right. Go on."

"You know, I guess it just makes me wonder. If Allen is going after Zack like this—and I *know* he really liked Zack at one time—then what is the limit of what he is capable of? Hell. He loved that kid, you know?"

"Oh, no doubt there. He asked me a number of times after Zack would pick up Mary Anne whether I thought Zack would ask her to marry him. The glint in his eyes; it was like Christmas morning."

"See, and that's what I mean. He really loved that kid. Now he turns on him like this. How can anyone do that?" He thought for a moment to tell her about Nicole and her father but decided not to. "I mean, I've broken up with women before and even had them break up with me. But I didn't spend my time hating them afterward. But Allen ... God, he treats people like they're his possessions. His property. Like they don't have any rights or dreams of their own."

"You're preaching to the choir, pastor."

"I guess," Dean said. "I guess I just think that if he can do this to someone like Zack, who he was pretty close to, what's to stop him from going after me?"

"Going after you? Why would he—"

"Forget it," Dean said, waving it away, "I'm just ranting." He took a deep gulp of the fresh drink. When he spoke again, he did so in a softer voice. "I've been thinking lately how easy it is to become something you never intended. How easy it is to become something you don't respect anymore. I don't know why that is."

There was silence for a moment between them. He became conscious of the other noises around them—the clink of ice in glasses, the muffled noises from the kitchen, other conversations, and somewhere down by the darkening windows someone laughed. Dean realized Charlotte had placed her hand on his arm and wondered how long it had been there.

"It's just with all that hate bottled up, all the arrogance, all the contempt for everyone around him, it's just ... Oh, I don't know. I don't think I can even put it into words," Dean said.

"Perhaps," she said, "it just makes a person wonder how much they really want to be a part of it."

The question hung there with neither of them touching it.

CHAPTER THIRTY-NINE

Dickens did not call Wednesday morning. Zack waited at home as long as he could before setting off at seven o'clock for the Bakers' sundeck. Paul said he hadn't heard from Dickens. Zack had called Jeremy at nine, and Dickens hadn't contacted him, either. When Zack checked his home phone after ten, he found two voice-mail messages. They were from the same person—but it wasn't Dickens.

Mary Anne's voice was urgent. "Zack, I need to talk you. Please call me at work."

She'd called again an hour later. "It's me again. I know you check your home voice mail regularly. I can't call you at the Bakers', not after what happened. But I need to talk with you in person. Any chance you can meet me for lunch, or maybe even dinner today?" There was a long pause. "Okay, look, I was wrong. I made a terrible mistake. I'm sorry! You've got to believe me. I know that it looks bad that I ... that I was in your home office, but you've got to believe me, I just didn't things would go this way." She sighed. "God, this isn't going well."

Long silence. Static. Click.

Life is bizarre, Zack thought. A week ago, he would have killed to hear her voice. Now, the sound of it saddened him—and made him want to launch the cordless phone over the fence and down the steep hill into the middle of Highway 680. He wanted no part of her. To think that she'd sneaked into his home office after they'd made love, spying on him. Spying for Daddy.

Zack surveyed the three engineers huddled in front of their computers. They should have been working in the new Santa Clara facility. He should have been hiring more engineers by now. They should have been getting the facility ready for the prototyping equipment and working with outside vendors to hurry up with equipment and samples. Instead, they were working in someone's backyard. They were canceling tests, samples, and equipment, leaving Brett—their one and only salesman—stranded, with nothing to show potential distributors and media types.

Zack saw Paul through the glass door, pacing back and forth in the living room, a cell phone glued to the side of his head. He seemed very animated, waving his arm about, his mouth moving fast enough to spray saliva, making him appear frantic. Who could blame the guy? Paul had invested over 3.4 million dollars of his own money into this company. And although Paul was too proud to disclose the entire financial picture, Zack was pretty sure he had gambled everything he had on Imagination.

It was stupid to be feeling sorry for himself and everyone else. After all, just yesterday, Dickens and his Manhattan colleagues had done the unexpected and decided to call Allen's bluff. And now, a day later, the lack of a simple phone call from Dickens was pushing him into a spiral of self-doubt to the point that he hadn't even passed on the encouraging news to his team yet.

God, Allen had really messed up his mind. What was so infuriating was the ease with which his former mentor had orchestrated the chaos. Zack clenched his teeth. Well, he was not about to let Allen control him. He was sure there wasn't anything wrong with Dickens. The man was old, and he'd probably just slept in after a long and late flight. And Zack needed to remain positive, especially for the sake of his team.

"Hey, dude, are you all right?"

Zack jumped. "Sure, Jimmy, what's up?"

"'Cause you look like you either had some serious constipation or were thinking up some way to kill someone. No one I know, right?"

Zack produced a fake smile. "Well, not anyone you can get an insurance settlement from."

"Damn. Well, if you're done with your murder plans, I need to ask you a question. You know, an engineering question. Remember that stuff? Not that you've had any time for it or anything."

He knew Jimmy was trying hard to keep up a cheerful attitude, but it was getting annoying. "Sure. What is it?"

"We're trying to figure out the protocol for the display drivers. Some of the guys," he jerked his thumb over his shoulder at the only other two guys, "want to use a standard protocol. But I want to change it. After all, our display technology is so radically new that I feel that we could break some new ground here. Why use a Model T engine for a brand new Ferrari, right?"

"Did you bounce it off Dimitre?"

"God! This is like dealing with my parents: Go ask your mom, go ask your dad, go ask your mom."

"What?"

"The big doofus told me to ask you first."

That was odd. Yes, this was an important technical decision, but it wasn't exactly earth-shattering. Why the hell didn't Dimitre deal with it? He looked over Jimmy's shoulder and saw Dimitre sitting at his desk, talking on a cell phone. His face was red, the color coming through the heavy beard, and he seemed to be talking in Ukrainian.

Zack immediately wondered if Dimitre had heard more yesterday than they'd thought. Paul had been all paranoid about how much he'd overheard, but these days Paul was always paranoid. Could he be job hunting and not wanting to deal with the problems of the small company? The idea that he had completely passed on a decision like this was bothersome, as though he didn't want to be involved in decisions that would affect the future of the company.

Stop it. Get hold of yourself. Keep everything under control. He'd just talk with Dimitre later to make sure he was okay with things.

"Dude. Are you like even here?"

Jimmy Morgan was looking at him like he was possessed.

Zack shook his head. "Forget it. It's just one of those mornings when you can't have enough coffee." He smiled again and patted the seat next to him. "Let's see if we can figure it out."

As Jimmy talked about the new protocols that he was dreaming up, the morning sun rose out of the valley. Zack put on his sunglasses and looked to the east. He could see lots of white, high tech-looking windmills perched on the tops of the yellow hills that surrounded Livermore. Jimmy was animated, talking excitedly about a number of ideas for compression geared specifically toward the new display. He had never seen Jimmy so worked up before.

"Have you ever thought," Jimmy said, "that this could have immersion applications?"

"What do you mean?"

"I mean, we've been thinking of just a huge display. Something really light and paper-thin and all, but why stop there? We could do things in three dimensions. You know, like a gigantic cube. People could put this not just on one wall, but because it's so light, it could go on the ceiling too. With another on two other walls, and maybe even one on the floor, suddenly you're not just watching TV, you're *in* the TV. Hell, why not do all six sides of a room? Though I suppose you'd need some way to actually get into the room. Plus," he said, with an expression on his face like he'd just thought of it, "what if we market this to the military or other people who need to do training? Police or pilots or something. What a way-cool battlefield simulation this could be.

"Okay, so not everyone would want to live inside a TV, but anyway, if we put in protocols now with an eye to that sort of thing in the future, we could save loads of programming in the future. What do you think?"

What did he think? He thought that he should have anticipated these applications himself. Because now that he gave it some thought, he saw the enormous potential. It was so simple that it had been stupid of him to overlook it. He'd had a visionary idea, but it was like he'd only been seeing it through tunnel vision. Maybe Allen was right; maybe he couldn't run a company like this. Maybe he really was out of his element. If they had left this door open, someone else would have quickly seen the opportunities, taking the idea right out from under them, and soon they'd be seen as second-rate.

Stupid, stupid, stupid. Zack silently kicked himself, numerous times.

"I think it's great, Jimmy. It's really great."

"Really?"

"Yeah. Besides, if your ideas work, we could sell six screens to people instead of just one."

"Cool. Can I be a vice president then?"

Zack laughed. "Do you really want the headache of being a vice president?"

"Well, actually, no. Not after what I've seen you've had to go through. How 'bout just permanent employee of the month, with all the perks and parking space—and raises—that go along with it?"

"You can't do that!" Dimitre exclaimed, causing both of them to jump and turn around in their seats. He was leaning over Jerry Steiner's workstation.

"Jeez, what the hell's bugging him?" Jimmy asked.

Jerry wiped his glasses with the sleeve of his shirt, replaced them, and then continued to type on his keyboard.

Dimitre stood up and arched his back, producing a series of noises that sounded like Bubble Wrap popping. "Change that design there," he said. "If you do not, the whole display will overheat like a sailor coming home to wife after three months at sea."

"What, here?" Jerry said, pointing at the screen.

"No, what are you—? Are you not hearing well, or are you—?"

"Or am I what?" Jerry leaned back and pushed the bridge of his gold-wire glasses farther up onto his nose.

"No." Dimitre leaned over Jerry's right shoulder and poked hard at the screen, making it bounce. "Here! Here is where you must change."

"I already did the thermal flow analysis. This will work."

"No, no, no! Look at corners. Use your eyes. Corners are too sharp. We are not making a dirt box for small children to play in."

"It's called a sandbox, not a dirt box. You should learn to speak English."

"And you should learn how to design, instead of pulling crazy ideas out of ass."

"Oh, for Christ's sake!" Jerry said. "Who made you God?"

"Christ and God have nothing to do with it." Dimitre stopped and shook his head. "Look, I am sorry. I ..." A hesitant smile appeared under his beard. "Say, am I ever telling you the story of how a Jew, Christian, and Muslim engineers design a bridge? It is—"

"I don't want to hear any more of your stupid stories!" Jerry got up, kicked the deck chair back, nearly hitting Dimitre, and jumped down the steps leading to the backyard pathway.

Dimitre just stood there, watching him go. When Zack walked over, Dimitre turned, his mouth opening and closing like a fish out of water. Zack located Jerry's bald spot through the gaps of the deck railing. His initial instinct was to go after him but he decided against it, figuring it was better to let him chill out on his own for a bit.

Everyone was acting as if they hadn't had a decent night's sleep for days. Who could blame them? He knew his own morning energy wasn't at its usual level. He'd been grateful he hadn't had to endure that commute down to Santa Clara every morning.

He made a mental note to jog this evening. With all this craziness, he'd fallen badly out of his daily routine.

"Care to talk about it?" Zack asked Dimitre.

"No," he said with an edge in his voice. He muttered something in Ukrainian that didn't sound overly pleasant.

Zack decided to let it all go. It wasn't worth it, whatever it was.

Through the glass sliding door, Paul on the phone—as always—was waving his free hand, looking exasperated. Even though Zack couldn't read his lips, he imagined what the conversation could be about. Perhaps he was talking to a nervous equipment supplier. There was no facility to deliver to, Paul said. No matter, the vendor replied, where do we ship our equipment? Nowhere, Paul said. Then, how do we get paid unless we ship? they countered. You don't, Paul said. That's why you don't ship.

They were losing the war after a few minor skirmishes. They couldn't go on like this. Allen's shadow hung over the deck, sapping their energy and their will to go on.

He'd never thought about it before since he'd come from a very loving family—his parents dated at least once a week—but it suddenly struck him that this must be what it was like to be in an abusive relationship. You constantly had a cloud hanging over you, always worrying when the next blow would fall, when the next argument would erupt, when safety would vanish. It was a future that held no hope of ever getting better, though you craved it with every ounce of your being, but were too scared and too hopeless to believe it was out there. And so you went on day after day, putting a brave face to the world, while inside you were crumbling away. A vicious cycle.

"Hey, Jerry?" Zack called. "Can you come up here? Jimmy? You too. Everyone come here a sec."

The team slowly gathered around like children who'd been fighting at the playground. "Listen, guys," Zack said. "We're each other's best supports right now. We need to stick together."

"We don't need lecture," Dimitre said, still hanging on to whatever bitterness was inside. "We don't need pep talk."

"That wasn't where I was going, but you're right. You don't. You're grown men. Anyway, what I was *going* to say was that I think the company ought to spring for a little R and R. We've been working damn hard as it is to get this company going; it's about time the company gave back a little."

Jerry eyed him. "Just what did you have in mind?"

"Well, how about if we go take in a Giants' game? The company's treat. They're playing the Diamondbacks today if I'm not mistaken."

"Awesome!" Jimmy said.

Dimitre's eyes widened. He was a huge fan of the Giants.

"And let's do it right," Zack said, "best seats in the house. Hotdogs, popcorn, and buckets of overpriced beers."

The three of them whooped it up and began packing up their things without further prompting. Zack went inside and grabbed the phone book. He was practically laughed at by the ticket agent when he asked for good seats four hours before game time. But she gave him the name of a ticket outlet that sometimes held premium seats. She warned him they would be expensive.

He hung up and started to dial the number when he saw that Paul was free. "Hey, Paul. You want to go to the Giants' game?"

"Huh? What the hell are you talking about?"

"We're celebrating."

"Holy shit. Allen died or something?"

Zack was taken aback by the sudden crassness. "No. You going to come with us? We've all been working too hard."

"No, I better not. I'd just be a downer. I've got way too much going on today. I'll wait to do a little R and R once I'm in my new office at the world headquarters of Imagination. I'm done with chasing phantom dreams."

Paul walked back to the kitchen, his comment as comforting as a blow to the stomach. Zack tried to ignore it and called the ticket outlet downtown. "Yes, I'm looking for some premium seats for today's Giants game. The best you have."

"Certainly." There was a pause, and Zack heard rapid keystrokes. "I have two in the VIP row behind home plate for 390 each."

"No, that won't work. I need five, er, I guess, four tickets."

"Oh, you know, I should have asked that first. Let's see what I have … I have four available in the field club, section 109. That's the sixth row over the visitors' dugout. I also have some behind the Giants' dugout, but it's the twenty-fifth row."

"We'll take the closer ones. Do you take checks?"

"I do, but we're not set up to take them over the phone. We have this scanner thing that runs it through to verify funds, but I do need the physical check."

Zack got directions to their office and said he'd be there in less than an hour. He went back out onto the deck, and the three of them were waiting for him. They piled into Zack's car and headed across the Bay Bridge, the windows down and Santana blaring into the perfect afternoon sunshine.

Zack went to the ticket office by himself. The others had gone to the sports store next door to load up on Giants' caps, T-shirts, and whatever else they could find. Jimmy said something about adding to his bobblehead collection. Jerry started teasing him about his dolls, and before long, Dimitre was building up to some dirty joke about dolls. Zack left before he got to the punch line. It was great to hear the guys act like themselves for a change.

"Hi, I called earlier about the four tickets? The ones behind the visitors' dugout?"

"Oh, yeah, hi. Do you have your check? Your total with tax and everything came to 1404."

Ordinarily, Zack would have choked at the price, but these were prime seats. Besides, after they were multimillionaires, that'd seem like pocket change. She took the check and ran it through the same kind of machine that they had at the grocery store. She punched in a few numbers and waited. It made a soft beep, and she looked at the screen, puzzled. She ran it through again, dutifully punching in the numbers again. It beeped again.

She came over, looking at the check. "I'm sorry, but it doesn't want to go through."

"What?" Zack said. "There's like thirty million dollars in that account."

She smiled. "Are you sure?"

She probably thought he was exaggerating. "Yes. There's plenty in there." He was about to say something about it being a new start-up, but that might not help his case.

"Well, I don't know," she said, shrugging, "it won't go through. This is a business check, right?"

"Yeah," he said slowly. How many people did she know named Imagination? Of course, this was California.

"Well, it's just that this must be one of your first checks. See? The number's only 1015."

"So?"

"Most business checks start at 1001. I could be wrong, but I seem to remember the guy who set this up saying it doesn't take starter checks, that they want you to write a hundred checks or something. Maybe the machine thinks this is still a starter check. Who can tell with computers? Anyway, I can take a debit card for the account if you have one."

Yeah, that's a great idea. Issue personal debit cards for a business account with thirty million in funds. The company would be out of business in a week, but at least all the employees would be driving new cars and living on Nob Hill.

Zack's spirits started to slide into his shoes. "I don't have one for that account."

"Do you want to put it on your personal credit card? You could have your company cut you a check to reimburse you." She said it with the confidence of someone who'd done this plenty of times before, neatly pinning him to see whether he truly trusted the bank account of his company.

"I don't have a credit card on me, actually." He was telling the truth. He saved those for traveling or emergencies, and he didn't keep that kind of cash in his personal checking account that his debit card drew on. He'd have to go find an ATM and transfer it from his savings first.

He took the check back. Something didn't feel right, and he was suddenly rethinking the idea of transferring money out of his savings account for a fourteen-hundred-dollar spending spree. The Giants had enough money.

"Let me go talk it over with the guys," he said. He found them in the store waiting for him at a respectful distance from the checkout, with armloads of Giants' paraphernalia.

"Zacko!" Jerry said. "We got you a hat and a shirt and a pair of thundersticks. You get the tickets? Let's see 'em!"

"Um, there's been a bit of a problem."

Their faces all fell at the same moment.

"What are you meaning?"

"Well, the check reader wouldn't read the check for some reason. The clerk thought it might be a failsafe set in for new business accounts. I don't have enough in my personal account to cover the fourteen hundred."

Jerry whistled. "Holy moly. You were really going all out for us. I'd spring for it, but my wife would take that out of my half of the divorce settlement."

"We'll have to get the upper-deck tickets instead."

"Hey, that's okay," Jimmy said. "At least we're going, right? Does this mean no bobbleheads?"

Jimmy's cell phone was ringing, and he handed his armload of stuff to Zack. "Hello? Yeah, he's here. Hold on."

He held the phone toward Zack. "It's for you."

Zack's stomach dropped; he hoped Mary Anne hadn't tracked him down through one of her girlfriends' girlfriends. That's all he needed right now. They swapped armloads, and Zack took the phone. "Hello?"

"It's Paul. Where are you guys?"

"We're down at the ticket office. Well, the sports store next—"

"Whatever. Listen, I need you back here. Right now."

Zack felt his knees go weak. Paul's voice sounded extra-nervous. "Why? What's going on?"

"Are Jimmy and the others right there?"

"Yeah."

"Then I need you to act like everything's okay. Smile, do a fucking tap dance, or whatever. *Trust me* and don't give me any bullshit about keeping everyone informed. Got it? You *cannot* talk to them until you and I talk."

"I don't understand," Zack said, trying to buy a little time and hoping Paul would give him a hint. He wasn't looking forward to the long, slow drive back to San Ramon without a clue of what he was heading into.

"Just get the fuck back here. Now. This is huge, and it's not good, and it's definitely not something to tell the guys." Paul hung up.

Zack closed the cell phone, steeled himself, and turned to face the guys.

CHAPTER FORTY

It was the third time Mary Anne had called her father.

"I'm sorry, but he's just busy today," Louise said.

"It's Wednesday! He's always in the office on Wednesdays, and that's usually his lightest day."

"I'm sorry, but not today. He has meetings scheduled and they've been overlapping, so everything is backing up."

It was amazing. No matter how many times she'd spoken to Louise and under different circumstances and no matter how happy or upset she was when she called, Mary Anne had never heard her change the tone of her voice. It was always the same tolerantly sweet tone she was using now.

"That's ridiculous. He doesn't have a *single* free moment? Not even for his own daughter?"

"I'm sorry, but I promise you I'll call as soon as he's free."

"Well, who's he been meeting with?"

"I'm sorry, but you know it's not company policy for me to divulge things like that. I promise I'll call."

"Yeah, but—"

"I'm sorry, but I really have to go now. I promise I'll call, dear."

Mary Anne hung up, wanting to strangle Louise with the phone cord while imitating her "I'm sorry ... I'm sorry."

It was ridiculous. Her father was always free on Wednesdays. Back when he'd tried to groom her to take over the company, he'd even told her once that a smart manager keeps Wednesdays open—to either deal with the problems that came up earlier in the week or to head off problems that would come up later in the week.

She'd promised not to confront Allen directly, but her mother's explanation made no sense, telling those pointless stories about her great grandfather in the Confederate army. How could she make things any worse by confronting him? How could things possibly get worse?

Now that she'd made up her mind to talk with the two most important men in her life, she couldn't reach either of them. She felt like screaming at the top of her lungs. She slammed her fist on the desk instead and started out of the office for a very long and very late lunch. But then she stopped, halfway out the door, realizing that if she left, she might miss her opportunity to talk to her father.

CHAPTER FORTY-ONE

Zack sprang for the souvenirs out of his personal account in an effort to keep everyone's spirits up since they weren't going to the game.

The subdued group headed back across the Bay Bridge. Zack had said he needed to go back to talk with Paul. "Something about a vendor or something, I guess," was the best he could come up with. The group, without Zack, headed to a local sports bar. Watching them head down the hill in their own cars, he wished he could go with them. He opened the sliding door and stepped inside the house. He smelled coffee coming from the kitchen. It was one of those specialty flavors, mocha walnut or something.

Paul was nowhere to be seen, but Jeremy was in the kitchen, leaning against the fridge door, his left hand wrapped over his head to hold his cell phone on the right side of his face. For his sake, Zack hoped he was speaking to one of his other clients; hopefully, one that pays.

He knew that his friend was sticking around until Dickens had rounded up all the legal cavalry that New York money could buy. Jeremy's tiny law practice was probably in jeopardy with all the time he'd spent on Zack's problems, but Jeremy was standing by him, valuing their friendship. He'd promised Jeremy a gold pot at the end of the start-up's rainbow, but unfortunately, the thunderstorm wasn't over yet. Jeremy had joked that having a nice cushy job as the general counsel for a wildly successful company sounded pretty good. Zack wondered what he thought about that now.

Paul emerged from the den. "After you guys left, I got a call from John," he said. "He got a call from the central bank. The person told him the main bank had suspended our account and they were calling to alert him to it in case any of the account holders came in. Apparently, someone had just tried to access it. I assume that was you."

"What do you mean they're suspending the account?"

"I have no clue. John's still checking into it. He couldn't get a straight answer, but he said that he was hearing rumors that the courts were freezing our financial assets until the TRO got settled. That's going to affect salaries, the rent, payment for the ordered equipment, and—"

"I know what it means! How the hell can they get at our bank account?"

Jeremy quickly collapsed his cell phone and joined them in the hallway. "They can't," he said. "I don't think that they can do that."

"You think or they can't?" Immediately, Zack regretted it. He took a deep breath. "I'm sorry. I didn't mean that to sound so harsh. So where's John?"

Paul dialed the number of the Bank of America. Zack took the cell phone, his hand swallowing the tiny silver phone. Zack hated cell phones. People's mouths were bigger than the entire device. It felt unnatural.

"John, is it true?" Silence. "John, can you hear me?"

"Yes, Zack, I'm here." His voice sounded tinny.

"Well?"

"Maybe ... I'm not sure, but probably. There's a court order coming down, so says the branch manager. I've got instructions to ..."

John said more, but Zack wasn't listening. Holy shit. If their money was frozen, what would they do? It was, literally, their lifeline. Without it, everything would fall apart. His engineers couldn't work for free, and he couldn't ask them to. Hell, even he couldn't work for free. It was great to have ideals and dreams, but they didn't impress landlords or utility companies.

Zack thanked him and hung up. In the fog of the thoughts spinning through his head, he figured he'd make sense of it later, or have Paul call him back. He turned to the others.

"Look, if this is true, and I use the word 'if,' then we have got to tell Dickens and the other investors immediately. It's mostly their money. If our current bank account is locked, then we have to tell them before the shitstorm comes. Otherwise, they'll pull up stakes completely, and we'll lose everything. Even our ability to fight the court battle."

Had it only been yesterday when things had looked so promising?

Paul pounded the wall with his fist. A picture of one of the Bakers' kids jumped and slid diagonally. "God damn it to hell!" he yelled. "It was bad enough telling Dickens about the TRO, the confiscation of our plant and equipment, and the eviction notice, not to mention having him in the front row when you're served like a common criminal. But this? My God, we're going to have to tell them that the millions of dollars is lost and—"

"Calm down, you two," Jeremy said. "It's not lost. Just temporarily inaccessible."

"Yeah, that'll be a real source of comfort to them!" Paul said, hitting the wall again.

The picture fell to the floor. There was a crack in the glass across the face of the Bakers' son, attempting to hit a ball with his oversize plastic bat at age five. They all stared at the picture.

"This isn't legal," Jeremy said quietly.

"What?" Paul said, bending down to retrieve the photo.

"A court can't simply freeze the bank account of a company. At least not because of a TRO that merely alleges a violation of a confidentiality agreement. They can't even do it for allegedly stealing trade secrets."

"Then how?"

Paul hung the picture back on the wall, crack and all.

"There's no way."

"John seems pretty sure it's happening."

Jeremy shrugged. "I just don't see it happening for a TRO. It's not legal."

"Then why would John say the main bank called and said they were shutting us down?" Paul said to Jeremy, who was standing his ground. "What, you think he just made it up for fun?"

"I don't know. Maybe his information is wrong," Jeremy replied.

"Then explain it," Zack said.

"I can't. I didn't speak to him."

Paul threw up his arms. "Zack. What did he say to you?"

"He said he had some sort of instructions. To be honest, I kind of tuned it out after he said the branch manager had said something about a court order coming down."

Jeremy covered his mouth with his hand and looked down at the floor in thought. He raised a finger in the air. "Ah. Well, that might be different then. If ... if they could tie the money to an illegal activity, then this—"

"What are you talking about?" Paul said. "What illegal activity?"

"It could be a claim regarding a payment for a trade secret that was obtained illegally."

"Speak English!" Paul said.

"Say a company had stolen a company secret and a buyer wants the secret. The buyer transfers money to the company's bank account—"

"We haven't stolen any secrets!" Paul said.

"That's beside the point," Jeremy said. "McSorley has managed to convince Rafkin that Dickens paid for these trade secrets."

"This is ridiculous," Paul said. "This is fucking ridiculous!"

"Of course, it is."

"Jeremy," Zack said, his eyes narrowing, "if what you're speculating is true, then what?"

"If the courts believe that there's enough evidence to warrant the holding of the funds, then we go through discovery again."

"Which means?"

"Our money is suspended until we get back to court."

"If we ever get there," Paul sneered.

"Let me do some checking," Jeremy said. He began making a few phone calls, starting with his office, and then he called the court directly.

"They can't prove anything," Paul muttered as Jeremy speed-dialed. "This is just like the original bullshit with the original TRO. The whole thing is bullshit. It's the biggest pile of bullshit there ever was. It's a mountain of bullshit. Hell, I've got bullshit coming out my ears, I've had to eat so much of it the last week. Bullshit for breakfast, bullshit for lunch …"

Zack said nothing, waiting for Jeremy to get off the phone. He hoped that John was wrong, but he didn't know how he could be. John was one of the most conservative and cautious people he knew. It wasn't like him to speculate on rumors.

"My office just got a call from McSorley," Jeremy said. "Judge Rafkin issued an ex parte order. We have to appear in court tomorrow. However, we've been given notice over the phone about the frozen bank account."

"This is fucking insane!" Paul said. "I thought Rafkin was baking his fat ass on some windsurfing holiday."

Jeremy shrugged. "Guess he's back."

"Would you stop stating the obvious," Paul said in a mocking tone.

"You're not helping the situation," Jeremy said calmly.

"Neither are you. You're the goddamn lawyer. You're supposed to head off things like this."

"I can't head off what I can't see."

"That's the fucking problem! You don't see these things coming!"

"Hey, hey!" Zack stepped in between them. In the close confines of the hallway, Paul's aftershave was really quite stifling. "Okay, come on, guys. Let's cool off a bit. C'mon, let's go sit down." He walked to the den, and his colleagues followed.

"If Judge Rafkin has issued an ex parte order, then this thing's a lot further along that we imagined," Jeremy said.

"What exactly *is* an ex parte order?" Zack asked.

"Normally in a court, both sides need to be present. An ex parte order means 'by or for one party.' It refers to situations in which only one party, and not the adversary, appears before a judge."

"Wait a second," Paul said. "Isn't that illegal?"

"It's unusual but not illegal. A judge is normally required to meet with both parties, but judges will sometimes issue temporary orders ex parte—meaning they're based on one party's request without hearing from the other side—when time is limited or it wouldn't do any good to hear the other side of the dispute."

"What?" Paul said. "That can't be legal."

"Sure it is. That's how restraining orders are issued for domestic violence cases where one party is immediately given temporary custody of the kids. But it's almost unheard of for this to happen on the corporate level. They must have really convinced the judge of some serious wrongdoing."

"Yeah. Or they just said please," Paul said.

"So will going to court tomorrow head this off?" Zack asked.

"I have no idea. I'll certainly raise our arguments again that we're not competing with DisplayTechnik and that we haven't stolen any trade secrets by any means. This court hasn't been terribly receptive so far, but he has to have *something* to base it on and not just because the other side said we're doing something. I mean, the judge can't support the illegal seizure of our bank account without cause. He'd get into all sorts of trouble."

Zack felt a little relieved. This was all psychological warfare, that's all. But it was warfare that was getting to him more and more easily.

Paul snapped his fingers. "Hey, you're right. This whole thing's a fucking conspiracy! Maybe we don't waste our time going back to court, at least not this court. We go to a higher court and appeal this thing. Jeremy, isn't that what you lawyers do? Get things turned around? We're getting railroaded here."

"Rafkin is one of the most senior judges in the San Francisco District Court," Jeremy said.

"I don't care if he's the mayor of Disneyland. We've got to go over his head. Rafkin has a boss, right?"

As Paul and Jeremy traded ideas back and forth on how to circumvent the judicial process, Zack's mind drifted to the short-term eventualities. The TRO had been extended another three months, so how long could Allen stretch out this ex parte order? They needed to pay the design team's salaries to take care of their young families and pay those ridiculous mortgages. Although they might volunteer to sacrifice, he couldn't ask them to do that.

He had to contact Dickens and fill him in on the situation. Dickens had to hear it from them, rather than a third party.

CHAPTER FORTY-TWO

Mary Anne called Louise again and listened to her phone ring and ring. She glanced at her delicate silver and gold watch—a gift from Allen that he had picked up on a combined business and skiing trip in Davol. It was 6:11 p.m. Louise had promised to call when Allen was free. She had probably gone home now, the bitch.

Mary Anne sprang out of the office chair, threw open her door, and marched out, heading for the Ivory Tower. If Louise came slinking out through the common corridor, she was in for an earful. When Mary Anne pushed down the brass arm of the heavy walnut door and stepped inside, she was immediately immersed in a cooler temperature and dimmer lighting. She bounded up the stairs, two at a time. The receptionist for the tower was gone, her desk tidy, the computer shut down.

It had been awhile since Mary Anne had roamed the upper level of the Ivory Tower, and after hours and alone, it was a little creepy. The conditioned air was stale, like filtration had stripped it of its nutrients. Leaning over the railing, she looked down onto the main reception area. From this viewpoint, the similarity to her home was startling. The style of furniture was the same, the color scheme of the carpet and walls was the same, and of course, there was a statue of a World War II soldier—an unnecessary reminder to visitors and employees how her father conducted business.

The upstairs was deathly quiet. And utterly deserted. Usually there was someone here working late. Shouldn't there at least be a security guard? She suddenly felt vulnerable. Allen just left doors wide open—and unlocked—so that any of his serfs could just walk right in?

Across the yawning expanse, she saw the office door of her boss's boss, the CFO, was closed, with the lights out. Mary Anne placed her hand on the brass railing that encircled the entire second level. She crept past the CFO's office and several others, keeping one hand on the railing. The plush carpet and deeply rich wood seemed to absorb all sound. She hurried up the stairs to the third level and approached the anteroom to her father's office. Louise's desk was off to one side, silently standing guard. Louise was nowhere to be seen. The PC was shut down, her desk orderly, with all pens and paper put back in their neat-freak places. No wonder she'd been Allen's secretary for more than twenty-five years—they were a perfect fit.

She knocked softly on the thick, carved door, listening for any movement inside. Nothing. She pushed down the brass door handle. The handle moved a few inches, but the door didn't yield.

She rattled the door handle up and down a few times before giving up. She was about to leave when she heard soft voices. She knocked again, louder this time, but was afraid to call out. The knock seemed to echo.

Still nothing.

She'd heard the rumors about her father's infidelities, but she always dismissed them. She didn't like to think that he'd do something like that to her mother, but then again, her mother had been in a fog of alcohol for a very long time. What would Mary Anne do if she actually caught him at it? Maybe she could use it as ammunition to save Zack?

She got down on all fours, her skirt riding up around her hips, and peered through the inch gap beneath the anteroom door, her heart pounding. If someone were to open the door right then, she'd scream bloody murder and then die of embarrassment.

There was light on inside, but it was hard to tell where it came from. Perhaps from her father's office or the anteroom, she couldn't be sure. She went to Louise's desk and knocked over the penholder, which clattered to the floor. She held her breath, but everything stayed quiet.

As she spread the pens across the desk to distract herself, an idea occurred to her. She picked up the phone and dialed her father's private extension, which was only accessible from this station. She heard it ringing in the other room. Five rings. There was no reply.

She stuck her ear against the carved door, dropping down on all fours again. There was a whoosh and a click, and she jerked up, hitting her head on the door handle. She bit her tongue. She'd jumped at the sound of the air conditioner clicking on. She listened a moment longer, but the fan motor's drone drowned everything else out.

Returning to Louise's desk, she began rummaging through the drawers. She found a box of paper clips and emptied them all over her desk, stirring them into papers, file folders, and the stackable trays. Making a real mess.

She smiled at her work and leaned back into the chair. Ever since she'd gone with her father to Dean McSorley's office, her life had gotten steadily worse, and it had become hard to concentrate on anything else. Today, she hadn't done any work, utterly consumed with the idea of speaking directly with Zack and her father. She'd failed miserably on both counts.

Her life was spinning out of control. She could just hear her mother urging her to return to the Young Christian Adults group, but now, that association seemed so trite. Everything seemed trite. A week ago, she was certain Zack had betrayed her father. Now, she was ten times more certain that he didn't.

She rubbed her temples, feeling the pressure mounting above her eyes. Why did she have to make a choice between Zack and her father? Why should anyone ever have to make that choice? She looked, but Louise didn't have any aspirin.

In the growing darkness, Mary Anne walked slowly down the stairs, feeling more secure now that she was leaving. She stepped out into the warm California breeze, which fanned the fat-leafed plants that lined the main wall of the complex. Only then did she remember that she'd parked her car on the opposite end of the building.

***

"Do you think someone heard us?" Sandy said.

"Who cares?"

"Allen, we need to be careful."

"We are careful. The guard is gone, I made sure of that."

"Damn it! I don't want to get caught here like this. It could … complicate things."

"Oh, stop it. So what if you were? We'd merely say you were consulting with me."

Sandy frowned at Allen but dropped it. He adjusted his surgical gloves and went back to work. Allen had no appreciation for the delicacy of the task. It required a jeweler's eye and a level of thoroughness that he could never understand.

Several piles of old archives, smelling of dust and age, were laid out on the desk. They'd already inserted one file a few days ago. Allen and some of his senior engineers had discussed the lawsuit, and with some leading questions and suggestions from Mr. Henley, some of them suddenly remembered work they'd done on basic OLED technology years ago.

He still needed to insert other files and notes into the archives to support the validity of the original file, making it look like Knowles's paper wasn't a fluke—or a plant. The archives from the critical time period were a phenomenal mess, stacked in boxes piled one on another, with little organization. Apparently someone had tried to alphabetize them but had quickly given up.

After carefully applying just the right touch of coffee and wet sugar to one note, he stuck it to the back of one of Knowles's pages from a completely unrelated project. The angle had to be perfect, the edge sticking up just enough to be seen but not enough to be obvious. He set it down on the rest of the file, restacked papers on top of it, and then set a large, heavy book on the whole pile to compress them all.

It's what he called a "second-pass insertion." He had purposefully left it out earlier so not all the related files could be located in one search. They wouldn't find it the first time, but when Allen ordered them to keep looking—surprise!

He had several other forgeries to insert. Using a stapler he had personally designed for the purpose, the fake would be attached to the mix of other notes, the holes perfectly aligned. In another case, to take advantage of how most people went through files, the real notes were on one side, and what they wanted to be found was stapled to the other. He had rubbed a little rust from a contemporaneous paper clip onto the existing file and the new note. The final plant was a simple misfile: Knowles's fake notes stuck into a mislabeled folder and filed in the wrong place. It was the easiest to insert, but discovery required the archives be searched folder by folder.

The night security guard was an understanding man, who assumed that Allen was entertaining a woman in his office. The next shift was due in at eleven. Before then, Sandy had to have everything in order. Allen himself would replace the archives in the huge, fireproof room on the lowest level of the Tower. It would take at least two trips. Sandy still needed to insert some computer files—he'd already typed them up on an ancient PC running Windows VISTA—but those were a matter of copying files, which he could do from any workstation.

All this to make it look like someone, whom no one cared about or cared to listen to, had once done some extraordinary work.

CHAPTER FORTY-THREE

Dimitre smiled at the waitress, who set down another beer and a pile of napkins in front of him. She didn't see his smile and left before anyone could respond to her automated question of "Anything else?" She knew they'd flag her down if they needed anything.

They had decided against going to a sports bar. It was too much of a letdown and just didn't seem right without Zack. They had settled for Zorro's, which was one of their occasional hangouts in Dublin, a town fifteen minutes south of San Ramon and a stone's throw north of Pleasanton. Zorro's was largely unremarkable except that it was one of the last East Bay bars that had a smoking section larger than a postage stamp; it was also something of a time machine, having never fully left the seventies. Bamboo textured wallpaper sagged and grayed under the weight of the smoke that perpetually hung in the air. Lime green carpet had well-established paths between the tables winding their way to the back room, with an electronic dartboard—pockmarks still visible in the old wood paneling from before the coming of liability lawyers. There were pool tables and an original Asteroids video game. Despite its name, Zorro's only halfheartedly served Mexican fare. Most people came for drinks and appetizers; their nachos were among the best in the area.

They were settled in a corner table as far away from the bar and smoking area as possible, eating a platter of nachos, spicy chicken wings, and zucchini sticks. Happy hour had come and gone. A handful of dedicated locals remained, serious about drinking, playing darts, and smoking their hearts out.

"Hey, Dimitre, what the hell was with you today anyway?" Jerry said, eating a nacho chip tethered with a string of cheese. "You were a real asshole. Just let me do my thing, all right? The design would have worked."

"No, it would not. Besides, why were you making complicated design when simple would do? Because you were tempted to, or because you had no other choice?"

"Come again?" Jimmy said. He licked spicy red sauce from his fingers.

"There are three guys, a drinker, a smoker, and a homosexual," Dimitre began.

Jerry groaned. "Not another story."

"God tells them that each must ignore temptation or they die. The drinker, not unlike some of the people in this bar, says, 'God is crazy.' He goes into bar, has a drink, and then … pow!" Dimitre clapped his hands together. "He die straight over dead! Now, other two friends are nervous. They leave bar, walk outside on sidewalk. The smoker sees a cigarette butt on the sidewalk. It still has fire. The homosexual turns to smoker and says, 'If you bend over and pick up cigarette, we both die.'"

Jimmy laughed, holding a half-eaten wing, his cheek smeared with sauce.

Jerry seemed unmoved. "You know, they say that when learning a language, humor is the hardest part to learn. Sorry, Dr. Koslov, I don't understand the relevance."

"No? I am saying temptation can be avoided by good communication." A grin spread across his face. He took a drink of beer, wiping the foam from his beard with his fingers. He handed a wad of fresh napkins to Jerry.

"I am sorry to be overreacting this afternoon. But things have been building up, and I am not being good communicator myself. I have something to tell you that you will not like."

He paused to make sure he had their full attention.

"Zack promised us that things would be different than at DisplayTechnik," he said. "Now, I am finding out that Zack and Paul are hiding several important informations from us. Zack does not warn us that we could lose our beautiful Santa Clara building forever. And maybe Zack could go to jail."

"What?" Jimmy asked, dropping the chicken wing onto his plate. "Zack's going to jail? You're kidding."

Dimitre didn't reply immediately. He raised the bottle of Sam Adams to his mouth and took a long sip.

"This is incredible! What on earth for?" Jerry said.

Dimitre put the bottle down. "I do not know exactly. It is complaint, not warrant for arrest. But Zack did get criminal notice. Of that I am sure."

"How do you know all this?" Jimmy asked.

"I overheard Zack, Paul, and Jeremy talking about it yesterday, in John's home. I had Anna check it at court to be sure. She was calling me today to confirm."

"Holy crap," Jimmy said.

"We have to talk to Zack immediately," Jerry said. "Find out what the hell is going on."

"Before you go to Zack, you need to know something else. Something that Zack and Paul do not know."

Dimitre studied the faces of the two engineers. It was hard to imagine relying on Jerry and Jimmy instead of Zack. How quickly things had changed. He began explaining about the faulty polymer formula. The work that they had all based their futures on had a fundamental flaw. What Imagination held as its closest secret was not worth the CD it was written on.

"So, everything we've sacrificed for has been a waste of time?" Jerry said in disbelief.

Jimmy appeared too stunned to speak.

"No, it does not have to be."

"What, is this more bad jokes?" Jerry said.

"I can speak Russian or German if that would make it easier

for you," Dimitre said. "Have you never wondered why we are in so much pile of shit? So often and so soon?"

"It's Allen," Jimmy said. "He's a vindictive asshole."

"Yes, Allen is a world-class asshole. But there is more. We are in this shit because Allen hates Zack. Before, Allen loved Zack, but now that he starts new company, Allen wants to kill him. Just like man and woman in bad marriage. This is why we have ridiculous TRO, this is why KGB comes to close our facility, and this is why he tries to put Zack in jail." Dimitre carefully studied his colleagues' faces before adding, "Because we belong with Zack, this means that we are in trouble too."

"We can still fight this thing," Jimmy said.

"Do not bend over and pick up cigarette."

"Huh?"

"You want to fight because you are tempted to? Or because you have no other choice?"

"You sound like Allen!" Jerry's face reddened. "I just don't get you. You're Zack's best friend, for crying out loud. You're telling us you want to abandon Zack when he really needs us? God! I can't believe I'm even hearing this."

"Zack was my friend. But he has been lying to me. Lying to all of us. He promised our company would not have secrets. Now, he is making all of us in danger. If he is hiding these things, what else is he hiding? He could go to jail, and he does not tell us this? What of us? Will we be receiving criminal complaints soon too?"

"So, what are you suggesting?" Jerry said.

"I am saying perhaps it is time we need to be looking out for ourselves. If Zack is hiding jail, he could be hiding other things."

While they digested what he'd said, Dimitre waved to the waitress for another round of beers.

"Maybe Zack just didn't want to worry us?" Jimmy said.

"It is not his decision to make," Dimitre said. "As soon as he becomes a filter, he becomes just like Allen."

"No way. Zack's not at all like Allen," Jimmy replied.

"Perhaps he is changing," Dimitre countered. "Perhaps Paul has changed him."

"Screw it," Jerry said, his voice full of indignation. "You're out of your mind. Some friend you've turned out to be. Remind me not to be yours."

"You know that I am right," Dimitre said. "Allen say worst idea is to attack a city."

"Please, no more Henley voodoo talk," said Jerry. "It makes me want to puke."

"We cannot win this thing," Dimitre said. "We are attacking a city that is a thousand times stronger, with a thousand times more resources than us. We cannot win."

Dimitre looked into Jerry's eyes. He hated doing this, but what choice did he have? It was obvious that Paul's influence had poisoned Zack. Now that Zack faced the possibility of imprisonment, Dimitre didn't dare risk being dragged down with him.

"I don't understand. What difference does any of this make?" Jimmy said. "If your formula doesn't work, then we don't have anything. None of this matters!"

"Come, come, my little friend, you do not really believe that?" Dimitre said, a smile coming out of hiding.

"What the hell are you talking about?" Jerry said. "You just told us that the damn formula didn't work!"

Dimitre leaned forward. "You were not listening. I said formula Imagination has does not work. It does not mean that I cannot fix it—if given time and money. But big question is, for who when Imagination is no more?"

"I hope you meant 'if,'" Jerry said, "not 'when.'"

"I think if you do not want to be hunted like wild pig, you will not squeal."

Jerry and Jimmy looked at each other, puzzled expressions on their faces.

Dimitre realized that even if he managed to solve the OLED lifetime issue, he was no businessman. He knew nothing about raising money and had no idea where to start. Jerry and Jimmy knew even less. Despite his loathing of Paul, the man did understand the financial community. Dimitre might be practically a genius—so his Anna said—but he was still just a technologist. And he could no longer count on Zack.

"Perhaps is time we are opening our own negotiations."

"What do you mean?" Jimmy said.

There was one obvious solution. In the nearly empty restaurant bar, Dimitre began to discuss a plan that a month ago would have been unthinkable. But today, it sounded surprisingly rational.

CHAPTER FORTY-FOUR

"What?" Zack said in amazement. He was on the phone with Dickens, sitting in the Bakers' home office with the door tightly shut. "I haven't told you anything yet."

"I know all about it. My money's been frozen."

Zack wasn't sure if he should have been relieved or shocked; he was some of both. "How did you find out?"

"Got to admit, this asshole Henley plays a good game of hardball. He confiscated our equipment and computers; the next logical step was to go after our capital."

"You seem pretty calm about the whole thing," Zack said, realizing that Dickens had avoided answering his question.

"Ha! Son, you should have seen me yesterday," Dickens said. He tried to clear his throat, sounding like a car trying to start.

"I did try to call you yesterday. Several times."

"Yes, I know. I suggest that you immediately cancel everything that … everything that you've ordered."

There was more hacking on the other line. Zack withdrew the phone from his ear. "Are you okay?"

"Yes, yes, though the airlines must be saving money nowadays by using first class as a big freezer." More coughing was followed by more clearing of his throat.

"Do you want to finish this later?"

"There may not be a later," Dickens said. "Go and cancel everything, understood?"

Every hair on Zack's neck pricked up. What had he meant by that? Was his champion going to die on him?

"Canceling could be a problem," Zack said. "Some of the equipment had very long lead times. Five or six months. We ordered them well before we officially started Imagination."

"Not to worry. Go ahead and cancel them, and then I'll reorder them immediately with one of my other companies in New York. Better yet, Houston, since we won't have to reship it quite so far. Just be sure to give me the details on what you've already ordered, purchase order numbers, invoices, all that. We'll handle the rest. Hold on—"

There was the sound of the receiver being set down on a hard surface, and he could hear coughing in the background. There were further rustling noises and some muffled sounds. Zack guessed Dickens got up to get tissues or a drink.

Zack heaved a sigh of relief. It was better than he could have hoped. He hadn't slept well again last night. Using Paul's cell phone, he had called Dickens yesterday afternoon, but his secretary had told him, in not-so-polite terms, that Mr. Dickens was in meetings all day and not to be disturbed—for any reason. Yes, she knew who Zack was, and yes, she would tell Mr. Dickens that it was an emergency. He hadn't called back.

Zack tried again after she'd left for the day, but the phone merely rang to voice mail. After her earlier tone, he didn't dare leave a message, but it had meant a very sleepless night filled with dread over what Dickens would say and the fear of facing his own team when the paychecks started to bounce.

There was a rattle as Dickens scooped up the phone. "I should sue the damn airline," he said, his voice still throaty. "Now where the hell was I?"

"You were talking about using another of your companies in Houston to—"

"Yes, right. After our lawyers bury Henley, we transfer the equipment back to Imagination. Anything else?"

Before Zack could bring up the subject of the team's salaries, Dickens made it easy for him.

"Oh yes, we use another company to pay for your engineering team's salaries. No sense in penalizing them for what we've gotten ourselves into. But considering that we intend to bail you out, I don't think that you or Paul should be drawing a salary for this cock-up. Agreed?"

What else could he say but yes?

"Of course, Jeremy is still retained as general counsel until my New York staff can determine the best course of action. And we've still got to talk about your legal defense for the criminal complaint."

In all the confusion of yesterday's problems with the bank, Zack had forgotten about the criminal charges against him. It was Thursday morning, and that Monday afternoon on the Bakers' deck seemed a lifetime ago.

"Is Jeremy there? Can I talk to him?" Dickens said. Another cough, less intense this time.

Zack waited a moment before answering. "Jeremy and Paul are in court right now. McSorley called us late yesterday. Judge Rafkin issued something called an ex parte order."

"Why the hell aren't you there with them?"

The remark took Zack by surprise, the tone more than the content. "Jeremy and Paul can handle it. I'm here, working with the engineers."

"Damn it, you're the CEO and president. Don't you realize what that means? It doesn't mean sitting in a cushy office while a cute secretary screens your calls. You're responsible for every segment of that company. You're also the one responsible for my money."

"We've talked about this before. We agreed that Paul and Jeremy would handle the court battles while I keep operations going."

"That was before you lost my money."

Zack didn't know how to respond. For what seemed to be an eternity, the line between them was silent.

"Any ideas on how Henley froze our account?" Dickens said finally.

The question surprised him. Zack had thought since Dickens knew about the frozen account so soon that he also knew how it had been pulled off.

"Son, did you hear my question?"

Zack could feel the knuckles of his right hand start to tingle. He switched hands to hold the phone. "Well, Jeremy speculated that they're trying to tie the account to an illegal activity of some kind."

"What *kind* of illegal activity?"

"We don't know," Zack said. "We'll find out at court today."

"You let me know as soon as you know something."

"I will. By the way, you didn't tell me how you found out about the bank account."

There was an abrupt click as the line went dead.

━━━━━━━━

Paul mumbled something about the air conditioner, his voice just above the low-frequency hum of the tires going over the concrete of the Bay Bridge. Jeremy placed his right hand over the vent of his green Daimler and noticed the air wasn't very cool, even though the dial was cranked to the maximum. As he leaned over to flick the controls on and off, he felt the back of his shirt peel away from the leather upholstery.

Paul opened the passenger window. Immediately, Jeremy felt the invasion of noise and warm air, but fresh air was always more welcome than manufactured air. Out of the corner of his eye, he saw Paul reach inside his jacket pocket and pull out his cell phone. Paul cursed as he struggled to remove his jacket, the sweat trickling down his temples; a short time later, he stopped to complain that he might have pulled a shoulder muscle.

Paul held his cell phone like it was a compass. "Christ, so much for modern technology," he said. "Can't get any kind of signal at all."

"It must be the interference from the bridge." Jeremy wiped his brow with his shirtsleeve, rolled up just above his mid-forearm.

"That never happened before."

"Try again." Jeremy rested both hands on the steering wheel at the twelve o'clock position, the car slowing to a complete stop. He looked at the traffic ahead. God, it was awful, he thought. He rested his forehead on his folded hands for a moment, hearing from overhead the rapid movement of cars. He always felt more insulated in the lower deck because the bridge's sidewall prevented him from seeing the bay. He hated looking down and seeing all that water.

Jeremy glanced to his right and saw a young man in a classic white Ford Mustang with red interior easing by, his head closely shaven, talking calmly on his cell phone. Jeremy crept forward while Paul turned on the cell phone again. This time, the phone reported finding a communication signal. He pressed the speed-dial function.

"Pick up, Zack. Come on, damn it, pick up."

Paul held the phone away for a second to turn up the phone's volume a level or two. Jeremy could hear Zack's "Hello?" and then there was the static.

"Hey, Zack. Listen, we're on our way home. I want to ..." Click. "Zack! Can you hear me? I said can you hear me?" Paul glanced at the phone display. "For Christ's sake! What's wrong with this goddamn thing?"

"Is the battery charged?" Jeremy said, looking over.

"Of course, the phone's charged," Paul said. "You just keep your eyes on the friggin' road."

"We're going about three miles per hour here," Jeremy said. "If you haven't noticed, the traffic's backed up all the way into Oakland."

"Just keep your eyes on the road. We've had enough accidents for one day." Paul wiped his forehead again. "Christ, it's hot in this fucking car."

Paul punched the speed-dial feature again.

Static. "... Hello?"

"Zack. Can you hear me?"

"... an't quite ... you ... are you?"

Paul punched up the volume to full. "Is this better? Can you hear me?" Static. "Zack, are you there?"

An alarm began to chime.

Paul punched the top of the glove compartment. "Fuck it! You think we could catch a break, just one lousy break. Zack, look, we don't have much time. I gotta tell you, something happened at court today."

There was a beep, and the cell phone display went completely dead.

Jeremy watched in astonishment as Paul threw his cell phone out the passenger window, the device slipping between the joints of the bridge.

———————————————

Louise's voice cracked through the office intercom. "Mr. Henley? There's a phone call for you."

"Is it McSorley?" Allen asked over his shoulder, casting his question in the general direction of the speakerphone. He stood by the window, looking out.

"No, sir. But—"

"I told you. No calls until after I speak with McSorley." What the hell was wrong with Louise today? She took directions better than that.

There was a pause and then she spoke again. "Is there a convenient time when I should have Mr. Koslov call you back?"

Koslov? He walked to the phone, his hands still behind his back. "Dimitre Koslov?"

"Yes, sir."

What was this? "Put him through. If McSorley calls, have him hold the line."

"Yes, sir."

The line clicked. "Hello?" He immediately recognized the Russian accent.

"Hello, Dimitre."

"Is this line secure?"

"I rather doubt my secretary would care or have time to listen."

"I should like to arrange meeting with you. Perhaps tomorrow?"

"Regarding what, exactly?"

"I would rather be discussing in person than over phone."

"I see. Let me be frank with you, Mr. Koslov. I don't have time to play games. You can either be straight with me or you can find someone else to bother."

"I wish to talk about future of DisplayTechnik."

That was unexpected.

"I think I have valuable information for you," the Russian continued.

This smelled like a trap. He should have known Zack would resort to sending an emissary to try to circumvent the court. Either that, or the Russian really did have information that he and McSorley lacked. Perhaps Koslov was afraid he would be next to be indicted on criminal charges, wondering why he hadn't been served yet. "If this has anything at all to do with saving Zack's skin," Allen said, "you can forget it."

"It does not. Zack is … on his own."

Once again, the master, Sun Tzu, was proven correct. Dissension among the ranks; he didn't even need to hear confirmation from Dean. He had already won the war, no matter what the courts dictated.

"Name the time and place. Here in Milpitas, of course."

CHAPTER FORTY-FIVE

The door to the Bakers' home office burst open, startling Zack half out of his skin.

"That backstabbing snake!" Paul shouted as he rushed in. "That low-life bastard!"

Jeremy was right on his heels.

"Lower your voice, damn it," Zack said, rounding the desk to shut the door behind them. "You didn't need to come back from the city; you could have just shouted to me from across the bay. What happened in court?"

"The big bad wolf just blew our fucking house down!" Paul said.

"What?"

"He huffed and he puffed and everything's gone."

"Save the nursery rhymes for your kids. What the hell happened in court?"

"That blood-sucking leech stole it from us!"

"Stole what?" Zack said.

"We go into court today, and that ... bloody shark, McSorley, starts explaining to the judge how we've stolen a vital secret from DisplayTechnik."

"What secret?"

"The fucking formula!"

"What? That's insane."

"It was so outrageous that Jeremy and I stood there like two of the little pigs. The big bad wolf comes and fires a cruise missile at our straw house. I mean, what the hell can you do? You can plan for all kinds of contingencies, but you can't plan for the 'Three Little Pigs Meet Hiroshima.' And what really pisses me off is that goddamn Judge Rafkin sat there, swallowing every lie spun by McSorley and Bennet like they were bonbons."

"Listen, Paul, if you don't tell me what the hell's going on, I will—"

Jeremy stepped in front of Paul. "Maybe I can explain."

Zack waved him on. Paul flopped down on the three-cushion sofa, his yellow tie flipped over his right shoulder.

"Dean McSorley's argument went like this," Jeremy said. "DisplayTechnik claims that a scientist working there some years ago came up with a polymer formula to manufacture a new revolutionary flat-panel television—a display so paper-thin that you could roll it out like a carpet. Sound familiar?"

Zack sagged against the edge of the desk.

"They claim that they have evidentiary *proof* of this fact. They claim that we stole it from them and that Dickens paid us money to start Imagination with this formula, which had been sitting in the company archives for years. They claim DisplayTechnik never pursued it because the scientist who developed it died and also because at the time he came up with it, it wasn't considered viable. Further, they claim either you or Dimitre must have come across the scientist's paper at some point during your tenure of employment."

Until that moment, Zack had believed that they could outlast Allen at any game he played. Sure, Allen was making things hard for them, he had thrown up a lot of smoke screens, a lot of spinning mirrors, but they were only shadows, with no physical form or basis in reality. Despite all the setbacks, all the attacks, and despite the fact that Allen, void of any moral principles at all, had used his own daughter to manipulate the situation, Zack still believed they were going to prevail.

Imagination was going to be based on the core values that he and Dimitre and the rest of the engineers had so badly wished for. Together, they had a unique and innovative polymer formula that no one in the world knew anything about. And they were convinced it would blow away any other technology. The way to the future had been paved with gold.

He leaned heavily against the desk. How could this be happening? Paul was saying something, his mouth moving rapidly, but Zack couldn't understand it. Everything he had ever believed or understood was collapsing on him. A small voice inside him kept saying they were going to win; they were still going to win. But the small voice was drowning in a sea of darkness and disbelief.

"Zack?" Jeremy put his hand on Zack's shoulder, a worried look on his face.

"Fucking unbelievable," Paul said, an unlit Marlboro bouncing in the corner of his mouth. "We invent the bloody polymer formula. Now Henley claims that we stole our own formula from him. You couldn't even dream up a Hollywood script like that!"

Zack needed to think. He went back to the desk, piled high with papers and files, and sat down. He'd seen the engineering archives at DisplayTechnik. They consisted of boxes and boxes of disorganized files and old five-and-a-quarter-inch disks in a temperature-controlled room at the lowest level of the Ivory Tower. It wasn't hard to gain access. You simply signed a sheet at the security guard's station, and anything you removed was also logged. The archives were rarely accessed since everything was done with word processors or drawing programs, and at 11:00 p.m., everything on file was automatically backed up.

Was it possible that Dimitre had been lying to him all along? Had Dimitre found some arcane formula years ago? Perhaps running tests at DisplayTechnik until he fully understood it, waiting for the right time to use it for his own advantage? Was it possible that Zack had based his entire dream on a theft? Zack buried his head in his hands. Forget dreams; he was living in a nightmare.

The haunting dream of Allen laughing at him after he'd been

disqualified from a tennis match for no apparent reason flashed before his eyes.

Wait a minute, he thought. How did Henley know we'd supposedly stolen this formula? How did he get hold of our formula in order to claim it was his?

"Jeremy," Zack said, "where do the marshals store the PC equipment they took from the Santa Clara facility?"

"Well, they usually keep confiscated equipment in a separate depot."

"Usually?"

"There's another option."

"What is it?"

Jeremy paused before he replied. "The court can issue a protective order, where the equipment is secured by the plaintiff's attorney."

"You got to be fucking kidding me!" Paul said, jumping off the sofa.

"Find out, will you?" Zack said, closing his eyes.

After making a number of calls, Jeremy confirmed the worst.

"Okay, so that asshole McSorley kept the keys to our equipment," Paul said. "So what? I mean, it's bad, but no worse than when Mary Anne divulged what was in Zack's home. Besides, the marshals are there to watch over our things, right?"

Zack looked at Jeremy. They had trusted him with their lives. They had trusted the system, at his insistence, because Jeremy had assured them that they would get in trouble if they didn't and that it would protect them. Zack had latched onto that with every ounce of his being because it had been the right thing to do.

"It wouldn't matter if it was on your systems or in your files," Jeremy said. "It wouldn't matter if you handed the formula to Allen. Remember, this is all part of the process of discovery. What's important is that DisplayTechnik claims prior art. Someone there worked on this before, and apparently they have proof of that. If it's true, I gotta be honest, it's pretty damning."

"Fuck it," Paul said. "I *knew* we should have hid things, I just knew it. He stole the formula, and now he's claiming it was his all along."

"Well, unfortunately, he's claiming you did the same thing," Jeremy said. "Except he evidently has some proof to back it up."

Zack stood up. They hadn't stolen anything. Allen had. He was a soulless bastard, but no one disputed his technical intelligence and business acumen. He had a gift for seizing an opportunity and maximizing its potential. If anyone could recognize the genius of a polymer formula and its applications, Allen was that person.

Obviously, he had, because the genie was out of the bottle. Allen's shameless boldness to prosecute the theft of Imagination's formula was perfectly in line with the manipulation of his daughter. He laughed. His two friends looked at him oddly. It was so incredible it was … it was beyond words.

"You all right?" Paul asked.

Zack closed his eyes, shaking his head. "You guys ever see Cary Grant in *To Catch a Thief*?"

Paul and Jeremy looked at him like he was talking Russian.

"Great movie," he went on. "A cat burglar gets caught by the police and claims, 'Monsieur Policeman, *excusez-moi* but zees woman's precious jewels zat you sink I stole are really my jewels. You see, I commit zee break and entry into her home to retrieve what was rightfully mine.' And the cop says, 'Ahhh, Monsieur Cat Burglar, I understand your point completely. *Oui, oui,* we march that foolish woman off to the guillotine. Now, Monsieur Cat Burgular, please go back to the woman's home. It rightfully belongs to you.' *'Bien sur,'* the burglar replies. 'I will.'"

Charlotte would have been proud of his accent.

"Okay, Zack, take it easy," Jeremy said, looking to Paul for help. "We'll get through this somehow with Dickens's help. He'll know how to handle this."

Allen hung up the phone, laughing as he slammed it into its cradle. He spun in his chair, laughing up at the ceiling. Dean had reported a complete victory in the morning's battle. Not just the permanent order to freeze Imagination's bank account pending the final outcome of the restraining order, but that their filing had caught the other side so completely off guard they were unable to respond. Dean had said that Jeremy looked like he'd just come out of a sound sleep with the help of a brick. Allen laughed some more. He could only imagine what Zack's face would look like when he found out.

The end was coming soon.

He felt like summoning Julie to his office but thought he needed something different to mirror his display of force this morning. Smiling, he picked up an envelope from his desk that had arrived this morning. He was in the mood to celebrate, and this was just the ticket.

He opened the envelope to be sure there was nothing personal inside, a bit disappointed when there was not. He had already offered the young paralegal a job in Bill Bennet's office, but Terri wasn't taking it just yet. She had a month of work ahead of her at Dean's office and was in the middle of finals as well. She was going to law school afterward but said that she wanted a part-time job with DisplayTechnik once her work at Dean's was finished.

She was intelligent and witty in addition to being beautiful. He distinctly remembered her smile as she'd teased him that he could hire her at a fat salary when she was a full attorney. He especially remembered her hand on his arm and the smell of her perfume as she stepped closer to say that she hoped they could work something out.

Allen enjoyed her brashness—that she made no attempt to hide that she was using him and his money to get what she wanted. Could it be he'd finally found a woman who was his equal? He liked the idea of having a woman lawyer. After all, anything that happened between them would be legally held in confidence. Not like Julie.

He tucked the envelope under his arm and left the office. He might be CEO and president, but he was an employee of decorum.

Still chuckling at the image of Zack's face, he smiled and winked at Louise, skipped down the stairs, and left the tower.

Dimitre walked over to Jimmy and Jerry, who were huddled on the back deck in front of Jerry's workstation. Under the pretense of needing some doughnuts and "real" coffee, he had left to place his call to Allen. As he joined them, Jeremy's Daimler pulled up, and car doors slammed. It was a safe bet the lawyer and Paul's court report would keep Zack busy and out of earshot.

"So, what did he say?" Jimmy asked.

"He is agreeing to talk to me tomorrow. I am meeting him at the Denny's across from the Milpitas facility."

"Whoa, you sure that's a good idea?" Jerry said. "That's our former neck of the woods. Some of the old crew might see you. What if word gets back to ... you know?" He inclined his head toward the house.

"I do not like to talk to the man, and it was the only place I could think of quickly. Risk is minimal. I am meeting him tomorrow at two. Most of DisplayTechnik's workers will be back at office or sitting in traffic on way home early for weekend."

They had discussed the meeting in great detail last night at Zorro's. Dimitre wasn't to agree to anything. It was just a test of the waters to see if it were possible to go back; if not, they would quietly begin looking for work elsewhere. Since it was Dimitre's idea, they had elected him their spokesman.

Jimmy looked at the Baker house. "What do you figure is going on in there?"

"I don't know," Jerry said. "Judging by how hard someone shut their car door, I'd guess it wasn't good. Then again, nothing's come out the window yet, so maybe it's not that bad."

"Where do you figure they were coming from anyway?"

Jerry shrugged. "Hard to say with those two." He turned back to his screen. He'd given up trying to work and was playing solitaire.

It was quiet, other than the wind and the sounds of the freeway drifting up the valley.

Jimmy took a deep breath and let it out slowly. "Man, I got to tell you. It has been totally weird being around Zack this morning. I feel like I'm stabbing him in the back."

Dimitre nodded. No one liked this. But the decision had been made. They had to protect themselves. What the others did not know was that after listening to Jimmy's pleading last night—he was the only one who did not have a family to protect, so he was the most loyal among them—Dimitre had devised a simple plan. If Zack voluntarily brought up the criminal charge or the eviction notice, then Dimitre would cancel his meeting, and together the three of them would find some way to stick it out.

A part of him hoped that Zack would pass his little test, but he was quite sure that he would not. He had betrayed their trust; he had lied to them and broken the very principles that he had used to lure them away. A man who had betrayed his fundamental values was not likely to pass a test of loyalty.

CHAPTER FORTY-SIX

Julie was surprised to see Allen walk into her office. She was on the phone checking a reference for a job applicant while Tiffany waited with a notebook and a stack of other applications. Tiffany blushed slightly at Allen and then glanced at Julie, looking very nervous.

"My dear, if you'll excuse us," Allen said, "I need to talk with your boss." He brandished an envelope. "I have something for her." He held the door for Tiffany, who quickly ducked out, without waiting for Julie's response. Allen shut the door behind her, quietly locking it.

"Listen, I'm sorry," Julie said into the phone, "can I call you back later? Thanks."

She hung up, looking at Allen's smug face. "What did you do that for? We have thirty applicants to go through. I need Tiffany back." She stood up and tried to get past him.

Allen grabbed her by the arm. "This is more important."

She didn't shake off his hand, but slowly removed her arm from his grip. "I'm busy here. I do work for you in case you don't recall."

He took her around the waist and pulled her into him, kissing her hard. He pushed her back into the desk; she could feel his excitement against her hip.

"Stop it. I—" she tried to say, but he cut her off, covering her mouth again with his. His hands groped at her, pulling at her tight skirt, fumbling with her blouse. He forced his hand inside, and a button popped off. She tried to push him away, muttering words unheard into his mouth.

Unable to make fast enough headway with her clothes, a zip sounded loud in the empty room. He took her by the hair at the back of her neck and pushed her down. She knew better than to resist.

When it was over, Julie crawled on the floor to retrieve her button and papers that had fallen. Allen watched her, leaning against the desk, a satisfied look on his face. She stood up, straightened her clothes, and moved to a small mirror she kept on the back of the door.

"Aren't you going to at least tell me what that was all about?" she said, wiping away smudged lipstick.

"It was a victory celebration. Zack's little dream is dead. His silicon dream is dead. I have crushed him. He put up a decent fight, but he was never any match for me."

"Silicon dream?"

He stood up, undoing his belt to tuck himself back in. "Yes, it's from conversations Zack and I used to have. All the time, in fact. The pursuit of the dream. The silicon dream, he used to call it. We disagreed on the definition of that dream. Zack would always talk about *believing* in something. He was right in a way, but he was also completely wrong. When I first started, a long time ago, arriving from the United Kingdom, I had those same high principles, the ones accompanied by a choir of bloody angels from St. Peter's. But pursuit of the dream can't overtake reality. Dreams and beliefs, no matter how principled, don't put food on the table, they don't send kids to school, and they don't buy nice houses with little white picket fences."

"So what are you saying, that people shouldn't have dreams? That it's not okay to believe in something?"

"I'm *saying* that there's no loyalty in America. None. People don't work for me because they believe in me. Hell, they couldn't care less about me. They work for me because it helps them get what they want. Money. Money for a bigger house, more cable channels, vacations from their pathetic lives. Today, people don't have any respect for their employers."

"I'm sure that people like Zack believe in something besides money."

"Bullshit. The reality is that if you took away the so-called belief, people would continue to stay because of the money. If people were offered more money at another company to do the same job and they didn't have to relocate their families, their employers would be smelling their exhaust fumes. The only reason why this doesn't happen more often is because people are sheep. Just dumb, pitiful sheep, who don't have enough imagination to sniff past their own assholes."

Julie shuddered. She was one of those sheep. Pliant. Weak. Vulnerable. Feeling the shame of it, tears filled her eyes. As she rubbed them away under the pretense of examining her makeup, her lower lip trembled.

Allen walked toward her. He reached out and stroked her left cheek. She jerked her head away.

"What are you pouting about?" he demanded. "It's very unattractive."

"I'm sorry, but I just think you can believe in something and be financially rewarded," Julie said. "Zack's following his dream. Was following it, anyway. If you hadn't been there, don't you think he would have had both?"

Allen's eyes flashed; the playfulness in his face disappeared.

"All right, let's talk about Mr. Zachary Penny. Do you think that his bullshit high moral principles have some magic spell on his little team of engineers? Despite his self-proclaimed sainthood, he's no different from the rest of us."

"He doesn't announce his principles. The engineers are just loyal to him." And not to you, she thought. "After all, they left you. It takes belief to follow Zack."

"That's not loyalty; that's just old-fashioned greed, plus a bit of stupidity thrown in for good measure." Allen spread his arms like a priest giving a benediction. "I am the shepherd of the flock. The technical geeks and freaks are sheep. Trust me." He smiled a devious smile. "With but one wave of my staff, any of Zack's engineers can be brought into my fold. And I mean anyone."

Julie looked into Allen's small eyes. They were cold and hard, looking out as though he held some secret knowledge that the rest of the world was not entitled to. It wasn't just his eyes that made her uncomfortable. It was the thoughts behind those eyes. She was beginning to understand what he was truly capable of.

"Please go. I have work to do."

"Oh, yes, that reminds me." He scooped up the envelope from where he had dropped it near the door. "This is a résumé from someone at McSorley's office. Find her a position in Bill Bennet's department. If there isn't one available, make one. She's too valuable to let go."

He turned and left.

Chapter Forty-Seven

Zack, Paul, and Jeremy were in no mood to think clearly, so they agreed to reconvene tomorrow morning. It wasn't until Zack was halfway home that he realized he hadn't said good-bye to his team, even though he'd stumbled out on the deck to pick up his station for the evening and had felt their eyes on him. He hadn't told them they should leave for the day too. He just needed to get out of there, to retreat to the safety of his own home. He decided they could go one more day before he told them all their dreams had been crushed.

When Zack reached for the doorknob to insert his key, the knob turned easily. Had he left the door unlocked? He couldn't remember. He put his keys back in his pocket. When he opened the apartment door, it was dark inside.

He flicked on the main light. Everything looked intact. The television was still there, the CD stereo, the love seat, the sofa, and the La-Z-Boy chair. Even the stains on the carpet looked the same. He went into his home office. The desk appeared undisturbed, two piles of trade magazines on one corner, one pile with the familiar, solid yellow spine of the *National Geographic*, high enough to partially hide the telephone. Zack picked up the receiver and listened to his voice mails.

Dickens had left a short message asking him to call. When Zack reached him, he got the news that Dickens and the rest of the New York investors had decided to pull the plug on the company.

It was the end of the silicon dream.

There was no secret polymer formula anymore, Dickens explained in an even tone. Allen Henley had it. There was the remote possibility that the New York investors could be dragged into the sordid mess and be publicly portrayed by Henley's lawyers as the purchasers of stolen trade secrets. Of course, that wouldn't happen, Dickens said, but they were too old for that kind of nonsense. Clearly, they had underestimated Henley.

"Son, I'm certain that once financial support is withdrawn from Imagination, Henley will call off his legal dogs because there won't be anything left to pursue."

Zack was sitting in his chair, one hand holding the phone, the other cradling his head. Tears streamed down his forearm. Yes, there will, he wanted to say. Allen could still pursue *him*. And now that Dickens was pulling his support, there was no way to hold him off.

"The best exit strategy is for us to bow out now," Dickens said. "I know I told you New York invented hardball, but we're used to doing business here in New York, not in sunstroked California."

Dickens carried on. Zack was not really listening as he justified why he was backing out. In the middle of a sentence, the elderly investor stopped. He burst into a racking fit of coughing.

Just as Zack was ready to say good-bye, Dickens offered some final advice. "Don't try to raise money from someone else," he said in a fatherly tone. "The word is out on the streets. And even if you were to find someone, Henley will unleash his legal hounds again. With so many options out there, no investor wants to take on Henley. Sorry, son."

Without another word, Zack hung up on him.

For a brief moment, Zack wondered if he should sue Dickens and his hypocritical band of New York investors. After all, they had a term sheet. It was a legal contract, wasn't it? Surely, Dickens couldn't simply pull out and leave Zack and Paul holding the liability bag. He could take Dickens to court and force him to uphold his multimillion-dollar investment—at least until the TRO lunacy had been settled. The thought of waging a two-front attack against two very wealthy men was absurd.

He started to snicker and then laughed uncontrollably. For a guy who was used to keeping things under control, his emotions were now pinned on his shirtsleeves.

Zack wiped his eyes and walked in a fog to the refrigerator. He reached in and grabbed a six-pack of beer. There was a takeout pizza menu stuck to the door with a magnet advertising a local realtor. Zack tore off the leaflet, crushed it into a ball, and threw it at a poster of the White Mountains taped to the opposite wall. It had been a lifetime ago that he and Dimitre had gone backpacking in the mountains near Tahoe, dreaming up the idea of leaving DisplayTechnik and forming their own company.

He rotated his neck, feeling the tightness. He went to the living room and collapsed on the sofa, turning on the TV just for some background noise.

Sometime later—he had no idea how long—he heard a knock at the door and opened his eyes. Six beer cans littered the floor, and his first thought was to wonder who'd been here to help him drink so many. He was slumped on the love seat, his legs dangling over the side, the television blasting. He looked at his watch, but it was too dark to see.

———————————————

Outside the front door of Zack's apartment, Mary Anne stood quietly. She could hear the television inside. She knocked again, her dress making a crinkling sound. A Hong Kong creation, it was made from a fabric with the texture of paper, but much stronger. She knocked for the third time. She could see light through the side window. She put her hand on the doorknob, turned it easily, and stepped inside.

"Zack?" she called. "Zack, are you there?"

She saw him sprawled across the love seat. One of his running shoes lay on the floor; the other was still attached to its owner, now rising to a sitting position, knocking over an empty beer can.

"Well, well," Zack said, his eyes only half-open, "I guess once a spy, always a spy. What's the matter? Daddy's little spy still needs more information?" He yawned, stretching his arms.

"The door was open," Mary Anne said.

"Sure, that makes it all right. I always walk into people's homes unannounced."

"I knocked, actually. Several times." Mary Anne glanced past Zack at the old black-and-white film on the television. "So, may I come in?"

"You're already in."

Mary Anne reached over and turned on the floor lamp. The redness of Zack's eyes jumped out at her. On the drive over, she'd rehearsed this moment many times. She went past the sofa and turned off the television and then sat on the edge of the La-Z-Boy, directly across from him. The vertical drapes over the balcony window were wide-open; the yellow traffic light on Stoneridge Drive was blinking steadily.

"What time is it?" Zack said.

Mary Anne looked at her watch. "It's just past seven."

"Did I ever tell you that you've got a great sense of timing?"

"I don't understand."

"The last time I saw you, you came waltzing onto the Bakers' sundeck just a few minutes before I was served a criminal complaint. Great timing."

"I told you, I had no idea that was going to happen."

"So, what was it? We had a solid year together, but just like that," Zack made a poor attempt to snap his fingers, "you believed Allen over me?"

This was not how she'd rehearsed it. "My father showed me some e-mails about Imagination. Some cryptic e-mails between you and Dimitre."

"Ah yes, the famous and brilliant Dimitre. I'm sure he'll find work."

"Listen, I came by to tell you something," Mary Anne said.

Zack got up and went to the kitchen. There was the sound of

bottles clinking and a door closing. He returned, holding a beer. "All right, let's hear it," he said, falling back on the green sofa. "I know you won't leave until you say it."

"I've made up my mind to confront my father. Tell him to tell the truth."

"Oh yes, the famous truth." Zack leaned his head back against the sofa. "The glue that holds society together."

"I used to think your beliefs were empty platitudes. Over the years, Allen and my mother have made me become so cynical. But you were right. If you don't believe in something, you are lost."

"Christ, that really is a load of crap," Zack said. "Did I really used to say that? Because I gotta tell ya, it sounds pretty pathetic."

"You've had too much to drink."

"Don't you see? I'm no different than Allen. Each one of us protects our own version of the truth."

"No. You're so different from my father. He might say things, but he never believes in them. He doesn't believe in anything or anyone. But you're different. I just never knew how much until now."

"You should hear yourself talking! Where were you a week ago when some of this might have meant something?"

"Please don't do this!"

"It's over, damn it. It's all over! Your daddy just got out his big elephant gun, pointed it at my small little company, and blew our brains out. Surprised?"

Mary Anne's face flushed.

"There's no company. There's no more funding. Got it? No more money! My backers have just jumped ship. They've bailed out. Now you come here talking about morals and how you're going to stop Daddy—after it's already all over. Jesus, your sense of timing is uncanny. Just uncanny. Daddy won. I lost. Hell, he even managed to poison our relationship. Turned us against each other. You've got to marvel at how brilliant your father is."

"I'm still here," Mary Anne said softly.

"Don't you get it? It's over. The company, my dreams, and

especially our relationship. It's over. I don't want someone who set me up!"

Zack drained the can of beer, crushed it, and threw it against the wall.

Mary Anne got up from the La-Z-Boy chair and took a tentative step toward Zack, her heart fluttering. "If you quit, then Allen wins," she said, extending her hand.

Zack turned away. "Quit?" He pushed her arm aside and got up from the sofa. "You must be joking. Hell, I'll probably be going to jail."

"Please, let me help," Mary Anne said, her eyes watering. "Please."

Zack rounded on her. "You wanna help? Then get the hell out."

The phone was ringing.

Zack's head throbbed, killing any motivation to rise from the pillow. He didn't know how long he'd been sleeping. It was kind of dark, but it looked either like early morning or just after twilight. He guessed twilight, but if he were right, he wasn't sure what day it was.

There was a sour, sticky taste in his mouth that made him wish for a drink of water, but that would mean getting up. He decided it wasn't worth the trip; he could wait. He rolled over awkwardly, the stiffness of his jeans chafing in sensitive spots. Now he felt the urge to pee.

The phone kept ringing.

He willed it to go to voice mail but vaguely remembered it had been ringing a short while ago and this must be their second attempt. He had to stop the throbbing. He rolled back over and reached for the source.

The receiver felt foreign against his ear. The person at the other end started to talk loudly and rapidly, confusing his brain. Zack didn't understand most of the one-sided conversation, but he managed to catch a few of the words. It sounded like there was going to be a meeting. Who's meeting? When the name was spoken, another elephant gun exploded in his brain.

"Who is this?" Zack said.

"You heard me," the voice said.

"Tell me again."

Dean McSorley wanted to meet.

Chapter Forty-Eight

At his desk Friday morning, Allen scanned through the 123 e-mails that Louise had sorted through and printed out for him. Without looking up, he reached for his coffee, sipped it too quickly, and burned his tongue. He jerked his head back, his reading glasses nearly falling off his nose. As he reset them, he noticed a few drops of coffee had splattered onto the top of the stack. He frowned and wiped them off with the cloth napkin Louise had set on the tray.

He was having a hard time concentrating. Dean had unexpectedly canceled their early morning tennis match, something he'd never done before. His voice-mail message didn't explain why. Allen had listened to the voice mail twice, making sure he wasn't missing something, but there it was. Dean had canceled on him. It was rare for anyone to decline a meeting, appointment, or tennis match with Allen. It just didn't happen.

Allen didn't believe in signs; he believed in subtle shifts.

A heavily religious childhood had instilled in him the belief in God, but he had come to view God the way the philosophers of the eighteenth and nineteenth centuries did: as the Great Clockmaker. God, or a god, had created the world like a giant clock, winding it up and then stepping back to see what happened. That belief system accounted for the input of mankind, that mankind could and did have influence on the outcome of events. There was that saying that there were no accidents, as though God had a hand in everything. As far as Allen was concerned, God wasn't even in the car.

People were creatures of habit, easily predictable. Small changes in habit patterns sometimes indicated larger changes underneath the surface. Dean canceling a tennis match was out of the ordinary, and he wished he knew the reason why.

Something else annoyed him. Or perhaps more aptly, something else puzzled him.

Last night, he and Charlotte had made love. They had not done so since the last full moon—or so it seemed. Not that Allen really needed it or wanted it, because he'd spent himself earlier in the afternoon with Julie. Still, Charlotte had approached him after he'd come home for the evening, at a decent hour for a change. Mary Anne was nowhere around. She'd been wearing that elegant baby blue and white lace nightgown that sculpted her figure so well. When she opened the accompanying robe to display herself to him, he didn't say no.

She surprised him not only by her willingness but also with her unusual eagerness—almost aggressiveness. Despite the alcohol and number of years together, the last three in separate bedrooms, Allen still found Charlotte sexually attractive. Her hips were a little heavier now and her readiness usually took a lot longer, but she was still an exciting woman to be with. When she'd left his room afterward, she'd looked back over her shoulder, a smile spreading across her face at his utter exhaustion—a tiger satisfied with the kill. He enjoyed it, of course, but still, his wife's behavior puzzled him.

Not one but two stones had been dropped into his pond. The ripples were unsettling.

He had built a life out of anticipating problems. Like an Indian scout trying to read shifts in the wind, he struggled to interpret the meaning of the subtle shifts of two people that he'd allowed to be close to him.

For now, he believed they were meaningless. Sometimes the wind just shifted. Certainly, they were small and insignificant things relative to what he was facing. Yet it was still not a good way to start the business day; he always wanted to start with a clear head.

Allen grunted as he flipped through the rest of the e-mails. There was so much to do, he realized. He had the polymer formula, but now he had to launch an entirely new division. He had to talk to the moneymen, the bankers. He had to assemble a capable management staff, a delicate mix of brownnosers and ass-kickers. Jump-start the development team. Tool up the new facility, order equipment and supplies. He also needed experienced design engineers who were capable of understanding this radically new technology of pancake-flat television screens with three-dimensional capability.

It was unfortunate about Zack. After all, he would have been perfect to head up the new division. Him and that ragtag team of rebels. Which reminded him that he had that afternoon meeting with that Ukrainian.

And with that thought, Allen slammed his palm on the desk, resulting in more coffee slopping onto the papers. My God, that was it. That was why the Ukrainian was contacting him. The vision of the path in front of him hit with sudden clarity. It was so surreal.

Yesterday when Dimitre had called, Allen had thought that he'd been trying to save his own skin out of fear of being indicted, that he would even turn Zack in, claiming that he had information that could help with Zack's prosecution. But the Ukrainian was actually calling to get a job. So much for belief, so much for Zack's engineers following him because they were following a dream. Like the rats that they were, they'd seen that the ship was sinking fast.

He was so sure of it that he could feel it. My God, it was so deliciously obvious.

Allen laughed so loudly that Louise peered in through the anteroom door, checking to see that he was all right. He waved her off, returning his attention to the stack of papers. He circled the e-mails that he needed to take care of and delegated the remainder to his VPs for further follow-up. He took off his silver reading glasses and made a mental note to visit the ophthalmologist because the letters in the e-mail messages were starting to flow together.

Thoughts about Dimitre had reminded him of the other important task for today. He wished Dean hadn't canceled their tennis match this morning because he'd wanted the lawyer to finish tying up a loose end, something Dean had thought was only a diversionary tactic. It was not.

Zack was going to jail. It was that bloody simple.

Dean stood at the opening to the circular parking lot of Coit Tower, its white fluted sides rising high above him. Perched on top of Telegraph Hill, it was a good vantage point to see the city and the waterfront. Alcatraz, the abandoned island prison glorified by Hollywood, was directly across the bay in front of him. Below, he could see the cargo and cruise ships docked at the various piers. To his right, he could see the steel-gray Bay Bridge linking Treasure Island to Oakland. If he leaned over the railing and peered to the far left, he could make out the Golden Gate Bridge, its red splendor piercing through the Friday morning fog.

Dean's thoughts wandered to the history of Coit Tower. He recalled young Lillie Hitchcock had been rescued by firemen at the age of eight, pulled from a burning building; two playmates had not been so lucky. Thus began her lifelong fascination with the bravery of firemen, who in those days were grouped—along with doctors, shopkeepers, businessmen, and lawyers—as the "city's best men." Legend had it that one afternoon on her way home from school, she came across the Knickerbocker Engine Company Number Five as they struggled to pull the fire engine to the top of Telegraph Hill. Like Joan of Arc, she dropped her books, rushed to their aid, and grabbed hold of the towrope. Turning her flushed face to the bystanders, she rallied them with the cry, "Come on, you men! Pull!" Others poured into the fray, grabbing hold of the ropes, and the engine surged up the hill. Though they had been passed on the way by other engines, they were the first to put water on the fire.

From that day forward, Lillie could often be seen at fires. She became such a conspicuous figure among the firemen battling the flames that she became something of a mascot and was made an honorary member of the Knickerbocker Engine Company Number Five. She was given a gold badge that she treasured to the end of her days. As Miss Hitchcock became older, she gave up the habit of following the engine, but the tie that bound her to the company was as strong as ever. If any member of the company fell ill, it was Lillie Hitchcock who gladdened the sickroom. And should death call him, she sent a floral tribute as a final expression of her regard.

Lillie married financier Howard Coit but never took to the norms of feminine high society. She could often be seen smoking cigars and playing poker with the firemen. To show her continued devotion to the fire company, she always had the number 5 embroidered on all her clothes. Although eccentric, her quick wit and flair made her quite popular. When she died, she was buried with her beloved gold and diamond Number 5 badge presented to her by the members of the Knickerbocker Engine Company. Childless, she donated a third of her fortune to the City of San Francisco, and the executors of her will determined at last to erect a memorial tower in honor of this colorful woman, to also serve as a memorial tribute to San Francisco's firemen.

Dean stared up at the 210-foot tower that resembled the nozzle of a fire hose. It had been Charlotte's idea to meet at Coit Tower. The best way to remain low-key, she reckoned, was to meet at a tourist attraction, normally avoided by the locals unless obligated by visiting family or friends. He watched them arrive: Charlotte and Mary Anne in one car, Zack in another. Dean waved to them and pointed to the edge of the parking lot nearest the bay. He passed the bronze statue of Columbus that stood on the spot where automated semaphores had once stood to signal to ships in the bay.

He waited by the knee-high wall that encircled the lot. For such a popular landmark, parking was hard to find. Cars were queued up behind the broad white line painted on the pavement entrance to the parking lot. Whenever a car space became available, the front of the queue moved forward. Very civilized. It reminded Dean of a conversation from a past litigation with the operator of a slaughterhouse. The steers would line up restlessly before an operator, who controlled a pneumatic metal rod. The operator explained, a silly smirk on his face, that the animals could smell death, defecating uncontrollably as they waited for the fatal punch. It was goddamn obvious what was going on.

As Dean watched the two cars finally find parking spots, the thought stayed in his mind but turned around: the bolt didn't punch-press the animals' brains; instead, it was turned on the operator—and he was that operator.

Dean was about to meet someone whose life he'd destroyed while benefiting enormously, and after that, he would violate the sanctity of his profession's confidentiality. It was made even more surreal because the wife of the man who had paid for Zack's legal dissection had orchestrated the meeting.

His urge to confess his true feelings and misgivings had taken priority the other night, but he still couldn't help but feel a rush of the old crush when he saw Charlotte coming up the walk.

"Hi, Dean," Charlotte called, heels clicking on the pavement. "Waiting long?"

Dean shook his head. "Just a few minutes before you arrived."

"Of course, you know these people," she said with a smile, gesturing to Zack and Mary Anne, who were a few steps behind her.

"Hi, Mary Anne. Hello, Zack." Normally, he would give Mary Anne an obligatory hug, but today wasn't normal.

"Hello," Mary Anne said.

Zack said nothing.

At first glance, he looked the same. Tall and thin as a rake, wearing an MIT T-shirt that was too broad in the shoulders, his arms covering the black letters. However, as Dean studied him more closely, he could see that Zack's eyes had lost their normal jump; instead, they appeared withdrawn and cautious. Mary Anne stood beside Zack, her pretty chestnut bangs parted by the wind on this elevated cityscape. There were worry lines on her young forehead that had no right to be there. Charlotte looked radiant. The wind swirled her long hair into an interleaved wrap that would have made for a terrific magazine photo shot.

"This round parking lot makes me feel like we're at a Roman coliseum," Charlotte said cheerfully, as if they were holding a Sunday church picnic. "I bring David into the coliseum. That's you, Zack."

"Oh, Mother, please," Mary Anne said. "No melodramatics."

"That's okay," Zack said. "I've come to understand your mother's humor. Only if you're referring to the Roman coliseum, Charlotte, I think you mean the Christians, not David. He was King of the Jews."

"Right you are," Charlotte said. "Come to think of it, the Christians would suit you better. After all, you do remind me of one of those southern preachers my mother used to drag me to."

"I don't preach to anyone."

"Sure, you do, honey. You do it all the time. That's why we're gathered here on this lovely Friday morning."

"Why *are* we here?" Zack said.

"You remember our earlier conversation, don't you? When I told you that you were running scared? At the time, I wasn't sure exactly why. But now I am."

Dean noted that Zack maintained his composure, despite the baiting. It was easy to see how people admired him. He looked at Charlotte, whose face was lit by the morning sun.

"I wonder," she said, walking slowly toward the wall and taking a seat next to one of the quarter-operated binoculars, "when the Christians were thrown in the coliseum with the lions and tigers, were they running scared? Or did their faith in God make them strong enough to stand up to the fear? What do you think, Zack?"

He said nothing.

Dean had had enough. "I suspect that they peed in their pants, just like any other sane person would," he said.

"Spoken like a true lion," Charlotte said.

"Excuse me?" Dean said.

"Well, we have the Christians entering the coliseum. Now, of course, we need the lions for this grand play. What was it you said the other night? *Nos morituri* something something."

"I'm no lion," Dean said. He looked down. Someone had eaten a sauerkraut hotdog, the fixings splattered across the observation walkway. He felt his stomach tighten.

"Sure, you are, honey." Charlotte smiled and rested her hand on his shoulder. "Now's not the time to be modest. Your law firm tore apart Zack's poor little company. And you enjoyed the kill."

Dean glanced uncomfortably at Zack. "'Enjoy' wouldn't be quite right. I was hired to do a job. Like most cases involving intellectual property, it was an unpleasant one. But I took no personal satisfaction. Considering I'm here, that should be perfectly obvious."

This is a very hard thing to do, Dean thought.

"It's ironic how history repeats itself over and over," Charlotte said, her eyes going back and forth between Zack and him. "Can you imagine how those poor Christians felt being thrown in the arena? They didn't ask to be there. And how about the lions? The poor creatures had been beaten and starved to death. Just like the young men in the Civil War, running scared, forced to kill their own countrymen, even someone they might have cared for."

"Mother, you're making no sense," Mary Anne said.

"Why don't you ask Zack what I mean?"

"I think," Zack said, "your mother is telling us, in her unique theatrical way, that we were all put in impossible situations where no matter what we did, or didn't do, we would end up hurting someone."

"Bravo," Charlotte said, clapping her hands. "Bravo."

"Okay, enough is enough," Dean said.

"Time to roar, lion," Charlotte said. She laid a steadying hand on his arm.

"I never thought things would come to this," he said. "I have been a faithful steward of the law my whole professional life. But this week …" His voice faltered. God. This was far more difficult under Zack's stare than it had been with Charlotte in the quiet corner of the restaurant. "This week, I have witnessed things that convince me I can no longer stand idly by. The idea that Allen would not only steal Zack's idea but then punish him for it … I just couldn't take it anymore.

"The thought actually sickened me, which was surprising since I'd always assumed I was indifferent to moral abuse. Support the client's wishes and let the court decide who was right and who was wrong. That had always been my creed. But this was different. Maybe because I knew you. Maybe because I knew the type of man you were. I don't know. I couldn't do it anymore. You know, I'm surprised your lawyer never filed to have me removed."

"What do you mean?" Zack said.

"You and I have something of a relationship. I'm a family friend of the Henleys, and you dated Mary Anne. Had your lawyer filed to have me recuse myself, I would have done so, if for no other reason than the sake of appearance. It was your ace in the hole, but he never played it. In fact, had he done so, it would have precluded anyone at my firm from representing Allen. That personal relationship would have been grounds for an immediate appeal."

Zack closed his eyes and slowly shook his head.

"Anyway, it's just as well that he didn't. Otherwise, I wouldn't be here today, telling you what I am about to tell you."

Dean told his spellbound audience he didn't know how Allen first came to suspect Zack, but he had quickly pieced together the direction Imagination was heading. He began questioning Mary Anne, using her as a tool to find out where Zack's allegiances lay. Then came the initial probes into the bank accounts and business filings and Allen overworking Zack to ensure that he'd take plans home with him. And Allen's careful manipulation of Mary Anne to have her invade Zack's office, where he knew she'd see those same plans. When Allen had enough to move on, he began the legal filings, assembling his case to have it in place if Zack wouldn't swear an oath of allegiance to DisplayTechnik. When Zack quit, Allen went into a rage. He'd come to the firm wanting to bury him. Then Allen had found the formula, realized its incredible potential, and used the services of Sandy Fong in order to claim the idea for his own.

Dean took a deep breath, now coming to the difficult part. He couldn't believe Allen wanted to punish Zack for his own idea. He couldn't support or be around an abuser like that. Once he started, Dean couldn't stop, and the words poured out; he even told them about Nicole and her abusive father.

When he finished speaking, he was exhausted, the angst of the past few days having passed right through him. He had done it. He had violated a sacred trust bestowed by a man who would never comprehend his actions any more than he was able to comprehend the black-and-white abusive world of Nicole's father.

He put his head in his hands, a deep shudder passing through him. He felt so ashamed of himself, so deeply ashamed. How many other lives had he ruined without a thought? How many other Zacks had there been, their dreams taken away? How could he have let Allen control his life for so long? He'd become a puppet. Allen merely had to pull strings, and he jumped and danced.

He angrily wiped his eyes and looked up to see Charlotte embracing Mary Anne, a show of affection he'd rarely seen between this mother and daughter. Zack observed the two women's embrace with an odd look on his face, as though he, too, never expected to see that happen.

Zack sat down on the wall, a respectable distance away. He was quiet for some time before he said, "I appreciate the fact that you weren't supposed to break confidentiality, but I'm not sure I trust you."

Dean hadn't expected Zack to welcome him with open arms.

"You've broken your vows, but so what? If you were as concerned as you claim, then why the hell didn't you do this on Monday, when I still had a company, or for that matter, before Allen filed a criminal complaint against me?"

"You can forget about that," Dean said. "It's just a scare tactic. Now that you've lost the company, Allen will withdraw the criminal charges."

"Dickens, my former financier, had suspected as much. But I still don't understand. Why didn't you say or do something before I lost everything? Why the hell should I trust you now? You got your money for prosecuting this, and now you try to cleanse your soul? Bullshit."

"Zack ..." Mary Anne began.

"It's okay, Mary Anne," Dean said. "He has a right to be angry. The truth is, I didn't know what to do. I knew I needed to do something. It was strange. I had decided that I needed to get out when Charlotte called me. I mean, not even an hour had passed, and here she was calling me to set up a meeting. I took it as a sign that I was on the right path."

Mary Anne turned to her mother. "When did you—?"

Charlotte shook her head and then nodded for Dean to continue.

"I met her Tuesday night, not knowing she also felt that what Allen was doing was wrong. We started talking, feeling each other out, and pretty soon, I found myself telling her everything. Charlotte filled in some gaps for me. For example, I didn't know how much Allen had used Mary Anne in all this, and I didn't know how much he'd truly cared about you, Zack. Meeting Charlotte confirmed what I was feeling, and I became convinced that I had to act. Up until then, I'd merely thought about withdrawing from the case or somehow stepping down, not wanting to be a part of it anymore."

"As we talked," Charlotte said, sitting down and taking Dean's hand, "we realized we needed to form an alliance. Allen had to be stopped." She squeezed his hand. "And we made plans."

He squeezed back. "Yes, we did."

"I told him that I'd had this grand vision of making Allen back off on my own so Zack could get on with his company, and who knows, perhaps eventually work in partnership with Allen rather than competing with him. I said I was considering threatening Allen with a divorce in order to force him to stop chasing poor ol' Zack. After all, I hold a considerable number of shares of DisplayTechnik, and after what happened to Jack Welch, I thought the threat of a divorce might make him see reason."

Dean took up the story. "But I advised against that unless she was willing to go through with it. Allen surely would have called her bluff. So I suggested a trial separation, something quiet and nonlegal."

"And I immediately saw the wisdom of that. You're such a brilliant lawyer." Charlotte smiled at him again. "The gossip mill would kill Allen. I could move out, perhaps with rumors I was seeing someone else, and if the world knew about my supposed infidelity, I could laugh in Allen's face. Can you imagine the scuttlebutt? Allen an inadequate lover? Oh, he'd just come unglued."

Dean continued, "And that's also why I didn't break things off with Allen. You see, as Charlotte and I made plans, I realized the best thing to do was to go through with Thursday's filing."

"How so?" Zack asked.

Mary Anne sat down next to her mother. Dean thought that odd but realized it was so she could hear everything better.

"Because then there would be a legal filing in court alleging you'd stolen his secret formula. If he hadn't filed it, then there would be no evidentiary proof for you to go after him. It'd just be your word against his. Now he's submitted evidence of his claim to prior art, which is all forged and I can help you prove it." Dean smiled encouragingly. "As bad as yesterday was for you, if you hadn't gone through it, you wouldn't have anything to proceed on."

"So we attack Allen on two fronts," Charlotte said. "We don't give him any way out. He'll be forced to concede and withdraw everything."

Zack sat there quietly, apparently absorbing it. "You know, this is all well and good," he said, "but you'll forgive me if I don't jump right in with both feet. I need to think about it. I just find this all a little hard to take in right now."

He got up and walked slowly away, hands in his pockets.

Charlotte watched him go and then turned to Dean. Her expression told him everything. She had issued a rallying cry, but Zack was simply walking away.

He knew it would take time for Zack to learn to trust again, but now he had people in his life who would help him fulfill his dream.

CHAPTER FORTY-NINE

"I'm glad you came," Allen said, "though I must admit I'm a bit surprised that you did."

Dimitre grunted. He hadn't told Anna about his decision to come here, and his conscience was bothering him. They were sitting in Denny's, located diagonally across from the Milpitas office. The red booth seats looked as if they'd been waxed with maple syrup. A pimply faced kid with a big rag sticking out of his back jeans pocket stood before them, two cups of decaffeinated coffee in his hands. Allen gave the kid a nasty look. He scurried away and returned a short time later with a fistful of sugar packs and a chorus of apologies. Allen waved him off.

"So, what is it you wanted to discuss?" he said.

This is big mistake, Dimitre thought. It was one thing to call him on the phone, another to be sharing a cup of coffee with him.

"I can see that Zack didn't steal you away from me because of your eloquence." Allen tilted his head to one side, peering at Dimitre. "I don't have time for games."

Dimitre took a sip of coffee and then put the cup down, pushing it away from him. It tasted like hot water. He wiped the corner of his mouth with the back of his hand. What was he doing here? Zack had lied to him or at least hidden the truth. Was that a good enough reason? The man seated before him was the master of lies. They had left Allen for that very reason.

"Dimitre?"

Of course, you could say that he'd not been so open either. Forget about the lifetime problem. That was different. He would fix it soon enough.

"Since you're unwilling, or unable, to talk, perhaps I should break the ice. You know that Imagination's days are numbered, and you'd like to protect yourself and get back with a settled company. I suspect that you'd also like to protect your two friends in some way. Am I right?"

Dimitre nodded. They had worked so hard to get Imagination off the ground. So many sacrifices. It was their one big chance in life to capture the dream. But now, their dream was going under. The man before him was destroying anyone who walked in Zack's shadow.

"I suspect you're afraid that, like Zack, you might also go to jail for the theft of company secrets."

"We steal nothing," he said. "That is not true." But it was true that he was worried he might be next.

"Hmm. That is for the courts to decide, I'm afraid." Allen stared at him. "But I'm curious what you meant when you said yesterday you wanted to talk about the future of *my* company."

It was clear Allen wasn't going to continue until he had a response. "I have … information that could help DisplayTechnik make paper-thin displays."

"And what information would that be that I don't already have?"

"What are you meaning?"

Allen frowned. "Is this a game?"

"Is no game. What are you meaning?"

Allen took a sip of coffee, obviously thinking something over, and then set the cup down and leaned forward on the table. "Before I say anything further, I want to know exactly what you want of me."

Dimitre cleared his throat. *Anna, forgive me.* "I want deal for

Jimmy, Jerry, and me. As you guess, we are thinking of leaving Imagination. There are too many troubles."

"Yes." Allen smiled. "It is rather difficult to build a company without money now, isn't it?"

Dimitre started. What was he talking about? "Money is not issue. There is plenty of that."

"My God, you don't even know, do you?" Allen laughed. "Do you mean to tell me that Zack, the king of all good morals, hasn't even told you that he can't pay your next paycheck? Today's Friday. I do hope it wasn't payday." He laughed again.

Dimitre shook his head, bewildered.

"How extraordinary. Just bloody brilliant. I'm sorry to be the bearer of bad news, my Ukrainian friend, but the courts have already seized of all Imagination's bank accounts. There is no money. Zero. I can't believe he hasn't told you. This was all decided in court yesterday morning."

Dimitre's hands clenched into fists. So, this was why Paul and Jeremy had come to the Bakers in such a bad mood; this was why Zack had left without saying a word.

"Brilliant! And to think that this is the same Zack Penny that my wife and daughter extol, praising his holier-than-thou value system. I wonder when he was planning on telling you—before or after you lost your house?"

"That … that cannot … it is impossible. We have funding. We have—"

"Mr. Dickens? Is that what you were about to say? Well, your Mr. Dickens and the rest of the New Yorkers have turned off the tap. Dickens has gone back to New York with his shriveled dick between his legs."

Allen threw his head back. He had the laugh of a jackal. Dimitre didn't know exactly what a jackal sounded like, but he was sure Allen had it right.

Dimitre's hands began to shake from the anger building up inside. How dare Zack not tell them? He had promised things would be different. Didn't he realize he was playing with their lives?

"Saint Zack was supposed to be so different from the rest of the corporate world," Allen said. "But he isn't. There's a reason why those at the top sometimes have to hide things. It's to protect those below them. How could you handle your day-to-day workload if you had to worry constantly about the bottom line or funding or orders not coming through or any of the other myriad problems a CEO faces every day? That is the life of the CEO. He shoulders the burden. He shields those beneath him, so they can get on with their work.

"But in this case, Zack didn't protect you. He set you up. He used your talents and your ideas to get the money for the start-up, and now that it's gone, there's nothing left to protect you with. Does Zack have assets that he can sell to pay you some sort of severance pay? Did he establish a contingency plan? Is he going to pay your mortgage while you look for work?

"Zack led you away from me to form a better company, one founded on his so-called morals and beliefs. But you don't reinvent the wheel. There are reasons why things are done the way they are in business. It's because they work. It's no wonder that Zack very soon got away from the business ethics he was so quick to preach. He's lied to you. He's hidden things from you." Allen waved a hand dismissively. "Oh, I don't blame him. That's business. But in business, you also look out for your own. One thing is certain. No one at DisplayTechnik has ever gone without a paycheck."

Allen leaned forward. "If you and the others have nothing left, why should I deal with you?"

"Because I have formula," Dimitre said, "secret formula to develop paper-thin displays. Displays so thin you can roll them—"

"Wait a minute. I'm confused. Is this the same formula that Zack stole from the archives of DisplayTechnik? The one he is going to jail for?"

Dimitre was flabbergasted. He tried to formulate words, but

nothing came out. Finally, he said, "What are you saying? I invent formula."

"Indeed." Allen held up his empty mug to the passing waiter. "Do you and Zack even talk anymore? I warn you, be careful what you say now, or you may find yourself in jail as well."

The waiter returned and refilled Allen's cup, saw Dimitre's was untouched, and left.

"Since Zack has not filled you in, allow me. Yesterday, the court froze Imagination's assets because it believed there was strong evidence that proprietary secrets were stolen from the archives of DisplayTechnik. Documents were presented that proved that the formula found on your computer systems was identical to one developed years earlier by one of our former scientists. Why, he'd even presented a paper years ago at a convention about the whole concept. More evidence will be presented when we finally go to court to settle this once and for all."

Dimitre said nothing while Allen spoke. He was afraid to. How could Allen have claimed the formula as his own? Where was the court to protect them? He knew it had been a big mistake to hand everything over. He knew they should have hidden things. Had he not warned Zack?

He knew he'd invented the formula, though Allen spoke so smoothly that for a brief moment, he doubted himself. It was as though he was being hypnotized. He wondered if he had ever come across the formula while at DisplayTechnik, sealed it away in his brain, and then later "invented" it. He shook his head, feeling himself drowning in Allen's lies. No, it was not true. It was not true.

But what could he say now? If he claimed it was his, Allen could immediately add him to the charges. And what of Jimmy and Jerry? Could they be charged as accessories?

"I ... I ..."

"Oh, I'm not blaming you. Yet. For now, I still believe this was all Zack's doing."

Dimitre had one last move, but he was afraid to bring his queen into play. He knew something Allen didn't: the formula wouldn't work.

"Since I'm willing to believe that you were merely caught up in all of this, I'll ask again, what is it that you want from me?"

Dimitre sat there, unable to respond.

"The cold war's over. You've got a great opportunity here. Don't blow it." Allen glanced at his wristwatch.

Dimitre had never gotten used to Allen's directness. But the pompous asshole was right. How often does one come up with a brilliant idea in one's lifetime? Perhaps once? Perhaps never? But another voice shouted from deep within, "Stop it! You can't betray Zack. You can't betray your friend." The voice was Anna's.

"Let's cut to the chase," Allen said. "It so happens I am currently developing another division to produce these displays. If I give you a chance to help me produce the world's first paper-thin, three-dimensional display, what do you want in return?" The smile on Allen's face disappeared. "It's not often that I am willing to negotiate."

Dimitre took a deep breath. "Give us guaranteed money up front," he said, speaking quickly, "then big salary and bonus when we are successful."

"And why would I do that? Sounds like I'm the one taking the big risk."

"Because I know something you do not. This formula of yours does not work. At least not the one in our computers."

Allen's eyes flashed and then narrowed. Dimitre knew the balance had suddenly shifted. But it was a tenuous shift at best. Allen could decide to press charges, and Dimitre had no lawyer friends and no money for a legal fight. Allen could, hypothetically, find someone else to work the formula, but in the meantime, Dimitre could take it to another company and they could leapfrog ahead.

But then he realized he'd made a fatal mistake. He could never go to another company with this. He would bring upon them the same ruin that Allen had rained upon Zack. Dimitre tried to keep his face calm; all the while, sheer panic welled up inside him.

"Explain."

"I will not."

Allen clenched his jaw. Dimitre could see the tendons working.

"I see. How do I know you won't stab me in the back by deserting me? You did it once already."

Dimitre cringed. This wasn't going to work. Anna would kill him if she knew. They would have to find employment elsewhere. He got up to leave.

"Sit down, you crazy Russian. No wonder you lost the cold war. You're too bloody sensitive."

Not Russian, Ukrainian. Dimitre sat down, the red seat crackling. Allen pulled a thick file from his briefcase.

"I will give you what you asked for. However, I anticipated that our conversation would lead us to this, so I took the liberty of having my general counsel draw up a binding contract for you that incorporates strict nondisclosure and noncompete clauses. You remember Bill. He assures me that this contract is not something that can be broken in the soft court system of Silicon Valley. It contains numerous bonuses in exchange for your guarantee that you'll be staying with us for quite some time. All we need to do is fill in some of the numbers. I also have contracts for your friends that you can take with you."

As Allen explained the terms of the incredibly strict but financially generous contract, Dimitre saw Anna's angelic face hover above the booth. She had a look on her face that could kill. He also remembered his discussion with Jerry and Jimmy about not signing anything and that this was for exploration only. But that was before any of them realized the extent to which Allen was willing to go. A five-year deal with the devil was better than ten years in jail.

They had lost. Imagination was finished. What hope did they have? Zack had abandoned them, that much seemed certain now.

The last remnants of his loyalty screamed at him, trying to be heard over the murmur of voices and the clatter of dishes, but it seemed the only sound in the restaurant was the scratching of his pen on the dotted line.

CHAPTER FIFTY

Zack's initial thought was to rush back to Paul and Jeremy and tell them what he'd learned. But as he drove back across the bay, his urge to shout to the world what he now knew was replaced with a sense of frustration. What good was it to know how the cattle were let out of the corral when the stampede had already destroyed the ranch?

Being Father Confessor to McSorley had been a real test for him. He'd had to bite his tongue more than once. Did the lawyer feel that clearing his conscience somehow absolved him of wrongdoing? The damage was done. Now there was nothing left. And what was that crap about waiting? It felt like all that did was protect McSorley from having to do something. Besides, wasn't he an accessory if this went to court, or did that whole lawyer-client crap protect him somehow? He'd wanted to lash out, but the look in Mary Anne's eyes had stifled that.

He pounded on the steering wheel. What difference did any of this make? Paul had probably burned all of his bridges. He certainly couldn't imagine Dickens wanting to get back on board—not now, not after the shitstorm he'd endured the first time around. Then again, maybe he'd want to stick it to that SOB Henley. No. No, he wouldn't. Dickens said that the word was out on the street about them.

Dickens would need him to actually have the company up and running before he'd ever show his face again. But in order to do that, they'd need his money and help to get the company going again.

Zack leaned his head against the window. Though he was too afraid to embrace it, maybe there was some small glimmer of hope here. He just had to see his way out of it. After all, weren't the good guys supposed to win in the end? Wasn't this a validation of what he believed in? His stomach and throat tightened, and tears started to build up as he thought that he just didn't know what he believed in anymore. He didn't know where to turn or what to do. Not anymore. Somewhere, someone had told him once that God only gave you what He knew you could handle and that you should count it a joy when you encounter troubles because it means God feels you're destined for greatness. Well, he was tired of being a cosmic proving ground. He used to think he was on a ship, steering it where he would, but now it seemed like it was all an illusion and he realized he was just a stick caught in a raging river.

He hit the steering wheel again. It wasn't supposed to be like this. Damn it, he'd just wanted the dream. Didn't other people make their dreams come true? Then why couldn't he? He'd just wanted to make a company for himself and the other engineers.

But had he? Had he really wanted it for the others, or was this a monument to his own ego? He was so sure of himself, so sure of his own ideals that he had become just like Allen.

That thought stunned him. Where had that come from?

Zack squeezed the steering wheel. He didn't know what to think, what to care about, or what or whom to trust.

The Santa Rita-Pleasanton exit came and went. He was conscious of the road and the cars around him, but they seemed to blur until he had no sense of how he fit into the flow of eastbound traffic on the 580, whether he was leading or following. He kept driving until he saw the white windmills perched on the yellow hills around Livermore, like serene scarecrows from an ancient society, left behind to warn strangers of a forbidden zone. He shook his head. He'd watched too many movies. He turned off the freeway and headed up into the hills toward those white scarecrows.

After a while—he didn't know how long exactly—he stopped beside the road and got out. The sun was not yet directly overhead, but it was still very bright and hot. He squinted, seeing the heavy grass up close, like thick stalks of spaghetti rising all around him. He began climbing the hill, using the grass to pull himself up, his face close to the yellow chaff. Halfway up, a clump uprooted in his grasp. He slipped backward but managed to twist to one side so he didn't fall. He was halfway up the hill. He decided to press on, this time keeping his center of gravity as low as possible. When he reached the summit, he realized the windmill was still some distance away, on a raised terrace not unlike some of the hillside vineyards around Santa Cruz.

Forget the windmill. He'd lived in the East Bay for five years and had never had the urge before to climb these ugly-looking hills. He didn't know why he was standing there. He knew he should go back to the sundeck and explain to the guys about McSorley. He owed it to them. But at that instant, he felt like sitting down with the sun behind him and enjoying the views of the surrounding hills.

He lay back, the dry grass crackling under his weight, and closed his eyes. Thoughts floated in his mind like a swarm of fireflies. Maybe now that Charlotte and McSorley had both decided to become personally involved, there was hope after all. But he just didn't have the energy to focus on that anymore.

He could still see Mary Anne's face in the shadow of Coit Tower. It had been a huge step for her to be there. Whether anything came from their meeting remained to be seen, but that she was there to help confront her father was huge.

He didn't know what to think about any of it. And that acknowledgment had some comfort in itself, like he was relieving himself of a terrible burden. He didn't have to know. Maybe it was just time to let the river run its course.

When Zack finally climbed down the hill, the top of his head and his face felt like they were on fire. He winced when he touched the tip of his nose. In his car's rearview mirror, he looked like Rudolph. He was only missing a sled—and snow, of course. Driving back along the 580, he saw the Hopyard exit. He swerved to the far right lane and just made it into the exit lane. A Ford pickup truck sped past him, the passenger communicating his displeasure with an upraised finger.

Forget about going back to the Bakers', he thought. Just go home. Get some rest; take care of yourself. What could he tell the team anyway? Hey guys, it looks like Allen's finished us off, but now it looks like Allen did a lot of illegal dealings and we might get him after all but it'll mean collaborating with our former enemies. And oh, by the way, the money's been frozen so you can't get paid. But hang in there!

Just hearing it in his own head, it sounded insane.

When Zack arrived in his apartment, the afternoon light was pouring through the balcony window. He turned up the air conditioner on the way to the phone. Before he dialed Paul's cell phone, he checked his voice mail. Predictably, Paul had left a few messages, wondering if he'd fallen off a cliff or not. Charlotte had called as well, leaving a somewhat cryptic message, asking if Mary Anne were with him. That surprised him until he heard Mary Anne's voice, saying that she was leaving work early and would wait for him at his apartment.

Zack looked at his watch. It was nearly two thirty. As he readied to dial Paul's number, there was a knock at the door. It was Mary Anne. When she extended her hand to him, he didn't know what to do. Instinctively, he took a step backward. She came in, and they stood awkwardly in the middle of the living room.

"What happened to your nose?" she said.

"The sun got in the way."

"I can see that. Let me put some cream on it. It looks painful."

"It's okay."

"Sure, it is." Mary Anne walked past him and returned a few moments later with a tube of Noxzema. Zack didn't recognize the blue tube, and then he realized it was hers, hidden somewhere in his bathroom cabinet.

"Sit down."

Zack shrugged his shoulders.

"Come on, sit down."

Zack sat on the love seat. Mary Anne spread a few drops on her fingertip and dabbed his nose.

He jumped back.

"Don't be such a baby. Look at your forehead. It's as red as a beet. Did you know that there are bits of grass stuck in your hair? Where were you?"

"Nowhere."

Zack closed his eyes as she spread the cool cream across his forehead. He could feel her breath on him. His nose picked up the aroma of fresh soap. He had always liked the way she smelled. When he opened his eyes, her face was very close to his, and he leaned forward and kissed her on the lips. Mary Anne returned his kiss, the cream on his forehead smudging hers.

They both laughed nervously. Zack rose from the love seat and gently pulled her down to the beige carpet. As he held her, Mary Anne gave a deep, quaking sigh. He wondered if this was a big mistake but decided he was just following the river. He was done thinking.

As she eagerly returned his kisses, Mary Anne started to cry, "I'm so sorry, I'm so sorry."

It seemed like forever since they'd made love. Hands and lips were searching for the right place, their enthusiasm tempered by Zack's sunburn. Actually, it had only been two weeks, but it seemed so long ago. So much had happened. They found their rhythm quickly.

Afterward, they lay quietly in each other's arms, with Mary Anne nestled under his chin. Tears of joy and sadness glistened on Zack's bare chest. Neither said a word. Zack closed his eyes, letting his mind go blank. Most of the time, he thought about everything too much, exploring every consequence with such seriousness. And although there was a twinge of guilt right now, he didn't need to rationalize why he'd just had sex with Mary Anne. He'd just done it, and for the moment, every muscle loosened, a wave of calmness flowed through him. That was reason enough.

"I don't know how you've kept from going insane through all this," she said, her arm on his bare chest.

"Who says I'm not?" He smiled. "I don't know, either. I guess I just hang on to the thought that I was meant to go through it, that this is all some part of a bigger scheme. It's always easier to give up or stop trying. But I just have this feeling that I'm on the right path, that I knew when I started that it was an uphill struggle. I just didn't know until I started up that the hill was actually a mountain. But you know what? Every mountain has a top. It won't go on forever. I just have to hold on till I get there."

"But what if you don't? What if you can't climb this particular mountain?"

"I don't think there's a mountain that can't be climbed. I don't believe in giving up. It's just that sometimes when you get to the top of your own particular mountain, the view isn't always what you expected."

"What's that supposed to mean?"

"It means that even though you realize you might be disappointed, you climb it anyway, knowing whatever the view is, it will be spectacular."

Mary Anne snuggled up to him. They were quiet for a moment, and then she said softly, "Well, you can't go to the police."

"What? Where the heck did that come from?"

"Oh, sorry. I was just thinking about today and this morning and all. After you left, my mom and Uncle Dean were worried you'd go to the police."

"Maybe I should go file my own criminal complaint. It seems to me we ought to start dishing out some of Allen's medicine; it'd be nice to see him sweat for a change. It'd be sweet to see his face when a process server shows up at a corporate meeting of his."

"You have no proof."

"We have a witness. We have the doctored evidence."

"Uncle Dean would never testify."

"I don't know; he seemed pretty eloquent today."

"He would never testify against Allen in a court of law. That's why this has to be handled outside of the system."

"You sound like you're back to defending him. You want to stop this, but not if it really means going after him."

Zack raised himself onto his elbow. Mary Anne rolled away from him, her legs curled up. He got off the floor and retrieved a blanket from the storage closet. He handed it to her, and she wrapped it around herself.

"I'm not defending him," she said. "All I'm saying is that Dean will never get involved like that."

"Well, if that's the case, then that whole meeting this morning was bullshit. He just wanted to clear his conscience. If Allen knows no one will really do anything, then he'll laugh at all of us. Jesus Christ! I must be out of my mind. For a while there, I really thought you guys were going to help."

"Please," Mary Anne said, "we're moving slowly, feeling things out. He's my father. Surely you must understand that."

"Yeah, sure," Zack said, stepping into his jeans and pulling them up. God, what a fool he was. "Nothing's changed between us."

"We'll get Allen to drop the charges against you. I'll confront him myself if I have to."

"Not only has your father destroyed Imagination, he's also given his daughter a vivid one. That will never happen. You know that."

"Just promise me that you won't go to the police, that you'll do nothing until we talk with Allen."

Why? So you can warn him? Zack thought. God! He was so stupid for opening up to her, for allowing himself to show his feelings for her. He couldn't believe he'd just had sex with her.

"I've got to go do something," he said.

Zack walked to his home office. When he entered, he swung the door shut, abruptly cutting off Mary Anne's voice. He picked up the handset and dialed Paul's cell. He let the phone ring and ring. He dialed the phone again, but again, there was no answer. Strange, Paul always had his cell phone on; that's why he didn't have voice mail. He called Paul at home. The phone rang ten times without success.

It was nearly four o'clock. It would take forty-five minutes to drive to Paul's house, but he had to talk to someone. He couldn't stay here. He took some cash from a CD box and stuffed it in his jeans pocket. When he returned to the living room, Mary Anne was fully dressed, the blanket folded across her arm.

"I've got to go," Zack said. "I would ask you to stay until I got back, but I don't think I'm ready for that. Besides, I only just got my new laptop, so there aren't too many files for you to rifle through."

"You're not going to forgive me, are you?"

"Why would you say that? After our little romp on the floor, we're as right as rain."

"Look, I know this will take some time. You've got to let me convince my father to drop all charges against you."

Zack shrugged. "Who's stopping you?"

He walked past her, opened the front door, and waved her through it in a grand gesture. He locked the door, sidestepped her, and bounded down the stairs.

She shouted down at him from the second-level railing.

"Where are you going?"

Zack didn't look back.

"Please tell me you're not going to the police! Please!"

Zack turned and shouted back, "Don't worry! Not tonight! Although I'm sure they'll be looking for me!"

Mary Anne started down the stairs. When she was two steps from the bottom, Zack's blue Toyota Cressida came whizzing out of the carport, the back end bouncing over the silent policemen that kept the apartment's traffic speed in check.

Tears filled her eyes. All her life, she'd hidden behind other people's strengths. When the people she loved exerted their will, she'd let herself become pliable, avoiding any possibility of confrontation.

There was a crashing sound behind her. Mary Anne turned and saw a Hispanic woman standing by her car's open trunk, her two children close behind her. Two bags of groceries had fallen at her feet, bursting, sending cans rolling across the parking lot. Wiping her eyes, Mary Anne hurried over to help.

She bent down and began gathering up the groceries. The two kids were running circles around them, trying to kick one of the cans under a parked car. The woman said something harsh to them in Spanish. Mary Anne loaded up her arms with cans and packets of food and followed the woman to her ground-floor apartment, her two kids racing ahead. Mary Anne put the retrieved groceries by the doorstep.

The woman smiled. "Thank you," she said. "You didn't need to do that. I could have managed."

"I just wanted to help."

"I know. It's the little things that keep us civilized. It was nice of you. There ought to be more angels around."

As Mary Anne walked back to her Ford Taurus, she thought about the woman's comment. She was definitely no angel, but it was true that help could sometimes come from unexpected sources in surprising ways.

It was time she took her own unexpected and surprising actions.

After she unlocked her car, she unfolded her cell phone and hit the speed dial. "Hey you," she said when Deidre picked up. "What's your dad's phone number? I need some help with something and figure he's just the man for the job."

CHAPTER FIFTY-ONE

L ess than an hour later, coinciding with Paul's arrival at home, Zack sat with his partner in the kitchen of his spacious home in Scotts Valley, south of San Jose. Paul's two kids, both still under school age, were running under the kitchen table, slaloming from one table leg to another.

"Tell me I'm not going insane," Paul said. "In the last few weeks, Henley and his attack dogs bushwhack us at every turn. They squash us with a legal sledgehammer. And then, miraculously, you get privy to a confession by McSorley, Henley's number one shark, and you don't immediately run to the police? What's wrong with you?"

"That was my first instinct too," Zack told him. "But then I realized we don't have a whole lot to go on just now. I think we have to wait it out to see what Charlotte and McSorley can do about it. I don't think we'll win in the courts. That seems pretty obvious."

"Are you nuts? That's our one advantage in this entire nightmare!"

"What advantage? Our company's dead, remember? We have no money. We have no investors. We lost our polymer formula. In fact, I'm charged with stealing my own formula!"

"Yeah, but we finally have some leverage over Henley."

Zack laughed. "Who are you kidding? You once told me to get my head out of the sand when it came to Mary Anne. You need to follow your own advice when it comes to Allen."

One of the boys knocked over a chair, and Paul picked it up. Giggles erupted from under the table. Paul leaned over and looked at them, upside down, their big blue eyes unsure whether they were about to be yelled at or teased.

"Where's your mom?" Paul asked them. "Joni! Can you please come here and take the kids? Zack and I are trying to have a serious conversation."

"I'm on the phone," his wife said from the hallway.

Paul rolled his eyes. "Kids, go see your mom. Ask her when dinner will be ready. Zack, let's go to my office."

Paul closed the door behind them.

"All I know is confessing at Coit Tower is one thing, testifying in a court of law is something else," Zack said. "Besides, I think Dean's bound by strict client confidentiality. We'll have to talk to Jeremy about that. And without his testimony, I'm not sure how we move forward. Without it, I don't know how we can directly prove that Sandy Fong, under Allen's directive, violated the protective custody and stole our polymer formula—especially with that prior art nonsense. McSorley didn't go into how he was going to force Allen into compliance. And Fong doesn't strike me as the kind of guy who would suddenly develop a conscience and confess."

"Anybody can be broken. Anybody."

"So, what do you propose we do? Hire a mafia thug, bring out the Chinese water torture home kit, and make Fong confess?"

"That's not a bad idea."

Zack scowled at him. "Not funny."

"Who said it was? Jesus, Zack! Wake up and smell the bankruptcy! I stand to lose several million dollars here. Henley has gone out of his way to bribe every judge, landlord, banker, and petty thief to steal what is rightfully ours, and you want to play by the Geneva Convention?"

"I agree, but for now we have to wait. We need to talk to Jeremy, find out some more from McSorley, and see what he and Charlotte have up their sleeves. For now, maybe we ought to put out some feelers to see if Dickens and the others would get back on board."

"Forget it. That isn't going to happen."

"You don't think they'll help?"

"Aren't you forgetting something? There's a fucking criminal prosecution going on! Henley's buddy decided yesterday that there was sufficient evidence to seize the bank accounts. Even if Dickens were to hand us a hundred million, the courts would seize it immediately." Paul took out a cigarette and lit it with a flourish. Zack couldn't stop him from smoking in his own office. "That's precisely why we have to nail Henley's ass to the wall, prove it's all lies, and put the bastard in jail where he belongs."

Paul took a deep pull on the cigarette and exhaled slowly. "I don't get you," he said, flicking the ashes into an ashtray on his desk. "Don't you *want* to go after Henley?"

"Of course, I do."

"Aren't you pissed off? Aren't you angry over what he's done?"

"It's weird. Yeah, I'm angry, but right now, I just feel kind of dead inside. Maybe numb's a better word for it."

"Do you want to go to jail? Because if you do, then you're on the right path. I don't care what McSorley or your girlfriend or anyone else says. Henley started this thing; you can bet he's going to finish it."

"I'm sorry?"

"What the hell's wrong with you? Do you think Henley's going to stop pursuing you? Don't you see where all of this is heading? He just got the judge to agree that there's reasonable suspicion of criminal behavior on your part. You can bet your ass Rafkin's going to sign off on it. Henley's gonna then head straight to the criminal court, and with Rafkin's seal of approval, it's a slam dunk you're heading to jail. And where's he going to stop? He'll go after me next, then all our investors, and swear out warrants against them too. What about the engineers? You think they're safe? They might get off with a fine, but they'll lose their houses.

"But if we go to the cops with what you've got right now, we can head him off tonight. We can get Jeremy to help us. We bring criminal charges against Henley."

Zack shook his head.

"Shit! For the love of God, why not?"

"I promised Mary Anne I wouldn't," Zack said, averting his eyes from Paul's glare. "She said it would screw everything up if I did."

"What did you say?"

"You heard me."

"You're fucking kidding me! When did you do that?"

"After the meeting with McSorley."

"What else did you promise the bitch?"

"She has a name."

"I just don't get you. She helps her father to destroy us, both professionally and personally. And yet, despite everything, you're still defending her! Why?"

"I'm not defending her."

"Then what the hell are you doing?"

"I don't know!" Zack said. "I don't know what to do or what to think! All I know is that I promised her I wouldn't go to the cops right away, so I'm not. Don't ask me why, because I don't know why! After everything's said and done, he's still her father."

"So, who am I? Look around you. I've got a young family to take care of. I've invested practically everything I have into Imagination. I can't afford to lose. And what about everyone else? What about Dimitre, Jimmy, Jerry, John, Molly, Brett, Jeremy, and the others? Don't they count too? Or are you going to sacrifice all of us for a piece of ass?"

"I'm telling you, knock it off," Zack said. "They're all good people. They can all find good jobs in no time."

"Is that so? What about my 4 million dollars? Got a home for that too?"

"When Henley withdraws, you'll get a lot of that back. We sure haven't spent that much. We never had a chance to."

"Wrong, buddy! We lost six months of lease payments, we put nonreturnable deposits on equipment, not to mention flyers, salaries, and all the rest. I'm liable for all of that shit. When and if the money is ever released, mine will be the last one left after everything else is doled out because I was a principal. I was essentially the first first-round. Oh, and guess what, that makes you liable too. They take it out of my salary first, not on equal percentages. When it's all said and done, I'll be lucky if I end up with any of it. You got one and a half million lying around that you plan on splitting the costs with me?"

Zack sat quietly, his jaw set. He hadn't anticipated those details.

"Jesus Christ. You might want to think this over. Henley bent every law, every principle that you ever preached at us, and used his own daughter as a spy, and you want to protect his daughter by not putting the son of a bitch in jail."

Giggling came from the other side of the office door. Paul's kids were trying to get in, probably attracted by the rising volume of their daddy's voice.

"That must have been some speech to get you not to go after Henley's ass. So, what else did she do to make you lose your brain?"

Zack said nothing.

"Oh, Christ. Don't tell me you slept with her."

"It's none of your business," Zack said, rising to his feet.

"Christ! You did, didn't you? Fucking incredible. Let me tell you, this is exactly my business. I have 3.4 million dollars that says it's my business. Do you understand me?"

Paul stood practically nose-to-nose with him. Zack took a step back.

"Just keep Mary Anne out of this," he said.

"How can we?" Paul said. "After what she's done? I thought you were finished with her. How did she get to you? Whisper sweet nothings into your ear, begging for forgiveness?"

"Careful," Zack said, his ears reddening.

"Man, you are priceless. I told you she was bad news! That little whore walks back into your life, shakes her booty for old times' sake, and you just roll over and play dead."

"Stop it right there."

"You stop it," Paul said, giving him a poke in the shoulder. "You've got your balls wrapped around your head. Trust me. That bitch is going to lead you straight to jail!"

"I told you she has a name."

"Do you even hear yourself? We're not talking about some tea social where everyone wears a cute little name tag! So, do you *want* to go to jail?" Paul poked a finger into Zack's chest.

Zack held his breath.

"Okay, how about this? Is the bitch really worth it? Is she worth 1.7 million dollars? Is she worth ten years in jail? 'Cause if she is, then I need to get me some of that." Paul poked a finger into Zack's chest again, this time harder.

"Stop that. And just watch your mouth."

"You've got to admire the Henleys," Paul said. "First, the father screws us." He poked Zack again, hard enough to force him back a step. "Then his daughter screws you so that her father can continue to screw us."

"Stop that or—"

"Or what? You'll get mad? I want you to get mad. We need your passion back to go after the bastard!"

"We don't need me to do anything. Mary Anne's going to get Allen to drop everything." Zack took another step backward to put some distance between them.

Paul broke out in laughter. "That's rich. She's like a whore who says she gives herself regular checkups. What's she going to do? Tell you to stop screwing her because she's not medically fit? You can't be serious! She's not going to do anything!"

"I'm getting pretty sick of how you keep referring to her."

"Yeah, and I'm getting pretty sick of how you seem to think it's perfectly fine to just throw everything away. Wait a minute, just wait," Paul said, his eyes widening. "Is it possible, I mean, is it possible that you don't care because you've cut a deal with Allen? In return for your passivity, you and his little princess will live happily ever after, getting a nice endowment, courtesy of my money? She lied to you once, she fucking betrayed you and stole from you, you think she's got your best interests in mind now? Allen used her once; why not again?"

"Paul, shut up. You're talking crazy."

"How did it happen? I mean, she must be pretty good having her old man as a teacher. So, did you beg Henley's daughter to ream you in the ass just like her father did to us?"

Zack lunged at Paul, wrapping his arms around him. Before he could lock down his grip, Paul broke free, twisting at the waist. Before Zack could blink, he was flying through the air. He hit the side of the desk and slid to the floor, but on the way down, he snared Paul's arm and dragged him down. Both of their heads barely missed the corner of the desk. Shoulders and knees banged into the desk and table, toppling several stacks of magazines and heavy books, sounding like cannon fire.

Zack tried to put a headlock on Paul, but he slipped out easily. Zack took an arching swing at Paul's chin, but he blocked it and rammed his forehead into Zack's face, hitting him solidly in the mouth. Stunned, Zack fell backward onto the floor, sending the metal wastebasket into a long roll that stopped at the foot of the office door.

At that instant, the door flew open. Paul's wife rushed in; behind her, the children clung to her skirt, bawling their heads off. Zack looked down at his shirt. It was covered with the blood dripping from his mouth. Paul asked Joni to go get them a towel, but she didn't move.

When they both got up from the floor, Joni stood solidly between them, the children still grasping her skirt.

"Just tell me one thing," Paul said.

Zack glared at his financial partner, backhanding the blood from his lips.

"For my own sanity, if McSorley and Charlotte aren't able to do anything, tell me you'll go after Henley. And don't give me some bullshit story about defending his daughter's honor."

Zack coughed blood, spray-painting the pinewood floor. Joni handed him a tissue that was stuffed in her pocket.

He mopped his mouth with it before answering. "I guess. I don't know. I'm just waiting to see what happens. I'm not sure what to do."

Joni put her arm around his shoulders. She asked if she could drive him to the Scotts Valley Hospital. Zack shook his head, saying he was all right. She tried to insist, but he declined again, thanked her, apologized for the chaos, and limped off.

Joni and the children followed him to the door.

Paul stared down at the spots of blood on the floor. He heard the front door open and Joni telling the kids to stay inside. He could hear their tiny footsteps coming back toward him. He closed the office door, anticipating the whining to come.

His right shoulder burned like hell. He wondered if his wife would eventually ask him if he was all right. He was certain that his shoulder was separated, or even broken.

He thought about the nearly 4 million dollars he'd gambled away. It had seemed such a sure thing. When he'd first met Zack at that pickup basketball game, he'd been so impressed with his attitude and principles that he thought he'd found the perfect business partner. He'd been so impressed that he'd gambled his entire future—and his young family's—on it.

Paul began searching through the spilled books and magazines on the floor. He cursed himself for throwing a perfectly good cell phone into the San Francisco Bay. He located the landline jack next to the desk and traced the wire to the phone, buried under a collection of Red Herring publications. He winced—pain shooting through his shoulder—as he picked up the telephone.

Zack was prepared to walk away from everything, and he was an asshole for doing so. In the end, he conceded he would probably never understand Zack's real motivations. However, what he did know was that his money and his future were firmly stuffed up Allen's ass. Zack wouldn't help him pull them out. Neither would Dickens.

Zack might have promised not to do anything, but he sure as hell hadn't.

CHAPTER FIFTY-TWO

Mary Anne marched past the anteroom to her father's Milpitas office. Everyone told her that she had the same walking style as her father, head slightly down, arms at the side, legs moving stiffly. Like a bulldog on a mission. At this moment, she would have settled for having a head half as hard as his.

She was surprised that Louise was nowhere to be found. Perhaps she was inside taking dictation or had gone on break. It was late Friday afternoon. No one left early at DisplayTechnik's corporate headquarters, except for some of the engineers, but that was because they'd already been there ten hours or more.

She reached the door and halted, her resolve suddenly faltering. Uncle Dean and Charlotte had warned her not to confront Allen, but she knew she had to, for her own sake. She couldn't live in fear of him anymore, and she was done living in his shadow. If Dean and her mother tried to confront him, she was sure it would end in disaster. He'd see them too much as equals. But coming from his own daughter, maybe he would listen to reason. And daughters had weapons wives would never have.

Allen had never taught her moral lessons when she was growing up. Most of that she took from her friends or her mother. Allen's lessons had all boiled down to "business ethics"—always paying your bills on time, even if it meant sacrifice, and treating your customers right. Little or nothing was said about the treatment of workers, except that extreme loyalty was required of them.

She eased the door open, her face feeling the stale heat. Going forward would be the hardest thing she had ever done. After this, nothing would ever be the same again.

Careful not to open the door more than a crack, she peered inside. A lot of people sat at the conference table, all of them looking in the opposite direction. She guessed Allen was standing at the other end of the room. She couldn't make out all the words, but it sounded like he was jump-starting his new venture with television sets that could be rolled down along Hollywood's walk of stars. Only his version of the walkway was having the tourists engage in real conversations with the movie stars who lay at their feet.

"Can I help you?" a voice said behind her.

Mary Anne's heart stopped. She spun around. "Jesus Christ, Louise!" she said in a hoarse whisper. "Do you always sneak up behind people like that? Where have you been?"

She thought she saw a smile tugging at the corners of Louise's mouth.

"I'm sorry, but do you always peek in at meetings you're not invited to?"

No one else in the entire company would dare talk to her like that. But Louise had more seniority than anyone other than Allen. Even though she'd known Louise her entire life, she had never liked the woman. Allen had tried to get her to call her "Aunt Louise," but it had never stuck.

Louise continued, "I was in the restroom, if you must know."

"Well, I need to talk to my father."

"You know that's not going to happen." Louise took her firmly by the arm and escorted her back to her desk. "He has a very important meeting right now and can't be—"

"I know precisely what he's doing," Mary Anne said, digging in her heels, trying to shake her arm out of Louise's grip. "Now let go!"

Louise released her.

"If you must know, I *was* invited," Mary Anne lied. "I just didn't want to barge in."

Louise eyed her suspiciously. "Then why wasn't I informed?"

"I don't know! Why don't you call and ask?"

Mary Anne turned and marched to the door, opening it before Louise could call her bluff. She was inside, closing the double doors before she'd made up her mind what to say to her father.

"And at home," Allen was saying to the group of marketers and engineers, "imagine display technology that could be literally wallpapered onto every living room in America. Wouldn't that be incredible? Use your imagination for a moment. A television screen so flat and flexible that it would forever change the way we look at the world. Because it will have perfect resolution regardless of size, it would change the way we think about the world, perhaps even the way we perceive ourselves. Imagine not only watching television but being surrounded by it. A theater in every home—television in three dimensions!

"Imagine the applications in schools. Children could not only read about the Battle of Gettysburg but actually be on the battlefield or step into the farthest reaches of the galaxy or be immersed in the smallest subatomic particle. Wouldn't that be incredible? Just imagine the possibilities."

A man in the front raised his hand. "Then how about calling the new product line 'Imagination'? That certainly seems to capture the essence of what you're describing." There were murmurs of approval from around the table.

Mary Anne had heard enough. She began to clap, the sound dulled by the thickness of the carpet and the expansiveness of the office. Every head turned toward her. At the podium, her father wore a deep scowl.

"Imagination?" Mary Anne said. "Now, that is an interesting name for a product line. However, may I suggest that you do a name search before you adopt it? We wouldn't want to steal anybody's idea now, would we?"

"Mary Anne," Allen seethed, "we're in a meeting here."

"Yes, I know. Do you mind if I join you?" She took a seat beside one of the marketers. "I would love to hear your ideas about Imagination. If only Zack Penny was still with us. I bet he'd have a great deal of input." Mary Anne gave her father a forced smile.

The other people in the room exchanged nervous glances. Mary Anne knew they weren't accustomed to seeing their boss being addressed in such a manner—even coming from his own daughter. The marketer next to her readjusted his chair, moving a few inches farther away.

"I don't have time to play games with you," Allen said. "We can talk later, at home. Now if you'll excuse—"

"Actually, we can talk now. Would you like to hear where my imagination leads me?"

Allen's eyes were alight, his mouth set in a thin line, as he dismissed the product team with a sweep of his hand. The surprised people shot out of their chairs, abandoned the conference table, and hurried for the exit.

"Give us five minutes," Allen said as he closed the door behind them. Then he turned on her. "What the bloody hell are you up to? You've embarrassed yourself—and me—by rudely interrupting my meeting. Five minutes! You've got my attention for a full five minutes."

Now that she was alone with him, she had no idea how to start. Mary Anne glanced at the whiteboard. She could see her father's familiar handwriting and lots of red circles and arrows pointed in every direction.

"So ... is this the master plan?" she said.

"This is pointless. I have people waiting for me."

"How does this work exactly?" Mary Anne angled her head, trying to make sense of the squiggles. "You build a big factory and either buy or destroy any competition in your way?"

"I don't have time for this idle prattle. We can do this at home."

"You're never *at* home. You're always too busy."

"Yes, you're right. I am busy. I *do* run a multibillion-dollar corporation."

"It's hard to forget that. The pursuit of the elusive silicon dream."

"Interesting choice of words. That sounds awfully familiar." He walked over to where she was sitting and stood behind her.

"I love Zack," she said. "And of course, I love you. Having Zack as your protégé was perfect. You were so proud of Zack, and I was proud of both of you. When you told me about Zack wanting to start a new company and compete directly against you, after all you'd given him, I didn't want to believe it. How could I? It wasn't at all like him." She took a deep breath. "Did you have any idea how difficult it was for me to believe you?"

"Yes, I did," Allen said. He walked around the table so he was facing her. He leaned on the chair in front of him.

"Did you really? Somehow, I doubt that very much."

Mary Anne saw her father's face soften. She felt her own tears start to well up. She didn't need that, not now. She needed to be strong. It was hard to imagine that the harsh, cynical man before her was also capable of great compassion and genuine sensitivity. That was the side of him she desperately needed to reach now.

"You can't imagine how hard I struggled with that decision," she said. "I should have asked Zack outright, even though I promised you I wouldn't. I was too weak, too scared to find out the truth." *Keep going,* she thought. "I kept waiting for Zack to confide in me, to tell me that he was leaving. If only he had, no matter what his reasons were, I would have accepted them. I love you, Daddy, but Zack is ... or Zack was ..."

The hard edge returned to his face.

"But, I never asked Zack the question. He wouldn't confide in me because he knew it would compromise my relationship with you. Isn't that the craziest thing you've ever heard? You convince me Zack is betraying you, so I hope you're wrong and pray that Zack will confide in me, but Zack won't tell me because he is worrying about straining our relationship, including between you and me. Can you imagine any greater insanity?"

"Yes, a daughter who would believe any of that nonsense. Enough of this. What foolish game are you playing here? What are you up to?"

So that was it. The gloves were off. Fine. She could play that way too. "I think you know precisely what I am up to. I'm here to put a stop to all of this."

"A stop to what?"

"Now who's playing games? I heard what you said to those people. You're taking Zack's idea right out from under him."

"Is that what you think? Did it never occur to you where he got that idea? He got it while he worked here. For me. For us."

Mary Anne felt her jaw drop.

"Does that surprise you? Sad but true. He stole it from us."

"You know that's not true. Zack would never do that. He—"

"Wouldn't he? Weren't you the one who found the proprietary drawings in Zack's office? Weren't you the one who found similar drawings for Zack's supposedly new company? That's right." Allen moved the chair aside and leaned on the table, his face nearly level with hers. "He stole it right out of the company archives and then tried to claim it for his own. He might have succeeded if I hadn't been personally involved with the original creator. You remember Dr. Knowles, don't you? He was a brilliant man and had developed a polymer formula to make ultralight, ultrathin displays. But at the time, too many people discounted his ideas and said it was technologically impossible, so I laid it aside. I should have trusted his brilliance. He was a man ahead of his times, unlike most of the dunderheads who work for me. Unfortunately, the poor man died. Had your Zack not tried to steal it from me, I probably never would have known the treasure that was in my own vaults."

Mary Anne watched her father, his eyes glittering as he battered her with his lies. Not long ago, they'd been in this very office, at this very table, when he'd first convinced her that Zack was set to betray them. Everything he'd said then was a lie too.

She'd been such a fool.

Allen mistook the tear in her eye, and his voice softened. "I know you're hurt. I know it hurts to realize someone you love has lied to you, betrayed you. But that's the nature of the world."

"No, no." Mary Anne shook her head, the tears streaming down her cheeks. "That's not it. I know Zack wouldn't betray us. That's not possible for him."

His eyes flashed his contempt that she would dare question him. He came around the table and grabbed her wrist and dragged her across the room, ignoring her struggles and protests. He tried to make her sit in his chair, and when she resisted, he planted a foot behind her ankle and cruelly forced her down. He slid her up to the desk, planting a foot behind the back wheels. She started crying again.

"Stop your foolishness. Stop it!" He rummaged through one of the top drawers and pulled out a thick blue court document. "Look here! Look. It's all right here. Here are some of Knowles's notes describing some of his first thoughts about the formula and its implications. Here's a memo he'd typed up to request funding for it. Here's another note, describing the paper he was going to present after I'd turned him down. It's all right here, and we're continuing to find more material as we search the archives."

Mary Anne watched her father spin his lies. He said them with such conviction; did he actually believe them himself? He was dangerous. His ethics weren't just duplicitous; they were nonexistent. She leaned forward and buried her head in her hands and began to sob.

"Stop this foolishness. Zack is a liar and a thief, and he'll be dealt with accordingly."

The intercom buzzed, and Louise's voice said, "It's been five minutes, should I—?"

Allen pulled the phone off his desk and threw it against the wall. It shattered and slid to the floor. He spun her chair around. "I'll protect you, you'll see," he said fiercely, his face close to hers. "Zack won't ever hurt us again. It'll be all right."

Mary Anne had come to confront her father, but now she didn't dare. She was too scared.

"What is wrong with you?" Allen said, straightening up.

"I'm sorry I came here. I'm sorry I had to witness this." Mary Anne sniffed, trying to get herself under control. She wiped at her eyes. "We live in a cynical world. We tear people down if we don't accept their principles. Zack had a dream, that's all. He had a dream to start his own company, to find his own way in the world. But Zack didn't betray you. He would never betray you. He came up with a revolutionary way to create extremely thin television screens. You didn't. And neither did anyone else at your company."

Allen backed away from her. "What is this nonsense? Weren't you listening?"

"You really make me ashamed of myself—and of you." There. She finally said it.

"That's not what you said when we were in Uncle Dean's office to sign the declaration."

"I was wrong."

"Enough of this prattle. I've got more important things to do," Allen said. He walked back toward the doors.

"Just tell me one thing," she said. "The whole reason I came here was to make sure that you'll drop the criminal charges against Zack."

"What?" Allen laughed and turned toward her. "You must be joking. Didn't you hear me? I said I'd protect you to make sure he wouldn't hurt you anymore."

"But Zack's company is gone," Mary Anne said, speaking louder, her heart racing. She got up and took a step toward him.

"So?" He walked to the doors.

"There will be no court hearing."

Allen stuck his head out the doorway. "Louise, get the team back in my office," he said. Then he shut the door. "Of course, there'll be a court hearing. What on earth are you talking about?"

"Surely you're dropping the criminal charges."

"And why, pray tell, would I do that?"

"Because there's no point!" Mary Anne shouted, feeling the blood drain from her face.

"Just because your ex-boyfriend failed at his pathetic attempt to profit from stealing my ideas doesn't mean he won't pay for what he did. What he did to us."

"Zack didn't do anything to us—period!" she said. "He didn't betray you! You won! Zack lost!" This was sheer madness.

"That is precisely the point. I won. Zack lost. He lost his pitiful company. Now he will pay for his treachery by going to jail. Repentance is good for a young man." Allen smiled smugly. "I've already started the process."

Mary Anne wanted to slap the smirk from his face. This wasn't her father. This couldn't be the man she loved.

"Oh, I get it," she said. "What will you do? Have a little chat with the law clerks so that you can get the right judge assigned to the case? You must be getting awfully good at that."

"What *possessed* you to say that?" Allen said.

A cold shiver swept through her. She realized she should not have said that.

There was a knock at the door.

Mary Anne's eyes darted toward the door and then at Allen, who was rapidly approaching, his mouth an angry grimace.

"I said, what made you say that?" Allen said, articulating each word precisely.

She raised her hands to protect herself. He grabbed both of her wrists and pulled her to him, looming over her. She felt faint.

The door opened. One of the marketers poked his head inside. "Is everything all right in here?"

"Yes, everything's fine! Now shut the goddamn door! I'll tell you when to come in!"

The door reclosed quickly.

Allen's eyes bore into her. Using the only move she'd learned in her women's self-defense course, she raised both arms and then twisted them down and outward, wrenching her hands free. She made a dash for the door. She reached the lever at the same time as her father, his hand pinning hers, his foot blocking the jamb.

She felt Allen's breath hot on her face. His body was pressed very close to hers.

God, let me go. Please let me go.

"We will talk about this at home," he hissed.

Suddenly, her hand was free. Mary Anne pushed down the door latch and pushed her way through the conference attendees. She rushed down the stairs and ran past the main reception desk, the surprised guard standing up after she was already at the front door. She slammed into it, the warm afternoon air hitting her face.

When she got inside her car, she collapsed against the steering wheel, her whole body shaking. What had she accomplished? Nothing. Her mother had warned her not to confront him head-on. For once, she had been right. Instead, all she'd done was accuse her father of tampering with a district court judge. How stupid was that? She had just made things horribly worse.

She started her car. She had to go to her mother. She had to warn her.

Zack explored the inner recesses of his mouth with the tip of his tongue. In places, it was tender and ragged. He thought he might have broken a tooth. He glanced in the rearview mirror. His right cheek was swollen and red. It looked like his ribs felt. Maybe he ought to go to the hospital like Joni suggested. He'd broken a rib in high school wrestling, and the pain was very similar. He raised his right arm. Ouch. He tried to flex to the left. A sharp pain stopped him immediately.

Well, he'd go home and try to sleep it off. If he wasn't feeling any better by tomorrow morning, he'd go see the doctor.

As he was about to pull into the parking lot, he saw someone standing at the door to his second-floor apartment. It was a man, about his own height but much more muscled. Zack didn't recognize him. He was knocking on the door.

Another process server? What could Allen be throwing at him now?

He switched off his turn signal and drove casually past, keeping his head forward and trying to watch the man out of the corner of his eye as he passed the complex. The man, focused on the door, didn't see him. He drove down two blocks and pulled over.

Who would be knocking on his door at this hour? It was nearly quarter after six. Do process servers work this late? Those guys kept regular hours, didn't they? Maybe it was another renter needing something, or a Jehovah's Witness. Something about the way the man was knocking told Zack it wasn't benign. He thought about driving past again but figured that would be too conspicuous.

In his side mirror, he saw a white, nondescript car exit the parking lot and turn right, back toward the highway. Zack waited until it was out of sight and then waited a few more minutes to make sure it wasn't going to just circle around.

The parking lot took on a very ominous feel. Several cars seemed suspicious; he couldn't recall ever seeing them. Then again, how often did he really take notice of other people's cars?

Getting out of his car was a real chore. It took him three tries to swing his legs out and turn to pull himself out. He never realized how much he'd relied on muscles around his ribs to do such a simple chore. As he locked the door, he looked around the lot, half expecting some mysterious figure to emerge out of the shadows.

He slowly walked over to his stairs and gripped the railing firmly to start up. Then he heard a door thrown open. He looked to his left and saw the complex's manager standing in the shadows of her doorway with her hands on her hips.

"Are you selling drugs?" she said.

Her tone made him instantly realize it wasn't a joke.

"Wha—? No, of course not."

She came out onto the sidewalk, glaring at him. She was already a good deal shorter than he was, and he was two steps up. Keeping a penetrating eye on him, much the way his own mother used to do when he came home late, she approached until she stood next to the railing, hands still firmly planted on her hips.

"Then are you on drugs?" she asked, as though the subtle difference would elicit the truth.

"No! I don't use them, and I certainly don't deal them."

"I don't tolerate that sort of thing here. Check your lease. Any drug use and you're out. Hear me?"

"I'm not— Why are you even asking me this?"

"The police were here. They were looking for you. Why else would they be here?"

Zack's heart jumped in his chest. They were coming to arrest him.

"The police?"

"Yes. About fifteen minutes ago, a guy knocks on my door and asks which apartment was yours. I told him I don't give out that information and solicitors are not allowed on the premises. That's when he pulled out his badge and says he's from the San Francisco police department; he said he needed to talk to you."

Zack didn't know what to say. Did she really need to know he was going to jail for his own invention?

"What happened to your face?"

Zack automatically touched his cheek. There was no sense lying about it. "I got into a fight."

Her jaw clenched, and her eyes flashed as though this confirmed her suspicions. She pressed right up against the railing and pointed a sharp finger at him. "You better hope they just wanted a donation, or I'll cancel your lease and kick your ass out of here faster than you can blink." She turned sharply on her heel, returned to her apartment, and slammed her door.

Zack glanced up at the landing. Whoever it was would be coming back. He knew since it was Friday, the courts were already closed, and that meant he could easily sit in jail the entire weekend without even being able to talk to a judge to explain why he shouldn't be there. He turned around, got in his car, and left. If the manager didn't believe him before, his leaving should push her over the edge. Only a guilty person would be fleeing the scene.

Just before he got on the highway, he pulled over at a Carl's Jr. and fished some quarters out of his ashtray. He dialed Mary Anne's cell from the pay phone and hoped she would answer. He couldn't go back to Paul's, he didn't want to face Dimitre or the other guys right now, nor did he want to see the Bakers like this. That only left one person.

"Hello?"

Thank God. "It's me. Where are you?"

"Zack? What? I'm on the 101. I'm almost to the city. I just—"

"Good. I'm heading there too. I can't talk right—"

"Zack, listen! I just came from a meeting with my father. He said he's going ahead with the criminal charges."

"I already know."

"What? How could you?"

"I don't think we should talk on this thing. They can be monitored. Meet me where we spent our first night together. Okay?"

"Okay, but Zack—"

"We'll talk there."

Zack hung up the pay phone. He merged onto the 580 and headed back into the city.

CHAPTER FIFTY-THREE

Allen was speeding up Highway 101 in his Porsche 911, heading north into San Francisco. Agitated by the slow flow of traffic, he shifted down, but the car slowed more than he'd intended, and he angrily shifted back into the higher gear and eased around another slow-moving idiot in the fast lane, passing him on the left shoulder. Traffic was horrendous tonight, even for California.

The clockwork regularity of his kingdom seemed to have slipped a gear, Allen thought. Charlotte had made love to him last night, Dean canceled the appointment this morning, and now his own daughter was accusing him of tampering with the judicial system, something he did not think she would piece together so quickly. Something was definitely amiss. He wasn't sure what it was, but he knew it started at home.

Zack stumbled into the Radisson on Beach Street, hoping Mary Anne was already there. He hadn't thought to look for her car until he was nearly out of the parking lot. The brown marble pillars holding up the towering ceiling and the set of beige leather couches facing each other brought back fond memories of their first night together. They'd spent the day down on Pier 39 tourist-watching, trying to guess where the visitors were from. He'd won their little game and elected to finish the evening in the lounge of the Radisson. Afterward, while they were snuggling on one of the couches, she'd surprised him by suggesting they get a room for the night.

As he limped forward, he felt a touch of smugness. Allen and the police would never look for him in the shadow of the Henley mansion. Allen's house was only about fifteen minutes away, past the marina and up over the hill.

He saw a familiar head on the sofa about the same time it turned toward him. Mary Anne got up and rushed toward him and then pulled up short, her momentum nearly causing a collision.

"My God! Are you all right? What happened?"

"I look worse than I feel. And I feel a lot better now."

She wrapped her arms around his neck and held him.

A few hours ago, Paul was his ally, and she was still on the outside. Now she was back to being his best friend, undoing eleven days of uproar with the smile in her eyes and the touch of her skin. Zack relaxed into her embrace.

"I've missed this," he said. "I've really missed this."

"Me too," she whispered, sniffling. "Me too."

Then she kissed him. Zack returned the kiss for a moment and then pulled back from the pain in his lips. "Oww," he said, laughing. "Too soon for that, I guess."

"Come on, let's get a room."

"Okay, but you're going to have to do all the work," he said, taking her hand.

"I always do."

As they checked in, the clerk tried not to take notice of his bruises, handing them two keys to a suite that overlooked the bay. With an arm over her shoulders for support, Zack walked slowly toward the elevator. Christ, his ribs hurt like hell.

"Are you going to be all right? Maybe we ought to go to the hospital instead."

"I should be fine," Zack said, clenching his teeth tightly. "I'm more stiff than anything else. Just … help me to the room."

He leaned against Mary Anne, but she was such a small set of crutches that he was afraid she could buckle at any moment. She pushed him into the elevator. He closed his eyes, glad he didn't have to walk up four flights.

"Where do you hurt?" Mary Anne said, swiping the key in the door.

"Everywhere."

"You need to go to a doctor."

"Just help me to the bed. I just need to be still. I think I stiffened up on the car ride over the bridge."

Zack reached the bed. Mary Anne tried to guide him onto his right side, but she went down with him, her arms caught around his chest.

"Oww!"

"Are your ribs broken?"

"They will be if you keep doing that."

"Sorry." She gently extracted her arms and sat up next to him. "You ever going to tell me what happened?"

"Paul and I had a bit of a tussle." He gave her the briefest outline of the fight and what led up to it, skimming over Paul's acerbic comments about her. Judging from the look on her face, she was able to fill in the details.

"I've never liked that man," she said when he finished. "Of course, he hates me anyway."

"These days, Paul seems to hate everyone."

"Yes, but I've ruined everything that you've worked for."

"You can stop being a martyr," Zack said. "Did you confront your father?"

"Yes," Mary Anne said. "I didn't do a very good job." She told him about how she'd confronted her father, how she'd interrupted the meeting with the marketing department to exploit Zack's own ideas, and all the lies he told. She also told him how he planned to move forward with the criminal charges.

"You okay?" Zack asked quietly.

Her eyes had become misty. She looked down at the mattress, sniffed, and nodded. It would have been easy for Zack to say *I told you so*. It would have been easy to say how right he'd been all along, that she should have just trusted him and believed in him, that she should never have believed her father over him. But he didn't. He merely reached over and placed a hand over hers.

Mary Anne's hands suddenly flew to her mouth. "Oh, my God! I need to call my mother."

"Why?"

"I need to warn her about my slipup. I don't know when she and Uncle Dean are planning to confront Allen, but I think it's ... dangerous for her to try to confront him right now."

"Dangerous? Why do you say that?"

"Because he was as angry as I've ever seen him. I thought he was going to hurt me. I think if she tries to confront him now, it'll go very badly. For everyone."

Mary Anne found her tiny silver cell phone and punched in the number. No answer. She hung up before it could go to voice mail.

"No one there?" Zack asked.

She shook her head and tried again. Four rings and still no answer. She hung up and tried one more time. When it rang to voice mail, she said, "Hi, it's me. I need to talk to you. Right now. I'm with Zack. Call my cell when you get this."

Mary Anne leaned back against the headboard, a worried look on her face.

To try and distract her, Zack explained about his coming home to find someone standing in front of his door and then the confrontation with the apartment manager.

"You know, I think that is all my fault."

"What do you mean?"

She looked at him, a smile spreading over her face. "I've done something else that I haven't told you about. After I warned you not to contact the police, I did just that. Remember Deirdre? Her father's a detective with San Francisco. I think that may have been him on your doorstep."

Zack looked at her in disbelief.

"Well, I wasn't turning you in, if that's what you're thinking."

"No, I am just amazed you did that. Did you tell your mother or McSorley what you were doing?"

"No. Besides, I didn't do that much. I just gave him a brief outline of what was happening, and I asked him to talk to you, off the record, so we could get a better idea of our options. I figure it's best to have all our bases covered."

Zack laughed, the pain in his sides stabbing him with every breath, but he kept laughing. Tears welled up in his eyes.

"I don't see what's so funny," Mary Anne said.

"Don't you?" Zack said, trying his best now to stop laughing, the pain becoming unbearable. "You and I are quite the pair. Maybe … just maybe, we do belong together after all."

Zack rolled onto his side. As he tried to find a comfortable fetal position, he could feel warmth pressing on his back. His nose picked up the faint odor of her body soap. Despite the insanity of the situation, he knew that he wanted Mary Anne to be with him. Paul was right. He was crazy.

CHAPTER FIFTY-FOUR

Dean knew he was insane to be here, in Allen's home, alone with Charlotte. She had called him at the office and told him that Allen was staying overnight in San Jose and invited him to dinner, saying that they needed to talk about the Coit Tower meeting. After the drinks at Ghirardelli Square, he'd fantasized about spending the evening alone with her. This morning at Coit Tower, she'd looked radiant. She was like a perfect recreational drug—too hard to resist, yet not hard enough to be concerned about. It was impossible to refuse her, so he hadn't.

Perhaps it was the element of danger of fantasizing about an affair with Allen Henley's wife that made him behave so irrationally. Or perhaps it was simpler. He never saw Marjorie anymore. Whatever the reason, he was a well-respected lawyer, a senior partner in a prestigious law firm, who'd violated his client's confidentiality and lusted after his wife.

The latter thoughts immediately sprang to mind when Dean heard the front door open. Out of the corner of his eye, he saw Allen walking through the doorway toward them.

"Dean!" Henley said. "What a pleasant surprise."

Dean started to rise, but Allen's hand on his shoulder firmly planted him back on his chair.

"No need to get up. I can see that you and my wife haven't quite finished dessert."

"I thought you weren't coming home tonight," Charlotte said, putting her napkin on the tablecloth.

"Life is just full of surprises."

"Have you eaten?" Charlotte asked. "Carl and Maria have left already for the weekend."

"Have they?" Allen glanced at his watch. "A little premature, wouldn't you say?"

"As I said, I didn't think you were coming home, and they'd already served us."

Allen bent down and gave Charlotte a deep, wet kiss on the mouth. Charlotte's face reddened, and she turned her head.

"Now that's a good appetizer. Wouldn't you say?" Allen gave Dean a wink. "Dean, would you care for one? A drink, I mean. I'm parched."

Dean shook his head. "We had a bottle of wine with dinner. That's enough for me."

"I'm sure it isn't," Allen said with a smile.

He walked over to the liquor cabinet built into the wall. The beech-wood cabinet was etched with designs that looked like hieroglyphics. In the center was a hexagonal mirror. Allen removed two glass tumblers. Dean could see Allen was watching him in the mirror. Ice clinked into the glasses, followed by the splash of scotch.

"Dear, I assume that you'll have the usual."

"You assume correctly," Charlotte said.

Allen brought the drinks back to the table. He passed a glass of scotch to Charlotte and sat down to her left, putting their guest across the table from him.

"Ah, yes. If only life could be as predictable as my wife's drinking habits." He turned to Charlotte. "So ... where is our daughter?"

"She didn't come home either," Charlotte said, holding her glass up to the light. "I'm sure she'll call later. I thought I heard my phone upstairs ringing in the middle of dinner—that was probably her."

"Dean, there's nothing worse for a father than to have an adult daughter living at home. It's better not to know what she's doing than to be her landlord with no eviction rights." Allen took a drink and then set his glass down. "Well, then. Isn't this cozy? Just the three of us."

Dean was sorry he had come. After unloading his soul this morning, he felt as transparent as a child caught with half a cookie behind his back. He felt Charlotte's eyes boring into him. Earlier, she'd said she wanted to start the confrontation as early as possible. Apparently, she was itching for a fight. He didn't have the energy for it and had told her so. She'd finally elicited a promise from him that they'd confront Allen together tomorrow evening. He never worked full days on Saturdays.

To break the awkward silence, Dean said, "I got your message today about the permits and your desire to proceed quickly through the county's requirements."

"They're finished?" Allen said. "Brilliant."

"No, not quite," Dean said. "We started the process, but I need your input on a few things."

"Ah. So you took the initiative then and decided to pop by the house?"

"Well, actually, I called to leave a message, but Charlotte answered and invited me for dinner."

"I see." Allen took another sip, sucking another ice cube into his mouth and crunching it loudly. "So, where's Marjorie?"

"She's gone with the girls for another round down at Spyglass." Dean shifted in his chair. "Listen, I've got the papers in my briefcase. Let me go get them and—"

"Rest your bones, old man." Allen motioned him to stay seated. "I can look at the papers later. I just came from a long day at the office, and you've been mighty busy yourself today. Although I don't know how you could have gotten all that work done, being gone all morning like you were."

"Come again?" He was used to Allen's bluntness and his propensity to change the direction of a conversation—but he wasn't usually the focus of the inquisitions.

"When you went and canceled our tennis match this morning, I called your office. They said you weren't there. Where were you?"

Dean felt beads of sweat pop out on his brow. Had Allen found out about the Coit Tower meeting? Had someone talked? He nearly glanced over at Charlotte but managed to keep his focus on Allen.

Get hold of yourself. You're a senior partner, for Christ's sake. This is just like court. "I don't believe I have to justify my time to you when I'm not working on one of your cases, but if you must know, I was meeting with some clients."

"Clients, as in plural?"

Dean leaned forward and folded his hands, his elbows on the table. "You are one of our firm's most celebrated clients and you are certainly my most important client, but I do have others."

"And who are they?"

Dean sniffed and gave a shake of his head. "You know the rules. Client-attorney confidentiality."

"Yes, the infamous client-attorney confidentiality. As I recall, that's where the lawyer is forbidden to disclose anything that his client has already disclosed to him. Is that about spot-on?"

Dean nodded. The chandelier was throwing strange lighting, making Allen's eyes look almost yellow. Allen watched him for a moment but was unable to break through his defense. Dean smiled inwardly.

"I bet you were a trifle disappointed when I walked in tonight."

"Of course not," Dean said, almost too quickly. "Why would I be?"

"Really? A nice bottle of wine, some friendly chitchat with my wife, the staff has an early night ..." Allen laughed. "We're old college chums. I think we can level with each other."

"I came here tonight to drop off the papers that you asked me to do."

"Oh, come off it!" Allen said, scowling. "You could have sent one of your flunkies to drop off the papers. I know how you are. Every time you see Charlotte, all you can think about is chopping down that tree of yours."

"What?" Alarm bells clanged inside Dean's head.

"Stop it!" Charlotte said. "You've got a filthy mind!"

"Really, Charlotte, I'm surprised at you. We've known about Dean's secret crush on you for years. Hell, we've even laughed about it after we've gone a few rounds in the sack."

Charlotte's face became beet-red. "My apologies, Dean. I suggest that you go home. Allen seems to be in one of his more disgusting moods."

Dean nodded and rose from his chair, discarding the dinner napkin from his lap.

"So where precisely is Mary Anne?" Allen said, standing up as well.

"I told you I don't know," Charlotte said. "She'll call. You owe Dean an immediate—"

"Don't know or won't tell me? Is this all part of client-attorney confidentiality? Don't patronize me!" he yelled. "My lawyer disappears this morning, something he hasn't done in years. Then my own daughter comes to me and accuses me of tampering with judges."

Dean felt the full force of his glare. When Allen spoke again, his voice had a menacing edge. "Now why would she do that, I wonder? That's very out of character for Mary Anne. And now, tonight, I come home and find my attorney nearly in bed with my wife!"

"What! I was—" Dean began.

"That is quite enough!" Charlotte shot up from her chair. "Dean and I will not be accused like this. You owe both of us an immediate apology."

Allen slammed the table. "I am not a fool! Don't play me for one. Come to think of it, where were you off to this morning, dear wife? You were up early."

Charlotte met Allen's stare with a tight mouth and hands on hips. "Good night, Dean. I hope you have a pleasant evening."

He took the cue and quickly turned to leave. In but a few

moments, Allen had disarmed them and they were on the defensive, fighting to keep their heads above water. Confronting him tomorrow night would not be all that easy. Dean thought of his jacket that he'd brought for the trip home, but Carl had put it away somewhere. Forget the jacket.

"Where are you going, old man? Leaving so soon?"

Dean kept walking, his hands clenched into fists. He wanted to knock Allen's head off but at the same time felt an overwhelming sense of guilt. The bastard might not know all the details of this morning's meeting, but he'd quickly pieced things together. Why had Mary Anne gone to see her father? That foolish girl. She'd put all of them in a horrible position. They'd been planning a surprise attack, and instead, they found themselves ambushed.

"Going to meet those same clients, are you?" Allen said, following on his heels. "Give Zack my best."

Dean knew Allen was firing blindly now, but his parting shot had hit the mark. When he opened the front door, cool night air enveloped him, tree branches whispering above his head. He shut the door behind himself, glad to be out of there.

He knew Charlotte would not have a pleasant evening.

Mary Anne watched Zack nap. He looked so peaceful. Listening to Zack's breathing, seeing his boyish face lying on the pillow, she had never felt closer to Zack than she did now. Was it only this morning she'd begged him not to go to the police? She'd been so worried that he would and jeopardize things before she and her mother could confront Allen. Now, she was the one who put things in jeopardy. But Zack would never have gone to the police. It was one of the reasons she loved him so much. He wouldn't betray her. Even as her father sought to destroy him, he still wouldn't betray her.

She'd curled up beside him after she'd ordered a pizza but got up, too agitated to lie still. She kept replaying the conversation with her father over and over. She couldn't believe her own father was going to attempt to put Zack in jail for something he and Dimitre had invented. She could still see Allen's eager smile after coming home late at night, as he kneeled down, arms spread wide, ready to scoop her up as she ran down the hall toward him in her pajamas after missing him so much during the day. She remembered Sunday mornings snuggled on his lap with the comics, while he held the sports page over her like a tent and the smell of fresh coffee washed over them. She remembered giggling wildly as his whiskers tickled her, making a game of trying to kiss her on the cheeks. He was her first knight in shining armor, always there to help her fight her battles. A tear rolled down her cheek.

When had it all changed? Had he always been this way, and she'd just put blinders on? Somewhere along the line, she had put him on such a pedestal that he was unassailable, untouchable. She'd created an ideal persona in her mind and failed to see the man her father truly was. Even now, she had a hard time remembering the brutal fights between her parents. Though she knew they'd happened, and frequently, she could hardly remember them.

How many other lives had he ruined that she'd never heard about? Comments between Uncle Dean and Allen about "going to the war room" or "the operation" and other such things came back to her now in a flood. She'd always thought they were joking, but perhaps not. And that Sandy Fong—she'd always ignored the bad feeling she had around him, he was just some old friend of her father's that helped out from time to time with a bit of work. There were others, too, that she couldn't quite remember. Names and faces blurred.

She'd sneaked a peek into Pandora's box and managed to slam the lid back down, afraid to open it all the way.

Chapter Fifty-Five

Charlotte stiffened as Allen stormed back into the dining room. "What a bloody coward!" he shouted. "He doesn't have the balls to stand up to me."

"If he had stayed," she said, "he would have stuffed those papers in your filthy mouth. Why did you embarrass him like that?"

"You and I both know that ol' Dean has had the hots for you ever since our days at Berkeley and Stanford." Allen went for a refill, looking a little dispirited now that his prey had moved off.

"You don't have to throw it in the man's face," she said, her cheeks flushed from the alcohol and her anger.

He screwed the cap back on the scotch. "It wouldn't surprise me at all that you're using his feelings for you to get something you want. How do I know that you and Dean haven't been having one of those special client-lawyer relationships? Kiss and hug under the covers of a confidentiality pact, complete with decoder ring and diaphragms."

"You're disgusting."

"The truth is the truth. Isn't that what that backstabbing ex-boyfriend of our daughter used to say?"

Charlotte knew if she could just make it up to her room, she'd be safe. With the door locked, she could collect herself and prepare for tomorrow's fight. She rounded the dining table, but Allen moved between her and the exit, still spoiling for a fight.

"Say what you will about him," she said, "but at least Zack never needed to attack anyone to prove he was a man."

"One of the converted, are we? Just like our daughter? Don't you think it's a little late to be cheering for the underdog?"

"Listen to you," Charlotte said, trembling inwardly. "This isn't some kind of game for your own personal amusement. You're talking about people's lives, your family's lives."

"That is precisely it!" Allen slammed his fist on the oak buffet table, making the dishes inside clatter. "My life. My family's lives. And the lives of the thousands of employees who work in my company. And Mr. Zack Righteous Penny was attempting to take away the livelihood of all those people that you wish to protect."

"What?" She studied his eyes. The alcohol was talking. She knew the signs.

"You heard me. If I hadn't crushed Zack, then he might have ruined everything I'd worked so hard to build. People's livelihoods were at stake. And it's my responsibility to protect the jobs of my employees. They expect me to do it; their families insist that I do it. So don't tell me about the high moral road. No one is listening."

"Who cares about your blasted business? I was talking about how you humiliated your best friend! And how you tried to destroy Zack's life, treating it all like some sort of game."

"Actually," Allen said, "we were talking about confidentiality. Who broke it?"

"I have no idea what you're talking about!"

"Who broke it? I can't believe that our Mary Anne could have coerced Dean on her own. That leaves you or Zack."

Charlotte took a few steps backward. "You're drunk," she said.

"Not yet, but I'm getting there." Allen took a step closer. "Zack could never have convinced Dean to become a Judas. Dean would have merely laughed at him. You, however, could lead Dean's little pecker anywhere."

"You're disgusting! This conversation's over."

Allen lunged at her and gripped her arm fiercely. She tried to free herself, but he spun her around, putting her back to the door. He seized hold of her other arm and squeezed. The pain was excruciating.

"I'm right, aren't I?"

"Let me go."

He drew her closer to him, until her forearms pressed against his chest. His face seemed to fill her entire field of vision.

"What did Dean say?" he demanded. "What did he tell you?"

Charlotte tried to free herself. When that failed, she tried to scratch at his face, but he squeezed even harder. She cried out.

"You had to stick your stupid nose into this, didn't you? Didn't you!"

"Let me go!"

"Tell me who else is involved!" he roared.

She tried to knee him, but he was too quick for her. He let go with one hand and slapped her hard across the face. The impact spun her around, and her back slammed against the buffet. Desperate, she grabbed the only weapon available, Allen's drink. She rammed the heavy tumbler into his nose, and the alcohol splashed into his astonished eyes.

Allen let out a yelp and clutched his face. She made a dash past him for the grand staircase. He tried to grab her, missing, but the impact threw her off-balance. She stumbled from the dining room, lurching into the forelegs of the statue. Pain shot through her shoulder, and the statue teetered on its pedestal. She looked back and saw him in the doorway, rubbing at his eyes. With a moan, she darted for the stairs.

"You bitch! You goddamn bitch!"

Gripping the wide wooden banister, she ran up the stairs, two at a time.

Something cold and wet clamped onto her left ankle, and an instant later, she was down on her rump. Allen's eyes bulged out at her like those horrible bullfrogs back in Louisiana that her brother used to tease her with. His hands batted at her, searching for an arm or a wrist to hold, but he found only her dress.

She kicked out as hard as she could, hitting him in the shoulder.

The blow stood him up straight on the edge of the step, and his arms flailed like a windmill. He tried to grab at the railing, but the stairs were too wide to reach it. Allen fell backward, his body tumbling head over heels down the stairs until his shoulder hit the bottom of the banister. He grabbed hold of a rung and tried to pull himself to his feet, but his head bumped into the railing. He squinted up at her, his mouth twisted like a Halloween pumpkin's. "You bitch! I'm going to get you for this!"

She couldn't stay there. She had to move. In a panic, she climbed the remaining stairs on all fours. Allen was coming; his feet pounded up the stairs. When she reached the landing, she staggered into her bedroom, locking the door behind her.

Her heart was racing.

It leaped into her throat when she felt him slam into the other side of the door.

Dean saw the sign for Highway 101 but pulled over to allow a car behind him to pass. He did a quick U-turn and headed back to the Henley mansion.

He should never have walked out; he should have faced Allen down. Damn it, he'd been tired before and still played through the pain. Maybe the truth was he wanted one more quiet evening with Charlotte before it all broke loose. He knew once it did, he'd never have the opportunity again. Allen would turn on all of them like a wolf out for blood.

He'd been stupid to leave. He knew you had to stand up to someone like Allen, to fight back, to not show any signs of weakness. And what he did earlier was show weakness. True weakness.

They should have confronted him right then. Tonight, like she'd wanted to. Allen had been off-balance and on guard, suspicious. That had been the moment to attack. Instead, he'd allowed Allen to take away the initiative. Well, he was going to take it back.

Dean hit the gas, and the car surged up the street. Allen wasn't going to know what hit him.

The burning in his eyes was excruciating. Allen stumbled back into the dining room table. He pulled the tablecloth toward him, the centerpiece of unlit candles toppling like bowling pins, the wineglasses shattering on the hardwood floor. He wiped his eyes with the heavy cloth, cursing the rough fabric.

"God damn it! She's gonna pay for this!"

He needed water. He swung around, nearly falling over a dining room chair. He kicked it aside and lurched into the kitchen. He wiped his eyes with his shirtsleeve. They hurt so badly he wanted to pull them out of his head.

At the kitchen sink, he flipped the faucet on full blast. The water came out hot. "Jesus Christ!" He pushed the lever to the right, ducked his head under the tap, and rinsed out his eyes. "The bitch. The fucking bitch."

After several minutes, the stinging in his eyes finally subsided. He pulled his head away from the running tap. He was soaked, the water having run down his neck, plastering his shirt to his body. He saw a red-checkered dishcloth tucked in the refrigerator handle. He grabbed the cloth and mopped his face and neck. He rolled his wet shirtsleeves over his elbows.

Charlotte had McSorley on a leash. She'd pulled his dick, and he'd told all. How else could Mary Anne have known about the court tampering? Sure, he'd bragged about it to Julie too, but he knew she'd never talk. She was a sheep.

He'd always known that Mary Anne was weak, but he hadn't foreseen his own wife and that coward McSorley trying to poison his daughter against him. She would hang on to her romantic delusions until Zack was finished. Once he was out of the picture, she'd come around. She loved her father that much. She couldn't turn on him any more than Julie could. She could be dissuaded, misguided, but she would always be true to him in the end.

He tossed the towel aside. Dean and Charlotte, on the other hand, had conspired to screw up the master plan he'd so carefully orchestrated. He wasn't sure yet how to deal with them. But come Monday, Dean's partners would be receiving a little visit.

His cell phone vibrated in his front trouser pocket, startling him. He thought it might be Dean calling to apologize. He'd driven down the road a bit by now and, realizing his precious job was in danger, was having second thoughts. He pressed the talk button.

"Speak."

"Is this Mr. Henley?"

Allen didn't recognize the voice. "Yes, who is this?"

"It's Detective Silver, sir. From the San Francisco PD."

"What can I do for you?"

"I don't know if this is news to you, but you told me to keep an ear open in case Mary Anne ever said anything to Deirdre about Zack that you should know."

"Yes, yes, go on."

"Well, sir, she called me."

"Who? Your daughter?"

"No, sir, Mary Anne."

For the first time in many years, Allen felt himself go numb.

CHAPTER FIFTY-SIX

Dean pulled up to the double gates outside the Henley mansion. He pressed the intercom button. He knew Charlotte would buzz him right in, but if Allen answered, he'd claim he'd forgotten his jacket. If Allen refused, he was prepared to climb over the wall.

A moment passed. He reached for the buzzer again, but before he could press it, Allen's voice said, "Come in, old man." And the gates rolled back.

Dean drove his car to the top of the drive. So what if he liked Charlotte? Was that a crime? It's not like he'd done anything about it. Allen had no right to embarrass him in front of her. Given all the years that they'd worked together, he deserved at least some measure of courtesy. Had he violated his client confidentiality by telling Zack, Charlotte, and Mary Anne some of the dirty dealings that Allen had orchestrated? Yes, he had. So what? Allen had stolen the polymer formula from Zack and wanted him hanged for simply being entrepreneurial. Allen had crossed the line first.

Dean got hold of himself. A defensive posture was no good. He had to be thinking offensively. He knew once he was inside, his instincts would take over, as they always did in court. He could devour and outmaneuver anyone. That's why Allen paid him so handsomely. Not because they were old college chums.

As Dean shut the car door and tucked in his shirt, he realized there was another reason that had brought him back. This morning, he'd lied to Zack that Allen would drop the criminal charge. He didn't know why he'd said it—maybe to ease his conscience. But now he felt an obligation—a moral one, and that was a real surprise—to convince Allen to drop the charge.

Time to step out from Allen's shadow.

When Dean reached the front door, he paused to wipe the sweat on his forehead with his shirtsleeve. The door was unlocked. He took a deep breath and stepped into the pit of the Coliseum. *Ave Caesar! Nos morituri te salutamus!*

Charlotte sat trembling on the edge of the cloud that was her queen-size bed, primped with downy comforters and fluffy pillows. She wished to God she hadn't mixed the scotch with the wine from dinner. She needed a clear head, and right now it was pounding. Or maybe she needed another drink to settle down?

Don't be a fool! She pounded a pillow with her fist.

It had been many years since Allen had struck her. In the days of their youth, when they were both filled with passion, they'd had some wicked fights. Even after Mary Anne was born, they'd still go at it tooth and nail. But as Mary Anne grew, she became wary of her daughter's eyes on them, and at some point, she'd lost the urge to fight, choosing instead the path of nonresistance.

She glanced over her shoulder at the antique vanity, a reclaimed maple bureau that supported a large half moon-shaped mirror with a gold trim. She didn't like what she saw in the mirror. Her face looked old now, the creases along her neck giving away her age. She turned away, the walls and time closing in around her.

She glanced at the headboard of her bed. She kept a spare flask back there since she hated to creep downstairs late at night. She rolled her tongue across her lips.

It was impossible to think with Allen yelling and stomping downstairs. She folded her arms across her chest, trying to stop the shaking. She looked at the headboard again.

Stop it! The tears ran down her face. She tried not to wipe her eyes, not wanting to smear the mascara. How pitiful she'd become, she thought.

She didn't know what possessed her to invite Dean to the house—especially so soon after the Coit Tower meeting. Maybe Allen was right. She'd seen the way that Dean looked at her, the way he practically gaped every time she crossed her legs. That didn't happen much with men anymore. The wild suitors of her youth had all been displaced, and now everyone knew her as Allen's wife. Even men on the street didn't pay her any mind. Lately, she'd had very little to be proud about. She looked over at the vanity mirror again.

She put her face in her hands, crying softly. God, sweet Jesus, is this what life has become?

Stop it. Just stop it, she told herself. There were good intentions behind what she'd done. She'd tried to help Mary Anne. She'd tried to help Zack. They were worth fighting for. Allen had used his daughter to run his stupid business, sacrificing her happiness in the progress. He had to be stopped.

There was more to it than that. She'd always been a game player. In the beginning of her marriage, one of Allen's attractions was how devilishly clever he could be, getting into people's heads, almost instantly knowing their motives, their inner being. She had admired that about him. She remembered when poor Zack had come over, searching for Mary Anne. She couldn't resist playing with his mind. And that was the real reason she'd invited Dean over tonight. It was a game. A self-serving game to feel wanted, to know that a man desired her. And she had played with his mind, his emotions, teasing him for her own satisfaction.

God, what a wretched lot we women can sometimes be.

Well, the flirting game had ended and no one had won, leaving only disappointed contestants. It was time to put away the balls and bats and do something real. She needed to warn Mary Anne off from the house tonight.

She picked up the phone from the bedside table overlaid with white snowflake lace. The blinking light indicated a message. Mary

Anne had tried to reach her and wanted her to call back. She deleted it and started over. The sound of the dial tone calmed her.

The phone rang two times. Halfway through the third ring, a hushed voice answered.

"Hello?"

"Mary Anne, it's your mother. Stay—"

"Hold on; let me move to the bathroom." There was a pause and then the sound of a door shutting. "Okay. Zack's sleeping. I—"

"Stay away from the house tonight. Your father knows." Charlotte spoke quickly, telling her bits of what had happened. Slow down, she thought. Be coherent.

Mary Anne told her she was coming over anyway.

"That's a mistake," Charlotte said. "You don't know what kind of mood your father is in."

"Yes, I do."

Charlotte realized that Allen had finally revealed himself to Mary Anne. She hoped he hadn't hurt her. "If you're coming, then hurry."

The phone clicked off. What had he done to their daughter? This was all such a mess.

She heard a noise and turned her head. She thought it was the front door opening and shutting—or maybe not. The water pipes often groaned when the fog drifted in from the ocean. Like a foolish child, she imagined some brave rescuer coming to save her.

At that moment, a terrible scream erupted from downstairs.

A chill started at the top of Charlotte's head, spread down through her neck and shoulders, and down her back.

CHAPTER FIFTY-SEVEN

Dean stepped into the foyer. Fading evening light streamed through the stained glass dome, supported by dark wooden beams that arched from floor to ceiling. The rays of color streamed down on the horse-and-rider statue, a gigantic chess piece on the black-and-white tile floor. The muscular hindquarters of the charger seemed to bulge and flex in his face. Allen really should turn the damned thing around.

He looked into the dining room to his left, half expecting to see Charlotte and Allen still there, but it was empty. "Hello?" he called.

A searing pain shot across his neck and shoulders. He screamed and staggered into the entrance hall, struggling to keep his balance. A figure came at him from behind the door, holding a wooden tennis racket in one hand.

"So, you return, old man?" Allen's face was red. "Couldn't wait to chop down that tree?"

Dean gasped, holding his left shoulder. What the hell was the man doing? Something must have set him off. He glanced at the rooms on either side of the entrance hall. Where was Charlotte?

"I told you," Allen said, jabbing the tennis racket at him. "*I* run the show. *I* call the shots. You got stinking rich because of me! I thought we were friends, trusted old friends. I led you to the Promised Land, gave you everything. Why couldn't you have just stayed a dumb sheep and done as you're told? But what do you do?

You stab me in the back. And then you convince my daughter to turn on me."

Allen slammed the tennis racket into his outstretched arm. He cried out but absorbed the blow and grabbed at the weapon, catching Allen off guard. Instead of meekly letting him vent his fury, Dean spun him around and slammed him into the wall, the chair rail cutting across his lower back. Dean grabbed the racket with both hands and used it to pin him against the wall. "You fucking bastard!" He shoved the racket hard into Allen's chest, not letting him get air. "You miserable bastard. You screw with everyone's lives—how long did you think people would take it?"

Allen's face was nearly purple between fury and lack of oxygen.

"I'm so sick of your goddamn arrogance." Dean was nose-to-nose with him. "You're right, Charlotte and I are moving against you, and when the two of us are done with you, you'll be lucky to have anything left. Now you can either back down," he jammed the tennis racket hard into Allen's chest, "or we can destroy you. Which is it?"

"Why?" he gasped.

"Because I've sat by and watched you destroy too many people, and I've had enough. Zack is a good man. He deserves better. Your own daughter deserves better. And look what you've done to Charlotte. You took a beautiful, charming woman and turned her into a drunk."

Allen feebly shoved at him and Dean stepped back, allowing him to catch his breath.

Dean pointed the racket at him like a sword. The mighty Allen was leaning over on his knees, struggling for air. Before this, he had never been able to beat the man in a tennis match or anything else. "But stealing Zack's invention and then punishing him for it ... that was more than I could take. You're a goddamn, spineless crook. I finally have the balls to say what I've thought for years."

Allen straightened up, shifting away from the wall. Dean carefully kept the tennis racket between them.

"God," Dean said with a laugh, "is it any wonder that Mary Anne finally saw through you? It was only a matter of time. You can't ruin people's lives and expect them to sit by and take it forever."

Allen looked up at him, his jaw clenched, the rage still very much alive.

"That's right, *old man*," Dean said, "your own daughter woke up to what a miserable bastard her father really is. Just you wait till she gets in court. She'll make a prime witness—against you!"

With a growl, Allen charged him, knocking aside the racket and hurling him backward.

They rammed into the horse's wide rear end, hitting it so hard that with an awful screech, the statue slid forward on its marble base, nearly toppling. It rocked for a moment before settling back into position.

The back of Dean's head slammed into the metal hindquarters. A bright light flashed inside his skull, and then darkness swam up. He shook his head, trying to find his center. Before he could do that, Allen landed a blow across his face that sent him to his knees. The racket was ripped from his hand. The painted sunlight glowed all around him, and a sea of black and white squares swam before his eyes. He was on a game board—left or right, black or white—adrift in the middle of an ocean of right and wrong choices.

He realized too late that he should put his hands out. His chest and face slammed hard onto the unforgiving surface. The tile felt cool on his cheek for a fraction of an instant, and then he was pushing up from the floor. Another blow hit him. Then another and another, across his back and shoulders. He collapsed again.

He could hear screaming. If it was his voice, he didn't recognize it. In the confusion of echoes, there was a loud, splintering sound. And another scream joined the chorus.

When Charlotte heard the first cry from downstairs, she jumped up and ran to the corner of her bedroom, as far from the door as she could get. She shook from head to toe, clutching at the neckline of her dress and cinching it closed. She thought she heard voices, but she couldn't make them out.

As she stared at the carved panels on the door, a dreadful realization dawned on her. She was trapped. There was only one set of stairs to the main floor. As magnificent as it was, it was the only way out, and it led directly into the lion's den. Her beautiful room, her sanctuary, was little more than a well-appointed prison cell.

Worse, the mansion itself was surrounded by several acres of lawns and woods and a high perimeter fence. Even if she could get to the front door, there was no one to help unless she sprinted several hundred yards across the lawns and climbed over a six-foot wall. The privacy of a large celebrity home in the island of an even larger sanctuary was precisely why she and Allen had chosen this mausoleum.

All the opulence she'd so greedily surrounded herself with was as useful as the treasures the ancient kings had hidden beneath in their burial mounds. She jumped at the sound of a fierce yell from downstairs. There was a horrible metallic screeching and then more screams—dreadful screams of someone crying out in agony.

She buried her face between her knees, covering her head with her arms. Sweet Jesus, help! Help us. Whoever that is down there, help them. Please!

But the prayer only seemed to bounce back at her from the walls.

Dean was relieved. On the last blow, the tennis racket had splintered and broken, its head spinning off across the marble floor.

Feebly, he got his shaking hands beneath him and started to crawl away. He couldn't see anything other than the black and white tiles that were inches from his face, but he was making progress. Because he couldn't lift his head, he didn't know if he was heading toward the dining room or Allen's study. He just knew he had to get away.

As he put one hand in front of the other, a thought rose out of the fog of his mind. He'd gone too far. Taunting Allen with Mary Anne's betrayal had been too much. Somehow he had to regain control of the situation.

A tremendous kick crashed into his tailbone. It propelled him forward, onto the soft carpet. He knew he was in Allen's private den. He blinked rapidly, images swimming in front of him. The big desk, bookcases, a glass trophy case, and like the other half of a crossed sword set, the mate to the broken racket still hung on the wall behind the desk.

Groaning, he rolled onto his back. Searing pain emanated from his shoulder as he tried to support himself on an elbow. He held his other hand in front of his face, trying to ward off Allen. It hurt so much to breathe, he guessed he had broken ribs. He just hoped he wasn't bleeding internally. He tasted blood in his mouth and felt it trickling down from his neck and the back of his head. He had several broken teeth; his right eye was rapidly swelling shut. He tried to focus and looked up just in time to see Allen striding toward him, backlit by the hallway.

Allen still held the broken handle of the tennis racket. Dean squirmed in retreat, trying to get up, but was backed up against the front of the desk. "You're insane," he said. "Do you think I won't bring charges against you?"

"My, my. Brave to the end, aren't you?" Allen raised the shaft as if to strike but then tossed it into a corner. He walked away, out of Dean's field of vision.

Dean turned over, grabbed the edge of the desk, and pulled himself upright. His right arm didn't seem to work. He heard a clatter of metal. When he turned, he saw Allen by the fireplace. Keeping his eyes on him, Dean rounded the corner of the desk, feeling blindly for some kind of weapon. When Allen faced him, he held the poker in his hand.

"For God's sake, you maniac! Put that thing down. What the hell's wrong with you?"

"What's wrong with me?" Allen asked, stroking the length of

the poker. "I'll tell you precisely what's wrong with me. You'll keep it under your hat, won't you, old chum? You being my lawyer and all. After you left, I got a phone call from an old friend, a real friend, a detective in the city," Allen said, his voice cracking. "His daughter works for Mary Anne. You see, this detective figures he owes me something. I gave his daughter a job when she needed some structure in life, kept her out of jail, actually. And he was calling me as a favor, just as a warning, a heads-up. Because that's what friends do."

Allen moved within striking distance. "Imagine my surprise when this detective tells me what my daughter told him. A story about how a certain lawyer, someone that I trusted implicitly, opened up his kimono to my daughter and her lying son-of-a-bitch ex-boyfriend."

"Wait, just wait," Dean panted. His vision began to blur, and he had to force himself to focus.

Then he felt something hard beneath his good hand—the communication workstation on the corner of the desk. When broadband had first emerged, Allen had wired all the phones and computers in the house through this station. He'd bragged about it incessantly—until ordinary people could also afford it. Dean groped for the telephone handset that he knew should be on top of the workstation.

"Wait for what?" Allen ranted. "It's bad enough that a stupid bloodsucking prick like you tells filthy lies to my daughter and to that ... ungrateful bastard, but Mary Anne was the one person in the world I trusted completely." His voice faltered, and he spoke again, almost in a sob. "And you poisoned her! Now my daughter is talking to the goddamn police!"

Allen raised the poker over his head with both hands. Dean ducked aside just in time, and the poker crashed into the workstation. Sparks shot up, and bits of plastic and glass flew.

Before Dean could move out of range, Allen took another swing. The hook caught him, tearing into his shoulder. Dean groaned in pain and wrenched himself away, putting the desk between them. The cordless handset was hidden in his left hand.

"Why?" Allen said, his voice shaking. "Why did you do it? You had no right to come between my daughter and me! Why did you do it?"

Dean could feel the energy seeping out of his body; sleep pulled at him like quicksand. No! Stay awake, his mind screamed. You've got to stay awake.

"What did you tell them? Answer me!" Allen shrieked.

Buy time, his brain told Dean. Buy time. Maybe Charlotte would come downstairs; maybe she'd already called the police. If she had, he just had to hang on until they arrived.

"Okay, okay! I told ... I told Zack and Mary Anne about some of things that we'd done."

"What things?"

"I ... I told them that we'd known about Imagination for some time. That we waited until Zack was ready to leave and that we would ... we would spring the TRO on him to shut him down."

"Zack knew that already. What else?"

"I ... I told him that we had leverage on Judge Rafkin. We could extend the TRO indefinitely. And that—"

Allen smashed the poker down on the workstation. "Tell me something important!" He hit it again and again until it broke in two, half of it falling off the edge of the desk. "Tell me!"

"I told him I gave Sandy access to the confiscated equipment." Dean backed up against the wall. "And how he found the polymer formula in Dimitre's disk drive, and that you put two and two together, knew of its technical significance. And ... and that we were going to use a dated conference to establish proof of prior art. Then use your connections to put Zack in jail for stealing his own invention. I ... I told them everything. Everything!"

Allen lowered the poker.

"But why?" Allen said, his voice becoming very soft. "Why did you betray me?"

"Because ..." His mind searched for answers. Blame it on

Charlotte, his mind said in a desperate effort at self-preservation. If he could just divert Allen's anger for a moment, he could survive this. She had come to him, seeking answers, seeking a way to stop her own husband. She'd convinced him to turn against Allen. She'd even flirted with him. In a moment of weakness, he'd agreed. He was sorry. Things had gotten out of control, out of hand before he knew what to do with it. He was just so sorry.

But then, in the clearest moment of his life, he realized he was done running. He was done hiding. Damn it all, he'd chosen his life to defend people, not destroy them. If this was the end, so be it. But he was not going to let Allen take away everything that he was.

Dean McSorley straightened up as best he could, his chest puffed out despite the searing pain that nearly robbed him of breath.

"I already told you. No one has the right to steal people's dreams. What you're doing is wrong, and I am finished with helping you. And it's about damn time I started letting my morals and beliefs drive my business conduct, and not the other way around."

"You dumbshit. What have morals got to do with business?"

When Allen came around the desk, Dean's legs failed him. Unable to move, he threw his only weapon at him. The handset flew harmlessly over Allen's head and smashed into the glass trophy case.

He saw Allen raise the poker. He felt his own mouth open wide to scream.

All was silence except for the whoosh of the poker and a loud thud as it hit the side of his head. There was a brilliant flash of light, and then everything was finally and mercifully darkness.

CHAPTER FIFTY-EIGHT

Charlotte heard the horrific scream from downstairs, like the cry of a dying animal. Then it went deathly quiet.

Oh God, oh God! It wasn't safe here in this bedroom, in this house anymore, and every last bit of her body screamed to get away, but she knew she was hopelessly trapped.

She glanced to her bed and saw the phone lying on the comforter. She ran to it and grabbed it. She pushed the call button, but instead of the comforting dial tone, all she heard was silence. She clicked the button several times, but there was still no sound.

Oh, Mary Anne, please hurry.

It was all so surreal, Allen thought, looking down on Dean's body. He nudged him with his foot. It was like he was made of rubber. So surreal.

He pulled up a chair to face his lawyer just as he had thousands of times before. A bloody gash split Dean's scalp from the top of his ear to the middle of his forehead. Amid the flowing blood, there was a brilliant, glistening sheen of pure white. It reminded him of the first time he'd ever seen live bone. He'd only ever seen the pale, yellow display bones, until he'd been playing baseball with some teenage friends of his at the school lot. Calvin had been playing third base when Ernie had hit a line drive right at him. It smacked into his glove, and Cal had thrown it off as soon as it hit. He was holding his hand, screaming, as everyone rushed over. It had bent back his pinky and split the skin, exposing a perfectly snow-white knucklebone underneath. Allen had stopped in his tracks and just stared, much as he was doing right now.

God, it was just so white.

He shook his head, trying to think. He'd always scoffed at the idea of temporary insanity, but what other explanation for his actions could there be? He hadn't intended to hit the poor bastard. He didn't know what had come over him. He'd taken the call from Detective Silver, listening as the man outlined what Mary Anne had told him. A fear and rage unlike anything he'd ever felt before built up inside him. He barely remembered thanking the man, excusing it all as a simple misunderstanding and he'd check into it but thank you all the same. When he'd hung up, he'd just seen red. Mary Anne, his sweet, wonderful Mary Anne, was going to betray him—no, she *had* betrayed him. And everything, everything just crashed down around him. The lawsuit, his company, all of it was going to go down the drain. Was he going to end up going to jail instead of Zack? What was he going to do?

And like an answer to a prayer, Dean had buzzed the gate. He looked so smug in the security monitor by Allen's desk, sitting there in his car. He'd let him in, grabbed the first weapon he'd seen, and then hid behind the door.

He honestly hadn't meant to hit him so hard. If Dean would just wake up, he'd probably apologize. He'd only wanted ... he'd just wanted to get his attention, to strike back, to let him know how badly he'd been hurt, and then things had all just gotten out of control. Can't you understand that, old man?

Allen stopped, realizing he'd been talking out loud to the corpse of his attorney. His hands trembled. Maybe he really was going insane.

That's fine. That would be his excuse. Any lawyer could successfully argue that case. And there were plenty more at Travis, McSorley, and Davis. He wondered if they'd keep that firm name.

Allen stood up. Good God, he just needed a moment of clarity to think, but his head was absolutely throbbing. Too much bloody scotch.

He circled the desk and then sat on the corner closest to the body. He nudged Dean's foot with his own. Still no response. He looked at Dean's face. For a man covered in his own blood, he looked oddly peaceful.

Of course, he'd be peaceful. The bastard had just stuck him with an unimaginable mess.

If Dean had managed to turn against him, he would have been horribly exposed. Plus there was his own daughter's testimony. Tears welled up in his eyes. God, he couldn't even think about her betrayal without breaking down. How could she turn against him? Looking at Dean's crumpled body, he began to shake. Mary Anne. His little girl. With their combined forces, they could have put him in jail, or at the very least, they would have forced him to concede. Either way, Zack would have won. As impossible as that sounded, Zack would have won. And now look at this mess. It was worse than anything he ever imagined.

God, what would people think of him now? They'd say he'd thrown it all away in a moment of passion and have a good one at his expense. Damn it. People were fools. They wouldn't see that he'd done what he'd needed to do. He'd made the hard choices to protect himself, the hard choices the rest of the masses would never have made, not in a thousand years. That's what set him apart. That's why he had his multibillion-dollar company, that's why he lived in luxury, and not like the simple sheep that merely grazed in the field. He made the hard choices and then faced the consequences head-on.

He stood up, turning his back on Dean. Mary Anne couldn't and wouldn't do anything by herself; he knew that. The bitch upstairs and this asshole had coaxed her into it, all in the name of Zack's almighty principles. It was pathetic, really. Didn't any of them realize that what they were really doing was turning on themselves? By ruining him, they were ruining all of their lives. Who'd pay for Dean's daughters' college funds then? Who'd keep

Charlotte in this house or those expensive clubs and charities of hers? And did Mary Anne actually think he'd be able to face Zack after Zack's little upstart destroyed everything he'd worked for? Didn't she realize she was ripping her family apart?

He looked at Dean again, strangely unable to take his eyes off of him. And then it hit him. Dean's smugly serene look counseled him once again. The lawyer had come here to chop down his tree. Charlotte and he were toying with an affair, but Charlotte decided to break it off, unable to bear the thought of hurting her successful husband of more than thirty years. Allen had come home and found them arguing—Dean was imploring her, begging her. It had turned violent. Dean had grabbed the poker, the spurned lover that he was, and Allen had grabbed the tennis racket in self-defense. They'd fought, and Allen had finally bested him, wrestling the poker from his hands. But the man just wouldn't stop. He just kept coming and coming. Years of jealousy over Allen's success and marriage to Charlotte had driven Dean to the point of madness. Allen hadn't meant to hurt him, but he was, after all, a tennis champ. He had a powerful swing.

One by one, the puzzle pieces fell into place. Allen was sure the two of them hadn't merely run into each other by accident, suddenly deciding to conspire against him. They would have had to meet; there would have been phone calls between them, maybe notes. All those could be found. Hell, who needed a lawyer? He could do this by himself.

Wait, the phone call from the detective. Allen thought a moment. He supposed he could claim he'd received it before he'd come home, or maybe he'd been in the driveway. He quickly replayed the call: there wasn't anything to betray that he *wasn't* in his car. At least nothing the man would be able to swear to under oath.

There was no security system to the outside. Alarms would ring internally and there were cameras that had been wired to the communications system, but they were all on a closed-circuit system. He'd never liked the idea of some pimply faced pervert at a security company watching them, and he wasn't about to let them know when he was coming or going.

This was good. Everything was fitting perfectly.

He turned and looked at the stairs. He'd tied up everything except for one thing. Dean was just one of the witnesses against him. If both were gone, anything they'd said to Mary Anne or Zack would be considered hearsay and would never hold up in a court of law. After many years of court battles, he knew that with absolute certainty.

Actually, Charlotte wasn't party to any of it; her testimony would also be hearsay. But he needed to be sure he could control her. She could still do plenty to damage him even without Dean. And he also didn't know what she'd heard just now or if she'd come out of hiding and seen anything.

Allen clutched the poker tightly. The smooth brass handle fit perfectly in his hand. Which reminded him, he needed to get Dean's fingerprints on this before it was all over.

He set down the poker and walked toward the staircase.

CHAPTER FIFTY-NINE

Zack drove in silence, as fast as he could go. More than once, the tires squealed on the pavement after the briefest pause at a stop sign. Mary Anne sat next to him, one hand under her leg, the other gripping the armrest. He felt the tension too.

On the way down in the elevator, Mary Anne had told him about her father's assault on her. As much as he hated Allen, Zack had never figured the man would actually hurt his own daughter. If Allen had manhandled Mary Anne in his rage, he hoped Charlotte knew how to take care of herself.

He turned onto Bay, passing Fort Mason. Once he made it onto Marina Boulevard, he knew he could safely speed, since the police were rarely there. As soon as he passed the marina, he hit the gas, only to hit the brake after less than a hundred yards. A policeman was parked along the road ahead.

Damn it. He slowed down to slightly under the speed limit. It figured. The one time he had a legitimate reason to speed.

He brushed aside the idea of turning back and asking for a police escort. He was still worried that there was an outstanding warrant for him. He wasn't convinced that the man on his doorstep had been Deirdre's father. He just prayed that Allen hadn't turned in his plates and car description as part of an APB. They'd be stuck here trying to explain things, rather than going for help.

He watched the policeman out of the corner of his eye as he slid past him. The cop didn't look up from his lap. He watched him in the rearview mirror, hoping he stayed parked. When the cruiser was out of sight, he sped up again.

Charlotte sat on the edge of the bed, clutching a Niagara Falls souvenir pillow to her breast. The dead phone sat beside her.

It had been a long time since she'd heard anything from downstairs. Part of her wanted to step outside the bedroom to see what was going on; the other half told her to remain right where she was and keep a close vigilance on the locked door.

Unable to stand the tension any longer, she dropped the pillow and felt behind the headboard for her flask of brandy. She unscrewed the brass cap and took a deep draw. The sensation of brandy going down, warming her insides, relaxed her.

After a minute or two, Charlotte got up from the bed and stepped to the door. She put her ear against it, listening through the thick wood panels. She heard the unmistakable sound of someone climbing the stairs. Heart pounding, Charlotte staggered back from the door. She ran to the window and tried to lift it, but it wouldn't budge. She couldn't remember the last time she'd opened this window. Years of neglect had swollen it into uselessness.

Even if she'd managed to pry the window, so what? Her bedroom was located on the back end of the house. The back wall rose the three stories of the house and a fourth for the basement, with no gaps or ledges or hip roofs. It was a straight drop onto the cement patio.

Desperate, she gripped the window edge and pulled again, this time putting her back and legs into it. It moved! Just a few inches, but enough to feel the evening air rush in. She kneeled down and stuck her face into the gap.

"Help! Help! Someone help me! Can anyone hear me?"

"No one can hear, you silly cow," a voice said from the other side of the door.

The knob rattled. "Open the door."

Charlotte pressed her hands tightly over her mouth, watching the doorknob twist back and forth. At first, the twisting was slow and forceful, but now the knob shook violently.

"Open this bloody door!" The door shook as he slammed it with his fist or his foot.

"Police! Police!" she screamed out the window. "Help!" Charlotte banged her fist against the frame. "Can anyone hear me?"

"No one can hear you, goddamn it."

The doorknob stopped shaking.

"Okay, enough of these games. I forgive you for throwing the scotch in my face. All right? I'm also sorry for taking those cheap shots at Dean. They were uncalled for. All right? Now just open this door."

"What happened downstairs?" Her voice sounded shrill in her ears. Shrill and panicked.

"I'll tell you all about it after you open this door."

"No," she said in the most defiant tone she could muster. "Tell me now. I heard screaming."

"That was me. You have no bloody idea how much scotch can sting."

"That wasn't you who screamed."

"You silly cow, of course, it was."

"No, you're lying. There were two voices downstairs."

Charlotte closed her eyes and held her breath.

Allen hit the door again. "Enough of your alcoholic hallucinations! Now unlock this fucking door!"

Tears choked her. She was trying desperately not to give into the fear that threatened to overwhelm her. "No!" she cried hoarsely. "It was Dean, wasn't it?"

A numbness crept up her left arm. She clutched at her chest, afraid that her heart was failing.

The doorknob shook again, violently.

"Listen, you bitch!" He slammed the door again. "Open this fucking door! Do you hear me? Unlock this door right now!"

"What did you do to poor Dean?" she shouted back.

Seconds passed, and there was no response. Had he given up? Charlotte carefully tiptoed to the door, positioning her ear between the door and the molding. She heard heavy footsteps descending the stairs.

She considered unlocking the door. If she could make it downstairs, she could get a knife from the kitchen to defend herself with, or better yet, run to Carl and Maria's apartment—maybe their phone line hadn't been cut.

Steeling herself, she opened the bedroom door and slipped out. Then she heard footsteps slapping the marble floor, storming up the stairs toward her. She turned back, slammed the door shut, and locked it. As she backed away from the door, the footsteps stopped.

What was he—?

With a crash, a panel in the door splintered inward.

Charlotte screamed.

The tip of something sharp lanced through the panel, again and again, widening the hole. It was the panel closest to the lock. Light from the hallway spilled through the ragged gap in the bedroom door. Then Allen reached his hand through and opened the lock. The door swung open and he stepped in, holding the bronze-handled fireplace poker. He was breathing heavily, his face shining with perspiration.

He walked over to her, grabbed a fistful of her hair, dragged her out of the bedroom, and flung her into the hallway. She fell, landing at the edge of the stairway, sobbing uncontrollably, petrified out of her mind.

Allen prodded her with the fireplace poker. "When did you and McSorley plan the betrayal? Before or after you screwed him?"

Charlotte couldn't answer. She was crying and hyperventilating simultaneously.

"Which was it?" he demanded, stepping on her ankle, forcing her legs apart with pressure from the poker.

Charlotte tried to curl into a fetal position, but the sharp point hurt too much. She shook her head.

"What does that mean?"

"I didn't have any affair with Dean!" she shouted between sobs. "You know that! *Tu es un fou.*"

Allen raised the poker over his head. "If I hear your stupid white-trash Cajun one more time, I swear I'll kill you."

Charlotte kept her head down, her eyes following his brown Gucci loafers.

"It doesn't matter. If you want to be McSorley's little whore, I really couldn't care less."

"What about you?" she said, praying to change the rules of the game. She raised her head to meet his eyes. "Whoring it up with Julie!"

He raised the poker again. Charlotte dropped back to the hallway carpet. Anticipating a blow, she locked her arms over the back of her head.

"Watch yourself."

"You deny it?" she said into the carpet. "It's common knowledge."

"And it's common knowledge that you're a drunk. But I don't make it public because I have respect for our family and our daughter."

"Respect? Save that speech for the television interviews. You don't respect our family and certainly not your daughter. You only care about yourself."

"Julie Reynolds beats you hands down. She's not some former bayou beauty queen, long past pull date, wallowing in self-pity, finding her reality in a bottle of brandy, you drunken slut. You called Dean and convinced him to spread his sorry ass in front of Zack and our daughter, didn't you?"

Allen held one of her legs down with the poker and used his foot to pry her legs apart again. She couldn't stop him.

"You fucking whore. Dean never would have acted without you stroking his sorry little cock, which means Mary Anne never would have found out without your meddling and dirty whoring. Now she wants to betray me because of you. But first she betrayed you."

"What? What are you—?"

"She came to my office today, very sure of herself in the beginning—really quite unlike her—trying to convince me that Zack wasn't a traitor. But then she told me something about a certain judge that only Dean knew. At first, I thought she was just guessing, but Dean confirmed it just now."

Just now? Charlotte thought. So it was Dean downstairs. "For once in your life, stop thinking about yourself," she said. "Your daughter worships you. But you can't manipulate her life just to save your blasted company."

"Oh yes, it was only a matter of time before he told me everything, including how you set this whole thing up." Allen smiled. "Just before he had a little accident."

Charlotte looked at the poker and for the first time noticed the blood on it. Fresh blood. It was on his hands and shirt too. She felt her dinner, diluted with red wine and scotch, coming up. She'd made a mess of everything. Even the flirting with Dean had led to disaster. Poor Dean.

"Aaagh!"

The gurgling scream came from downstairs. Followed by shouted, incoherent words. Then the house fell silent again.

Dean was alive! At least for the moment. Charlotte looked up at Allen. His attention was focused down the stairs, at the entrance to his study, and the poker hung loosely in his hand.

She sprang from the floor and dashed past him, for the stairs, grasping at the banister for dear life as she descended. Footsteps pounded right behind her.

A half-dozen steps from the bottom, something sharp hit her legs, just below the knees. She screamed and fell against the banister. Allen grabbed her hair, lifting her up by it. She stretched for the handrail, but it was out of reach. Then he shoved her, throwing her forward. She flew headfirst through the air, past the last six steps. As she fell, she tried to reach out and break her fall but misjudged the distance. She landed with a thud, her head striking the floor. A brilliant light flashed before her eyes. The world spinning, she raised her head and saw Allen behind her on the stairs, a strange, satisfied smile on his face. Dean was nowhere to be seen. The foyer's statue towered over her, sword raised in salute to Allen's victory.

She wanted to scream, but there was no air in her lungs. Then, as if she had slipped into dark, bottomless waters, there was nothing.

CHAPTER SIXTY

Zack pushed in the code Mary Anne had given him, and the gates slowly parted. As soon as the opening was wide enough, he jammed down the accelerator, his side mirror missing the receding metal by mere inches.

Roaring around a stand of trees at the last bend, he saw an unfamiliar car on the blacktopped parking area by the detached garage. Zack pulled up behind it.

Mary Anne got out before he did.

"Stay here," she said, quickly striding down the walk. "I don't know what Allen would do if he saw you here."

Allen walked around the slumped body of his wife. With his back to the front entrance, he knelt down beside Charlotte and gently turned her over. Her makeup was smeared like a clown's. What an ugly way to die. He lifted her left wrist, checking her pulse. It was there, but very faint.

Blood oozed from the side of her head where she'd hit the floor. Perfect. Now all he had to do was slam her head against the marble sufficiently to finish the job. Without Dean or Charlotte, all his problems would go away.

He smiled. He could honestly say she'd fallen down the stairs. Or maybe it was Dean who'd pushed her—yes, that was better. *That* was why he'd gone after Dean. By the time he returned to her side after the fight, she was already dead. He put one hand under her chin, and the other grabbed the back of her dress and lifted her head, aiming carefully. He didn't want a medical examiner finding two wounds close to one another, although he supposed he could say she'd hit her head on the steps on the way down.

Before he could crack her skull on the tile floor, the front door opened and then closed, and a cool breeze touched his neck. The quick clip of high heels told him Mary Anne had returned.

He rolled Charlotte over into his lap, holding her hand like he was seeking a pulse. "Mary Anne?" he said. "Thank God you're here. Hurry, help me."

Out of the corner of his eye, he saw her come around the statue.

"Oh my God!" she gasped. She ran to him. "Is she all right? What happened?"

"It was Dean. He came here. When I came home, they were arguing. I don't know why. But I saw him push her—Charlotte, she called him horrible names. Something about a dirty mind, that she never wanted him. Was she, I mean, were they?"

"Slow down, just tell me what happened," she said, kneeling beside him.

"He pushed her, damn it! On the stairs. I saw him do it. They were on the stairs, and he pushed her down. I tried to catch her. Then he came after me. I grabbed the tennis racket to defend us, but he grabbed the poker. We fought. And I beat the murdering bastard."

Allen checked his daughter's face. It was ashen. The lie was working.

Then Mary Anne screamed, pointing a finger in the direction of the den.

Dean charged out, his shirt soaked in blood, arms outstretched, the white bone glimmering on his forehead. In his right hand, he held a large tennis trophy with a white marble base. He raised it high over his head. Allen tried to get up, but he was pinned with Charlotte lying across his lap.

Before he could move, Dean hit him between the shoulder and

the base of his neck. He yelped and fell to one side. His momentum unbroken, Dean tripped over him and stumbled. As he tried to catch himself, the trophy fell from his hand and slid halfway across the floor. The poker lay where Allen had dropped it, much closer, at the foot of the stairs. On hands and knees, Dean made a grab for it. When he turned, he held it ready to strike.

Allen was still trying in vain to get to his feet. The pain in his collarbone was excruciating. He was sure he'd heard something snap. He realized Dean had a clear shot at him with the poker. He braced himself for another, perhaps final, blow.

"Stop!"

Mary Anne dove into Dean, grappling with his upraised arm. The poker slipped from his grasp and clattered to the floor.

"Dean! Uncle Dean. What are you doing?"

When Dean turned slowly to face Mary Anne, Allen scrambled out from under his wife and grabbed the poker.

"Mary Anne?" Dean said as if he was unsure what he was seeing.

"Yes."

"Your father ... he attacked me ... I—"

Allen swung the poker, hitting Dean in his shoulder. He staggered, tried to right himself, and then collapsed backward onto the floor, at the front of the statue. Allen raised the poker, ready to finish the job.

Mary Anne grabbed his arm before he could strike. "Stop it! What is wrong with you?"

Dean was trying to sit up. He got an elbow beneath him, but his legs wouldn't cooperate. He slid back until he was half sitting against the statue's base. He opened his mouth to speak, but nothing came out. His eyes rolled up into his head.

Mary Anne rushed over to him. Dean looked up at her for a moment, smiled wanly, raised a hand to touch her face, and then his head lolled to one side. She whirled around. "What is going on here?" she yelled at Allen.

"I told you. Dean attacked your mother, and then he attacked me. I thought I'd killed him. Then I came to see if your mother—"

"But she called me. She said you were the one acting crazy." Mary Anne started crying. "You didn't come home and find them—"

"Of course she called." He took Mary Anne by the shoulders. "I was outraged. Why wouldn't I be? I came home and saw them having what I thought was a romantic dinner. I said cruel things. Then I went into the kitchen to get myself something to eat. I heard arguing, and then your mother went upstairs. She must have called you then."

"No ... but I, she—"

"When I came back out, I heard arguing, but this time coming from upstairs. He must have followed her up there. Pushed her down the stairs."

Mary Anne grabbed her hair. "We need an ambulance!" she said. "This is insane!"

"You just saw him attack me!"

"No! That's not—"

"Mary Anne!" He shook her firmly. "Listen to me. I'm your father. None of that matters now. We need help. Quickly. Go and call the police. Get an ambulance."

Mary Anne nodded through her tears. "Yes. You're right." She ran into the den. Allen knelt by Charlotte, feeling her wrist. She was still alive.

A moment later, Mary Anne came back. "The phone in there—it's smashed."

"That's right, I'd forgotten. Where's your cell phone? Your cell phone! Did you bring it?"

Mary Anne shook her head. "No ... yes. It's with Za—it's in my car."

"Go get it. Run! I'm not feeling a pulse!"

Mary Anne took a last glance at her mother and ran for the door.

"Wait!" Allen shouted, stopping her. "You'll need to go down to the gate to let them in. The security system's broken." He watched her throw open the door with so much force it bounced off the wall and didn't quite swing back to shut. Allen quickly got up and closed it behind her so he'd have some warning when she returned.

He looked down at the crumpled shapes of the two star witnesses against him. With soft evening light illuminating the grand foyer, the two bodies looked like they were part of a movie, a murder scene at a museum.

Allen smiled. It was wonderful how all this was fitting together. Dean had not only attacked him in front of Mary Anne, but he'd also put his own fingerprints on the poker. Others might call the outcome perfect providence, but he knew it was a direct result of his ability to command and shape events. Mary Anne had let it slip that her mother had called her. He'd seized that opportunity too, although until he knew exactly what had been said, he'd have to step carefully around that one.

Yes, how bloody perfect it was, he thought as he stood between the two bodies. But he still had to close the deal. There could be no witnesses.

"She'll never believe you."

The voice was so soft that at first Allen thought it was his own, deeply buried doubt bubbling forth. Then he saw that Dean's eyes were open and locked onto his.

"Why?" Dean whispered. Blood dripped between his eyes, but he didn't blink. "Why did you attack Charlotte?"

"Don't be an asshole. I didn't do anything. She merely fell down the stairs."

"I saw you. You pushed her."

"Well, it doesn't matter anymore, does it? It doesn't matter what you saw."

"She'll never believe you."

"Who?"

"Mary Anne. You've already lost her. The truth will win out. It always does."

"You're wrong, old man. I've already won." Allen picked up the poker. "And this time you will die, you son of a bitch."

He rammed the poker into Dean's chest with all his strength. It slid between rib bones, buried up to the hook. Dean arched his back in pain as blood spurted up. Then he made a whimpering sound and collapsed.

Because of the blood already on his shirt, no one could say what had just sprayed Allen was new. Perfect. Now there was only Charlotte left to deal with. He stood over her unmoving body.

Everything was perfect.

Chapter Sixty-One

Zack was leaning against the car when Mary Anne came racing around the corner.

"Zack!" she gasped, gripping his arm. "Do you know any first aid?"

"What? First—"

"My cell phone! Where is it?" She ran to the other side of the car. "Tell me I didn't leave it at the hotel."

"Calm down. What's—"

"My mother!" Mary Anne shouted as she dove into the car. "She's not breathing! And Uncle Dean's in there. He's been hurt too—he might be dead. Oh, thank God! Here it is. Dean attacked my mother; my father saved her. Do you know CPR? Go help! Give me your keys; I have to go down to the gate."

Zack fished his keys out of his pocket. She snatched them and jumped into the car at once. She quickly backed it around and then sped off toward the gate, leaving him there.

He took a step toward the front door, wincing at his bruised ribs. He walked in slow, measured steps until he reached the entrance. An hour ago, Mary Anne had seemed to finally see Allen for who he really was. Now she had come back around to believing her father, sure that he'd gallantly protected her mother from McSorley. Much more likely, Allen had attacked the two of them, and now he was blaming Dean. Before today, Zack had never dreamed that Allen would resort to physical violence. Now, everything it seemed was unraveling. Zack put a hand on the doorknob. Holding his left side, he took a shallow breath and stepped cautiously into the house.

When he entered the foyer, everything seemed frozen in place—gleaming white walls, the massive statue, the grand sweeping staircase, as if the stage had been set, the lighting dramatic; now all that was missing were the actors.

A sickly smell hung heavily in the air. It was blood. He didn't know why he recognized that, but he was sure of it. Next, he saw the statue had nearly been shoved off its granite pedestal. It had moved so far forward it was a miracle that it hadn't tipped over onto the floor. The severed head of a tennis racket lay along the wall. Dark puddles of blood marred the alternating perfection of black and white tile.

When he came around the statue, he saw a man sitting in its shadow, his back and shoulders resting against the base. One of the forelegs of the horse, frozen in parade march, hung directly over his head. His legs were splayed, and he sat in a puddle of blood. Zack stared at Dean McSorley for a moment, seeing him but not wanting to. The lawyer paid a dear price for resurrecting his moral conscience.

Nearby, a woman in a blue dinner dress lay sprawled on the floor. One of her arms was trapped beneath her, the other to one side. It was Charlotte, he was sure.

Had it only been that morning that he'd talked with both of them at Coit Tower? It seemed so long ago. He'd seen dead bodies before, but they had been cleaned and dressed up at funerals, like they were merely sleeping—never like this, never so soon after their spirits had departed.

He looked at Dean more closely. There was a huge gash across his forehead all the way to his left ear, and blood had run down his face, which was bruised and swollen. Zack felt a sudden twinge of nausea.

Then the fingers on Dean's right hand twitched.

The random nerve firings of a fresh corpse. It was too much. Zack's stomach heaved before he could stop it, and he vomited on the floor. His ribs shot stabbing pains through him, but his stomach lurched again and again.

"God, you really are weak. To think I once considered you my protégé."

Allen was sitting on the stairs behind him, resting his elbows on his knees, a poker beside him on the step.

"What have you done?" Zack asked hoarsely, trying to get his stomach under control.

"I haven't *done* anything. I am merely the victim in all this. Dean came here, trying to have an affair with my wife. He'd always been in love with her, you know. I came home to find them having dinner, there were harsh words between us, including me accusing them of betraying me to you. Oh yes, I certainly suspected as much. When I went into the kitchen, I heard them arguing. By the time I got back—"

"For God's sake, shut up! Mary Anne might believe your lies, but they don't work on me. Not anymore."

"How dare you accuse me of lying! You who betrayed me and my family." Allen looked possessed.

"Shut the hell up!" Zack couldn't believe that he'd once feared and respected this man. Allen was studying him, looking for weaknesses. Zack knew Allen expected him to be falling into line, and because he wasn't, that made him dangerous and unpredictable.

Zack motioned to Charlotte. "Is she okay?"

"She just has a little bump on her head. She'll be fine. Mary Anne's gone to fetch an ambulance."

Zack knelt down next to Charlotte. "Mary Anne said that she's not breathing."

"I said she's fine," Allen repeated.

Zack saw a wet matte of redness on the side of her head. He felt for a pulse in her neck. Thank God. Up until that moment, he wasn't sure she was still alive.

"Have you heard from Dimitre and the others today," Allen

asked, "or didn't they show up for work?" He smiled at Zack. "Oh, half a moment, I forgot. They work for me now."

"What?"

"Yes. He came to me and signed an ironclad contract. Looks to me like you not only lost your company, you've lost your friends, as well."

"Look, none of that matters now. Dean's dead, and your wife's dying. What the hell did you do? I don't get it—why would you throw everything away like this?"

"Throw everything away? I've done nothing of the sort. I've made the hard choices to protect what's mine. That's what separates me from the sheep. Now you tell me, why did you do it?"

"Do what?"

"Why didn't you confide in me about that wonderful polymer formula?"

"Jesus Christ! Who the hell cares about the goddamned formula right now? There's blood everywhere—just look at yourself. You're covered with it."

"Indeed I am," Allen said, looking down at his shirt as he stood up. "But I asked you a question. Why didn't you come to me first with your idea of an ultraflat television display?"

"You're insane," Zack said. "People are dying here."

"I most certainly am not insane. And since you're going to jail, this might be the only time we'll have to talk freely. You know, I do hope Mary Anne didn't call the police too. Aren't they looking for you?"

Allen picked up the poker, examining its shaft. From where Zack stood, it looked slightly bent.

"How did you turn Mary Anne against me?" Allen said as he slowly descended the stairs.

Zack stood up and took a step backward. He didn't like the way Allen was holding the bloody poker. Allen seemed fine physically, but Zack couldn't help but wonder if the man had a head injury of some sort.

"I didn't turn your daughter against you," he said. "In fact, I took steps to make sure I didn't interfere with your relationship. Anything she's done, it was her own choices."

Allen moved faster than he could react. The poker jabbed him in the side.

"Jesus!" Zack yelled, backing away, half bent over and clutching at his ribs.

"Can you imagine how I felt when I learned that my own daughter was going to side against me? Or how hurt I was to learn she actually believed the lies you and McSorley were trying to spread about me?"

Zack was silent. It wouldn't do any good to tell him he knew exactly what it felt like.

"But you know what?" Allen said. "It's okay. In the end, she'll choose me. Now that you're going to jail and Dean can't bear witness against me, she'll come back around. After all, jail time is notoriously hard on relationships. And while you're gone, I'll make sure she'll see the error of her ways."

Allen looked at his wife and said, "And if poor Charlotte doesn't make it, then I'll be the only one she has left, won't I?"

He jabbed again with the poker.

"Stop it!" Zack said, swatting at it.

"What's the matter? Don't like fencing? You know, in the Middle Ages, might truly did make right. When there was a dispute that couldn't be resolved between two nobles, they used trial by combat. The victor was declared the winner because, obviously, God couldn't be on the side of the loser."

It wasn't much of a competition if only one side had a weapon. It dawned on him that Allen was holding the weapon he'd used to murder Dean. "For God's sake, I don't know what's happened here, but this isn't going to make it any better."

"You're wrong. This will make it infinitely better. I'm going to fix everything. You interrupted some unfinished business. Now back off."

Zack tool another backward step and nearly tripped over Dean's leg.

Allen knelt beside Charlotte, set down the poker, and turned her face down. He gripped her by the back of the neck, turning her head at a slight angle to the floor.

"What the hell are you doing?" Zack asked.

Allen looked up. "I'm going to kill my wife."

"What? You can't be serious."

"Of course, I am. Why would I joke about such a thing?"

"Because, you goddamn psycho, I'm fucking standing right here."

"So what?" Allen smiled at him. "You don't understand how the world works, do you?" He let Charlotte's head rest on the tile. "And you obviously have no idea how the legal system works. You're not a policeman, you have no authority, you have absolutely no standing in the community. You're a nobody. Your little testimony wouldn't do anything.

"Think about it. You come here; you're angry with me. You're losing your company, you're going to jail for something you claimed was your own invention, you've lost your friends, you've lost all your money, and you've nearly lost my daughter. Murder my wife in cold blood? Of course, you'd make up a lie like that. Do you think any jury would believe a word you said?

"I have evidence—cold, impartial evidence—that will shortly be sending you to jail. Who believes convicts? I have a successful business, employing thousands of people; I'm a respected member of the community. I'm wealthy and have everything I could ever want. You have none of these. I am by my very nature more believable.

"So tell me, who would believe you? No one. Not even Mary Anne would believe such an outrageous lie. Kill my wife right in front of you? That's utterly preposterous." He laughed. "Not only will I take care of the two witnesses against me in your little rebellion, but this will be the final dividing line between you and my daughter."

He picked Charlotte's head up again. "Go ahead! Tell Mary Anne. Tell the world."

Allen turned Charlotte's head so the killing blow would fall on top of the wound she had already suffered. "It will all be over soon, my darling," he said, and then he slammed her into the floor.

———————

Mary Anne heard the operator come on as she spun the car backward, the phone in one hand as she wrestled with the steering wheel with the other.

"Nine one one, how can I help you?"

"Yes, I—"

There was a beep as she accidentally hung up the phone. Swearing, she put the car in drive and sped off toward the gate. She hit redial as she drove, spinning gravel all over the lawn.

"Nine one one, how can I help you?" The voice crackled a bit.

"My mother's hurt. I need an ambulance!"

"Okay, I want you to not panic. Tell me what happened."

"Goddamn it, I don't need a quiz. I just need an ambulance!"

"Okay, why don't you tell me where do you need it sent to?"

Mary Anne quickly gave the address and then waited for her to respond. "Hello?"

She held the phone away from her ear and looked at the screen. Damn these hills! The signal had weakened, and the call had disconnected. She redialed it again.

When she had 911 again, she started over, telling the new operator that she needed an ambulance and she gave her the address.

Nearing the gates, she slowed down. When she was ten feet from them, they opened automatically.

"My mother's hurt," she said. "She fell down the stairs. My uncle's here too, and he's bleeding. I don't know what happened, my father said—" She didn't want to implicate Allen in something she wasn't sure about. "Look, I don't know what happened. I wasn't there. I just came home and ... Hello?"

"Hold on a sec, I'm checking something ..."

Mary Anne stared at the gates. The pressure of her car on the drive had opened them from the inside, but if she moved the car in or out, they would both close. Then the EMTs would need to be buzzed in from the house. She wasn't sure an ambulance could get through the gates and past her car. Which meant she had to stay there until help arrived. She didn't like the idea of her mother hurt and alone. She could leave the car here, but it was a five-minute jog back to the house and all uphill.

"Did you call once from this number?" the operator asked.

"Yes. I was disconnected."

"Okay, let me see if an ambulance has already been sent." After another pause, the operator returned. "No, she never got your address. I'm sending one now. Hold on."

"How long before it gets here?"

"Probably about ten minutes."

That seemed like forever. She glanced in her rearview mirror at the house. She needed to get back. Leaving Zack alone with her father hadn't been a good idea, but she hadn't had any other choice.

Yes, she had. Oh, my God. Why hadn't she sent Zack with the phone down to the gate? She could have gone back in and been with her mother. She was so accustomed to taking orders from her father that she hadn't even thought about it.

The gates tried to close automatically, but sensing her car was still there, they opened back up.

"Okay, thank you. Hold on a second." She put the phone in the cup holder, and when the gates tried to close again, she slammed down on the gas, aiming for the one on the left. She crashed into it before it could reverse course—metal screeched, and the left quarter panel of her Taurus buckled under the impact. She hit the brakes before the car slid into the street. The gate was bent and no longer moving. She'd knocked it off its track and bent the first five feet around the brick wall. But the other side of the gate was still swinging closed.

Damn it. Pulling out into the street, she put the car in reverse, stomped the gas, and roared backward. She crashed into the middle of the gate, and the impact slammed her head into the seat. Her trunk popped up, obscuring her rear view. She stuck her head out the window and saw she'd knocked the gate completely off.

She picked up the phone from the cup holder, amazed it hadn't hung up.

"Miss? Miss? Hello?" the operator was saying.

"Tell them I've left the gate open for them." She hung up.

Mary Anne reversed the car over the bars of the gate, onto the lawn, and then sped up the driveway back toward the house.

Hold on, Mom. Hold on, Zack. I'm coming.

Zack dove at Allen, who seemingly in slow motion, was ramming Charlotte's head into the floor. Though his aim was slightly off, he corralled Allen's neck and managed to yank him off her. They tumbled to the right of the staircase, and Zack momentarily ended up on top of Allen. Ribs screaming in agony, he scrambled away. He glanced at Charlotte, who wasn't moving. The puddle beneath her head seemed larger. On her right side was the poker.

Allen saw the weapon in the same instant. Diving for it, they collided in midair. Zack landed belly down on top of the poker. Failing to wrench it out from under him, Allen drove a fist into his side. The pain made him cry out, and he rolled away.

As he got to his feet, Allen waved the poker at him. "That's game, set, and match. Now I can do away with you too, for attacking me when I was vulnerable. Who wouldn't believe that?"

As Allen lunged at him, Zack slid to the left and drove a fist into the middle of the oncoming face. The impact stopped Allen cold, and he dropped the poker. He stumbled over Charlotte and fell backward onto the stairs.

Zack picked up the poker and pointed it at Allen, who slowly stood up, clearly calculating his next move.

Behind them, the front door opened.

"Mary Anne! Thank God you're here," Allen yelled. "Help! He's attacking me."

CHAPTER SIXTY-TWO

The last thing Dean remembered was Mary Anne leaning over him, looking anxiously into his face. She was such a sweet girl.

He heard voices. But they seemed to come from a long way off, as if there were a long tunnel between him and whoever was speaking. The words made no sense at all.

He tried to move but couldn't and realized that this was what utter helplessness felt like. Had others felt that way when the mighty Dean McSorley had crushed them? He lay against the cold stone base of the statue, dying. The faces of all the clients he represented over the years sprang to mind. He knew full well that most of them were guilty of something. He'd gotten them off, secured the forgiveness of the court. They weren't even sorry. He was. Sorry for the direction his life had taken. If only there was someone to defend him now, he'd throw himself on the mercy of the court and beg forgiveness. He only hoped there was some forgiveness left to be had.

He wasn't sure if he'd opened his eyes or not. There was a light around him, and when he looked up, he could see a marvelous door. Stained purple and gold, surrounded by white, it glowed down on him. Eight beams of pure white stretched around him like loving arms, ready to pull him in. The light seemed to be drawing closer, or maybe he was drawing closer to it. He tried to lift his hand to reach out and touch it but couldn't.

Marjorie's face seemed to take shape in the purple and gold. Oh, God. Marjorie. He had loved her so much. Somehow over the years, they'd become so distant from one another. If only he'd treated her better, maybe she wouldn't have played golf so much. He longed so much to take her in his arms and whisper how sorry he was. His daughters. His lovely daughters, if only he could touch them. He hadn't talked to Kaitlin in a month, and now she wouldn't know how much he missed her, how much she meant to him. He loved her so. Please don't be mad at Daddy. I'm sorry.

And Mackenzie. He could still see her face, stained with tears, after some boy had been mean to her at school. They'd sat on her bed and she'd just held him, crying. He could still feel her arms around his neck. Please don't cry, sweetheart.

Little Brianna, his darling. She'd always have that mischievous grin on her face, that look she gave him even as a preschooler when she was getting ready to play some joke on him. She often pretended emotional things didn't affect her, but he knew she had a big heart and he wished he'd spent more time nurturing her, hearing her laughter. He'd give anything to hear it one more time.

He hoped they'd remember the bits of wisdom he'd tried to pass on to them, or that in some still, quiet moment, when all was dark and they needed help, the memory of his voice would whisper in their ear. If only they could know, really know, how much he truly loved them. And as his spirit left his body, his heart rushed out to them.

He reached up to touch their faces and felt something cold and hard under his hand. He took hold and pulled, trying to lift himself up.

As Mary Anne threw open the door and ran in, she heard her father call out, saying something about Zack attacking him. She rushed forward and saw Zack threatening her father with a poker, and then to her horror, she realized the statue was toppling over in slow motion, the Confederate officer, sword raised, shouting a final battle cry to rally the troops. She was vaguely aware of Dean crouched behind it, but all she could focus on was that the statue, and its sharp sword, was crashing down onto the two most important men in her life. She knew she couldn't save them both.

Everything happened in a blur.

Allen lunged, seizing Zack's poker hand and a fistful of shirt collar. He turned and held him in perfect alignment to meet the point of the descending sword.

She threw herself at Zack, grabbing his waist and pulling him from her father's grasp. Allen tried to drag him back, determined not to let go, but the momentary struggle twisted him around. He squealed as the sword pierced his back; the weight of the statue as it crashed with him to the floor drove the blade all the way through. The impact on the marble shattered the fragile, bronze figure, leaving Allen amid the fragments of rider and horse, screaming and writhing, impaled to the hilt by a sword clutched in a disembodied metal hand.

As his cries faded away and the writhing stopped, Mary Anne buried her face into Zack's chest. He put his arms around her tenderly.

"I couldn't save you both," she told him. "Then I saw his face. He was going to kill you." She wept into his chest, her entire body shaking with sobs of grief.

CHAPTER SIXTY-THREE

Seated in a funeral limousine, Mary Anne looked back across the bay. San Francisco was truly one of the most wonderful and beautiful cities in the world. She could see Coit Tower standing proudly on the spur of Telegraph Hill. Had it really been just three days since they'd had that fateful meeting in its shadow? It seemed a lifetime ago, so much had changed. She'd never be able to look at it quite the same way again.

There had been a huge gathering at the service inside St. Matthew's Baptist Church downtown. Reporters were everywhere, cameras flashing indiscriminately. Horrific murders were always big news, and these were even bigger because they involved Allen Henley, the most familiar icon of California's Silicon Valley.

Eventually, the very long line of cars pulled away from the church and headed across the Golden Gate Bridge. As she looked back at the city, the early evening light turned all the buildings aglow. The Transamerica pyramid, the centerpiece of the financial district, rose above everything. She searched for a metaphor. Money ruled everything?

She might have thought that at one point in her life, but not anymore. No, its rule was an illusion.

She smiled and glanced at her mother, dressed in mourning, with a wide hat and veil and wearing dark glasses.

The island prison of Alcatraz rolled past their window. With all the sadness of the last few days, she was truly grateful that Zack wouldn't be going to jail. She knew society needed such facilities as Alcatraz, but right now she couldn't find the will—or the heart—to judge anyone. If everyone went through the trying times she had and had met with such tragedy, perhaps they would find a way to get along.

As the sun began its final dance, it turned the Pacific Ocean into rippling sheets of light, bright red on the horizon. The light faded to orange on the sand-colored hills of Marin County and finally to muted pink as it reflected off the line of cars climbing up to the cemetery.

Behind them, the traffic was backed up all the way to the freeway. The driver helped Mary Anne out of the limousine and then helped her mother into a wheelchair. Her mother was enjoying the attention of a young handsome man. Mary Anne began walking slowly along the small-pebbled pathway, hearing others joining the path all around her.

The crowd at the cemetery was huge. There had to be several thousand at least. Black suits and dresses stretched as far as she could see, and more besides were still coming to pay their respects. There were somber faces and genuinely sad ones as well, many with tear stains as they listened to the minister recount Uncle Dean's successful life, his many triumphs, and his heroic last moments. For having to piece it together from probably a dozen sources, he got it remarkably right.

How different this was from her father's funeral yesterday morning. He had been buried just over the rise on the next hill. It had been intended as a simple, private affair, but the media hadn't allowed that. Guests uninvited came by the hundreds: competitors, associates, partners, acquaintances. She wondered how many had come for one last glimpse of him to make sure he was really dead, how many had come to mourn him, and how many others had come to celebrate his passing. Most telling was that none of Allen's family from Britain attended the funeral.

She'd loved her father, she knew that. But these last two weeks and those final moments—she shuddered. She'd never have believed her father was capable of something like that. She wanted desperately to think that he wasn't himself, that maybe he really was, as the police psychologist surmised, temporarily insane.

She'd thought a lot about her father these last few days. She remembered the many good times. That's what made it all so confusing. There was enough good in him that it made the bad hard to believe, or to even see. It was something outsiders could not understand.

One of Dean's partners rose to speak at his graveside, extolling him as a consummate attorney. Having discovered just what kind of business their firm did, Mary Anne had a hard time not getting up and walking away. She saw Dimitre, looking somber, very unlike the smiling teddy bear she was used to seeing. Next to him were Jimmy Morgan and Jerry Steiner, both awkward in probably the only suits they owned. Brett Davis stood behind them, head down, appearing to be intensely studying his shoes. Off to the right, she could see John and Molly Baker, and farther back, away from the crowd, was Paul Ryerson, his arm in a sling.

She looked to the graveside again and saw Marjorie brush away a tear. She was surrounded by her daughters, who wept uncontrollably. Marjorie looked up, and for a moment, their eyes met. She gave Mary Anne a weak nod of acknowledgment and then turned her attention to her youngest daughter.

Oddly, Marjorie had been Mary Anne's main source of comfort. Mary Anne had felt she owed it to her to explain in person Dean's final moments and her father's actions, which in turn had led her to tearfully recounting the confusion she felt. Marjorie had told her that she understood. Her own mother had been terribly abusive to her when she was younger, but to the outside world, she was a doting parent. Marjorie had even once worked up the courage to tell a teacher about the abuse, but the teacher had refused to help her because she was sure she'd made it all up.

"But you know," Marjorie had said, "people are not only who they actually are, but they are also the people we make them to be. Dear, your father's gone now. If you remember the good your father did, and focus on that, then that's who he'll remain for you. Don't dwell in the darkness of the past when the promise of the future holds so much hope."

Marjorie had patted her hand. "Just a little something I learned at a women's conference," she said.

Mary Anne called Dean "Uncle," but she'd hardly known Marjorie. She turned out to be a remarkable woman, and Mary Anne hoped to get to know her better.

Listening to the minister's benediction, she reached down for her mother's hand. She squeezed it and got a squeeze back. A loopy scarf was slung around Charlotte's neck, hiding the brace and heavy bruises, and the wide-brimmed hat covered the cuts and bruises on her scalp. The doctors hadn't wanted her to attend either service, but she'd been insistent. She wasn't wearing makeup for the first time Mary Anne could remember. Partially hidden by the black veil, her face now looked old and exhausted. She had removed her wedding ring. Considering the trauma she'd endured, she seemed remarkably at peace.

Zack had wandered away. He'd had a hard go of it at her father's funeral. Today, he was still struggling with the fact that the man who had helped ruin him had in the end apparently acted to save his life. Mary Anne had told him—and the police—that she'd seen the mortally wounded Dean reach for the statue. Zack wondered if at that instant, Dean had actually been trying to kill Allen. They'd never know.

With the final benediction, most of the crowd began to disperse. The caretakers moved into position to lower the casket. The family filed past, laying a hand on the casket, a final good-bye. Each daughter laid a white rose on the casket; Marjorie laid a red one.

Zack stared down at a gravestone decorated with a pot of wilted yellow daisies. A strong gust picked off some of the petals and scattered them down the hill. Unstoppable forces. He closed his eyes and listened to the wind whistling between the headstones.

When he opened them, he saw Paul coming toward him, his arm in a sling.

"You know, it's amazing what extreme stress can do to people," Paul said.

Zack nodded, wondering if he was talking about their fight or about what happened to Allen and Dean.

"I remember," Paul went on, "goading a man that I respect immensely, turning my own goddamn home into a circus."

He should have figured Paul was talking about himself. It wasn't like him to see beyond his own skin.

"God," Paul said as he looked around, "I don't know how people can act like nothing's happened. Just look at Dimitre, Jerry, and Jimmy. What the hell are they doing here?"

"You're here."

"I'm here because a part of me wants to open that coffin and spit in that asshole's dead face. He destroyed our lives. I don't buy that crap that the media's saying, do you?"

Zack patted Paul's back, grimacing as the new bandage tightened around his ribs. "Paul, let it go. Dean did a lot to hurt us, but he really was seeking redemption. He was going to help us fight Allen. He was ready to throw away his career for us."

"Did you know that Dimitre signed a goddamn contract with Allen? He was trading the polymer formula for a chunk of cash. Did he tell you?"

"Actually, Allen did. I haven't spoken with Dimitre about it yet."

"Doesn't that bother you?" Paul asked. "They sold their souls to the devil and didn't even bother to tell you. McSorley's heroics would have been for naught."

"God, Paul, you just don't get it, do you? With everything we've been through, haven't you learned anything in all of this? Dean's actions weren't for nothing. In the end, he stood up for something. He realized he'd made a mistake, and although he paid for it, at least he tried to do something about it."

"Well, excuse me. Most of us don't have the same inner strength that you have."

Right now he didn't feel that strong.

The last remaining petal of the daisies floated away. Zack watched it skip past a black granite headstone that was inscribed with the American flag. When he closed his eyes, he could still see Dean McSorley's brutalized face and the stain of his blood that was smeared over the marble tiles. He remembered his left side burning as he launched himself at Allen. All he could think about in that moment was helping Charlotte, but then there was the sickening thud as Allen drove her head into the floor. He'd been told he probably saved her life by changing the angle of the blow, but he couldn't remember if he heard the sound before or after he'd hit Allen. He supposed it didn't matter. She was alive, and that's what really mattered.

Zack watched the crowd disperse from around the graveside, the family having thrown in their handful of dirt. The service was over.

"It's ironic, isn't it," Paul said, "that Allen gets stabbed in the back?"

Zack didn't respond.

"Look, I've got to say this. Throughout all this insanity, there's only one thing that I've been certain of. Mary Anne is bad news for you. I've told you that from the very beginning, and we fought about it at the end. Just seeing you two together makes me sick to my stomach."

Zack started to head down the hill, but Paul's hand on his shoulder stopped him.

"Hero, my ass. Dean was no hero. He'd never save anybody except himself. Come on, you were there. Look at you. You look like shit. What really went on that night?"

Zack felt a genuine sadness for him. Paul would never change. He would always only see exactly what he chose to see and never anything larger than himself.

He brushed away Paul's hand and started in the direction of Mary Anne's car.

Farther down the hill, he saw Dimitre. Anna was pulling him by the arm. Zack attempted a smile and waved. Dimitre looked at him and then looked away, toward the cemetery exit. Anna was talking in her husband's ear and pointing in Zack's direction. She was trying to play the peacemaker, but Dimitre wasn't ready for détente just yet.

There would be time later, Zack was confident of that. It would all work out exactly the way that it should.

Epilogue

harlotte Henley had always hated her husband's business. Now she found herself holding 84 percent of the privately held company: Allen's 51 percent plus her own 33 percent. Her first order of business was to appoint herself CEO and chairman—temporarily, of course, just long enough to tidy up a few loose ends.

The first matter of business was to withdraw the lawsuit and criminal charges against Zack Penny, Paul Ryerson, and Imagination. She met privately with the remaining partners of Travis, McSorley, and Davis to determine the best way to "cover their collective rear ends," since it was against California state law for an attorney to knowingly submit falsified evidence to the court. Unable to resist the chance to bill DisplayTechnik one more time, it took the partners three full days to decide on the best course of action. They approached Judge Rafkin and claimed that, although they had substantial material evidence to proceed with the case, much of the case was dependent upon the testimony of their witness, who was now deceased, and considering that, they had no choice but to withdraw the case. The judge was very understanding.

Jeremy asked for, and received, reimbursement for all legal expenses. Dropping the suits freed up all the Imagination seed money, and minus expenses and equipment, Paul recovered just over half of his investment. Charlotte quietly made up the rest by insisting the building manager return their deposit and six months' rent.

Her next step was to meet with Zack in her office and have a heart-to-heart talk with him—a real one this time, with no theatrics. Zack expressed his misgivings, his hopes, his goals, and for once Charlotte did more listening than talking. It felt good to both of them to have an honest conversation where nothing was decided, but both felt they'd been heard by the other. When Zack left, she knew what to do next.

Dimitre Koslov, Jimmy Morgan, and Jerry Steiner had signed ironclad contracts that paid extremely well and would use their considerable talents in the new ultrathin display division, but they were made very nearly prisoners of DisplayTechnik. She called them into the palatial office and offered to nullify their contracts, since she knew they were signed under duress. She also offered to give them their severance packages and allow them to seek employment elsewhere but said she greatly valued their skills and hoped they would choose to stay on. Then she offered the stunned trio a further idea.

The next morning, Charlotte met with Zack and the others and appointed him the chief technology officer in charge of the new OLED division, which the three engineers insisted be called Imagination. It was, after all, a position well suited to Zack's goals and personality. One of his confessions to Charlotte had been that he'd found out that he really just didn't like some of the aspects of being a CEO.

After some careful thought, she chose Matthew Dickens to be the new chairman and CEO of DisplayTechnik. Allen would have hated that selection, which was precisely why she chose him.

Dickens purchased the equipment from Paul but otherwise kept him out of the new company, having never really trusted him. Embittered, Paul took the money, but it did little to improve his mood. He moved to Florida and became a financial consultant for retirees, but his marriage ended in divorce within a year of their move. He found his second wind by investing in some telecom stocks that were on the rebound and netted himself a small fortune.

Dickens quickly transformed the Santa Clara facility into a first-rate manufacturing headquarters for the new division, which quickly became the most popular in DisplayTechnik, with employees lining up to join in. It wasn't just the company barbeques in the parking lot or the surprise day at the Giants' game with Dimitre tearfully belting out "The Star-Spangled Banner" or the pickup basketball games at noon; it was because people were genuinely valued for their talent and ideas.

Two years later, the company was spun off and went public, making Zack, Dimitre, Jimmy Morgan, and Jerry Steiner instant millionaires. Along the way, the company encountered several bumps in the road, but Dickens remained faithful to the pursuit. Ironically, the final polymer formula looked nothing like the version that Zack and Dimitre had originally concocted.

John and Molly Baker quit their jobs at the Bank of America, sold their San Ramon home with the spacious sundeck, and headed back to the Midwest. They never once failed to send the team Christmas cards.

Julie Reynolds was quietly asked to step down as manager of human resources. The speculation was rampant that Charlotte had insisted upon it, but Dickens was too much of a gentleman to ever confirm the rumors. She was given as much as a month to find a job, which she did in less than a week. Until then, she religiously kept up her duties at DisplayTechnik, and one of her final hires was to hire a bright young female intern for the legal department, recently of the staff of Travis, McSorley, and Davis.

Bill Bennet stayed on as legal counsel at DisplayTechnik. He was a competent, if unimaginative, attorney. He was a bit surprised to receive an intern, since it appeared his workload was going to decrease.

Jeremy continued at his small Foster City law practice. Unlike the others, his lifestyle never changed. He didn't even invest when Imagination had its initial public offering—just too busy to notice.

After things settled down, Charlotte took Mary Anne on a cruise around the world that lasted three months. Zack was happily buried with work in the new company, and mother and daughter needed some alone time to make up for many years of estrangement. When they returned, Charlotte moved out of the mansion, finding a well-appointed home within easy driving distance of the city and the Santa Clara facility. She sold her 33 percent stake but decided to keep the 51 percent—just in case.

Zack met the cruise ship at the dock and asked Mary Anne to marry him. They planned to marry quickly, knowing that life was too short to wait for what mattered most.

―――――――――――

As they curled up together on the floor of his apartment later that night, Zack thought about everything that had happened. He had left Allen to start Imagination because he had a dream of living and working free. Free from petty jealousies. Free from bulging egos. Free from hidden agendas. Free from all the trappings of corporate culture. Now, he was back at the company where he started.

It wasn't quite the view from the top that he'd expected, but it was still spectacular.

ABOUT THE AUTHOR

Glenn Ogura is the executive vice president for a New Hampshire-based laser micromachining company. He is a graduate of Electrical Engineering from Queen's University in Canada. He lives with his wife in California. This is his first novel.

CPSIA information can be obtained at www.ICGtesting.com
Printed in the USA
LVOW10s1616170614

390451LV00019B/1070/P